DISCLOSING
THE
SECRET

VINCENT AMATO

DISCLOSING THE SECRET

First Printing, 2015

ISBN-10: 0-9944757-1-3
ISBN-13: 978-0-9944757-1-8

ThinkShark Publishing Pty. Ltd.
203a Victoria Road
Northcote VIC 3070
Australia
www.vincentamatoauthor.com

DISCLAIMER

ADDITIONAL FREE CONTENT

For additional free content that was not permitted to be published visit:
vincentamatoauthor.com

ACKNOWLEDGMENTS

First and foremost, I owe a deep debt of gratitude to Colonel Jesse Marcel Jr. (Ret.) for granting permission for his family name to be the focus of this story. Colonel Marcel Jr. joined the US Navy in 1962 and retired in 1971 to enter private practice. He then joined the Montana Army National Guard in 1973, went through helicopter flight training and retired for the second time at the age of 60. Shortly after his 68th birthday, he again came out of retirement to undertake yet another tour of duty in Iraq. There he served as a flight surgeon for the 189th Attack Helicopter Battalion flying 225 hours in combat. He is, by every definition of the term, a true American hero.

If it were not for the tireless life's work of noted physicist Stanton Friedman, who was the first to personally visit and interview Jesse's father, Colonel Jesse Marcel Sr., then the incident that occurred in the desert during that summer of 1947 may have never been brought to the public's attention. His disciplined approach of investigating only verifiable facts has been the backbone of the historical events portrayed in *Disclosing the Secret*.

Also deserving of thanks are Travis Walton and Clifford Stone who had the courage to commit their personal experiences to print, as well as Lucy Pringle who allowed me to republish her fantastic crop circle photo in the book.

My sincere appreciation goes to Leslie Watts and Jenny Scepanovic for being so thorough with their editing.

Thanks also to my devoted wife, Linda, for her support and for enduring my many late nights writing.

Finally, my profound thanks to Dr. Steven Greer for his dedication to CSETI, his vision in driving the message of disclosure, and to his office for granting permission for his name, as well as his previous work on the Disclosure Project, to be a part of this story.

www.siriusdisclosure.com

Make up your own mind.

Dedicated to Colonel Jesse Marcel Jr., MD (Ret.)
1936–2013

FACTS

Fact 1

Since the 1940s, more than 100 US military personnel have gone on record stating that nuclear weapons had been compromised by undefined aircraft. They have reported countless incidents of these vehicles hovering over (or maneuvering near) missile launch sites, nuclear bomb manufacturing facilities, nuclear weapons laboratories, and nuclear test ranges. These military personnel are witnesses of the highest caliber: the US Government entrusted them with the operations and control of their country's own weapons of mass destruction. They had been thoroughly scrutinized, and highly trained, before being permitted to serve for their country. In a court of law, their detailed testimonies would be considered as accurate accounts of witnessed events.

Fact 2

In Charles Darwin's work *On the Origin of Species,* he hypothesized:

> *If it could be demonstrated that any complex organ existed, which could not possibly have been formed by numerous, successive, slight modifications, my theory would absolutely break down.*
>
> (Darwin 1859, 213)

Gaps exist in the fossil record where *Homo neanderthalensis* (Neanderthals) and other primate species appear in genetic succession. *Homo sapiens* then appears in the record with no intermediate evolutionary steps in between. Geneticists have determined that Neanderthals and *Homo sapiens* are two separate species because their genetic comparisons show signs of biological incompatibilities. The mechanism by which Neanderthal DNA morphed into *Homo sapiens* genetics has yet to be explained by contemporary science.

Fact 3

On September 29, 1995, President Bill Clinton issued presidential determination No. 95–45 exempting the US Air Force's operating location near Groom Lake in Nevada from all laws that normal American citizens, companies, and government entities must obey. The term *operating location* was used to describe the secret base because it did not officially exist during the time of his presidency. This ruling was issued on the grounds that:

i. *Information concerning activities at this operating location near Groom Lake (a.k.a. Area 51) had been deemed classified, and*

ii. *Its disclosure would compromise national security.*

Fact 4

On May 9, 2001, an assembly of US military, intelligence, government, corporate, and scientific witnesses came forward at the National Press Club in Washington DC. They went on the record to give firsthand eyewitness accounts of non-terrestrial life forms, non-terrestrial vehicles, associated advanced energy systems, and exotic propulsion technologies. Their testimonies have now been made available to the wider public.

PROLOGUE

At the end of World War II, President Harry S. Truman faced a situation that he perceived to be a national threat to the United States. So profound was the threat, and so significant, that his advisers insisted that an entirely new level of "top secret" classification be created to specifically deal with the situation. At a time when the Cold War was brewing, when it was known that Soviet spies had successfully infiltrated the US Government, it was decided that the only way to guarantee that the potentially menacing situation remain hidden, along with its technological secrets, was to hide it from their own governing administration.

Truman decided that a self-sustaining "government within a government" be formed, independent of any presidential oversight, to manage such scenarios regardless of which side of the political spectrum was in power. This entity became the precursor to the lesser-known intelligence agencies that currently still operate within the US.

CHAPTER 1

"Come on, come on, come on! We gotta *go*!" Mark's frantically nervous voice crackled through Jake's radio.

Jake Marcel was crouched beside the open safe behind a research scientist's desk. His fingers sifted through the contents of the unlocked drawer as he skimmed through the files as quickly as he could.

"Almost there." His eyes jumped from file to file, scanning every document.

Words leaped off the front cover of a folder:

UNIDENTIFIED EXOTIC MATERIAL
I-BEAM METALLURGICAL ANALYSIS
CONFIDENTIAL

He snatched the file from the drawer and stood up, flicking through pages. The document was written in a language that he was not familiar with. His eyes randomly darted from page to page: *Test sample ... unknown atomic structure ... half-life suggests ... high probability ... correlation consistent with ... sample originated within the region of the Orion system.*

I found it! Jake thought.

Fixated on the top-secret report, Jake dropped the grappling gun he had been carrying. He felt a mix of elation and wonder wash over him. Jake Marcel was holding an irrefutable, measurable, peer-reviewed analysis of the metal sample.

My God! This would prove ...

A rumbling under his feet tore Jake away from his thoughts. He felt rising trepidation as the building around him seemed to tremble.

An earthquake?

Jake winced at a *snap-hiss screech* that sounded like a gigantic blowtorch had just been ignited outside. A low grumble of rolling thunder that ricocheted around the walls accompanied the blast and was felt in the pit of his stomach.

The noise was the distinctive howl of a twin jet engine streaking past the building. Jake froze, realizing that the jet was obviously flying lower than aviation regulations permitted.

A jet this close to the ground ... it can't be civilian!

Jake sensed that its timely presence could not be a coincidence.

"Mark?" he called, fumbling his radio.

"On it, buddy," Mark crackled back through the speaker.

Jake's eyes panned around the room as picture frames

rattled from the walls and shattered into pieces as they hit the floor.

His tone intensified. "What the hell was that? An F-15?"

⌘

Mark and Natasha sat in a van backed against the building Jake had broken into. With the building behind them, they had a panoramic view of the menacing aircraft that began to circle.

Craning his neck to glimpse the jet whip past, Mark managed to strain out a few words. "We've got a …"

Feeling his jaw drop mid-sentence, Mark stared at the sinister-looking aircraft and couldn't believe his eyes. He had seen aircraft shaped like that before, but only in magazines or on the web, never up close.

Jake's best friend checked one more time before answering with awe in his voice. "A Raptor!"

⌘

Jake slowly raised his eyes.

Pausing for a second, he wondered why anyone would send an F-22 Raptor, the flagship fighter of the entire US military machine.

In a freeze frame of disbelief, he was overcome by a horrified realization.

Instinctively, he reached into the safe again to retrieve the gun and a bullet clip resting on the narrow shelf over the file drawer. Along the pistol's black side was printed *Glock 22*. Working quickly, he deciphered which way the clip should be inserted into the butt.

The instant the clip snapped into place, he paused, frozen in place again for a moment.

There isn't much time!

Jake's eyes dropped down to the Glock gripped in his hand. Reconsidering, he threw the gun back into the safe. He folded the report, stuffed the document inside his shirt, slung the grappling gun over his shoulder and broke into a sprint back down the corridor toward the entry foyer.

❦

Mark snapped open the backpack at his feet and reached for his binoculars. Tracking the speeding jet as it curved around the building, he struggled to center the magnified image on the fighter's undercarriage.

Mark's awe now gave way to rising apprehension. "Buddy, those aren't fuel tanks hanging under the belly of that thing."

Speaking in code, he was referring to the complement of missiles being carried by the fighter, a very rare sight over homeland soil during peace time. Mark didn't want to alarm Jake's girlfriend, who sat in the front passenger seat beside him.

Natasha was confused. "What's a Raptor?"

Without missing a beat, Mark said in rapid fire, "A fifth generation, joint strike, first wave, assault fighter."

She returned a blank look, unimpressed.

Mark elaborated. "Okay, you know the saying never bring a gun to a fight unless you intend to use it? Well, they would never send a $340 million fighter unless they really mean business. For someone to sign off on scrambling a Raptor, it can only mean one thing."

She crossed her arms and raised an eyebrow as if to say, "Go on."

"They're going to kick somebody's ass!" he said.

The color drained from Natasha's face.

Mark cringed internally. He knew he had a habit of blurting out the most inappropriate thing at the wrong time. This was one of those moments.

The next word that parted from Natasha's lips was almost an inaudible whisper: "Jake?"

Mark's eyes remained locked on hers as he activated his radio. "Time to go, buddy!"

CHAPTER 2

"Already on it!"

Whatever Mark said next, Jake did not hear. Adrenalin coursed through his body, and already he was sprinting down the corridor. Jake knew he would not have enough time to run back down the stairs to ground level. Instead, he headed for the armory safe.

He bolted through the office entry and the bulky armory doorway. Dropping to his knees, he slid the rest of the way across the length of the room-sized safe, stopping in front of the crate that had caught his attention earlier. He snapped open the top of the crate; its contents shimmered.

Jake felt as if he were skirting the edges of rationality. With a deep breath, he heaved the object out of the crate and over his shoulder. Hauling an extra 30 pounds, he dashed out of the armory and back to the office foyer. Now planting himself in front of the windows, he faced the incoming threat.

Balanced on his shoulders sat a Stinger rocket launcher.

The FIM-92 Stinger is a personal, heat-seeking, surface-to-air missile launcher. Easy to operate and light to carry, it was designed to be shoulder-fired by a single person.

First time for everything!

He grasped the pistol grip with his right hand, unfolded its antenna, and flicked the sight assembly into position in front of his aiming eye.

The fighter was circling to make another pass. Jake found it through the Stinger's viewfinder, tracking it across the sky as it turned toward the NRO building.

His left hand fiddled with the unit's switches to bring the launcher to life. Nothing happened. Trying the right thumb trigger, he pressed hard.

Still nothing.

Through the sight, he saw the fighter heading straight for the building, approaching fast.

He tried to release the safety again, and this time he heard its gyro start to spin, commencing the weapon's warm-up sequence. Seconds later the weapon started to buzz. Jake recognized the sound; it was the confirmation signal that the Stinger's sensors had picked up a heat source.

Target locked.

He drew in a slow, deep breath and started to squeeze the trigger gently.

Then Jake's eyes rocketed wide open. Abruptly, he spun around 180 degrees, squeezing the trigger the rest of the way.

With a hiss, the missile shot down the corridor. Both its forward and rear tailfins extended before its main two-stage solid-fuel motor ignited with a loud *pop-hiss*. Milliseconds later, the projectile collided with the rear wall of the building, detonating in a brilliant flash.

Time seemed to slow down. He watched the resulting explosion erupt from the building's rear wall to rush at him. Lowering the nose of the launcher, he used the long metal barrel to shield him from the heat and airborne debris being propelled in his direction.

◈

Mark and Natasha's darkest fear had just been confirmed. They watched in horror as the fighter circled to make its final approach, its undercarriage open and exposing two large missiles. They were helpless to prevent what was to follow.

All they could do was watch in terrifying slow motion as two missiles dropped, one after the other, from the fighter's internal weapons bay. After a short descent, they exploded into life, each leaving thin white contrails as they catapulted toward the building.

Natasha's heart stopped as she froze in shock. Mark noticed she stopped breathing. An equal mix of intrigue and terror filled her chest; she had never seen a missile being launched before, let alone toward her!

There was barely time to scream.

The missiles shot over their heads, disappearing into the building above them. Mark lunged toward the passenger seat, and forced Natasha forward into a brace position.

◈

Jake Marcel had crept over to the other side of sanity. He waited for the Stinger missile blast to pass overhead before dropping the launcher then sprinting as fast as his legs would carry him through the smoke toward the origin of impact.

Almost nothing was visible through the dust and haze. Jake saw light streaming through the newly created opening in the back wall. He ran straight for the light. Then, with all the power he could summon, he leaped out of the building into the open space.

Jake knew he needed to gain as much distance as possible from the building before gravity would take hold of him. His legs pedaled through the air like an Olympic long jumper's, straining for distance as he flew through the haze and smoke.

When Jake punched through the dark smoke cloud, he found himself 30 stories above the ground.

Behind him, the Raptor's missiles smashed through the glazed facade, each impacting their designated targets—the building's internal columns.

The resulting fireball blew out all the windows above the van where Natasha and Mark waited and rapidly expanded to blow through the newly created opening in the rear wall. It narrowly missed Jake, passing over his head as he descended.

With gravity now overcoming inertia, he stretched his arms forward to rotate his body, forcing himself into a controlled fall. He plunged headfirst, like a diver falling toward water, except Jake was accelerating toward the ground.

With a rapid fluid motion, he unslung the grappling gun and took aim, knowing that he was going to get only one chance. Aiming for an internal concrete column through the gun's crosshairs, he sighted his target at level 10 and squeezed the trigger.

The grapple hook hit its mark, lodging in the column near its base. At that moment Jake fell past level 10, and the slack in the grapple hook's line quickly went tight. The force dislodged the hook and the line then dragged it back outside. As the hook whipped toward the window, it slashed through carpet along its path to the ledge. That's where two of the hook's teeth bit hard into the window sill and held tight. It stabbed through the sill to grip the small concrete wall supporting the window.

Jake braced, gripping the grapple cord hard. He had gambled that the concrete window ledge would have enough strength to hold him despite his speed toward the ground.

The small concrete wall held; the resulting tension in the line then hurled Jake back toward the building, converting his vertical velocity into angular acceleration, effectively turning him into a giant, 180-pound pendulum.

Now in a sweeping arc, he accelerated toward the building, catching a glimpse of the window he approached moments before impact. With barely enough time to curl into a human ball for protection, he had more than enough momentum to smash through the second level facade glazing.

Jake felt the bone-shaking thump as he impacted the window, expelling the air from his lungs. Glass exploded around him as he burst through the facade. He felt the sensation of rolling along the floor, again and again, and struggled to maintain consciousness as he catapulted across the second-story office.

Did I just do that?

Jake wasn't NSA or CIA. Nor was he FBI, KGB, MI6,

Special Forces, a Navy SEAL, stationed at NORAD or a part of any other hyper secret government agency whose name consisted of indeterminate letters. And he definitely hadn't been trained by any nameless underground military units funded through black budget back channels.

Although he did have a university degree in engineering and had taken up martial arts, he had never owned a gun nor had he known anything about explosives. Like most guys his age, he was interested in motorcycles, girls, and nightclubs.

Jake had no way of knowing it, but the incident triggering the chain of events that led him to break into a National Reconnaissance Office building occurred decades before he was born.

He used to believe that things happened for a reason. But he never believed that one person could have enough influence to alter the course of modern history. What Jake Marcel was about to learn was that it takes only one person to ask the right questions, and it's the answers to those questions that have the potential to change everything.

CHAPTER 3

July 2, 1947
11:54 p.m.

The armada of B-29s, known as the 7th Bombardment Group, stretched across the fields nestled on each side of the main runway strip at the US Eighth Air Force headquarters in Fort Worth, Texas.

The soldier assigned to the evening's security shift never tired of watching over the hulking silhouettes perched along the runway. After arriving to start his watch, he unpacked his small transistor radio and noticed that his partner was absent from the small outpost. With his partner, the soldier was to look after the dark beasts lined up in perfect rows before them—all aligned and facing the same direction.

He's probably already started his rounds, the soldier thought.

Most nights, the moonlight would shimmer off the aircrafts' wings, but tonight the soldier was treated to a more active panorama. After tuning the radio, he settled in to watch the storm gathering around him; he could almost feel the voltage in the clouds. The soldier was not yet concerned that his partner had not reported to his post so long as he materialized soon.

Huge storm clouds clamped down overhead. The soldier's eyes lit up as awesome thunderclaps crashed in the distance. Lighting blazed in chain reactions across the horizon.

He jolted as ear-piercing thunder sounded in the clouds above him then seemed to roll overhead toward the main hangers and heavy armory bunkers located close to his outpost. The soldier was surprised by the speed at which the weather approached. Moments later, a trickle of rain gained momentum then turned into a steady soaking. Nevertheless, he reached for his M1 Carbine service rifle and small radio and prepared to walk his usual rounds, an activity he repeated several times per shift.

As the soldier passed the first armory bunker along his route, the transistor radio began to choke on static, killing off a soft tune midway through. Lifting the radio to his ear, he gave it a shake before opening its rear compartment to check the batteries. The rain added an extra layer of difficulty, challenging him to keep the small radio dry as he fiddled with its switches.

Something in his peripheral vision drew his attention. Instantly, he wheeled in its direction. For a long moment the lone security soldier stood frozen, trying to process what he was seeing.

Emanating from the roof of the heavy armory bunker before him was a pencil-thin beam of light that shot into the sky. The soldier stifled a gasp. The beam of light appeared to be bluish-red and similar to a spider's silk; it was unlike any beam of light he had ever before seen.

His blood chilled as he realized the bunker was the Strategic Air Command's Special Projects storage facility that housed the 7th Bombardment Group's super-secret armament, atomic weaponry, which was said to be generations ahead of the bombs used at Hiroshima and Nagasaki to end the war almost two years prior.

The soldier instantly reached for his radio. "Alpha-Four-Charlie, do you copy?"

No response.

"Frank"—his whisper trembled—"are you there?"

The radio was dead. It was then that he also noticed his watch had stopped.

This can't be a coincidence, he decided.

Filled with uncertainty, the soldier drew in a deep breath and edged toward the storage facility, the random lightning strikes above erratically lighting his path.

He stood in front of the facility's side entrance, and with his gaze still fixed on the luminescent beam of light that disappeared into the storm clouds, he reached to pound on the door. When the door opened, the soldier was surprised to recognize a familiar face.

"Frank!" the soldier spat. "I've been trying to reach you. Where the hell have you been?"

"I saw the beam of light," Frank said, "and came over to see what the hell is going on. I tried to call it in, but my radio is down."

"Mine too," the soldier said, his eyes urgent. "You don't think this is some sort of exercise?"

The pair looked up to follow the bright, thin beam to

the clouds above. Strikes of lightning illuminated the storm clouds from within. With every flash, they glimpsed a dark silhouette hidden within the clouds.

They both gasped in unison as sporadic portions of the object were revealed, giving them an impression of a solid, circular-shaped mass that hung silently above them.

The arriving soldier flashed Frank a startled look and said, "Try the landline. Call the tower and ask if they're picking up anything on the radar."

With an acknowledging nod, Frank immediately disappeared inside the bunker. The soldier's eyes rose back up to the beam of light, fixing on the point where it contacted the bunker's roof.

Having run a mental calculation of where in the bunker the light beam met the roof, he entered the storage facility and paced out the distance to the area under the beam.

❧

"This is Alpha-Four-Charlie. I repeat, do you have any unusual contacts on your radar?" Frank was relieved that the telephone was still working.

"That's a negative Alpha-Four-Charlie."

"Are you sure? Because I'm telling you there is a flying craft about 55 feet in diameter and hovering anywhere between 50 to 100 feet over our heads. Alpha-Four-Bravo and I were staring right at it. It's as black as night and shooting a beam of light into the storage bunker housing the atomic ordinance!"

There was a long pause from the other end of the phone. "Um … okay. Stand by."

❧

With growing apprehension, Alpha-Four-Bravo let himself through a series of locked enclosures until he reached the location under the beam of light. As he stepped through the door into the highly restricted storage area, he felt himself momentarily go rigid. The ceiling over the atomic ordinance storage housing looked as if it was glowing, and the room was bathed in an eerie bluish-red wash of light. A thin luminescent beam pierced the glowing ceiling. His eyes filled with horror when he realized the beam's target— the live atomic ordinance.

At that moment, the base's auxiliary lights, which were perpetually illuminated to mark walking paths and emergency exits, went dead.

Alpha-Four-Bravo bolted for the exit, nervously feeling his way through the darkness to find the doors he had passed through minutes earlier. When he finally found himself outside the bunker, his gaze shot straight up. The only remaining light sources were the rolling storm and the thin beam stretching down from the clouds. The lightning strikes had now intensified, sharpening the shape of the craft's eerie silhouette looming motionless above.

"The landlines have gone dead as well as the …" Frank burst through the exit straight after Alpha-Four-Bravo, but stopped mid-sentence when he realized that the entire base had gone dark. The two soldiers exchanged a nervous glance in the erratic flashes of lightning.

The beam disappeared without warning milliseconds before the dark silhouette morphed into a brilliant bright sphere of silver light then shot up in a vertical blur and made an impossible right angle turn. It instantly disappeared over the western horizon as a streak of light like a shooting star. The pair watched in bewilderment. The object's silent departure had happened within the blink of an eye, leaving a faint smear through the storm clouds in its wake.

❧

Back inside the bunker, power had returned to the atomic ordinance storage enclosure after the object's departure. The two soldiers stood speechless in front of the deadly bomb that had been of interest to the light beam.

Although Alpha-Four-Bravo was not an atomic physicist, being assigned to maintain security of the US's most secret weaponry required training to cover the very basics of the ordinance's internal mechanics. He frowned, recalling that their atomic weapons used an isotope of uranium to create a chain reaction. The isotope atoms contained extra neutrons, making it less stable than its associated element because it tended to shed the extra neutrons over time. When the uranium isotope reached a certain critical mass, which is the mass that will provide enough neutrons to sustain a cascading reaction, the isotope atoms would shed neutrons, shooting them into other atoms and causing them to split, in turn shedding another wave of neutrons and splitting even more atoms in an escalating chain reaction. When an atom is split, called nuclear fission, a colossal amount of energy is released.

All the bomb did was transport a precise amount of the uranium isotope to the target in two separate portions. When the bomb reached its target, it fired one portion of the uranium isotope into the other, slamming them together to form the critical mass and initiating the imminent chain reaction.

The way the two uranium isotope portions were brought together was foolishly simple. Alpha-Four-Bravo pictured it as a small bullet of uranium, packed with conventional explosives behind it, like a shotgun shell loaded in a long barrel that ran the length of the weapon. At detonation, explosives propelled the bullet down the barrel through the center of the bomb to strike the sphere of uranium at the other end to form the critical mass, initiating the fission reaction and resulting atomic explosion.

The mechanism that fired the uranium bullet was an electronic triggering device powered internally by a 24-volt battery. The soldier's blood chilled as he read the needle on the voltmeter monitoring the weapon's triggering assembly. It was at zero volts, not 24 volts where it should be.

Mortified, Alpha-Four-Bravo turned to his confused partner and stammered, "Whatever that thing was, it's killed the battery ... It's dead; the bomb is completely neutralized!"

CHAPTER 4

July 3, 1947
12:27 a.m.

The night sky lit up with violent red and passive blue clouds huddled together in random lumped masses. Laid out like a soft quilt, the storm stretched to touch the horizon in all directions. The New Mexico desert danced along with the thunderstorm, frequently revealing itself under the random bursts of lightning.

Above the layers of chaos, peace resided. The stars burned with constant brilliance. Through the still air, and over the clouds lit with random bursts of color, streaked an unearthly object. It was metallic silver and shaped like a disk with a dome structure positioned at its core.

Glistening in the moonlight, the silver disk tore through the air at a blistering speed toward the west horizon. A glowing bluish haze emitted from the perimeter of its circular edge like a halo as the craft's magnetic field, generated by its non-terrestrial propulsion system, ionized the surrounding atmosphere.

With military precision, it descended to meet a second disk, the two crafts then skimmed through the upper wisps of storm clouds. Lumped cloud masses, erratically lit from within, continued to rip past at hypersonic speed.

Even with advanced avionics, there was no way the objects could detect what was about to unfold. In an earthshaking thunderclap, a brilliant lightning bolt leaped from a passing cloud mass to strike at the heart of the lead craft's core.

Its metallic shell burst open in a blinding flash. Overloaded by the sudden electrical surge, the propulsion system exploded with fury, disintegrating a great portion of its mass and causing it to rocket toward the second craft.

The two objects came together in an explosive impact as the first sliced through the second, leaving a wedge-shaped rip in the second craft's hull. A violet-blue blast erupted from within what remained of the first craft after impact, disintegrating what was left. A cloud of ejected debris stretched across the sky in its wake, left behind to fall toward the desert below.

Catapulted off course, the crippled second craft sliced its way through the clouds to emerge from beneath the storm. It struggled to maintain altitude then continued at speed as it descended.

When it struck the ground, the explosion momentarily illuminated the desert floor. The force of the impact spewed debris; inertia propelled what remained of the intact body, dragging it across the rocky surface.

Heating as it scraped across the desert plain, the craft's

underside glowed white hot as it sliced a path through the rocks and rubble. It continued scraping with sparks and smoke bellowing from its rear, the friction doing little to slow it down.

The fallen craft trenched a mile-long path across the desert before inertia finally succumbed to the persistence of resistance against the dry earth. It slowed before coming to a smoky halt against a small cliff face.

CHAPTER 5

July 7, 1947
7:36 a.m.

"We've had weather balloons come down over these parts plenty, but never anything like this."

William "Mac" Brazel stood with two uniformed intelligence officers as they looked over the desert plain of the Foster Ranch in Corona, New Mexico. Before them lay a scattered debris field that stretched almost a mile in length and at least 300 feet wide.

"The sheep and cattle around here are scavengers," Mac continued, his words peppered with grit as the ranch foreman spoke. "They'll eat anything in their path. If we don't clear out your downed weather balloons in time, their bits and pieces end up choking my stock."

The rancher exhaled slowly and lowered his voice. "But this stuff is different … the herd won't go anywhere near it."

RAAF Counterintelligence Officer, Major Jesse Marcel, kneeled to inspect a torn piece of material. Beside him

RAAF Counter Intelligence Corps (CIC) Captain Sheridan Cavitt already held a fragment of the scattered wreckage. The two intelligence officers had traveled to the ranch with Brazel the prior night, after the rancher had reported the crash debris to the local county sheriff's office on the previous day.

Marcel exchanged a glance with Cavitt, the captain's concerned expression confirming Marcel's assessment of the scattered materials. The remnants of whatever had crashed must have exploded in the air mid-flight because there were no impact craters or burned ground depressions. More puzzling was that the scattered material was not consistent with any conventional aircraft crash site he had ever seen.

As the Counterintelligence Officer at the air field base that housed the 509th Bombardment Group, the unit tasked with the operational deployment of atomic weapons, Major Jesse Marcel was an expert in identifying all types of conventional and top secret aircraft, missiles, and their composition materials.

Marcel stood up, holding what seemed to be a severed segment of heavy-gauge fishing line. As he inspected it closely, he noticed that specks of light shined dimly at its ends. To his utter amazement, he found that when he cupped his hands around it to block out the sunlight, he could peer inside his cupped hands to find the inside also illuminated. It was unlike anything he had seen.

Major Marcel stared at the luminous fiber in astonishment. "You say that this came down four nights ago."

"The night of the thunderstorms," the rancher declared. "In between the thunderclaps, we heard what sounded like a strange explosion. The next morning, this is what we found."

Captain Cavitt had picked up what looked like a short broken piece of strut or beam before turning toward Marcel. "What do you make of this?"

Marcel studied the small silver object, which was the shape of an "*I*," and noticed the rippling of a purplish-violet hue that appeared iridescent along its length as Cavitt held it in the sunlight. The object was just short of 12 inches long, approximately an inch deep, and three-eighths of an inch wide. It looked as if it had been broken, or possibly shattered, at both ends. Between its flanges shimmered what looked to Marcel like symbols along its length.

It was immediately evident to the counterintelligence officer that the small, broken I-beam segment was made of a material that was not conventional by any definition of the word and more exotic than anything that the US military was fabricating, let alone testing.

Marcel took hold of the I-beam to inspect the symbols more closely. He suddenly paused as soon as he held it in his hand. He was amazed at how little it weighed: it was like holding a feather.

The captain already looked troubled. "You think it's Russian? Or Chinese maybe?"

The question was met with a few moments of silence as Marcel noticed yet another peculiarity about the symbols. They were neither printed nor engraved along its length; instead they had three-dimensional form, as if they'd been molded.

Finally responding, he chose his words carefully in

front of the civilian. "Its form looks more like symbols than writing, similar to hieroglyphics."

"Well," the rancher interjected, his voice stern, "whatever it is, I'm sure you can appreciate the problem here. I can't get the herd through these parts to the river on the other side. But nobody I've shown this stuff to has seen anything like it. This mess has to belong to somebody. Who's responsible for cleaning it up?"

CHAPTER 6

July 7, 1947
11:20 a.m.

The two beaten-up military police jeeps bounced onto the delicately manicured lawns in front of the Chaves County Courthouse. Located at 401 North Main Street in Roswell, New Mexico, the county had spared no expense in the design and construction of the majestic building that had been the pride of the town's center since its completion in 1911.

As the two vehicles shuddered to a halt, their fully uniformed occupants leaped onto the grounds to trample past the courthouse toward the separate jail extension and sheriff's office that stood behind the main building. The door to the office burst open as eight armed officers spilled inside.

❧

Unaware of the imminent disturbance, Sheriff George Wilcox sat at his desk wrestling with his draft report detailing the particulars of the previous day's events. Yesterday had not been a typical day for the sheriff, and therefore he felt it best to carefully filter what was appropriate to include in his incident report.

Moments later, his peaceful office was assaulted by a sudden intrusion as the sound of heavy footsteps thundered toward his building. When the doors exploded open, army personnel entered like charging bulls into a ring.

His eyes bulged at the number of armed officers that poured into his office. "What's the meaning of—"

"We've been sent on the orders of Colonel William Blanchard," the ranking office proclaimed, cutting the sheriff off mid-sentence. "You have a package of interest to the US Army; we're here to collect it."

Wilcox found his feet, glancing at each of the armed officers one by one. "Eight of you to transport one box?"

"The colonel understands its contents are …" He paused. "Sensitive in nature. We are to ensure the package is delivered without, as he put it, interference."

The sheriff felt a rising air of uneasiness.

Moving toward the desk, Sheriff Wilcox tried to lighten the mood. "Well, I've got to hand it to you boys, you certainly are quick. Your two intelligence officers are still out in the desert. They only trekked out there with Mac yesterday afternoon."

Motioning toward the wooden box, the sheriff's eyes fixated on the exotic purplish-violet hues that seemed to ripple up and down the length of a protruding crash fragment, depending on the direction of reflecting light. "This, my friend, is what you are here to collect."

The box contained torn fragments of thin foil, broken segments of small I-beams with odd symbols along their lengths, and fragments of what the sheriff initially thought was hide but felt synthetic and could not be torn. It had been brought into the office the previous morning by Max Brazel, the local rancher who managed the Foster Ranch. He demonstrated that neither the hide-looking material, nor the very thin foil could be cut or torn. When he held a lighter to the material fragments, Sheriff Wilcox was astonished to see that they could not be burned either. The metallic colors of the small I-beam segments were also puzzling to the sheriff because it was not something he had seen before.

Wilcox didn't know who the debris might belong to, but he thought it may be something the military was testing. He promptly called the local army air field and was put through to Intelligence Officer Major Jesse Marcel.

During the course of that conversation, Wilcox explained that the rancher had reported strange pieces of wreckage and that he had a box of samples sitting in his office. After hearing a detailed description of their unusual properties, Marcel drove the short distance to the sheriff's office to meet the rancher and inspect the debris samples for himself.

The sheriff was both surprised and amused that the intelligence officer was equally bewildered by the sight of the mysterious samples. When Marcel asked permission to use the sheriff's telephone, he had obliged. He offered a polite smile as he overheard Marcel describe the contents of the box to his superior officer and felt a rising apprehension as Marcel's face turned stern. He had obviously been given orders.

"Yes, sir." Marcel's tone was submissive. "Understood, sir."

The intelligence office had put the telephone receiver down and paused for a long moment. "I do apologize, but may I impose upon you to make one more telephone call?"

"Of course," Wilcox said, his tone laced with curiosity.

Major Marcel lifted the phone to his ear and dialed the same number. "Hello, this is Jesse Marcel. Could you please put me through to the CIC officer?"

After a short pause he continued, "Hello, Sheridan? It's Jesse. We may have a situation. Are you available to accompany me to inspect a possible crash site?"

Marcel had listened for a moment. "Not sure. You may want to have a look for yourself." He glanced at the rancher. "We could come by and pick you up on the way if that works."

Mac Brazel gave a slow nod. Marcel continued, "Good, we'll see you shortly."

The sheriff's eyes remained fixed on the violet-purplish I-beam sticking out of the box. "Not one of ours I trust?"

Marcel had selected his words carefully. "That remains to be determined."

The intelligence officer thanked the sheriff for alerting him about the find then promptly left his office accompanied by the rancher. The two men were to pick up the CIC officer then make the 80-mile journey together out to Foster Ranch.

Sheriff Wilcox thought it would be dusk by the time they could get there.

Mac Brazel had, however, had left the box of samples

behind. He felt there was no use in hauling them all the way back to the property.

"We'll take the box and be on our way then," the ranking officer declared, picking up the box without waiting for permission.

The sharpness of the armed officer's voice snapped the sheriff from his fixed gaze on the wooden box and jolted his mind back to the present. He watched in silence as the ranking officer helped himself to the box full of debris, spun on his heel, and marched out the door without another word of gratitude or goodbye. His flanking muscle filed out the door after him, one by one, until the office was again silent and peaceful.

CHAPTER 7

July 7, 1947
3:32 p.m.

The shaken archaeology student stumbled toward a weathered phone booth that stood in front of a dusty, rundown service station in the community of Mesa, New Mexico. With a trembling hand, she picked up the receiver, fed the phone a coin and hesitantly dialed the operator asking to be put through the county sheriff's office.

After several rings, she heard the authoritative but personable voice of Sheriff George Wilcox crackle through the line. "Sheriff's office."

She felt drained. During the 35-mile drive from San Agustin, she had practiced in her mind, over and over, how to explain what she had seen. Now that she had contacted the authorities, the prepared explanation instantly evaporated.

She could not believe what she had just witnessed, and wondered how anyone would possibly believe her. "Um …

sir, I'd like to report a …"—she drew in a long breath and finally managed—"crash."

"A car accident?"

"No." She tried to ease her nerves. "A craft."

"I'm not sure I understand, ma'am. An aircraft?"

"Not quite." Her voice was a quivering, barely audible whisper. "A silver craft."

Sheriff Wilcox had paused. "I'm not sure I understood, ma'am. You'll need to speak up."

She gathered her strength. "A silver craft." She went on, getting louder. "A round, metallic, silver craft crashed in the desert." She spoke faster. "A flying silver craft has crashed in the desert. The side of it has ripped open, and there are bodies. Tiny little bodies. Three of them are dead, but one survived." She hadn't realized she was on the brink of crying. Almost shouting now, she went on. "And those eyes, those big dark eyes. It knew what I was thinking; I could feel its thoughts!"

She stopped herself, clasping her mouth as if trying to restrain the psychotic rants of a crazy woman. She feared she may have told too much, that she would simply be dismissed as a drunken mad woman.

But to her surprise the voice on the other end of the line did not sound skeptical. "Ma'am, please calm down. Tell me exactly where you saw this silver craft."

CHAPTER 8

July 7, 1947
3:48 p.m.

Roswell Army Air Field Commander, Colonel William Blanchard, stood before the contents of the wooden box laid across his office floor. It had arrived after midday; now four of the MPs who had retrieved the box were assisting with the assessment of the unusual material properties of the contents.

"Sir," an assistant called, "we managed to get through to General Ramey. We have him on the line for you."

Without acknowledging the assistant, Blanchard moved toward his desk to take his seat. His face stern, he drew in a deep breath before reaching for the receiver.

Four hundred miles away in Fort Worth his superior officer, Eighth Air Force Commander, General Roger Ramey, had received urgent word that concerned him enough to warrant his exclusion from the weekly Joint

Chiefs briefings. General Ramey had rushed back to his Strategic Air Command office and was waiting on the line.

Colonel Blanchard didn't know where to begin. "Sir," he said, his voice uneasy, "we have a developing situation."

The general remained silent.

"Yesterday we received a report from the Chaves County Sheriff's office of a possible aircraft crash site out on a ranch outside Corona. From the description given by the ranch foreman, the debris remnants didn't sound …"—Blanchard paused a moment to search for the right word—"conventional."

"We dispatched our intelligence officers to meet with the sheriff and inspect the samples of the crash debris, and they confirmed that the materials were indeed … Well, the term they used was exotic. They're now accompanying the ranch foreman to the crash site to have a look for themselves. In the meantime, I had the box of samples sent here for a preliminary assessment."

The general finally spoke. "And?"

"Well, sir, we have several pieces here; none of the men can break, tear, or scratch any of it. There is one sample that looks like silk but has no strands of visible fibers. We can't puncture it. The men brought in a sledgehammer to pound one of the larger metallic pieces, but they couldn't even dent it, no matter how hard they tried."

The colonel shifted his weight. "The really strange thing about this material is how light it is, like picking up a feather."

Blanchard picked up one of the small, torn pieces from his desk. He folded it in his hands as he spoke. "And some of the tinfoil-looking sheets, ones as thin as the lining inside cigarette packs, can be folded." He made a fist, crumpling the small silver sheet before opening his hand again. "And it immediately resumes its original shape, without any creases, as if remembering it was a flat sheet. I've never seen anything like it … it's definitely not made by us!"

The general's eyes slowly widened as he thought back to the strange reports he had heard recently about a circular craft seen over his Fort Worth base. He had dismissed the notion, thinking the report was more likely the product of alcohol and bored officers than lights in the sky.

The general heard Blanchard draw in a slow inhalation. The colonel was clearly uncertain how proceed. "I was going to ask if there was a special program that I had not yet been made aware of, but then things took a turn."

"How so?"

"Well, it would seem that the Corona site was not the last of it. We've received another call from the sheriff's office. A distressed young lady has reported another … um … crash site."

"With similar materials?"

"Yes and no, sir. It's not the materials that have prompted my call. It's the, the …" Blanchard paused a moment to compose himself. "It's the pilots, sir."

General Roger Ramey felt his heart sink low into his chest cavity. "Pilots?"

"Civilians have found a silver disk with injured occupants. Not Russian, not Chinese. Not like anything, sir."

The statement was met with a brief silence from the other end of the line as the general weighed the information.

"Where is your field team now?" the general snapped.

"Major Marcel and Captain Cavitt are still out in the desert."

The general's grip tightened on the phone. "Then find a photographer, scramble a Sentinel, and do a fly-over. Find me that disk!"

❧

Within an hour of Blanchard's call to Ramey, a lone single-engine Stinson L-5 Sentinel, affectionately called the "Flying Jeep" by the troops, was already in the air conducting the reconnaissance mission ordered by the general. Along with the pilot, the four-passenger liaison plane flew a photographer and an accompanying officer past the Foster Ranch to systematically crisscross the skies over Corona.

A few miles west of the debris field, on the Plains of San Agustin, a shiny metallic object caught the photographer's attention. As the small plane approached, he became transfixed by the glimmering object, seemingly out of place on the backdrop of the sunburned desert floor, and started snapping shot after shot, chronicling the mysterious object as he watched it grow in his viewfinder.

Shooting faster now, he felt an upwelling of nervous excitement as the object took form.

The photographer froze. Overcome by a wash of incomprehension, he slowly lowered the camera to behold the approaching vista with both eyes.

Below him lay a flawlessly polished silver metallic disk lodged into the side of a rocky outcrop. It had evidently carved an increasingly deep trench as it scraped toward the small rocky hill, where it was now wedged in a steep sideways angle. He could clearly see a tear that extended from its domed apex and widened to its curved extremity. It looked as if a similarly sized disk had sliced through it.

Five people in civilian clothing were scattered around the crashed disk, observing the unearthly object. Under the raised end of the silver craft, lying motionless, were four small gray bodies.

CHAPTER 9

July 8, 1947
1:00 a.m.

"Jess, wake up."

Jesse Marcel Jr. slowly emerged from sleep to the soft tones of his father's voice. The 11-year-old boy rubbed his eyes to find his father, Major Jesse Marcel, sitting at the end of his bed. Tired from a full day of riding his bicycle with his friends and chasing fireflies after dusk, he thought it was unusual for his father to wake him up in the middle of the night, especially while still in his uniform.

With a gentle smile his father said, "I've been out on a ranch and picked up pieces of something that crashed out there. It's in the kitchen; come take a look."

Never having woken up this late, the curious boy slid off his bed. He found his robe and shuffled behind his father toward the kitchen, eager to investigate what surprise would be important enough to get him out of bed in the middle of the night.

The kitchen within the Marcel household at 1300 West Seventh Street was located at the rear of the house. Swing doors separated it from the adjoining dining room. The sink and fridge were placed on one side with white cupboards on the other; gold and white linoleum covered the floor, which led to the house's rear entrance. The boy's father usually entered the house through the rear door, which the family left open during the summer nights to let the cooler, fresh breeze flow through the house.

As Jesse Jr. approached the dimly lit kitchen, he could hear that his mother was also awake. His curiosity was spiked by his father's excitement. What was all the commotion about? As he entered the kitchen, the boy's eyes immediately fell to the cardboard box sitting in the middle of the kitchen floor. The box measured two feet by two feet with most of its contents being delicately laid out across the floor.

His father felt a tingle of anticipation as he watched his son's eyes dart across the exotic objects.

Beaming, Marcel could no longer hold in the excitement he had for his boy. "Jess, something extraordinary has happened."

Jess looked up as his father as he crouched beside him.

Motioning to the floor, he said in soft tones, "These are parts from a real-life extraterrestrial spaceship. It traveled a long way to get here. So these bits and pieces were made a long, long, long way away. Somewhere no person has ever seen!"

The boy's eyebrows furrowed; he didn't understand the terms "extraterrestrial" and "spaceship" or even why his father was so excited about something being made a long way away. Nonetheless, he knew from his father's enthusiasm that it was something special. Furthermore, he was completely content just to have his father home, be out of bed so late, and see the mess his father had made on their kitchen floor.

Wide-eyed, he looked over the fragments spread before him. There were what looked like broken pieces of plastic that resembled dark brown wood with jagged edges. It felt smooth to touch with no wrinkles or depressions. The biggest piece his father had collected covered both of Jess's hands when he held it flat from underneath.

Jess then reached for a piece of what looked like the ordinary aluminum wrap his mother used in the kitchen—there was more of it than the other types of material on the floor. As he picked it up, it felt as if the foil didn't have any weight; it was lighter than a small feather. It was also stronger than any aluminum wrap he knew: the foil didn't bend or fold when lifted but remained as stiff as cardboard, although it was thinner than a stand of hair.

"This one looks like a little I-beam, doesn't it, Jess?"

His father handed him a metallic beam that was sticking out of the box. Jess now noticed a few of these shiny objects; the one he held was around the same length as a ruler he would use in school. Turning it on its end, Jess recognized that its cross-section did in fact look like the letter "*I*."

Jess gave a wide smile. "Yeah, it does!"

The small "I" was half an inch tall and three-eighths of an inch wide. Its top and bottom flanges had a ridge along the beam's lengths, as if the shape of its cross-section were made from two very flat triangles pointing in opposite directions and attached to the thin vertical. It too felt as light as a feather.

As he turned it, the light caught what appeared to be writing along the vertical connecting the flanges. On second thought, the markings looked more to Jess like little pictures than writing. Running his finger along the markings, he felt the smoothness of the raised markings that appeared only on one side of the beam.

The color was fascinating and like nothing he had ever seen before. As he rotated the small I-beam in the light, he watched as a purplish-violet ripple danced up and down the length of its reflective metallic gray surface.

His father's eyes twinkled. "Jess, one day, you'll understand the importance of all this. And one day, many years from now, when you grow up and have a family of your own, you will remember this night and tell your children about it."

CHAPTER 10

July 8, 1947
9:50 a.m.

The sunburned Plains of San Agustin is a vast flat region of western New Mexico nestled between the Tularosa, Black, and Datil Mountains. At 7000 feet above sea level, the snub nose of the military green Chrysler Plymouth effortlessly shoved the thin dry air out of its way as it hurtled toward its remote destination southwest of Magdalena and 150 miles west of the Foster Ranch.

A white five-pointed star branded the front doors of the speeding vehicle. It led a small convoy across the barren expanse. Trailing in the dusty wake of the Plymouth was a similarly colored jeep fitted with long-range communication equipment. Two long low-frequency antennae extending from its rear whipped in the wind as its driver fought to speak over the background roar into his receiver.

Behind the communications jeep followed two troop transport trucks carrying armed MP officers in khaki uniforms. Crammed under the transport's canvas roof, they sat shoulder to shoulder, holding their rifles upright between their knees.

Captain Armstrong sat in the front passenger seat of the Plymouth leading the convoy.

"Sir, we're approaching the crash site now," said the Lieutenant seated in the back seat behind Armstrong. "According to the aerial photos, it should be dead ahead."

The redheaded captain didn't respond. He was fixated on the approaching hillside and rocky outcrops and felt overcome by a profound sense of apprehension and uncertainty.

Armstrong was not a man who could be rattled easily. He was a product of World War II hardening, and his European campaigns had dragged him through the front lines in France and Poland against the Nazi occupation. But, as he approached his current mission coordinates, all the unthinkable gore and atrocities he had carried out under orders for the allied effort against Hitler's regime were a distant memory.

Within hours of the mission briefing, everything he thought he knew about life and the dark side of the world had been turned on its head. Along with his detachment of troops, Armstrong and his men were among the few who now lived in a new and very different reality.

During their mission briefing, they had learned that mankind's place at the apex of the evolutionary ladder was now in question.

The upper echelon commanding the armed forces had initially suspected that the often-reported sightings of flying disks were an advanced form of Soviet aircraft or missiles developed by captured Nazi scientists at the end of the war.

However, Armstrong and his unit learned that there were confirmed crafts other than those made by the Soviets, Germans or Chinese flying through American skies. The recent retrieval of crash debris made of super-light, super-strong materials of unknown composition indicated the existence of technology beyond anything that America, or its enemies, currently possessed. More alarming was the discovery of several small nonhumans amid the wreckage captured in aerial reconnaissance photographs. The images revealed who or what may be piloting these vehicles, which were immeasurably superior to anything manufactured on Earth. And though they knew of only one craft that had crashed, the debris samples the military had assessed suggested the unconventional aircraft was the product of a civilization with a far greater knowledge of science and technology.

With the development of the world's first atomic weapons, the United States might have staked their claim as the globe's leading superpower, but now they possessed material proof that a civilization from elsewhere was technologically superior.

The president of the United States, Harry S. Truman, now faced an impossible decision. Was he to stand before the masses and inform the country that unexplained vehicles, from unknown origins, flew through American skies? Should the president also inform the public that the world's greatest air force may be powerless to challenge these unknown crafts' activities in any way?

Informed individuals at the highest levels of

government decided that such an admission of powerlessness against a threat to national security would cast into question the total sum of the combined American armed forces. A loss of faith in a government by its people of such magnitude was an equal, if not greater, threat to national security.

By keeping all knowledge of this amazing, yet terrifying, discovery secret, the government would not only buy itself time to study these *others* to learn about their intentions and capabilities, but also it could postpone the day when the public would learn that mankind's place in the universe might not be as secure as they had believed.

Therefore, Armstrong's detachment had received orders to lock down the crash site, retrieve the crashed vehicle, and ensure containment of any and all knowledge of its existence. The men were to use terminal force if challenged by anyone. The captain was in command of, to his knowledge, the US military's first Extraterrestrial Recovery and Disposal Unit.

Use terminal force if challenged by anyone.

His superior's orders ricocheted around his mind. The use of the word "anyone" had meant just that—the general public.

In the past, the captain had never hesitated to spill blood in the line of duty. Although his men knew him for being a hard man, Armstrong sensed they would need reassurance that their mission orders were not to be questioned. Even if he trembled with uncertainty about the orders to lead his unit to exert lethal force against American citizens, he could never show it.

"Well, I'll be damned!" the lieutenant choked out from

the back seat, staring in disbelief at the unearthly object now appearing before them in full view. They were off-road and had been bouncing alongside a dry riverbed that cut through the valley toward the small rocky hillside captured in reconnaissance photographs.

When Armstrong saw the craft appear from behind a row of trees they were passing, all he could do was stare. He was speechless. Embedded in the hillside was a metallic, silver disk. Although he'd already seen the unknown object in photographs, he felt an unexpected wonder ripple through him as he gazed on it with his own eyes.

Armstrong's world twisted. *It's real*, he said to himself.

From the photographs, he had estimated its diameter to measure 50 feet across from tip to tip, which he could now confirm, having seen it again from a different angle. From ground level, he approximated the height of its domed center, which looked as if it measured 10 feet from the apex to its flatter underside. He could also observe the circular craft had rammed through several trees before it lodged itself into the hillside, resting on another tree that held it at an angle. The craft had dug a trench through the dry riverbed, leaving a parallel line of scorched shrubbery extending from some point of impact out of view to the east. The length of the blackened trench, which disappeared past an adjacent hillside, gave Armstrong the distinct impression that the object must have hit the ground travelling at a blisteringly high velocity.

When the captain's African-American driver slammed on the brakes, Armstrong flung his door open. He found himself standing right in front of the halted convoy to survey the crash site he was ordered to lock down, civilians included.

The captain counted 12 people of various ages surrounding the unknown vehicle, which was seven more than had been previously photographed.

They're multiplying!

He felt a surge of adrenalin when he realized that the civilian population was not the only variable that had since changed. Under the silver disk, shaded from the midday sun, were four beings: two were dead, the third looked like it was seriously hurt or dying, and a fourth appeared to be uninjured. The creatures were roughly four feet tall, had gray, dolphin-like skin, and heads that seemed disproportionately large for their bodies.

By human standards anyway, the captain thought.

Their eyes were jet-black and oddly almond-shaped. Huddled in the disk's shadow, the injured creature seemed to have difficulty breathing: it held itself like a person with broken ribs would. Beside it, the other creature sat, looking uninjured by the ordeal.

Armstrong watched in astonishment as some of the swarming civilians attempted to communicate with the uninjured creature. A small boy, who couldn't have been older than 10, was summoning the courage to take a step forward while three of the adults attempted to communicate in different languages—German and Spanish as well as sign language. The boy inched toward the creature slowly, expecting the gray visitor to suddenly react. But the creature remained still. It calmly looked in the boy's direction, as if acknowledging the boy, and watched the human slowly moved closer.

The boy's fear subsided, and he showed a growing confidence as he edged closer. Armstrong couldn't fathom how the boy could suddenly feel more at ease with the unearthly visitor. Perhaps, with some higher level of perception, the visitor understood that the intentions of the boy and his family were nonhostile. Was it also with that same level of perception, usually out of reach to most humans, that the boy could sense he had nothing to fear from the visitors?

Behind the captain, his soldiers spilled out of the troop transport, amassing in formation under the lieutenant's direction.

He heard the lieutenant's footsteps approach. "Sir, the men are ready."

Captain Armstrong heaved an ominous sigh and turned to meet eyes with his second-in-command. Barely audible, his words cut through the still air, "Round them up. All of them."

"Understood."

The lieutenant's follow-up command to the soldiers dissolved the amassed military formation into a chaotic horde that charged the short remaining distance to the crash site. Within moments, they had stormed the civilians to surround the crashed disk completely, startling the adults and scaring the younger civilians in the process.

With his curiosity peaking, the captain calmly walked through the frantic scene and moved into the shadow of the silver disk. From his vantage point, he now saw that a rip had opened all the way down one side, leaving a three-foot-wide gap at the disk's edge. It looked as if a wedge had been cut out, or the disk had split down one side on impact, the force wrenching the two sides of the split apart to form the opening.

The metal along the edge of the rip was jagged. Underneath was a second hull that mirrored the shape of the polished external hull. Beyond those two layers, the captain spotted bundles of fine, thread-like material tied together, the way cables and wires were bunched together in a conventional aircraft. He smelled a distinct odor filling his nostrils—a strange mix of alcohol, acetone, and ozone.

Examining one of the bundles dangling from the ripped opening, Armstrong noticed that the ends of the fine threads were illuminated. They glowed in various intensities of crimson red and brilliant white, with some flashing on and off, as the bundle swayed in the light breeze.

Armstrong tried to peer deeper inside the craft, his eyes following the threads up to the rows of components they were attached to. There was no way he could distinguish the functions of the brown, wood-like cubic components. The captain squinted and tried to interpret the pinkish-violet inscriptions immaculately printed across each cube. To Armstrong, the closest thing it resembled was Egyptian hieroglyphics.

No chance.

It was at that moment that he noticed the same kind of inscriptions had been printed along the sides of the struts and structural beams that were also visible.

Although it was a dry, hot day, the captain was surprised that, while he stood close to the craft, he felt cool. When he reached up to brush his fingers across its flawlessly polished surface, it was ice-cold.

Feels like it just came out of a giant freezer!

He glanced at one of the dead aliens; it lay motionless near the craft. Clearly it had sought shelter from the scorching sun. Armstrong was astonished to see its four-fingered hand and that its ears were just tiny indentations. Its ripped clothing seemed to be a one-piece outfit; gray in color, it didn't have any buttons, zippers or a belt. He could also see that a very deep gash ran the length of its short, gray leg. Curiosity got the better of him, and he found himself bending down to touch the deceased being; it too was ice-cold.

Although he wasn't yet concerned, he could hear the tension between the civilians and his troops escalating. The curious gathering was protesting about being rounded up and ushered away from the craft. They were now huddled in three distinct groups: a family group of two men and three boys, a professor accompanying five college students, and a man on his own who identified himself as a civil engineer.

Turning his attention to the uninjured creature, the captain moved toward the small entity. Its uniform was torn in a couple spots, but seemed to be unscathed. It was then that Captain Armstrong was to endure a frightening, soul-chilling experience.

As Armstrong moved closer, the creature turned to lock eyes with him, penetrating the captain's soul with its large, black eyes, which radiated a frightening telepathic ability. Armstrong could sense an external presence in his own mind; it knew his thoughts. The creature seemed to be in Armstrong's head, doing Armstrong's thinking for him. The captain felt the mental sensations of being in the spacecraft, the anguish of falling and tumbling end-over-end out of control. He felt its fear, its peril, and its isolation. He relived the crash.

More frightening still, the communication flowed both ways: the small, pale being knew the captain's intentions as well as that of the military once they had it in captivity. The creature knew it was going to die. In that second, on a higher level of perception, the captain was already living the visceral terror that was to come for the condemned visitor.

Behind the captain, as if unsurprised by the unearthly appearance of the disk-shaped craft, the soldiers pushed and shoved the family of five, along with the others, into tight groups away from the fallen craft. They hadn't stared at it in awe, or stood motionless gazing in bewilderment as the young boy and his family had.

As he was being pushed away, the 10-year-old boy strained to see past the soldiers toward the creature. He hopelessly tried to wrestle out of the arms that held his body turned in the opposite direction, marching him away from the crash site, and couldn't even rotate his shoulders enough to look back toward the hillside. The soldier kept shoving him forward, possibly harder than was necessary, eventually shoving the defenseless child to the ground.

"Hey!" the boy's father snapped.

Turning his attention away from the soldier he was arguing with, the father rushed over to the aid of his son, who was now on the ground nursing a grazed knee.

"What's going on?" the father demanded. "Do you have to be so rough? Who's in charge here? I want to speak with your CO and—"

Using his machine gun to shove the father in the same

direction, the soldier ignored the hysterical man and sent him reeling backward onto the ground.

Clearly shaken, the trembling father picked himself up. The civilian group now understood the gravity of their situation. They were being rounded up and marched away from the crash site, with or without their consent, and by force if necessary.

✍

The sound of the father crashing to the ground jolted Armstrong out of his telepathic experience. Shaking it off, he tried to return to normal consciousness. However, not all the higher order telepathic links between the captain and the creature had been severed because Armstrong could still sense what the creature was feeling. It knew its situation was hopeless. It had just lived through the nightmare of watching two of its crew die; another crew member was dying before its eyes. It knew there was no chance of rescue now that the military had arrived. It was totally alone on a hostile planet, and now the only humans who had shown it any compassion were being marched away at gunpoint.

Wait a goddamn minute! Armstrong reminded himself that he was commanding the Extraterrestrial Recovery and Disposal Unit. Atomic threats from the intercontinental bombers of the enemy were alarming enough for the general public—the prospect of interplanetary or interstellar threats was deemed to be too horrifying to share with an already excitable population. He was there to do a job—to ensure national security by sanitizing the crash site, civilians included if necessary.

With an upwelling of determination, the captain

stormed toward the father, who was 30 feet away picking himself up off the ground.

The father had recognized the lieutenant as a higher ranking officer and rounded on him. "Look, my name is Glen Anderson. I've moved my family out here because I've been hired to work on nuclear weapon design at the secret base at Sandia. If you could just explain to me what's going on and where we're all being taken—"

"I don't care who you are. Shut your mouth and keep moving." His tone and grim expression left no doubt that he was not to be tested.

Glen's teenage son now challenged the lieutenant: "You know this is bullshit! I'm in the Marine Corps, and we don't treat our own kind like this! What the hell's going on here?"

Adding to the hostilities, the boys' uncle also tore into the lieutenant. "Where the hell are you taking us? You can't shove us around like this! What did we do? What the hell is going on?"

Before he knew it, the uncle found himself thrown to the ground by the lieutenant, who yelled, "THAT'S ENOUGH!"

As the uncle hit the ground, he looked up to see four soldiers stepping forward to flank the lieutenant, two on each side. Incredulous, the uncle found his feet. Filling with rage, he lunged at the lieutenant with an adrenalin-fueled right hook. The lieutenant simply evaded his blow, blocking it with his left arm.

Armstrong had now reached the conflict. He snatched the rifle clean out of the hands of one of the soldiers who flanked the lieutenant. White-knuckled, his muscles rigid, he shoved the butt of the rifle into the uncle's chest. The intense blow hurled his victim backward before he hit the ground, limp.

Glen's teenage son stepped forward to stand up to the captain. As he moved in to strike, two of the flanking soldiers intercepted, restraining the teenager's arms and forcing him to the ground face first.

"Okay! Okay! Hang on a minute!" Glen yelled, his eyes filled with fear. He was waving his hands in the air as he stepped into the middle of the fight to save his family from further injury.

The captain ordered his soldiers to step back and waited for the uncle to find his feet again. The injured man got up, holding his chest and leaning on Glen's shoulder. Glen's older son snatched his arms back from the soldier who had restrained him and picked himself up. Glen's 10-year-old son and eight-year-old nephew clung to the teenager, who was now dusting himself off.

The redheaded captain looked at the three boys then back to their terrified fathers. He took a menacing step forward.

Captain Armstrong's tone was as cold as it was precise. "What you have just witnessed is a secret military aircraft. You are never, and I repeat never, to divulge what you have witnessed to anybody, EVER! If you do, your children will be taken away, and you will NEVER SEE THEM AGAIN!"

CHAPTER 11

90 Days before the Building Collapse

The building foreman was sitting at a desk in a guard house beside the construction site entry gate, making his way through his breakfast sandwich. His gaze shot up from his newspaper at an approaching noise, and he grumbled aloud at being disturbed as he probed the street for the annoyance.

He locked unamused eyes on the offending intrusion. Emerging out of the traffic was a rider throttling his motorcycle. The foreman was even less amused when the motorcycle stopped short of the entry gate in front of him, waiting to be given permission pass.

With all the elegance of a grazing wildebeest, the building foreman cleared his throat and said in a monotone, "All deliveries go to the site office. Head back the way you came and turn right."

The rider slipped of his helmet to reveal the face of a

man in his late twenties. "I'm Jake Marcel; I was called out to meet your site manager."

"You the engineer?"

The younger man nodded.

"You sure don't look like one."

Thank God for that, Jake thought, pausing for a moment before motioning beyond the gates toward the building under construction. "Our office understands that there's a problem with the entry."

"Yeah, that's right. Straight ahead then. He's expecting you."

⤨

"The damn fool can't read drawings!" The site manager's voice exploded.

Jake Marcel stood with the builder's site manager in the foyer of the new building being constructed. The two men studied the building's glazed entry.

The site manager cursed. "The steel fabricator idiot not only screwed up how the main beam over the opening carries the weight from above, but he also got the beam's shape wrong!"

Jake couldn't help but give a half-smile as the other man struggled to contain his anger. Errors during construction were common. As an engineer, Jake had seen mistakes made during construction on almost every project he had been involved in. However, today's problem appeared serious enough to be ranked among the worst he had seen in some time, bordering on professional incompetence by the builder's subcontractor. The engineering company Jake worked for was hired by the architect and had designed the structure of the building, and today he had been called out to the site to provide a solution to the builder's current predicament.

The site manager's rage continued. "So now I've got this circular beam that's bowing because the weight from above is being concentrated at its mid-point, the worst possible place. And who the hell uses circular beams anyway?"

Jake studied the steel framing in the entrance. The architect's intent called for the entry to be entirely glazed with the supporting structural steel being thin and inconspicuous. The beam in question supported the weight of the floors above. The problem was the extent of the beam's deflection, or bowing, would not only look unacceptable to the building's owners, but also meant that the glazing panels would no longer fit underneath it.

The builder was right to question the circular section. Not only did the tubular beam not have the geometrical properties to be strong enough to carry the load, but anyone installing the steel should have had enough experience to realize that a square or I-shaped beam would be more suited to provide the structural capacity required.

Reaching inside his motorcycle jacket, Jake pulled out a folded set of structural drawings to compare to the constructed frame before him. A further problem immediately became apparent. The plans showed the steel beam in question was to support the weight from the floor above via five vertical struts evenly spaced along the length of the beam. Looking up he saw that the contractors had installed only a single strut at the beam's center, which effectively concentrated the entire load from above to a single point in the middle of the steel beam, causing the already inadequate circular beam to bend more than it should.

Jake looked up from the design drawings. "There was supposed to be a larger I-beam spanning this entry, supporting five struts. When did it change?"

"And that's another thing!" The builder's rant intensified. "The damn architect decided that the highlight windows over the door needs to have, how did he put it … 'a cleaner form.' So he deleted the five struts to have only one instead. AND he changed the I-beam to a circular beam."

Jake was unsurprised. "And he didn't think to run that little detail by us?"

The site manager cursed under his breath.

Sounding hopeful, Jake said to the grumpy builder, "Is there a reason why we can't replace the circular section with a larger I-beam that can do the job?"

The builder's eyes turned grim. "When we suggested that to the architect, he lost his shit because the deeper beam would hang underneath the ceiling line. He doesn't want to see a bigger beam because then we'll have to wrap some lining around it to hide the beam, and the whole thing will be too bulky and poke under the ceiling."

Jake turned back to the steel framing. "Then cut the strut and install the bigger beam higher so it sits above the ceiling line."

"Jake, we're already weeks behind. I don't have time to do a measure, cut, and install. I was hoping more for a quick solution so we can just replace it with something around the same size."

"You're not making it easy," Jake said, his voice turning conclusive. "There really isn't any steel section the same size with enough capacity."

A wide grin crept across the builder's face. "C'mon, Jake, you've bent the laws of physics for us once before."

Jake's eyes met the builder's. "And there's a reason that it was only one time; it's not very easy to do."

Now it was the builder who sounded hopeful. "Can't you come up with one more of your magical solutions?"

"You're not giving me much space to work with. Let me go back to the office and look at the numbers. We do the impossible every day." Jake looked back up at the over-stressed circular beam, and added, "But miracles take a little longer."

CHAPTER 12

89 Days before the Building Collapse

Jake's computer screens told him what he expected—there wasn't a steel beam size available that was small enough, as well as strong enough, to replace the failing circular section he had seen at the building site earlier.

He heaved an ominous sigh as he sat back in his chair. Scattered across his office desk were steel fabricator catalogs containing the specifications of all the readily available and off-the-shelf structural sections that could be sourced worldwide. Jake's abilities in math and physics were such that he was able to "feel" the right answer without having to solve complex mathematical equations. Both his laptop and desktop computer screen displayed diagrams and analysis that confirmed his initial feeling: anything that could work was going to be too big to fit. Jake's brow furrowed as he looked at the screen. His numbers also indicated that the capacity of the closest matching I-beam size that would fit was just short of capacity by only a few percent.

There has to be another solution!

On a scrap piece of paper, he drew the cross-section of the circular beam. Over the top of the circular section, he drew an I-beam, paying particular attention to how much room there was available to fit in an alternate section shape.

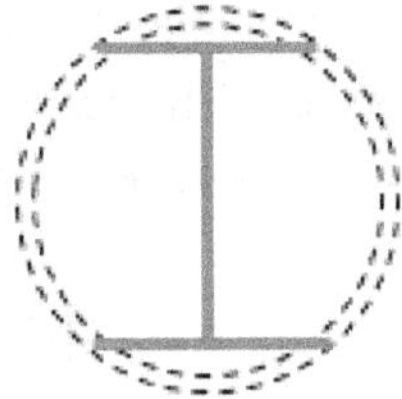

Feeling a growing sense of defeat, he shut down his desktop computer. As his laptop logged off, Jake caught a glimpse of his silhouetted reflection in the darkened screen. The man staring back at him usually had deeply inquisitive eyes, but this afternoon he looked drawn and mentally drained. The organized mess that was his dark hair was scruffier than usual. But his strong jawline remained unchanged, framing his face to reflect a family trait. Despite his weary appearance after an afternoon of problem solving, he was staring at a younger version of his father.

Recognizing the familiar face, Jake felt an unexpected memory rise to the surface. His mind filled with an image from a bedtime story that his father, Jesse Marcel Jr., used to tell him when he was a boy.

A wave of inspiration took hold of him. He instantly

switched his computer back on and snatched a pen to draw the image he remembered from his father's bedtime story.

Sketching frantically, he recalled the story of his grandfather coming home in the middle of the night with a box of top-secret metal parts. Jake's father was only a boy then, but distinctly remembered that Jake's grandfather had spread the bits and pieces across the kitchen floor.

When Jake had finished sketching, he entered the geometric properties into the analysis program and let it run. When the screen refreshed with the results, Jake Marcel felt a chill propagate through his flesh.

It works!

Reaching for the phone, he dialed the number printed on the back of one of the steel supplier's catalogs on his desk. After a short moment, he was connected. "Yes, hello, I'm calling to ask about your customized sections."

The voice on the phone launched into a scripted description of how their company's steel mill was capable of producing a variety of structural beams and columns.

"So you can fabricate customized shapes?" Jake asked.

"We've been involved in a number of projects that required special architectural elements to be made."

Jake was pleased to hear the confirmation. "If I email you a dimensioned cross-section of what I have in mind, would you be able to tell me if it's possible to fabricate?"

"Send it over. Do you have our email address?"

Jake checked the email address listed under the number he had just rung and confirmed he did have all their contact information. He took a snapshot of his screen and attached the image to an email. "Okay, I'm sending you a picture of what I need."

Moments later the voice on the line told Jake what he wanted to hear. A broad smile spread across his face. "Thank you very much. I understand there'll be a premium for the unconventional shape, but this is exactly what we need. We'll draft a more detailed schematic and email the drawing so you can get started."

Jake put the phone down and double-checked his analysis one last time. The reason the conventional I-beam section was failing was due to the way the I-beam behaved under bending stresses. There were three parts to an I-beam: two horizontal "flanges" and a vertical "web" that joined them. Together all the three parts form the "I" shape. As an I-beam starts to deflect, or bend, one of its flanges is stretched as the beam changes shape. If bent downward under a heavy weight, then the lower flange would stretch. At the same time, the upper flange would compress as the I-beam bends.

When Jake was studying engineering, he was taught that steel was extremely strong in tension, but not so sturdy in compression. Thus, as the I-beam bent under heavy loading it would be the upper flange being compressed that would fail long before the lower flange being stretched. Jake always pictured the compression failure mechanism as being the same as what happened when he compressed both ends of a plastic ruler with his hands back in high school—it tended to buckle sideways.

The analysis on Jake's screen indicated that the closest sized I-beam available was under capacity by only a few percent, and its failure mechanism was the same as that of a plastic ruler being compressed—under full loading, the beam's top flange would buckle sideways under compression as it tried to bend.

The solution Jake sketched and emailed was both simple and elegant. It was the I-beam that his father described in the bedtime story of when his grandfather brought home a box full of crash wreckage.

When Jake entered the geometric properties of his memory inspired I-beam into the analysis, the results indicated that he could strengthen a steel beam without having to make it bigger. The geometry of the beam his father described solved the top flange's lateral buckling problem by strengthening the flanges. This simple adjustment added overall strength to the beam section without increasing its depth.

Jake held up his sketch. He was staring at two flattened diamond-shaped flanges pointing up and down on his scrap piece of paper, connected by a vertical web. It fit within the height limit of the existing circular section.

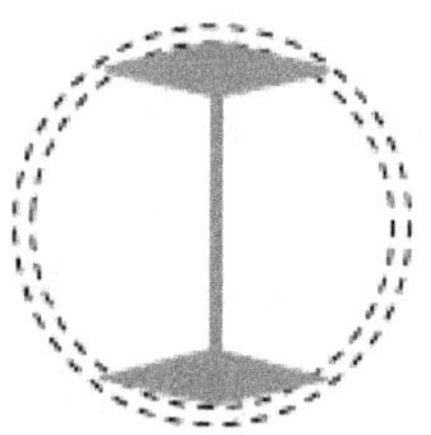

It's crazy enough to work!

CHAPTER 13

The scorching desert sun pelted down on the huge white spheres that sat atop a number of smaller buildings, all sporadically located within the top-secret facility.

Although located near Alice Springs in the center of Australia, Pine Gap was an underground facility managed by the US. Built in 1968, it was officially known in the Australian defense community as the Joint Defense Space Research Facility. Its various white spheres, some of which are up to five stories high, protect super-sensitive satellite dishes. The odd-shaped structures appeared out of place in the backdrop of the Australian outback.

Under these huge satellite dishes and beneath the desert floor, existed a multi-level underground labyrinth. Each level housed countless arrays of networked super-computers that were generations ahead of commercially available workstations and mainframes for the mass civilian market.

The facility was a small cog in the greatest global surveillance effort, codenamed ECHELON, ever undertaken by one of the most well-funded intelligence organizations in the United States, the National Security Agency (NSA). ECHELON had been credited with the success of managing the most sophisticated global spy network in existence. Its purpose was simple: to capture and analyze every phone call, fax, email, and text message sent anywhere on the globe.

Controlled by the NSA, ECHELON was operated in conjunction with government agencies such as the United Kingdom's Government Communications Head Quarters (GCHQ), Canada's Communications Security Establishment (CSE), the Australian Defense Signals Directorate (DSD), and New Zealand's General Communications Security Bureau (GCSB). In 1948, these agencies executed a secret agreement called the UKUSA alliance, whose terms and polices remained active in the 21st century. Thus far, only Australia had admitted its participation in the alliance; the NSA still refused to answer inquiries from Congress about ECHELON's active programs.

Project ECHELON's ability to intercept most of the world's communications traffic was mind-bending. Being one of ECHELON's many tactically positioned interception stations, Pine Gap's satellite dishes captured all satellite, microwave, cellular, and fiber optic communications traffic.

ECHELON's strength was in its ability to sweep, intercept, decrypt, examine, and filter messages into preselected categories on a macro scale for further analysis by intelligence agents. The intercepted intelligence was processed through an array of next-generation supercomputers that automatically searched for preprogrammed keywords and code phrases. Having both voice recognition and optical character recognition capabilities, ECHELON's powerful computers could transcribe conversations into text as well as target an individual's unique voice pattern such that every call made by that person could be automatically recorded and transcribed for further analysis.

The system churned away 24 hours a day, day after day, year after year, crawling the internet, telecommunication networks, and satellite signals for targeted keywords, diagrams or specified voiceprints. Any person, located anywhere, was susceptible to being monitored by ECHELON. However, only messages containing keywords, or hits, were flagged for further scrutiny. ECHELON's true power lay in its ability to efficiently cull the avalanche of intercepted messages and signals down to only those deemed critically important or of tactical interest to the intelligence community.

The Pine Gap station, along with all monitoring posts within the ECHELON system, were provided with a unique list of keywords and diagrams that were constantly used to sweep intercepted communications. The onsite intelligence analysts were responsible for adding, deleting, or changing keyword search criteria whenever updates were issued by the NSA.

⤎

Rubbing his eyes, the Pine Gap Signals Intelligence Manager sat at his desk, robotically scanning through the evening's list of flagged messages, searching for anything of tactical relevance. His small office was separated from the main underground open space containing countless rows of networked servers.

Having worked past midnight, he felt the weariness of early hours weighing heavily as the minutes passed. He sifted quietly through the flagged interceptions that had been automatically compiled and prioritized by the supercomputing workhorses. On the desk next to him was a half-full coffee cup, which had long since reached room temperature.

He almost tipped his coffee cup over when his concentration was unexpectedly disrupted by the beeping of his half-hidden desk monitor. He adjusted his glasses then cleared away the disorganized collage of sticky notes to reveal a blinking screen.

An alarm popped up, sending text flashing in the middle of the screen. Framed within a big red box was an unexpected message:

SERVER 1701. PRIORITY MATCH. TOP SECRET UMBRA DIRECTIVE.

The Signals Intelligence Manager's brow furrowed. He recalled that the 1700 array of servers were assigned to intercept emails. Server 1701 had made a significant match, indicating that its find had been ultra-sensitive.

"Top Secret UMBRA," he whispered to himself in amazement.

His senses tingled at the sight of the word "UMBRA." He knew that such a high level of classification existed for only the most sensitive of materials, but he'd never come across any matches that had been predetermined to require such a high level of secrecy.

He threw down his pencil and launched himself out of his chair, immediately dashing from the office to find server

1701. He ran along the length of the computer aisles, reading the array designations as they flew past.

1450.

1500.

1550.

1600.

1650.

1700.

There it is!

He slid along the tiled floor to slow his pace and grabbed the edge of a desk to swing himself around the corner. Three seconds later, he found himself standing in front of server 1701, gasping for air, trying to refresh his lungs.

He stood there staring at 1701's screen a long moment, processing the displayed image. The interception didn't make any sense. On the screen before him was a copy of Jake's email to the steel fabricator, showing his sketch of the exotic looking I-beam.

CHAPTER 14

88 Days before the Building Collapse

The setting sun had almost disappeared as its orange-crimson light streamed through the Gulfstream's side cabin window. It illuminated cigarette smoke that ascended to the cabin's ceiling in a tight narrow column and dispersed as it reached the overhead no smoking sign.

Mr. Sabre was inclined to hold his cigarette at the base of his first and second fingers. He sat alone in the modestly outfitted jet. His surroundings were adorned with luxurious couches, a self-contained bar, and several full-sized desks.

Cell phones don't work at 32,000 feet. However, being linked to a secure satellite network via the jet's own communications system, Mr. Sabre's personal phone beeped from the inside pocket of his dark suit jacket.

His tone was crisp as he answered. "Sabre here."

The voice on the line was dry but efficient. "We have a developing situation."

"Understood, sir."

The line went dead.

Sabre reached back inside his jacket, pocketing his phone.

Developing situation, he thought.

Sabre's eyes drifted out toward the darkening sky, and he felt a shiver of apprehension. He tried to recall a previous occasion when his immediate superior, the head of a secret unacknowledged department of the NSA, had personally called to use the words "developing situation." He couldn't.

It must be serious if Thirty-Three makes the call himself.

Thirty-Three's discrete NSA department managed a multitude of Unacknowledged Special Access Projects (USAPs) that were completely black in that their funding was kept off the books, that is, not subject to oversight by Congress for reasons of national security. It has been estimated that between 3.5 and 4 trillion taxpayer dollars are spent annually on USAPs.

Such special access projects that fell within the charter of Thirty-Three's department were engaged in extraterrestrial contact and the reverse-engineering and replicating of ET technology for assimilation into human, terrestrial technology. This secret organization that employed Mr. Sabre was known as the Extraterrestrial Contact Intelligence Organization (ECIO).

With its headquarters in New Mexico, the ECIO had agents in all member countries of the European Union and throughout Southeast Asia. Predominantly unknown, even to very senior directors within the NSA, the ECIO is the least known government organization within the intelligence community and has enjoyed complete anonymity since its inception.

Its personnel and agents were drawn mostly from scientific and military elite who are paid extraordinary salaries to match their equally high IQs or security clearances. Moreover, the extraordinary salaries were incentives to guarantee their complete anonymity as employees.

The head of ECIO was a genius who was unparalleled in both knowledge and intelligence. Thirty-Three was identified early in his academic years as being extremely gifted. As a teenager, he wanted to build computers that could think and learn for themselves, a concept that was unheard of in the mid-1960s.

He was not taken seriously by his professors and had been told to get in line with academic protocols and pursue more conventional lines of research. Bell Labs heard about his awesome intellect and hired him without hesitation in a covert effort to remove him from the university before he'd had a chance to establish himself within academic circles. But he quickly outpaced Bell's research agenda, wanting instead to develop exotic technologies years ahead of what was achievable at the time. He was then introduced to the ECIO through its alliance with Bell Labs and joined the ECIO at the age of 21.

Decades later, he was head of the ECIO, and he continued to ensure that the ECIO not only possessed unmatched technical capabilities, but also had access to technologies that were decades ahead of any other agency or research facility on the globe. His name, Thirty-Three, signified his security clearance level: the highest of the upper echelon of the ECIO's security levels.

Mr. Sabre reached for the plane's intercom switch to hail the pilot. "Turn around, we're heading back."

"Sir?" The pilot sounded confused.

"Our mission has changed."

"I understand, sir."

The jet banked west toward the small patch of sky that was still ablaze after the sun crept beneath the horizon. Its fuselage glimmered as the jet turned. With no insignia or identification markings whatsoever, the plane's exterior was simply matte black.

CHAPTER 15

Hundreds of miles away, a retired scientist labored alone in his urban apartment.

Despite having previously served as a scientific consultant to four previous presidents and the National Security Council, as well as serving as a flight surgeon and counterintelligence officer to the Central Intelligence Agency and National Security Agency, the ailing scientist now worked from home, a shadow of his fit and active former self.

He worked at his desk within his study; the modest room filled with computers, two electron microscopes, medical reference literature, and lab equipment. His walls honored his late wife and young son, their images comforting him no matter which room in the apartment he occupied at any given time.

Distracted, he glanced at a notification that appeared on a computer screen at his desk:

NRO TSSCI PRIORTY DISTRIBUTION.

The scientist whispered the acronym as he reread the letters. "TSSCI"

Top Secret Sensitive Compartmented Information, he thought

He felt the familiar sense of urgency in receiving encrypted messages from the National Reconnaissance Office, the government's espionage agency now declassified since 1992. He was on indefinite leave due to his failing health, so he no longer received the stream of daily intelligence reports the NRO routinely issued to the CIA and NSA. But his Above Top Secret clearance status had been maintained from his previous role as the leader of the National Security Council's Special Studies Group and kept him on the very short distribution list for ultra-classified reports deemed to be extremely sensitive in nature.

The 56-year-old scientist slowly extended a weakening hand to his desktop computer to execute a decoding application to decrypt the incoming report. An instant later his screen was filled with an intercepted email. Astonished, the scientist cocked his head, intensely studying the image attached to the intercepted correspondence.

On the screen before him was a hand-drawn image of a fully dimensioned sketch that appeared to be an exotic but familiar I-beam. The scientist scanned for the author of the correspondence; the name listed was Jake Marcel.

CHAPTER 16

56 Days before the Building Collapse

Standing to face their opponents, two lines of student warriors stretched the length of the dojo. The late afternoon light streamed sideways through the hall's roof level clerestory windows, filtering the sunlight into rays of muted yellows and orange. Through patches of light and shade their teacher strolled down the middle of the formation, closely inspecting each kendo student's stance.

The sensei checked that each student's upper body remained upright with shoulders kept squarely aligned to their hips and knees. Both feet faced straight forward, the right foot in front of the left. The left heel was to be kept slightly off the floor with the right foot anchored flat. This posture was intended to allow the students to achieve an optimum balance between mobility and stability.

Because kendo swings were designed to develop maximum power around one's centerline, one of Sensei's first lessons was the importance of facing one's opponents squarely. Thus, when students faced their opponents during sparring practice, they always lined up such that their opponent's centerline was directly in line with their own. When their opponent moved, Sensei instructed them not to compensate by altering their swing, but instead to adjust their body positioning to keep moving with their opponent's and always face them squarely, allowing the students to swing about their body's centerline and develop maximum power with every strike.

Moving through the center of the lined formation, Sensei scrutinized the students' uniforms, checking that their armor was being worn correctly. All were fitted with traditional kendo armor that shielded the head, throat, wrist, and abdomen to protect against being struck by an opponent's shinai, the split-bamboo swords wielded by the students during practice.

With years of dedicated training etched into the deep lines on his face, the kendo instructor radiated an aura of pride as he passed each of his students.

As he approached the end of the lines, Sensei's gaze met that of the younger warrior and he spoke, his voice reverberating off the dojo's walls. "Kendo wa ken no riho no shuren ni o ru ningen keisei michi de aru." *To polish one's skill with the sword is to polish one's soul as a human being.*

Turning back, he peered down the middle of the lines of students facing each other. With shinai raised at their opponents, they stretched out along the length of the hall, ready to fight on command.

Switching to English, the sensei's accent was coarse. "Kendo, the way of the sword, has its origins with the samurai. Its ways have been passed down through the Japanese culture for centuries."

Now moving back through the center of the formation, the instructor passed between the raised wooden swords.

He locked eyes with each student he passed. "The concept of kendo is to discipline the human character through the application of the principles of the Katana ... the sword. As you train, you must remember the purpose of practicing ... To mold the mind and body ... To cultivate a vigorous spirit ... And through correct and rigid training, to strive for improvement in the art of kendo."

With hands held behind his back, the sensei continued. "Thus, one may be able to hold in esteem human courtesy and honor ... To associate with others with sincerity ... And to forever pursue the cultivation and control of oneself."

Still moving through the raised weapons, he was silent a moment as he gathered his thoughts. "The ability to control oneself will set you apart from any aggressor. You need to keep practicing until you can summon the release of adrenalin at will. Once you master this ability, it will make you, for a very short period, super-human. In that short period, you can do anything, achieve anything and defeat anyone."

Having reached the opposite end of the lined formation, he paused to give the students time to absorb the lesson.

After a long moment, he turned back again to face the parallel lines of drawn swords extending down the length of the dojo. "One more round for today."

Drawing in a deep breath, he commanded, "Chudan no kamae!"

The students' reaction was immediate. The parallel lines readied their stance, the tips of their swords leveled at their opponents' throats.

Jake Marcel stood in formation at the opposite end of the line from where the sensei stood. Gripping his shinai firmly, he was conscious not to squeeze too tightly as it would inhibit fluid movement. He locked eyes with his opponent, a slightly shorter fighter who returned an equally piercing stare. Both stood in ready anticipation for what was to follow.

With a force generated from deep within, the sensei's command hit the students like a sonic shockwave: "HAJIME!"

Instantly, the two disciplined rows dissolved into a chaotic swarm as the student warriors broke into pairs engaged in combat. Because all were adorned in protective armor, they swung at their opponents with full force, wooden swords colliding together.

Jake opted to retreat from the mass of furious exchanges and deafening cracks. Beckoning his opponent to follow, he backed into a less populated area of the hall where there was more room to fight.

In a series of flowing exchanges, Jake and his opponent blocked, attacked, and blocked again. Known as one of the class's more proficient fighters, his opponent was swift and confident, waiting for the moment when Jake dropped his guard. But Jake held steady.

Being higher in rank, his opponent asserted himself by advancing with every repetitive strike to create an opening through Jake's guard. And yet Jake did not back down, blocking and counterstriking in flowing movements.

Not taking any notice of the duels erupting around them, Jake and his adversary moved through the middle of the surrounding skirmishes now evenly scattered throughout the dojo.

Although only a couple minutes had passed, Jake felt as if he had been dueling with the higher-ranking fighter for much longer. Side stepping incoming advances, they orbited each other, switching positions as their furious exchanges increased in intensity. With crashing force, his opponent was on him again, and still Jake blocked each blow.

Eventually, it was his opponent's overconfidence that was his undoing. Jake noticed that the other tended to overcommit his follow-through when he swung, favoring throwing his full body weight into his attacks without restraint. By putting all his weight into each swing, inertia dictated which direction his opponent's body would move with each blow.

Jake waited for the opportunity.

Then it happened.

As his opponent lunged forward with a blisteringly fast swing, Jake moved by instinct, barely aware of his own actions as he stepped to position himself for a counterstrike.

Having put all his weight into the mighty swing, his adversary inadvertently exposed his neck and side as his body stretched out. With measured determination, and timed to the millisecond, Jake struck at his opponent's neck with all of hell's fury.

Stunned by the impact, his opponent was infuriated,

knowing it was his own error that allowed the vulnerability. Not wanting to allow a lower rank to get away with the brilliantly executed maneuver, his answer was relentless, fighting back with ferocious intensity. Jake continued to block again and again, counterstriking when an opening presented itself.

✑

From the other end of the hall, Sensei was monitoring the time. The three-minute round was over.

He commanded the students to stop. "Yamé!"

All students immediately stopped in their tracks except for one pair that continued sparring.

Incredulous, the sensei noticed that Jake's opponent was oblivious to the world around him, continuing to advance on Jake despite the others having stopped.

Countering strike after strike, Jake maintained his defense, continuing to block and deflect, waiting for his opponent to make another error.

Repeating his command, the instructor strained to be heard over the clashing of wooden swords. "YAMÉ!"

No reaction. They continued fighting.

The surrounding students looked on in surprised silence, slowly moving to surround the ongoing duel.

The kendo instructor was unimpressed by his student's defiance and approached the duelling pair as the thrashing of swords continued.

Lost in his determination, Jake's opponent pressed on with increasing intensity until Jake executed a maneuver completely unorthodox in kendo.

He readied himself for the next blow and drew in a deep breath as he willed adrenalin to course through him.

When it happened, the series of movements that followed was kinetic artistry.

His aggressor lunged with an overhead strike. Jake, however, was a split second ahead of his aggressor. Instead of blocking, Jake gripped the attacker's wrist. In a motion that was as swift as it was powerful, Jake swept his opponent's feet from under him with his front leg while using the forward inertia of his attacker's own body weight to simultaneously flip him over his shoulder.

The motion was utterly unexpected; Jake threw the aggressor into the air, the opponent appeared as an arched blur as Jake then dragged him back down to earth and slammed him into the floor.

By the time Sensei had reached the pair, Jake had his opponent's chest clamped down under his right foot. He aimed his shinai at his aggressor's throat as he stood firm, despite now being short of breath.

"YAMÉ!" Their instructor's final command carried all the power of a charging bull.

Realizing that the rest of the dojo had long since finished sparring, Jake released his opponent.

With beads of sweat streaking down his face, the fallen student quickly stood to face his victor, his expression filled with a shamed surprise. The two bowed to each other then ran back to their respective places in the line. The surrounding students followed, finding their places in the original formation that ran the length of the hall.

Sensei stepped to Jake's opponent, his eyes angry. "Yamé … mean … STOP!" He turned to slowly walk through the middle of the two rows, hands again held behind his back. "Seiza."

The students reacted as one, all instantaneously assuming the traditional kneeling position in their respective rows, sitting on their heels.

The sensei's face was deep in thought for a long moment. Finally, he spoke. "There is a lesson to be learned here … remove your head gear."

All the students complied.

Jake's opponent was the first to unfasten his helmet. Being of Asian descent, his proud composure was suggestive of his experience and higher ranking within the class, and yet he looked toward the floor, his eyes showing his shame for not obeying the sensei. He knew better than to let his anger consume him.

Jake removed his head gear, panting heavily. Although still one of the more novice students, he had fought to defend himself with proficiency against a superior aggressor. He raised his eyes to his opponent, sensing that his aggressor had been momentarily driven by fury that Jake had used to his advantage.

Jake felt the weight of another pair of eyes on him. Slowly glancing across the students removing their amour, he found his friend Mark beaming. Flustered, with beads of sweat dripping, his bulging eyes displayed shock and surprise.

Jake watched Mark silently mouth the words, "Oh … my … God."

Next to Mark sat Chris, another friend also with sweat dripping down the sides of his face. Jake watched a quiet smile cross Chris's lips that turned to a grin. A half smirk crept across Jake's own face in response.

Two places down the line from Chris sat Paul. His

scruffy hair was moist with perspiration. Paul's eyes said, "I can't believe you did that!"

Movement in Jake's periphery caught his attention. Across from Paul, leaning forward was TJ, the largest of his friends. His body armor straps strained across his bulky, muscular frame. Smiling through gritted teeth, TJ shot out a short jab in the air as if to say, "Give it to him!" He then quickly retreated to his seated position away from the eyes of their instructor.

The sensei continued walking between the seated students as they removed their protective gear and wiped their faces. "When you are consumed with anger, your aggression clouds your judgement."

He gestured toward Jake. "Jake saw this. He could also see that his opponent was overcommitting his strength in his swings." Sensei nodded to himself. "We all know who is the better fighter by rank … so how did Jake overcome a superior aggressor?" He paused, as if to punctuate his next point. "He used his aggressor against himself."

"Fighting is an act of faith in one's self, not just a trick of technique," he added as he passed each student, meeting the gaze of each one in turn. "Jake's move may have come from judo … or aikido … no matter. What matters is that he used what he could … it may have been unorthodox … but he succeeded."

Reaching the end of the two seated rows, he turned to look back at all his student warriors. His voice was commanding, its deep tone rich with insight. "The lesson here is this: When you can't fight fire with fire, USE THE FIRE AGAINST ITSELF!"

CHAPTER 17

"He was so full of himself!" Jackie declared.

Natasha and Jackie sat in the living room of Natasha's suburban home gossiping. A set of speakers played chilled-out club mixes in the background, and scattered around them were handwritten notes, half-empty coffee cups, chocolate wrappers, and a laptop that had gone into sleep mode.

The young women were meeting that afternoon to plan their upcoming workload. Having created a small events company together, they met weekly to track progress and map out the projects they should pitch to interested client groups. Despite their diligence and commitment to their work, Natasha was curious to know as much as possible about the handsome guy that kept giving Jackie attention during the previous night's networking event they both attended. She especially wanted to know who he was.

Jackie looked unimpressed. "Just because he's the doorman at that nightclub, he thought he was a big shot."

Jacqueline Reade, sometimes called Jackie or Jack by

her friends, was Natasha's closest friend. Slightly taller than Natasha, she was stretched out on the couch, her feet dangling off the edge of its arm rest.

Natasha sat on the single seater next to the couch. "But wasn't he mingling with the guests as if he was part of the event? Isn't he just a bouncer there?"

"That's right, and he thought that was supposed to impress me." Jackie couldn't stop smiling. "And then he used the 'I also used to play football' line on me."

The two girls burst into a fit of hysterical laughter.

"Really?" Natasha gasped in amusement. "I'm telling you, there must be some correlation between big muscles and low IQs. I'm sure there's been a study on it."

"Well, if we're going back to the club next week, he might be working."

"What was his name?"

"You know, I was so unimpressed by his inability to hold a conversation, I didn't even take notice."

The two girls laughed in agreement as the doorbell rang.

"That would be Jake," Natasha speculated. "He said he would come over after training then we'd do something for dinner."

Frowning down at her watch, Jackie's face turned grim. "Shit! I've got to go. I told Tom I'd meet with him for one drink."

"Tom?"

Jackie pouted. "You remember Tom; we met him last week at the same club."

Now walking toward the front door, Natasha smiled inwardly, shaking her head. "I can't keep up with you!"

Leaving the living room, she passed through a hallway that ended in a set of double front doors. The floorboards were polished, the hallway walls lined with framed photos of her travels and times with friends.

Opening one side of the double door, her supple lips pursed as she called, "Hey there!"

Jake returned a smile and moved in close to give her a hug. The particular perfume she wore always smelled sweet to him.

"Hmm … you've got your 'smell' on," Jake said softly.

Every person had their own distinctive fragrance; it's something that characterized a person as much as their personality. Jake loved her favorite perfume, but not on the merit of the fragrance itself: it was because it had become Natasha's characteristic scent. Whenever he came across someone wearing the same perfume elsewhere, he would instantly think of her.

"Of course," she arched a surprised eyebrow as she looked up at him.

Jake felt the familiar sensation of being mesmerized when she stared deeply at him. It was the one attribute he remembered from when they met—being immediately struck by her bright arctic blue eyes. They were still just as magnetic as the day he was first mesmerized by them three years prior.

That day Jake was meeting with university friends for drinks at a bar they used to frequent. He had sensed the room shift to focus on two figures appearing at the entrance. Jake felt himself bristle, as if their arrival triggered a change in the properties of the air particles within the bar, their presence electrifying the air molecules. When

Jake turned to see the two newcomers, Natasha's presence seemed to eclipse every other female in the room. With an almost impossible combination of bright luminescent eyes and tempered olive skin framed by flowing dark hair, her warm gaze was as haunting as it was breathtaking.

"Come in," Natasha DeMorea said into his thoughts. She was holding his hand, dragging him inside as he clutched his helmet under an arm. "Jack is still here, but we're finishing up. She may need a lift into town. I had intended to drop her off before you got here, but time slipped away from us, and I need to finish a couple of things before tonight. Would you mind?"

Jake caught his involuntary grimace at the request before Natasha had a chance to notice.

"Hey there! How are you?" Jackie greeted Jake as he was led into the living room.

"Hi. A little tired and sore." Jake strained to smile.

"Why? Did you jog here?" Jackie grinned.

"No, I came straight from training," he said, sensing Jackie's attempt at drawing attention to his scruffy appearance. He found a comfortable armchair and sat, assuming a relaxed posture.

Whenever they all went out for drinks, which was often, Jake never tired of being quietly amused by men attempting to engage Jackie in conversation. Ambitious guys would trip over their own words or offer a verbal recital of their resume in an attempt to impress. More often than not, she barely acknowledged their existence.

There was no question that she was a formidably attractive female. That is, until she opened her mouth to speak.

Jake always felt that her appearance and social status were too closely linked to her sense of self-worth.

That was the reason Jake felt drawn to Natasha when he met them both for the first time. With Jackie everything was all about her. Natasha could easily have been mistaken for a runway model, but she was the type of girl who didn't hold herself on such a high pedestal. She was caring, always put the needs of others ahead of her own, but was somehow oblivious to most men's reactions at her appearance.

Jackie on the other hand was stunning, knew it, and was well on her way to mastering the fine art of manipulating men to get whatever she wanted.

A 21st century man-eater in the making, Jake thought.

Natasha returned to her seat. "Okay, so where were we?"

Jackie turned back to Natasha. "The guy from the nightclub."

"Oh yeah, the intellectual giant!" Natasha laughed. "He was cute, but I think he wore his IQ on his ID tag. What was his number?"

"Thirty-six!" Jackie burst out.

The two girls broke into another fit of laughter. Jake sat unamused with a polite but confused smile.

Jackie turned to Jake. "We're talking about one of the guys who works security at that new club that opened downtown."

Jake's eyes lit up. "The one with the special entrance for motorcycles … you can ride straight in and park inside. Isn't it called Capitalism?"

"That's the one," Jackie confirmed. "One of the security

grunts that works there had also worked at the function we were at last night and seemed very friendly."

Jake rolled his eyes at Natasha. "I'm not surprised."

Jackie shot Jake a sarcastic smirk. "Anyway, you know what they say, men are from Mars, and women are from—"

"That's right," Jake interjected, "women *are* from Venus. On Venus, the atmosphere is toxic! The clouds rain sulphuric acid, the pressure at ground level is 90 times that of Earth's, so you'd be crushed in an instant. And the surface temperature is over 860 degrees Fahrenheit. It is literally the place in our known solar system that is closest to hell. So when you say 'women are from Venus,' you really don't know how right you are!"

A satisfied smile stretched across Jake's face.

Natasha threw a couch pillow straight at Jake's head and narrowly missed him as he ducked to avoid it.

"Anyway," Jackie said, disregarding Jake, "we might be going to Capitalism next week."

"Might we?" Jake's tone was as sarcastic as it was patronizing.

Trying not to smile, Natasha shot Jake her best angry face. "Didn't you just graciously offer to drop off Jackie in town, honey?"

"Okay, come on, princess." Jake sighed, his condescending tone was playful. "Grab your things; we'll try not to mess your hair too much!"

He handed her a helmet. She inspected it distastefully, as if she'd been handed a soiled diaper. Looking up at Jake, her unimpressed eyes seemed to say, "Do I have to?"

CHAPTER 18

The front wheel of Jake's Ducati momentarily lost contact with the road's surface as the motorcycle powered over a small crest. The engine screamed while the tachometer needle swung into the red zone. The thrill of almost being airborne sent adrenalin coursing through Jackie's bloodstream.

With no other cars to be seen, Jake hogged the entire width of the suburban road through the turns. He swung out wide on approach to the curve, and then kissed the inside curb at the apex of the turns.

Banking from left to right as they soared around corners, Jacqueline felt like she was flying. She loved the contrasting tug-of-war between simultaneous thrill and terror—the lightning quick acceleration, the thundering of the engine as it peaked through gear changes, the feel of the engine's vibration through the seat. The experience was almost arousing as she gripped on to Jake for her life.

Jake, however, reminded himself not to push too hard with an inexperienced passenger. It wouldn't take more than a nervous jerk from the passenger in the wrong direction to disturb the delicate balance he needed to keep the weight evenly distributed. A scared passenger leaning against the turns could cause both rider and passenger to come off.

Satisfied he'd done enough showing off by treating the empty roads as a racetrack, he eased off the throttle. They continued over the next few miles in a more civilized manner, observing the posted speed limits.

The evening air was starting to feel crisp. With no other traffic on the road, the night seemed very still. Stars hung bright and clear in the voids between sporadically distributed clouds.

Suburbia dropped away as they continued along the highway approaching the city. They banked to the left as they turned through a large intersection then followed the road through a small series of bends. The road then straightened before gradually dropping into a steep decline to cut through a small valley. At the bottom of the hill lay another intersection. Beyond that, the road gradually rose to the top of the next hill.

While riding downhill, Jake geared down as they approached the intersection below. If it had been daytime, Jake thought, they would have been treated to a scenic view of hills on either side of the valley; in front of them the city skyscrapers would have peeked over horizon beyond.

It was at that moment that they both saw something in the sky above them.

Jake instinctively kicked the brakes, locking the rear wheel. Skidding in a straight line, he brought them to a controlled, sliding stop.

It lasted for only half a second, but what they saw in the sky drew both their attention.

A brilliant light illuminated a small patch of cloud from within, accompanied by a narrow beam that shot straight down in a distinct straight line, as if emanating from a huge, powerful torch in the sky. Although the cloud diffused the glow, its location was indisputable. The source was not above the clouds but within them, as if a flare had been lit.

Jake and Jackie watched in transfixed silence.

Then, as quickly as it had appeared, the width of the beam shrank until it disappeared, followed by the original light source within the cloud vanishing. It didn't seem as if the light had been switched off: more like the source of light had diminished in size until it simply was no more.

Beyond the cloud that had been illuminated, halfway between their location and the horizon, a large commercial airplane appeared through another cluster of clouds. Its navigation lights blinked as it headed toward the airport situated behind them. The size and speed of the aircraft, possibly a Boeing or Airbus, gave some scale to the scheme of things. It appeared to be cruising at the same altitude as the mysterious lights. But when the light departed, Jake had the impression that it moved away at near light speed.

A heavy silence hung between them for a long while.

"What w-w-was that?" Jackie finally managed to say.

Jake paused a moment, weighing his words carefully. "Well, it wasn't a plane … it wasn't a helicopter … it obviously wasn't a shooting star or a satellite."

Jackie's voice was a confused whisper. "It seemed to shoot off when that plane came through the clouds."

"And it sure as hell wasn't lightning." Jake continued, as if not hearing her.

Jake studied the approaching airliner then traced its path toward the cloud that shrouded the mysterious lights. His mind ticked over as it sifted through every possible explanation for what they had witnessed. There was no hint of any other aircraft in the sky besides the airliner. The clouds didn't seem to be the type that could evoke lightning.

Jackie was still puzzled. "Jake, what did we just see?"

Great question: what the hell was it?!

He refocused on the area of the sky where they had seen the bright light. The airliner was now flying through the same patch of cloud. Its lights disappeared when it entered, making no difference to the brightness of the cloud as it flew through it.

Jake had no answer. More to the point, he didn't have an answer that he was comfortable sharing.

He didn't respond to the question.

Jackie also appeared lost in thought. "What could have made the light shoot down like that?"

Jake's gaze traced a line from the cloud in the direction the beam of light had followed, down to the ground. He approximated their distance to the cloud, which roughly triangulated the beam to be over a cluster of suburban rooftops in the distance.

Was it shooting down onto a house? Into somebody's backyard?

Without an exact frame of reference, Jake couldn't be sure.

Slowly shaking his head, Jake finally answered Jackie's question, his tone ominous. "I don't know."

CHAPTER 19

The small suburban parklands spread among the sea of domestic residences were intended to be a green initiative enforced by the city council. Though it was too small to have any significant impact on its surrounding concrete jungle, the small park that was walking distance from Natasha's home was a place she frequently enjoyed spending time.

Following Jake's return from dropping Jackie off downtown, the two had decided to take a walk to the nearby park after dinner. Jake lay on one of the half-dozen scattered lumps of timber that approximated a park bench. He was staring up at the sky, out into the emptiness of space. Natasha sat upright beside him, his head rest on her lap.

She was enjoying the simplicity of his company, but in the silence, she sensed that something was weighing on him.

"Jack said that tonight you guys saw something in the sky on the way to the city," she said.

Jake was pulled from his fixation on the star-sprinkled sky. "When did you talk to her?"

"Are you kidding? I've already received a full report on the guy she's meeting. She texted me while I was cooking. What do you think it was, a UFO?" Natasha giggled.

Jake drew in a deep breath, then once again allowed his head to relax on her lap. He felt an unexpected heaviness, as if her question had aggravated a familiar injury from the past.

Jake's response was a tense whisper. "I don't know."

For years, Jake tried not to think about the troubles his family had endured, or about the times he was taunted as a young boy. For as long as he could remember, and whenever anyone recognized his family name, he hated to hear people belittle his grandfather.

Whenever the topic came up, and without fail, people would discredit his grandfather as they questioned his father. "That's right, wasn't it your dad who mistook that weather balloon for a flying saucer? It was all over the newspapers."

Jake's father responded by recounting the events and justifying facts as he understood them. But then the inevitable round of demeaning jokes and laughter would come.

In Major Jesse Marcel's younger years, he ate, drank, slept, and bled the military. But after the infamous "Weather Balloon" incident, Major Marcel seemed to have been pushed aside, his life's hard work and achievements demeaned. After a life of devotion to his military career, Jake's grandfather's disillusionment with the army he once loved gathered momentum. Although he would never openly condemn the military for chewing him up before spitting him out, the incident did take its toll in other ways.

The story never went away for the Marcel family. Jake watched as his grandparents grew apart, and how people would discredit both his grandfather and father. The distance between his grandfather and the rest of the family then grew over the years.

Even though Jake's father followed in his grandfather's footsteps and went on to enjoy a distinguished military career, ascending to the rank of colonel, Jake held a deep hatred toward the military for how three generations of his family were affected by a single event. Jake had vowed he would never be a part of it, never join any military branch or government organization. He was ashamed of how he eventually neglected to defend his grandfather against discrediting comments and prying questions whenever the topic of conspiracies and downed unknown aircraft in the desert came up because it was easier to play along instead of constantly fighting narrow minds.

"That's just crazy old Grandpa," Jake used to agree, biting down hard on his pride and trying not to display any signs of anger at simple-minded judgements.

Jake shut out those early years of his life and convinced himself that whatever his grandfather found in the desert all those decades ago wasn't real.

Natasha understood that the pain was still a presence in his family.

"Sweetheart, are you okay?" She was gazing down at him, lightly stroking his hair.

The words shook Jake from his daydream. "Yeah, I was just thinking."

She pushed on. "Well, do you think there is life out there in the universe?"

Jake looked toward the scattered pinpoints of light above them once more. "Well, since we've been able to detect planets orbiting other stars, we thought there may have been one star in a hundred that have orbiting planets. Now we know from years of observation and our understanding of how stars form that every star has planets, and of those, one in five likely has the right conditions to support life. So scientists have worked out that the number of planets outnumber the stars, and there are as many stars in the universe as there are blades of grass on Earth. So there could be as many Earth-like planets in our galaxy alone as there are trees in the United States."

In a nearby tree, a pair of owls cooed at one another, capturing Natasha's attention. "So you're saying we're like a couple of owls wondering if it's possible that there are other owls living in any of the other trees?"

"That's a funny way to look at it, but yes."

Natasha now gave a playful smile. "So, do you think there is life on other planets?"

Pressing his lips together, Jake heaved a ponderous sigh. "I used to, but I don't know anymore. If we were the only life in this immense universe, then I guess that would be an even more incredible discovery ... it would make our little blue planet infinitely more valuable and precious than we could imagine."

CHAPTER 20

55 Days before the Building Collapse

Groom Lake is a vast, flat salt bed located in the southern portion of Nevada, about 80 miles from Las Vegas. Home of the iconic SR72 Blackbird spy plane and colloquially known as Area 51, or to its employees Dreamland and The Ranch, the base is a leading-edge military avionics and aeronautics weapons system integration, production and research facility. It has produced avionic advances such as the U2 spy plane, the F117, the B2 stealth bomber, the secretly produced and unacknowledged TR3B "Space Plane" and the hypersonic Aurora.

The 575 square miles of airspace directly over Area 51, known as "the Box," is restricted. Unauthorized entry of aircraft into the Box triggers the immediate scrambling of four F18 Hornet fighters with standing orders to escort noncompliant intruders away from the area—or terminate them.

Approximately 10 miles south of Groom Lake lies Papoose Mountain. Built into the mountain and on the edge of Papoose Lake is the lesser-known, five-level, ultra-secret underground facility referred to as Section 4. Its nine-hangar bay doors were built at a 60-degree angle and set flush with the side of the mountain. The door's color and texture were specifically designed to blend in seamlessly with its surrounding topography. Another smaller dry lake bed sits at the toe of Papoose Mountain; a barely detectable tarmac that leads to the hangar bay doors has been built over it to facilitate the entry and exit of the exotic craft hidden within.

The general public have spotted countless strange-looking aircraft in the sky above Area 51. Observers focus their attention on the well-known Dreamland and away from Section 4. This misdirection was by design to prevent the public from learning of Section 4's existence.

A matte-black Gulfstream approached Papoose Mountain. Even though the pilots could see only a pitch-black desert floor under the clear star-filled night, their navigation screen plotted the outline of the unseen runway ahead. The pilots executed a textbook landing guided solely by their instrumentation. They then taxied toward the toe of the mountain and came to rest in front of Section 4's camouflaged hangar bay doors.

Mr. Sabre stepped out onto the aircraft gangway ladder. The agent appeared to be in his forties, but nobody really knew how old he was. With dark hair and piercing eyes, he had a powerful presence that drew respect from those under his command.

Four bulky-framed and heavily armed sentries in black fatigues met Mr. Sabre as he stepped off the gangway ladder.

The soldiers stood at attention, not one moving a muscle. They cradled well-used FN SCAR assault rifles, their sidearm holsters clutching semiautomatic Glocks. With two soldiers in front and two behind, his greeting party silently marched him along a path marked with parallel lines painted on the tarmac. As Sabre's eyes adjusted to the night, he recognized the familiar pair of parallel blue lines painted inside red lines identifying the walkway that led to the entrance of the underground facility. All arrivals, no matter their rank or security clearance, were to remain inside the blue lines at all times. Sentries had standing orders to use terminal force against any noncompliant visitors who stepped over the red lines that fell outside of the blue.

A small recess that allowed entry to the base had been hollowed out of the mountain rock at the southern end of the hangar bay doors. As the party approached, Mr. Sabre stole a quick glance at one of the sentry's name patches. His designation was 45851.

All sentries were Special Forces personnel from all four military branches, usually ex-Delta Force or ex-Navy SEALs. Sabre always wondered if the sentries gave each other nicknames since personnel requisitioned to the NSA's subdivision at Section 4 were stripped of their names and called only by their designated service numbers. To ensure long-term security, sentries were never to know the identities of the others within their own detachments. Even though they all lived at the underground base, socializing was discouraged.

They wore brown uniforms during the day, black at night. Duty was four hours on with eight hours off repeated around the clock. Talking among themselves while on duty was strictly prohibited; even during their downtime and recreational periods, they had standing orders never to discuss their missions or anything they might have witnessed while on duty. Sentries were never briefed on the events of the prior shift, as all personnel operated on a "need to know" basis.

In addition to sentries, there were four snipers on duty with starlight infrared scopes at all times. Any intruders beyond the sights of the snipers encountered the laser motion detectors that encircled the perimeter of the underground base. That is, provided the intruders could safely traverse the surrounding area within a radius of almost 600 feet of the entry, which was peppered with C26 landmines, a classified, high-yield plastic explosive that was denser and packed more destructive power than conventional C4.

Being the most highly secure and heavily fortified underground facility in the United States, Section 4 shut down any external activities every 48 hours to allow Russian and Chinese spy satellites to sail over without witnessing any activity or unconventional aircraft within the surrounding area of Papoose Mountain.

As he arrived at a heavy metal entry carved into the side of the first hangar bay, Sabre was met by two additional sentry guards. Despite his being well known to all personnel stationed at Section 4, security protocols remained mandatory. After checking his credentials, the entry guards allowed Sabre to pass.

With a *snap-hiss,* the heavy metal doors slid open, one metal panel sliding in front of the other before both disappeared into the stone wall. Only two of the sentry detachment followed Sabre through another checkpoint and down a long, dull, gray corridor that ran the rear length of the hangar bays. Although solid walls occupied both sides of most corridors, in apparent overkill, parallel blue lines inside the red ones still ran along the edges of the floors.

Would they shoot me if I tried to walk through the wall? Sabre mused.

Twenty seconds later, the wall to Mr. Sabre's left dropped away to reveal the expanse of the first hangar. The corridor transformed into a catwalk that bridged all nine hangar bays.

Sabre's gaze dropped to the hangar below. He never grew tired of taking in the exotic form of the silver, disk-shaped craft docked in hangar one. Seamless and sleek with an almost-mirrored finish, it was the product of numerous Black Project programs active at the underground base. Within the confines of Section 4, specialist scientists worked at reverse-engineering exotic technologies from non-terrestrial origins.

The term "Black" signified that, for reasons of national security, the budget allocation provided by the US Government to exotic unacknowledged programs of non-terrestrial nature would never draw the scrutiny of Congressional auditors.

As he passed the next hangar bay, Sabre feasted his eyes on the captured, non-terrestrial, interstellar vehicle housed below. It shimmered, its skin almost radiant under the hangar bay lights. With its disk-shaped form and components manufactured somewhere no human had ever seen, it was a sight to behold, serving as the blueprint for its distant, earthly clone sitting in hangar bay one.

The program to apply exotic, non-terrestrial technology into instruments that human pilots could control was in its seventh decade at Section 4. The core directive of the program was to bridge the gap between alien technology and proven terrestrial technology. Over the years, the program scientists came to understand solid state electronics, integrated circuitry, lasers, and infrared optics. These spin-off technologies were primarily cultivated and developed for military applications, but eventually trickled down for global commercial use.

The rear wall adjacent to hangar bay three opened to a perpendicular corridor that stretched deep into the mountain. The two armed escorts continued to follow the agent down the full length of that corridor. Sabre's eyes rose to the ceiling to find the small audio detectors placed at regular intervals as well as devices that looked like crystals and functioned as holographic security cameras.

If the guards spoke to each other on duty, they would be disciplined.

After a series of right and left turns, they came to a stop at a bank of three elevators. Three keys, a palm print, and a retina scan were needed to access any elevator. Silently, Sabre provided the latter two requirements, which biometrically confirmed his identity. One of the sentries then handed him a flat laser-etched electronic key. The three men exchanged glances then inserted their keys simultaneously into the console to unlock the elevator.

✎

Although he was alone when he stepped out onto Sub-Level 3, a new pair of armed sentry guards greeted Sabre and escorted him to the door of Thirty-Three's subterranean office.

Sabre paused momentarily; behind that door sat one of

the most gifted men he had ever met. The door slid opened, and the armed escort ushered Sabre through.

"Please, sit." Thirty-Three's voice was dry as he gestured for Mr. Sabre to join him at his slender desk.

As Sabre sat, Thirty-Three's transparent desk illuminated with three-dimensional images of a young man in his mid to late twenties. Although the desk was relatively thin, the images seemed to hover just under its surface, giving the desk the illusion of depth.

Thirty-Three slid a finger across the desk and black-and-white two-dimensional images materialized, hovering in between the growing number of mixed three-dimensional images; they were a collage of people and events.

Thirty-Three continued: "Do you recognize any of these people?"

Sabre allowed himself a moment to study the images. He touched one of the pictures, the screen reacted by magnifying itself. "That looks like the vehicle that crashed at Corona, 1947 I believe."

He moved on to inspect a second photo. "That is Colonel Marcel—Senior—most likely a major when the photo was taken."

"And that looks like his son, Colonel Jesse Marcel Junior," he said scrutinizing the three-dimensional holograms. "But I'm not familiar with this guy." Sabre pointed at the younger man.

Thirty-Three met eyes with his subordinate. "No-one does. He is Jake Marcel, the son of Colonel Jesse Marcel Junior. He has recently come to our attention because of this …"

Without clicking a button or tapping the desk, an

image of Jake's email to the steel fabricator appeared, covering all the other images.

Sabre studied the hand-drawn sketch of the I-beam. "That looks oddly familiar."

"Indeed." Thirty-Three tapped the desk then swiped through crash wreckage images. "Almost two generations separate him from what his grandfather picked up in the desert. Which leads us to believe that his family are still in possession of non-terrestrial materials. This, of course, would be lucrative to an enterprising individual. But more to the point, if we allow exotic materials to remain in private hands, it would threaten over 70 years of national secrecy."

Sabre again studied the holographic image of Jake as if measuring his ability to withstand a visit from the NSA's deep black agency.

Thirty-Three's voice held growing concern. "This young man is a particularly sensitive target due to his relationship with one of history's first military personnel to be linked by the media to an alleged interstellar conveyance crash event. We had always suspected that remnants of a crashed interstellar conveyance may still linger in the hands of civilians, but we need to be certain."

Thirty-Three now spoke to Sabre over steepled fingers. "Your unique skill set will be required to assess the possible civilian exposure to any non-terrestrial materials. You are to quarantine the extent of, if any, contamination to the civilian populous."

And by "contamination," you mean "information spread."

Mr. Sabre's tone had the detachment of a seasoned agent. "I will give the situation my immediate attention."

CHAPTER 21

52 Days before the Building Collapse

Although Jake Marcel preferred not to park his motorcycle on the sidewalk, the paved courtyard immediately adjacent to his office building afforded ample space for trees, street lights, and the endless stream of foot traffic, chatting on their cell phones as they hurried past.

He was pleased to find a small cordoned-off area to park his motorcycle. It was neatly out of the way of the sidewalk, nestled in between a row of courtyard benches. After dismounting and taking off his helmet, he tucked his gloves into his pocket and headed for the building entry.

"Jake?" A figure seated on a courtyard bench called out as Jake strolled past.

Stopping to turn toward the voice, Jake trained his eyes on the unknown figure. The seated man wore loose casual pants with a bulky jacket that seemed oversized for his frail frame. He had short brown hair that looked like it had recently started turning silver, and dark unassuming eyes; if the man had been dressed in a suit, Jake would have assumed he was an accountant from one of the nearby office buildings.

Jake looked around before responding. "Yes?"

The unknown man stood and gave a warm smile that radiated a placid sense of welcome, as if greeting a long lost relative. "I'm just a messenger. I could give you a false name, but I won't. Please, if you have a moment, we really should talk."

❧

Jake found himself drawn to the stranger for reasons he could not put a finger on. He found himself agreeing to listen to the other man, walking with him to a nearby park, where they found a bench to sit.

The stranger's eyes were weary. "Thank you for staying to listen. My apologies for the unannounced arrival, but you will come to understand it was a precaution."

Jake felt a rising uneasiness. "And you are?"

"I'm here because of this." The stranger winced as he slowly handed Jake a folded piece of paper, as if the movement caused pain.

Unfolding the sheet, Jake immediately recognized his email containing the hand-drawn sketch of the I-beam.

Jake shot the man a quizzical look. "Okay then, if this is because you guys can't manufacture this shape, the guy I spoke with on the phone clearly said—"

"You are Jake Marcel, the grandson of the late Major Jesse A. Marcel of the 509th Bomb Group who retired as a colonel."

Jake stared at the man, trying to process what he had just heard.

"That's right," Jake finally managed to say while feeling a surge of anxiety. "He used to warn my father and me of mysterious men who'd know all about us. That they would want to meet us in public places. So, which version of the lie are you here to ask me about? Weather balloons? Project Mogul? Or are you actually going to argue my personal favorite, swamp gas? Whichever it is, it's my father you should be talking to!"

The other man smiled, his voice softening. "I do agree with you; the government gave four official explanations of the crash your grandfather investigated. They kept changing their minds."

Jake listened in silence, unable to imagine where this conversation was going.

The man spoke as if he had personal experience with government cover-ups. "But no, that's not why I'm here. And I do believe I have the correct Marcel. I'm here to help you."

CHAPTER 22

Mr. Sabre entered the briefing room on Sub-Level 2 of the underground base, his dual security detail trailing behind. Assembled rows of off-duty sentry guards stood at attention the moment the entry door slid open. He felt the weight of their inquisitive eyes; they were eager to know why they all had been summoned at once.

Sabre scanned the emotionless expressions staring past him. "Anyone in this room with fewer than five field combat skills, LEAVE!"

Instantly, the uniformed bodies dissolved from their rows and silently shuffled out the door. Standing ready, only six hulking figures remained.

Sabre's eyes perused their muscular forms and battle-scarred faces. His voice was suddenly harsh: "You'll do."

CHAPTER 23

After hearing what the stranger had told him, Jake felt short of breath as he shared the park bench with the man who had not yet introduced himself. He felt uncomfortable about how much the other man knew of his background.

The stranger paused to meet eyes with Jake. "Your interesting use of geometry in that email you're holding reminded me of things I've seen in my work over the years."

"Your work?" Jake felt his pulse escalating.

"How do I put this?" The man paused, as if to choose his words carefully. "Everything I'm going to discuss, well, has a classification that is in the stratosphere above top secret. Thus, the reason for all the precautions."

The stranger continued. "For a long time, I worked for the US Defense Department within an agency called DARPA, which stands for Defense Advanced Research Projects Agency. It's unofficially associated with 'Unacknowledged Special Access Projects.' Or you could call them 'Black Programs.' I'll assume you know what they are."

Despite his shortness of breath, the stranger's words had piqued Jake's curiosity. "Secret programs that officially don't exist?"

"Correct. That's what they call it when something is ultra-classified. Those types of programs are managed by the National Programs Office, so when government auditors do their thing, they find nothing."

Jake remained silent as the man went on. "Thus, government scientists like myself could access virtually unlimited funds to create some fantastic—and sometimes terrible—things, and it'll never been known. They call it 'black' because our secrets will never be learned by the rest of society; that is, never see the light of day. No one can expose them or the greed and corruption that is sometimes associated."

"So you're a scientist then?"

The man nodded softly. "My name is Dr. Charles Reilly."

Jake sensed nothing but truth in the man's eyes.

Charles drew in a deep breath. "The primary role of the agency I once worked for was to maintain the United States' technological superiority in military capabilities, and to guard against unforeseen advances by potential adversaries, both terrestrial,"—Charles's eyes met Jake's—"and non-terrestrial."

Jake's eyes widened.

The scientist paused to allow the younger man a moment to absorb his words. "DARPA's mission was to go beyond traditional thinking to develop imaginative and innovative research projects that are often high risk."

Jake was still trying to process the previous sentence. "You worked with ET technology?"

The scientist again flashed a warm smile. "Not exclusively, but you could say that."

So Grandpa was right all along! Jake thought.

Jake sat back, a look of amazement growing in his eyes.

In his teens, Jake had become a skeptic, and yet deep down he had always wanted to believe in his father's bedtime stores. The thought that the individual seated next to him might be a Black Projects' scientist who could confirm what his grandfather maintained as the truth completely knocked the wind out of Jake.

The crash was an alien craft all along. What Grandpa brought home to show Dad was real.

Charles's tone hardened, tearing Jake back from his trance. "The reason I'm here is because of this—your email."

Jake shuddered. "Ho-How did you come by it?"

Charles's gaze stretched out across the park. "They can intercept and assess every type of transmission available: phone call, fax, email—"

"They? As in your formal employer? How?" Jake asked.

"How is not important," Charles said as diplomatically as he could. "What is important is if this has crossed my desk, then it would have been brought to the attention of other agencies too. And I suspect it will raise a red flag or two."

Jake protested. "But it's just an email!"

"It's not just an email, Jake; it's what it represents."

Where is he going with this? Jake wondered.

Charles sensed the younger man's mind was beginning to connect the dots. "You come from a family that had contact with the alleged New Mexico crash site. Almost 70 years later, a member of the same family produces, or is involved with, the production of what resembles alien geometry in a commercial application. It's more than a coincidence, Jake. I am willing to bet that your family still has in their possession a piece of the crash debris, kept hidden from the government all these years. If I think this, then it's a sure bet that other agencies will think it too."

The scientist detected the boy's growing apprehension. "I've come here to tell you that they're not going to want any of it out in the open. Because of who you are, and now because of this." Charles gestured at the email Jake was still holding. "They're going to be convinced that you, or your family, still have some crash debris in your possession. Something that the United States' Government would prefer you didn't have. They've spent over 70 years, and trillions of dollars, keeping what it represents in the dark. Don't think that they won't hesitate for a moment to send out a team to retrieve it."

Charles's expression turned to one of deep concern. "I'm telling you all this as a warning. Be careful."

Jake felt the nervousness returning. "Who are 'they'? The CIA?"

"The CIA is just a figurehead. They're lawyers, accountants, clerks, and graduates. Their job is to gather information. But as far as intelligence is concerned,"—Charles paused as if to emphasize his next point—"the NSA is far superior."

"And your DARPA isn't a part of that?" Jake inquired.

"Well, yes … and no." Charles weighed his words carefully. "There are many agencies with numerous departments whose objectives overlap, but sometimes they also clash."

Hesitant so that he did not to divulge too much, the scientist slowly explained, "Within DARPA, some of my team's objectives were to determine the extent of off-world visitation at any given time, track the numbers as well as the races of visitors, determine the reason for their visits, and gain an understanding of what human interaction occurred—both now and in the past."

Jake's head was spinning; he could not believe his ears.

"You may find this difficult to fathom all at once," Charles said, "but each race of visitors has their own ethics, morality, social structure, and of course technical advancement in comparison to our own. My team was charged with gathering this intel to achieve our prime objective: to determine how to negotiate with them."

"My God!" Jake exploded, finally regaining control of his lungs. "You're not kidding, are you?"

Jake spoke in rapid-fire bursts. "This is beyond historic! Why isn't this more widely known? Are any other countries involved?"

"Not yet. That's why it's an enormous task, because every nation must have input. But for the moment, and although I'm now retired, the most pressing objective for the team is to resume negotiations with *them*."

Still speaking rapidly, Jake blurted out, "Resume? Did they stop? When did they start?"

Charles shifted uncomfortably. "Okay, perhaps I'll come back to that another time."

Considering carefully what to disclose, the scientist

continued cautiously. "The keepers of the secret will never come forward on the question surrounding the ET presence because the government broke the law. They committed crimes in the process of the cover-up and will never want to admit it because they won't want to answer questions about what they did at Corona. Amongst other things, the government violated the Constitution when they used the military to threaten civilian witnesses, going so far as to tell them they would never see their children again if they talked about what they saw at the crash site."

The scientist riveted Jake as he listened to Dr. Reilly continue.

"Putting that aside, over the years, extraterrestrial conveyances have been visiting our nuclear missile sites and shutting down our ICBMS, that is the intercontinental nukes, to send us a message."

"A message?" Jake stammered and started to feel dizzy.

"That they have the power to easily neutralize our forces if they choose. So, neither the Pentagon nor the Kremlin would ever voluntarily admit that this is occurring. You just don't admit to other countries that your strategic nuclear weapons, your first line offensive arsenal, are compromised regularly by unknown entities that possess technologies immeasurably superior to our own."

The scientist's eyes met Jake's. "There have been countless claims of sightings, but it will take only one that's been scientifically proven for the ET presence to become a reality. All it will take will be one piece of their technology or a scrap of their material to be analyzed and deemed to be not man-made, not of this Earth, for all of the sightings to be verified."

Jake could only nod vacantly.

"But we don't have any solid, physical, irrefutable evidence of the actual ETs or their crafts in private hands." Dr. Reilly's eyebrows arched in intrigue. "And anything we do have is either circumstantial or has been covertly retrieved and kept hidden from the public."

The words seem to hang in the air before they fully registered in Jake's mind.

But didn't you say we have ET technology? Jake was baffled.

"If you worked with ET tech, then don't you have access to reams and reams of intelligence reports about your work? Isn't that in itself proof enough?" Jake was shaking his head.

The scientist had asked himself the same question, and the answer was unsettling.

"That I did." Dr. Reilly answered after a brief pause. "But the US Government would do what all governments do when presented with official intelligence documentation referring to an ET presence; claim it's a fraudulent document and deny its authenticity. I should know this because I was one of the debunkers acting in the interest of national security … or so I thought."

The more pieces of the puzzle that Reilly laid out, the more interconnected the picture became.

Dr. Reilly stared intensely, as if peering into Jake's soul. "The problem is getting a sample of non-terrestrial material into the public long enough to make noise. Something you can hold in your hand that is irrefutably, undeniably not of this Earth. When the governments of the world are faced with physical evidence, only then will it be a very difficult thing for them to fight. It will take only one sample to validate every single unexplained sighting that has been recorded through the ages."

A wave of realization rolled over Jake. "You really think my family is still holding on to a piece of the crash?"

A knowing smile slowly crept across Dr. Reilly's face, but he said nothing.

"That's it, isn't it? That's why you are telling me all this … You think that my grandfather held on to a piece of the crash." Jake's eyes went wide. "That would be one thing that could prove everything! And you want it before the other agencies get it!"

"It takes only a single thread to unravel even the sturdiest of tapestries." Charles's tone was soft. "If you do have a family heirloom, perhaps an object that, according to the US Government, is not supposed to exist, then all you need to do is hold on to it tight with both hands … History will then decide what happens next."

Jake felt a chill.

Dr. Reilly waited a moment while his young companion gathered his wits. "I think you may not know what could still be in your family's possession. Even if there was the smallest, slimmest chance that there could be something left behind after all these years, the consequences would be so profound. So far reaching … it would change everything."

Jake sat in semi-paralytic silence. He held on to the park bench as if his world were spinning.

A comfortable silence slowly grew between them as they stared past each other, both contemplating the gravity of the possibilities. Across the park, children played on a swing, their parents chatting and smiling as they supervised.

They have no idea, Jake thought. *How would they react if they knew?*

It was the scientist who broke the silence. "I know this is a lot to take in at once, and there is no reason why you should believe or even trust me. If there were anyone on this planet who had the means to trigger a full public disclosure, I'd put my money on its being you."

"Trust you?" Jake exploded. "You appear out of nowhere holding a document of mine which you, or your so-called agency, somehow intercepted. You know all about me and my family, and you're telling me things that are so farfetched that they are beyond belief! Why the hell should I trust you?"

Charles's soft tone never wavered. "Because out of the entire population on this globe, you're probably the only one who wants to rectify the wrongs done to your family as much as I do about what happened to mine."

Although seated, Jake felt as if his feet had been swept from under him. He fell silent as he listened.

"You may not understand my reasons for what may seem from the outside as my working against the establishment to reveal the secrets I once helped to keep. But understanding will come with time, depending on the path you choose to follow."

Jake felt a gentle hand on his shoulder as Dr. Reilly stood. Wincing in pain, the scientist turned toward the younger man. A business card appeared before Jake's face. "Think about it. And if by chance you do find something that may have been hidden away all these decades, this is how to find me."

Jake took the card.

Before turning to leave, Dr. Reilly reached inside his jacket to produce a small USB pen drive. He handed it to Jake. "Now, I'm not saying that every documented UFO sighting has been real, because the majority aren't. There are plenty of film students out there, as well as crazy nut jobs, doing some convincing work with special effects. So I'm going to leave you with some documents that have been declassified ..." The scientist looked around, quickly sweeping their surroundings. "Well ... mostly. They say that, after you've read enough military investigations on sightings and spoken to enough credible witnesses, one of the most profound experiences a human can have is to come to realize that the ET existence is *real*. When you're faced with the reality that there is life out there, that we are not the only ones, and you truly know it for yourself, it'll change everything you believe in. If you reach that point, you might want to use that card."

Charles paused. "Remember, if you choose to go down that path, it will be a dangerous one. But I'll be in your corner. Whatever you decide, be careful, they're already watching you."

With that, the scientist turned and walked away without looking back. Jake looked at the business card; it was plain white with only a single cell number printed in black. No name, no title, no business address.

CHAPTER 24

49 Days before the Building Collapse

"This is beyond belief!"

Mark was scrolling through the contents of the small USB drive Dr. Reilly had left with Jake. The two curious minds were in Mark's home office pouring over PDF images of once-classified documents and reports that were now appearing on Mark's twin desk monitors.

"So, what do you think?" Jake asked.

Mark read aloud the titles of the documents as he shuffled through. "'Extraterrestrial Entities and Technology Recovery and Disposal, dated April 1954'; 'Unidentified Aerial Objects Project "Sign," Wright Patterson Air Force Base dated February 1949'; 'United States Air Force Projects Grudge and Bluebook Reports 1–12, Dated 1968'; 'Analysis of Flying Object Incidents in the U.S, dated 1948.'"

Feeling restless, Jake paced within his friend's home office as he read.

Mark looked exasperated. "There are hundreds and hundreds of pages here! How about this one ..." Mark strained to read the poor lettering on a document that looked as if it had been typed on an old-fashioned manual typewriter. "'Air Force Regulation number 80-17, Unidentified Flying Objects.' This regulation establishes the Air Force program for investigating procedures and release of information. It provides for uniform investigation procedures and the release of information. The investigation and analysis prescribed herein are related directly to the Air Force's responsibility for the air defense of the United States. The UFO program requires prompt reporting and rapid evaluation of data for successful identification. Strict compliance with this regulation is mandatory."

Mark whistled to himself as he pulled up the next file. Once again he strained to read the photocopied Courier font. "How about this memo dated October 1969? 'The investigation program has two objectives, a) to determine whether UFOs pose a threat to the security of the United States, and b) to determine whether UFOs exhibit any unique scientific information or advanced technology that could contribute to scientific or technological research.'"

Excited, he pulled up the next file. "And look at this picture." Mark cocked his head to the side. "Looks like a crop circle with the picture of an … alien? Really? In the middle of a field in Hampshire in the UK?"

With his thoughts racing, Jake averted his focus away from the offending screens, as if glancing at them made him physically ill. "What would he have to gain from producing hundreds and hundreds of bullshit documents if none of it was real?"

"Hey, there's an affidavit from some military officer." Mark's voice reverberated with excitement. "It's dated December 2002. It says, 'My name is Walter Haut … was born on June 2, 1922 … Am retired … Received a preliminary briefing … Samples of wreckage were passed around … It was unlike any material we had ever seen before. Pieces looked like thin metal foil and yet were extremely strong … Some pieces had unusual markings that no one could identify.'"

Jake had stopped pacing and was leaning on the desk, his back to the screens.

He listened as Mark read on. "On Monday, July 7, I was aware that …"

Jake recited the remainder of the sentence along with Mark as he read. "Major Jesse A. Marcel, head of intelligence, was sent by the base commander, Colonel William Blanchard, to investigate."

Mark looked up stunned. Connecting the dots, his face went white. "Shit! That's your eff'ing grandfather!"

Despite already having read the document before, Jake's stomach did a backflip. "So it would seem."

Mark's expression twisted into an impossible combination of horror and excitement. "Jake, if this is real, then—"

"I know." Jake's voice was a fearful whisper. In that moment, Jake's wall of doubt seemed to crack.

The friends looked at one another for a handful of heart beats. Each knew the other was contemplating the possibilities. If the documents they were looking at were authentic, then the US government had successfully hidden the biggest event in human history: contact with an extraterrestrial civilization. It was both exciting and shocking at the same time. Either way, the prospect was no longer science fiction; it could be very real.

Mark finally regained function of his vocal chords. "You need to talk to your father."

CHAPTER 25

42 Days before the Building Collapse

Seated at the rear of a quaint, run-down café on the outskirts of Las Vegas, Dr. Steven Greer fidgeted with his place setting as he anticipated the arrival of his guest. In accord with the strict instructions he was given, he had arranged a private table away from the front window facing the street.

Dr. Greer shot to his feet. "Dr. Reilly, I … I didn't see you come in."

Dr. Charles Reilly remained silent, returning a narrow smile.

People rarely do, Reilly thought.

Greer swept an open palm toward the vacant seat opposite his, inviting his guest to join him. His voice crackled with nervous excitement. "Please, won't you—"

"I have been following the Disclosure Project since its inception. But despite your tireless work, you may be stepping into territory that you are not prepared for."

Greer had not expected Reilly to be so forceful. He flashed a broad smile. "Why don't we get right into it then?"

Greer patiently waited for Dr. Reilly to slowly take his seat. He observed Reilly in silence for a moment in an attempt to hide his nerves before continuing. "We have been seeking to arrange a briefing with you for years; imagine our excitement when we finally received your acceptance. I nearly fell off my chair. You men in black never want to talk to us."

Reilly looked down at his sports coat then shot Greer an incredulous look—he was not wearing black.

Why don't you say it louder, the waitress didn't hear you! Reilly thought.

Smiling, Greer politely removed his foot from his mouth before starting again. "Thank you for agreeing to meeting with me; it's a rare privilege to speak with one who has been a contractor for the CIA, NSA, and NSC."

Reilly offered a vague nod. He remained silent, giving his nervous companion an expectant look.

Greer read the scientist's expression to say, "Why are we here?"

The air grew heavy as Dr. Reilly waited.

"Okay." Greer finally found his voice. "We have assembled a considerable number of transcripts from military intelligence and corporate witnesses with very sensitive positions within three branches of the US military—Air Force, Navy, and Army—all with top secret clearances."

Dr. Reilly was unimpressed. "I am fully aware that your Disclosure Project has been circulating volumes of documentation and affidavits to members of Congress, scientists, and even to the head of NASA."

Formerly the chairman of Emergency Medicine at Caldwell Memorial Hospital located in North Carolina, Dr. Steven Greer was a medical doctor by profession who worked as a staff physician in Asheville, North Carolina. But it was not his day job that had led him to pursue a meeting with the scientist.

In the mid-1990s Dr. Greer founded an organization known as the Center for the Study of Extraterrestrial Intelligence (CSETI), which gave rise to coordination of a disclosure event involving witness testimonies from former military leaders and intelligence operatives the magnitude of which had never before been conceived.

Greer gave Reilly an edited outline of his organization's work: "The Disclosure Project is not only about circulating information; these witnesses are ready and willing to testify before Congress that we have not needed to pump oil out of the ground and burn it for energy from before I was born. We know there have been classified projects that have procured advanced propulsion systems from downed spacecraft that were not manufactured on Earth and that you guys figured out how they worked! We have documented evidence to demonstrate that, by the 1950s, more money had been spent on antigravity and electrogravitic technologies than the total sum spent on the Manhattan Project. And the reason for hiding these technologies is to keep the world operating on a fossil fuel-based economy."

Although surprised at how successful Greer had been in convincing his witnesses to come forward, Charles could not fault the accuracy of Greer's information.

The US Navy retrieved the first crashed extraterrestrial vessel in 1941 from the Pacific Ocean. In the late 1940s, when the army retrieved other downed ET craft that had crashed inland, the upper echelons of the US military were baffled by its exotic avionics and advanced power plant. It wasn't until the 1960s when human advances in electronics, electromagnetics, and quantum theory allowed clandestine government scientists, Dr. Reilly's predecessors, to reverse engineer the off-world technology and gain an understanding of how it worked.

Greer went on. "We can even subpoena a witness who was a subcontractor for Lockheed Martin, or Skunkworks as you guys call it, who was at a secret facility along with former Secretary of Defense Frank Carlucci at Norton Air Force Base in 1988. There he saw a demonstration of alien reproduction vehicles manufactured with materials from Earth. There were three of them: one about 25 feet in diameter, one about 60, and another about 120 feet in diameter. He witnessed them hover via the use of advanced electronics without any visible power source or external thrust."

The scientist appeared to consider it then shrugged. "There are top secret projects, that is, 'black projects,' and then there are the 'ultra-black projects.' Your witness is talking about what is termed an Unacknowledged Special Access Project of the *ultra-black* variety. Even if you were to persuade a senior member within the chain of command to make an inquiry about it, they will be told that the project simply doesn't exist. This is up to, and including, the White House and the Joint Chiefs of Staff."

Greer sat back in excitement. "So are you confirming that such man-made replicas of ET craft have been in production? Letting the cat out of the bag so to speak?"

"Oh, from where I'm sitting it would appear that the

cat has already wandered out a few times. I'm just giving the cat a name." Reilly's tone was as controlled as it was calculated.

Steven leaned forward; his tone intensified. "You know, I spent nearly three hours briefing a CIA director about all this because even he didn't have access to anything on the subject."

The scientist's eyes narrowed. "You really don't need to be talking to the CIA director; he won't know anything about off-world tech, and he's not going to know anything about man-made replicas. If I were you, I'd be talking to people like me, people who are involved in doing a lot of high-tech work, covertly, as contractors to the US government."

Greer's tone sharpened. "The point I am making is that this is exactly what Eisenhower warned us about. 'Beware the military-industrial complex,' he said, because of the likelihood of its escaping the checks and balances required by our system of government, by our law. I'd say it has already come to pass. We can prove it with the testimony not only of these witnesses, but also from the unaccounted billions that disappear from the national budget annually."

Dr. Reilly understood where Greer was headed with the conversation. The next line of questioning inevitably becomes: "Who is managing all this, and how is it being governed?" The answers to these questions had the potential to cause the most adverse reactions from the public. If they were to learn that a breakaway organization—or government within a government—exists that has significant representation within the military and intelligence communities and is not subject to the normal checks and balances necessary to run a democracy, the consequences would destabilize the current democratic system of government.

Ironically, the threat to national security exists not from the extraterrestrial presence, but from the current covert management of its secret. The administration of the ET cover-up operates outside of the constitutional chain of command. It was this breakaway organization, which Charles once worked for, that controlled these operations and was actively involved in the reconnaissance and reverse-engineering of ET technology.

Greer was still talking. "A case once reported in the media was published in the *New York Times* and the *Washington Post*. The Senate Intelligence Committee confronted the National Reconnaissance Office with the fact that they built a $300 million office building, what we now know to be an unacknowledged control facility, which had never been authorized by Congress or the White House, along with an accompanying $1.7 billion funding allowance that had not been authorized."

The medical doctor looked away a moment, his expression as determined as it was pained. "When we were setting up the Disclosure Project, and before Neil Armstrong passed away, I asked one of his friends if Armstrong would be willing to come to Washington to brief members of Congress. I was told very bluntly that Armstrong wished he could, but that if he spoke about what *really* happened during the moon landing, Neil, his wife, and children would all be threatened. At the time, I thought it was unbelievable, unthinkable even."

Dr. Reilly's tone had an eerie edge. "Hence my warning to you at the beginning of our conversation."

Charles moved to skip past this contemptible reality, trying not to show how he detested the extreme measures taken by the NSA's breakaway governing group to protect their trillion-dollar secrets.

Greer appeared not to have heard the warning. "In the early 1990s, we tried to get President Clinton to spearhead an effort to disclose what the government knew about the ET presence. The CIA Director at the time, Jim Woolsey, was very much in agreement, but told us that he and the President did not have access to these ultra-black projects, that they had been kept out of the loop and essentially were being lied to. Laurence Rockefeller then asked us to provide him with some briefing documents so that when he met with President and Mrs. Clinton they could review them. But President Clinton worried that if he were to bring on the disclosure about the ET question, he may end up like Jack Kennedy. That's when I realized how serious the dysfunction in our government was—that there was a secret government within the government that was really in control."

You have no idea how right you are, Charles thought. *The screenwriters of the* X-Files *couldn't come up with that plot twist!*

Dr. Reilly knew Greer was right. The President had decided not to act, even though he was told not only that we were not alone in the universe, but also that, for 70 years, the scientist's former employers had successfully suppressed revolutionary new energy and propulsion systems that could have avoided conflicts in the Middle East over oil reserves, eliminated the need for fossil fuels, avoided damage to the biosphere from pollution, reversed global warming, and reduced poverty in the world resulting from the shortage of cheaply available energy sources. These technologies reverse engineered from ET tech, which had been the object of covert research and development for seven decades, would one day be of great benefit to humanity. But there would be one inescapable catch.

The scientist's eyes grew heavy. "Did you ever stop to consider that we weren't ready? That some secrets needed to be kept?"

Drawing in a deep breath, Reilly paused as he calculated how much he should, and shouldn't say. "During World War II, Churchill was shown a photo of what was termed a *foo-fighter* that had trailed a British reconnaissance plane. The photo was so detailed, so clear, that Churchill ordered the photo to be quarantined for 50 years. As it turns out, the quarantine is still in place. The reason is that Churchill was convinced, without a shadow of doubt, that whatever was photographed was not of this earth. He believed that all religions would implode if people knew there were beings visiting us from other worlds."

Greer's jaw dropped. He was stupefied as Dr. Reilly continued.

"If we did what you want, disclose the ET presence, then in the same breath we also will have to admit that we cannot control whatever, or whomever, they are from entering our airspace whenever they want. Mix in the implications to right-wing religious organizations, and don't you think that would be a recipe for widespread panic? Not everyone handles revelations of this nature the same way; the outcome would be unpredictable."

Charles's question was met with a long moment of

heavy silence. The doctor's eyes fell to the glasses and silver-ware set out on the table between them. His gaze seemed to focus past the table as he contemplated the question.

"Fifty years ago I would have agreed with you." Greer's voice cracked slightly, and he took a moment to regroup. "But we are no longer living in a post-war, closed-minded era, and today's realities are very different from what they were back in the Cold War when the government's truth embargo poli-cies were forged. The current generation is the first to have unprecedented access to most information instantaneously via the web. It's now common knowledge that we've found ice on the moon, water courses on Mars, and a liquid environment on Jupiter's moon Europa that may support bacterial life. And how many planets have we now found outside our solar sys-tem? Two thousand? Three thousand?"

Steven's eyes rose with a newfound determination. "I agree that the process of coming to grips with a post-disclosure reality of an extraterrestrial presence will force the world to evolve its moral, spiritual, and psychological capacities, the likes of which have never been experienced. The vast and profound consequences inherent in the fact that we are not alone will be of unparalleled significance in the history of the human species. The world's religious leaders will need to come to terms with the theological and philosophical implications of a universe in which humans are no longer the only intelligent, sentient children of God. In this respect, concepts of God, creation, life, and religious meaning will need to evolve in the direction of accommo-dating the existence of intelligent life throughout the uni-verse. I'm sure there will be the unfortunate reactions from various fundamentalist religious groups. But such reactivity should eventually give way to a more reasoned and mature response as the world's religions adopt an understanding of intelligent life that is universal under an infinite creator whose glory is not confined to the boundaries of Earth."

Steven spoke more confidently now. "And yes, governments around the world will immediately be affected in more ways than one. Those covert, previously unacknowledged black projects can finally be moved into the public domain and be governed under conventional oversight and control. I can honestly say that we have photographic evidence, government documents, and more than 100 top secret military and intelligence witnesses which, if they were permitted to be presented to the United Nations, would definitely trigger the disclosure snowball rolling."

The doctor's face darkened. "The first problem we have is that the US government doesn't allow a process that would have any of this come out in an official way. The second problem is that every time we get within an inch of irrefutable proof, something empirical and undeniable, it either mysteriously disappears or the person who possesses it disappears!"

Reilly looked skeptical. "Are you in a position to show me a sample of your so-called documented evidence?"

Greer retrieved an envelope from his pants pocket. "These were found in 1977 by a lawyer."

Reilly watched Greer unfold its contents before he slid the document across the table. It appeared to be a photocopy containing a collection of hand-drawn symbols.

When he studied the photocopy more closely, the scientist's eyes went wide in recognition. "Where the hell did you get this?"

CHAPTER 26

1977
Library of Congress
Washington, DC

The Library of Congress loomed before the lawyer. The 33-year-old was preparing for a seminar on the potential religious implications of contact with extraterrestrial civilizations. If there was compelling information hidden within the library's little-known archives on the extraterrestrial presence, he was there to find it.

It was the scientists at the Jet Propulsion Laboratory (JPL) working on a program known as the Search for Extraterrestrial Intelligence (SETI) that originally requested the lawyer personally deliver the seminar. The request was made via Jane Austen, the Director of the Science and Technology Division of the Congressional Research Service of the Library of Congress.

Just prior to meeting the lawyer, Jane's Science and

Technology Division had been commissioned by Congress, at the personal request of President Carter, to take on a project to review research on UFOs and extraterrestrial intelligence and to evaluate two separate issues. One was the potential existence of extraterrestrial intelligence; the other was the evaluation of collected data on the UFO phenomena. The purpose of the project was to gather all available information to determine what information, if any, should be made available to Congress? And more importantly, how much should to be released to the public?

Having been told that the lawyer was General Counsel to the United States Jesuit Headquarters at their national office in Washington DC, Jane had asked the lawyer whether he could obtain access to the section of the Vatican Library in Rome that held the church's historical information on extraterrestrial intelligence and the UFO phenomenon.

The lawyer was pleased to assist Jane gather data for her division's project, as he had a personal interest in NASA's Space Program and the implications of potential contact with extraterrestrial civilizations.

Soon after he contacted the Jesuit who was head of the Vatican Library, he explained that he had an official request from the Congressional Research Service of the Library of Congress on behalf of the Congress of the United States, and the President himself, that he be granted access to the particular portion of the Vatican that held their information on the sensitive subject matter.

Much to the lawyer's surprise, the official response from the Vatican Library was a simple "no," that the Jesuit National Headquarters would be refused access to that area of the Vatican Library. So, he regretfully had to let Jane Austen know that he would not be able to assist her.

Several months later, Jane Austen called the lawyer again for his help.

After the US Congress cut funding for the SETI program at the JPL in California, Austen contacted the lawyer to ask for his help in his professional capacity. She wanted him to join a group of former astronauts in lobbying Congress to reconsider funding SETI.

Shortly after funding was fully reinstated to the SETI project, Austen sought assistance from the lawyer again.

Jane called from the Library of Congress. "The scientists in the SETI program at JPL would like you to give them a seminar on the potential religious implications of contact with extraterrestrial life."

"I'd be delighted to," the lawyer said. He paused a moment. "Look, if you want me to put something together for them, I'd like to get access to any data you have uncovered in the course of your investigation for the Science and Technology Committee in Congress."

"What would you like to see?" Jane asked.

The lawyer instantly knew what he wanted. "The classified sections of Project Blue Book."

"Oh … I don't know whether the Air Force, or the Department of Defense, would agree to release those to the Library of Congress." She then sounded hopeful. "But I'll try."

❧

The Library of Congress, on Independence Avenue, was not yet open to the public when the lawyer arrived early in the morning. Jane had given him instructions that on a specific time and day he would be allowed access—Saturday, 7:00 a.m. sharp.

The lawyer approached the Executive Protective Service guard blocking the building's front entrance.

Puzzled, the guard measured the approaching stranger. With short, dark curly hair atop of a tall frame, the stranger carried a briefcase with a notepad nestled under his arm. However, the offices were currently closed. Nobody was supposed to be in the building.

The guard stepped toward the curly-haired stranger. "Are you lost?"

"I believe I have an appointment." Juggling his briefcase and notebook under one arm, the lawyer offered his identification.

After calling a supervisor to check on the visitor, the suspicious guard was surprised at his radioed response.

The guard reluctantly unlocked the front entrance. "Yeah, they're expecting you. This way."

Without another word, the lawyer followed the guard through the hall to the stairs that led to the basement. The guard gave the lawyer directions to the room where he was expected.

When the lawyer found the basement room, he was met by two security guards standing ominously on either side of a heavy door. A third sat at a desk to the right of the door being guarded.

The lawyer never would have imagined that he'd be allowed to see what secrets were hidden beyond the heavy door and could feel the weight of the guards' military presence bearing down on him. It was the seated guard who addressed him: "Can I see your ID?"

Feeling an unsettling mix of nervousness and excitement, the lawyer again offered his license.

The guard plucked the ID out of the lawyer's hand and checked it against a series of documents neatly set out on the desk before him. Then handing back the ID, the guard's tone was robotic. "Okay, you are supposed to be here. You may go through."

The lawyer turned toward the heavy door, but hadn't made it past his first step before the guard barked at him.

"I said YOU may pass. Leave your briefcase here."

Apologizing, the startled lawyer laid his case on the table as the other two guards opened the heavy door. He felt a shiver of excitement as he entered.

The lawyer stood dumbfounded. He heard the door close behind him as he was left alone in the room. It wasn't until his heart settled that he realized he still held his yellow notepad under his arm. In all the tense excitement, he had forgotten he was carrying it. Resting it on a nearby table, he surveyed the room for a good place to begin his search.

Dominating the room before him was a reel-to-reel film projector sitting on a table and facing the blank wall ahead. Next to it was an overhead filmstrip viewing machine pointed at the same blank wall. The walls to the side were lined with tables with documents, filing cabinets, and stacked khaki green boxes that were not much bigger than shoe boxes.

The projector is as good as place as any, he thought.

Choosing a box next to the projector, he opened it and sorted through the reels. Since he didn't see any helpful descriptive labels, he chose one at random and loaded the film projector.

He killed the lights and fired up the projector. It groaned to a ticking start, as if reluctant to reveal the reel's hidden images on the wall. The film was silent, the only sound in the room was the projector's fan. The lawyer watched as scene after scene of out-of-focus vehicles danced in strange patterns across the sky off in the distance.

After watching a third reel, he had still not encountered any outstanding revelations let alone anything of real interest.

I'm not getting anywhere with this.

Sensing that his time was limited, the lawyer moved on to the stacked khaki green boxes and chose one at random. Inside he found small metal canisters, like smaller versions of the film canisters, filled with filmstrips. They didn't have any classification markings or labels.

He picked up the box and moved back to the central table, this time loading the other machine, which projected still black and white images onto the blank wall. He turned a small manual crank to progress to the next frame.

The lawyer was astonished to find a collage of photographs and short film stills of increasing clarity. It wasn't until he had explored the contents of a fourth box that he found himself staring open-mouthed in amazement at the image.

It was unmistakable.

A disk-shaped craft appeared to have plowed through a field and stood out of the ground at an angle. There was snow all around.

He was holding his breath now, turning the crank in machine-gun-burst successions. He watched with a combination of shock and wonder as the camera panned to reveal that another craft had crash-landed in a desert, wedging itself into an embankment after having torn a trench through the earth that stretched across the field to the horizon.

The next succession of frames showed military personnel inspecting the crash. With measuring tapes, cameras, and notepads, it appeared every aspect of the crash scene was being forensically recorded. The clarity of the images was pristine; the lawyer was astounded that he could read the name badges on the jackets being worn by the personnel attending the site. There could be no mistake—they were US Air Force.

He shuffled the crank; the next frames were close-up images of the craft. As the camera panned across the seamless, silver, metallic form, something caught his eye. He stopped advancing the film, working the lens to zoom in closer.

There were small symbols embedded across the external skin of the craft. They reminded him of Egyptian hieroglyphics, but were more refined with angular, geometric shapes.

Now skipping ahead, he was hopeful that there was a closer shot. He felt a rising exhilaration when he saw it. The lawyer stared in a trance. Frozen on the wall was a crystal-clear close-up of the alien symbols. Shimmering and exquisite, the angular geometry appeared to be molded into the otherwise flawless metallic surface. He felt as if the alien language called out to awaken a dormant genetic memory from deep within him; that there was some obscure familiarity about the symbols that he couldn't quite put his finger on.

His thoughts were jarred by the muffled rustling of the guards on the other side of the door. Feeling a rising nervousness, he stared at the door a short moment to be sure he wasn't going to be disturbed. He grabbed the yellow pad, convincing himself he still had a little more time. The lawyer anxiously worked the filmstrip projector lens until it had shrunken the close-up image of the symbols to the same size of his notepad.

Stepping to the shrunken close-up, he flipped open the notepad and raised it to the wall. After some minor adjustments, the image was projected onto the notebook's gray cardboard backing. Heart pounding, he meticulously traced the symbols in detail.

After what felt like forever, he stood back and studied his work. He held an exact copy of the extraterrestrial symbols.

Again he heard muffled echoes from the other side of the door. He turned and shot a glance at the door handle.

There was no movement.

I need to get out of here, I don't want to push it, the lawyer thought.

With an intensifying urgency, he returned the filmstrip to its canister, turned off the projection equipment, and returned all the boxes. Within minutes, he was back at the seated guard's desk outside the secure room where he asked for his briefcase back.

"What's that that you've got there?" The seated guard pointed to the yellow pad under the lawyer's arm.

The lawyer did his best to keep his tone calm and controlled. "The notepad I had with me."

The guard sneered and reached out his hand. "Let me see that."

A new wave of anxiety surged through the lawyer as he complied. The guard flipped through the yellow pages, occasionally raising his eyes to the visitor.

When he handed it back, the lawyer felt he could breathe once again. The guard never looked at the inside cardboard backing.

Three minutes later, the lawyer exited the main entry doors and made his way outside. Striding briskly, he headed toward Independence Avenue and away from the library.

CHAPTER 27

42 Days before the Building Collapse

Sitting opposite Dr. Charles Reilly in the café in Las Vegas, Dr. Steven Greer had just finished giving a concise but comprehensive version of how he came to be in possession of the exotic symbols reproduced on the photocopy that lay between them on the table.

Reilly studied the familiar symbols as Greer continued: "The name of the attorney who procured the images of those alien symbols is not important. But what is important is that he is one of over 50 expert witnesses ready to step forward to testify before Congress on the full extent of their knowledge and experience working with, or having been witness to, non-terrestrial technologies and extraterrestrial vehicles, or ETVs now that we don't call them UFOs anymore. I guess that's because they are no longer unidentified."

Slowly, Dr. Reilly turned back to the medical practitioner. "Then what do you need me for?"

Dr. Greer collected his thoughts. "I understand, and deeply respect, that the National Security oath you were required to sign prevents you from publishing papers in scientific journals on your findings during your classified research. And the Disclosure Project has been wildly successful in spreading awareness of the extraterrestrial presence. When I started on this journey, only 30 percent of American citizens believed that there could be civilizations elsewhere in the universe. Today it's up to 80. But I'm sitting here before you to ask ... Is there some way you can support the Disclosure Project's next endeavor?"

Without committing treason? Reilly asked himself.

Steven was gaining momentum and sensed he was making progress. "I was brought up to believe that the United States of America was the land of the free. But it's keeping a lid on the fact that we have been visited, that we are not alone, because of what comes with it."

He paused to emphasize his point. "Which is the 'crown jewels' of the technology, that we now have a working knowledge of the advanced physics that governs the ET technology, which would also have to be disclosed. And will mean the end of the world's $200 trillion oil business, the end of our oil age and the 19th century oil-based technologies that come with it."

Greer was right. Because the US contributed one-third of the world's economic output, there was more pressure from Dr. Reilly's former employers than from other nations to maintain the status quo, despite having to cook the atmosphere and go to war over oil more than once. It was these unintended consequences of keeping the secret that had been eating its way through Charles: increasing dependency of foreign oil, resource depletion, global warming, and the increasing disparity between the rich and poor nations. The list went on.

Steven was still firing: "The world can't wait another 50 years for the truth about these technological advances to come out. Because, once the technology is shared, then every single person on every continent can potentially have access to energy extracted from the ambient environment. You know better than anyone that it will permit a community, even in the jungles of Tanzania, to have energy for electricity, irrigation, crops, and manufacturing, with no pollution or need for multi-trillion dollar infrastructures like power lines, fossil fuel pipe lines, or nuclear power plants."

Greer caught himself, calming his excitement down a notch. "We know of the meeting that was held at the UN when 30 nations were represented and one of the subjects touched on was the ET matter. Although it was widely accepted by those in attendance that the extraterrestrial presence around the globe was real, US interests used, shall we say, alarmist tactics to convince the other nations that disclosure within the next decade would still be premature. But I can tell you there is active discussion happening at the senior levels of the G7 countries to initiate open contact sooner than that. We have been working behind the scenes with the more supportive governments to facilitate a landing event with the full support of their ministries of defense, air forces, and senior political and scientific leaders present."

A wide smile crept across Steven's face. "In May 2001, we held the Citizen Hearing on Disclosure at the National

Press Club. Attending media heard testimony from more than 100 witnesses, including 20 retired Air Force, Federal Aviation Administration, and intelligence officers who stepped forward to describe what they had observed. And yet, it made little impact. With your knowledge and help, you would bring a weight to our movement that the United Nations could not ignore and help negate the US's push to keep delaying disclosure."

Dr. Reilly knew that Greer's request was akin to asking him to breach multiple national security acts.

Reilly paused, as if weighing his words carefully. "That's a very dangerous question you are asking. And as I said earlier, you are embarking on a traitorous road. It's fortunate that up until now your personal safety has been predicated by your maintaining a very public profile. But you need to understand that a public profile is not an absolute guarantee of one's personal safety."

Greer swallowed, nodding. This time he heeded the warning.

Charles pondered the implications of this fortunate, but dangerous, development.

Does he know what he is getting himself into? Charles thought.

If he were to assist Dr. Greer, Dr. Reilly would no doubt put Steven in the crosshairs of the unacknowledged NSA branch charged with the job of keeping such secrets. And yet, Greer's next Disclosure Project venture presented an unparalleled opportunity to reveal the truth as the project was a grass roots movement gaining critical mass in the public domain. Outside the sanitized walls of the NSA, Groom Lake, or Section 4, the Disclosure Project was freely accessible and could be joined by anyone who had an interest in gaining access to the information the Project uncovers.

Reilly made his decision. "I cannot, and will not, violate the oaths I took to preserve national secrets by feeding you information or materials from within the vaults of our most secret underground facilities."

The words seemed to drain the blood from Steven's face. He felt his hope in the scientist's support instantly evaporate.

"There is, however," the scientist added, "no reason why I couldn't direct you toward a sample of irrefutable, undeniable evidence that was already in the hands of the public, or help stand you in front of the United Nations General Assembly to share it with the world."

CHAPTER 28

35 days before the Building Collapse

ight miles away, and six miles north of the Las Vegas Strip, Jake Marcel sat at the desk in his downtown office. He stared blankly out the window, building design drawings were scattered over his desk, the coffee at the bottom of his mug had reached room temperature, and his computer had finished its three-dimensional modelling analysis on the structure he was working on.

Jake's mind was elsewhere; he hadn't noticed that the analysis had finished 25 minutes ago and was sitting idle. Gazing out the window, he watched the reflection of the late afternoon sun bounce off the adjacent buildings as it made its journey across the sky toward the horizon. Around him, the office was bustling with activity, but Jake stared at the sun's orangey-red reflection, his mind filled with the conversation he'd had with Dr. Reilly and the content of the USB drive he'd given Jake.

The sun's reflected image off the adjacent building was

that of a focused beam of light that shot through the clouds toward the ground. It was eerily reminiscent of the light he had seen in the sky with Jackie the night he dropped her off in the city. The strange scene replayed in his mind.

What the hell was it? Was Grandpa really right about what he saw? he thought.

"Would you like another tea or coffee?"

Jake didn't seem to hear.

"Jake … are you okay?"

The question tore Jake from his thoughts. Startled, he turned to find the company's secretary hovering beside his desk.

"I said, would you like another tea or coffee?" she said with a hint of a smile.

He shook his head slowly. "I've had my caffeine quota for the day. But thank you," he quickly added the latter with a lopsided smile.

"You've been staring out the window all afternoon." Her tone was playful.

He slowly turned to face the window again. "Just thinking."

The secretary arched a delicately shaped eyebrow. "Ah! A new girl in your life?"

"No, just something I saw." His voice was flat.

"She must have been really something!"

He pushed the thoughts of Dr. Reilly out of his mind and turned back to her, forcing a polite smile. "Now why does it always have to be about a woman?"

"A young man like yourself … that's the only thing you guys think about. It's either that or money!" With a mischievous smile, she turned and walked away.

Jake let the comment fly past. On any other day he would have returned a witty comeback, but at the moment his thoughts were elsewhere.

He turned back to the desk to assess his workload. It had been an uneventful day at the engineering firm that employed him; no site inspections, no architects calling to scream for designs or structural drawings, no contractors calling with their latest problems, which usually spawned from their inability to read structural drawings or specifications.

I really haven't done much today, he thought glancing at his watch.

Turning to his phone, he activated the intercom and dialed the director's office. "Excuse me, William?"

"Yes, Jake." His boss's voice was as efficient as it was emotionless.

"I'm not really being terribly productive. I'm going to call it a day … but I'll have my phone with me if anyone needs anything."

"We'll see you in the morning then."

Jake flushed with relief. "Okay, thanks. Bye for now."

❧

Forty minutes later, Jake was walking up the footpath to his parents' modest suburban residence. The familiar feeling of home was already making him feel better as he opted to walk the length of the driveway to enter the house through the back door instead of ringing the doorbell in the front. It was a habit he had picked up as a boy from his father, who in turn had learned the same habit from his grandfather.

The aromas of a home-cooked meal rushed at him through the door, enveloping his senses.

"Hello?" Jake called out.

"Is that you, Jake?" Linda Marcel, Jake's mother, sounded both surprised and pleased.

Jake was entering the kitchen when he answered. "Who else were you expecting?"

His mother promptly dropped the kitchen utensils she had been using, rinsed her hands, and threw her arms around her son. Although she attempted not to let her damp hands touch him, her familiar embrace was no less welcoming. She kissed him on the cheek. "What are doing here?"

Jake tried to hide the apprehension that had been growing within him since his impromptu meeting with the scientist. "I need to ask Dad something."

"He's outside tinkering away as usual; he'll be happy to see you. Are you hungry?"

Jake couldn't help but smile. Using those three little words, "Are you hungry?" was the universal method by which a mother communicated affection for her child.

When Jake walked back outside, he was finishing off a pastry that had just left the oven. His mouth was still full as he called out to his father. "Dad?"

The response was a muffled bark: "In the garage."

Jake stared blankly when he found his father in the garage. Dr. Jesse Marcel Jr., the retired colonel and former flight surgeon for the 189th Attack Helicopter Battalion, had disassembled the lawn mower and spread out its parts across the garage's concrete floor. In the middle of the organized chaos sat the retired colonel, perched on an old metal bucket that sat upside-down, cleaning a small engine fragment with a dirty rag.

Jesse looked up at Jake over dirty reading glasses. "Are you still wearing those old things hanging from your neck?"

The question caught Jake off guard. His father was referring to the military dog tags that hung from a chain under Jake's shirt.

He shifted uneasily, clutching at the offending accessories for a moment. "You know I never ride without them; they keep me safe on the road."

Wiping his hands clean, Jesse moved toward his son, careful not to step on any parts.

"Four wheels will keep you safe!" The retired colonel scowled, giving his son a playful, open palm slap on the back of his head. Jake winced, instantly annoyed.

A bright smile crept across his father's face. "It's good to see you!" He opened his arms to offer a hug.

Jake embraced his father, not forgetting about the slap. "Was that necessary?"

"Come on," Jesse said, his wide smile as warm as it was welcoming. "How often do I get to discipline you these days? You're not working today?"

Jesse led the way outside to an outdoor table under one of the randomly positioned fruit trees within the backyard.

Jake let his father's question go unanswered.

"Here, sit." His father seemed insistent, motioning for Jake to take a seat.

Jake sat and didn't hesitate to dive straight into what had been weighing on his mind. "Some guy showed up in front of my work. He claimed to be a scientist for a secret government agency. Said he used to work for the NSA on secret black projects."

Jesse's expression darkened.

"He knew who I was, who you are, and all about Grandpa's military history. Then he gave me this story about his agency working with ET technology and said that the government would never admit to what is really going on."

The retired colonel felt a rising alarm. "What does any of it have to do with you?"

"Apparently, he had access to a private email I sent." Jake explained. "He said that if he knew about my email, then other secret agencies within the government would also know and not be too happy about it."

"I'm not following." Jesse shook his head. "OR more to the point: How could your email have anything to do with the NSA or black projects?"

Reaching into his pocket, Jake retrieved a neatly folded piece of paper and offered it to his father without a word. His father's eyes shone with recognition when he saw the image.

"Dad, have you ever heard of a scientist called Dr. Charles Reilly?"

Jesse didn't look up from the familiar image that riveted his gaze. He was studying the cross-section of an I-beam he had once held as a young boy. It was part of a collection of objects his father had brought home that had supposedly been retrieved from a crash site. There was no way Jesse could have known as a young boy that the shiny object he innocently held would change their lives.

Jake tried again. "Do you think this guy is who he claims to be?"

The retired colonel remained silent a long moment, as if calculating a stream of possibilities. Finally, he drew in a long breath. "Once something similar happened to me. It was the summer of the early '90s. Just before I flew out to attend a UFO conference in Washington DC, I received a call from an individual who didn't identify himself right away, but said it was imperative that he meet with me while I was in Washington."

Jake was surprised. "So you went off to meet with this person without knowing who he was? You didn't think that was dangerous?"

"The arrangements were to meet at a Capitol Building address, which at the time I thought was reassuring," his father explained. "I really didn't think that someone within the government would kidnap me from there."

"But when I got to the hotel in Washington, a message had been left for me to meet with him the following morning," Jesse said.

Jake hesitated a moment. "So whoever left the message already knew not only that you were attending the conference, but also your arrival time and where you were staying … At which point did the alarm bells go off?!"

"If anything, I was more curious than alarmed," his father answered. "So I went to the Capitol Building that morning after the conference, cleared security, and was shown to an office where I was given instructions to wait in the outer lobby."

"And none of this seemed a bit … odd?" Jake pressed.

"Sure, I felt a little bit anxious as I sat there. But it wasn't long till a gentleman in a dark suit greeted me."

Jake looked skeptical. "And by a dark suit you mean a man … in black?"

Jesse didn't seem to catch the devious reference. "He was pleasant and got straight to the point. He told me he knew exactly what your grandfather saw that had crashed out in the desert—and what I had seen as a young boy."

"Who was he? Did he ask you a thousand questions about Grandpa and what he brought home?" Jake asked.

His father took a moment as his synaptic gears turned. "I think he introduced himself as Richard … That's right, Richard D'Amato. He was a security specialist with the National Security Council. I just told him that I had nothing further to say that I hadn't already said. Actually, he surprised me."

Jake held his father's gaze. "How do you mean?"

Jesse paused. "He said he'd wanted to see me because there were things he needed to discuss, but more importantly, that he might have things to tell me. He took me to a secure room, deep underground, beneath the Capitol Building."

With the demeanor of a caring father, the colonel went on to recount the events that followed.

When the elevator doors opened to the secure basement level, Dr. Jesse Marcel Jr. was met with an imposing concrete corridor that shot out into the distance. Service pipes and data cables lined its ceiling, and a labyrinth of subcorridors branched out on both sides of the main passage.

Two minutes later, Jesse was shown into a conference

room lined with flat panel monitors and resplendent portraits of the country's Founding Fathers. As he was led to a seat at a table that stretched the length of the room, he sensed that he was in a place where only the most privileged conversations were held by powerful people.

On the table before him sat a yellow notepad and book. Marcel's eyes scanned the book's cover: *Majestic* by Whitley Strieber. Having written the foreword for the book, Marcel knew that it was a fictionalized version of the events that followed the discovery of the crashed extraterrestrial vehicle that his father was sent to investigate in the 1940s.

"As it turns out, this book is not fiction," the government official said as he took a seat opposite Marcel.

The subtext to his host's statement was not lost on the colonel. It had all the subtlety of a stampeding elephant: *I know that the story of the crash is true!*

"Can you tell me what you remember about the pieces of debris from the crash that your father showed you all those years ago?" D'Amato asked.

Though he sat in the conference room, Jesse felt himself reeling back to that night he helped his father lay out all the crash fragments on the kitchen floor when he was a young boy. As he recounted his story, he pictured the tiny details of the I-beam he held in his hands: its color, it weightlessness, the sound it made when it hit the floor, the texture of its flanges, and the shapes that formed hieroglyphic symbols molded along its sides.

D'Amato's eyes were captivated by the colonel. "Where do you think those crash fragments are now?"

Marcel was surprised. "Don't you know? You are the guys who have them."

D'Amato's face clouded with apprehension. He paused in silence has he contemplated his next words. "You've been in the middle of this since day one. And I'm well aware of the burden this situation has placed on your family. I'm not in a position to comment on what we did to your father, or whether it was the right decision at the time. But I will share something in good faith."

Jesse tried to repress a shiver.

"I'm not sure how much you know of our levels of security, but there seems to be a controlling group entrenched within our government." D'Amato said, hesitating. "It's this black government within our government that has secured all known ETVs retrieved from crash sites and maintains the global secrecy about the ETs."

Marcel looked around in disbelief. "You're the security specialist sitting in a top-secret, subterranean installation *under* the Capitol Building in Washington DC, and you don't know?"

"Sir," D'Amato said with a controlled smile, "I've been charged with investigating the operations of this group, this government within our government, which we suspect is the beneficiary of unreconciled funds spent annually without appropriate Congressional oversight. It's my job, sir, to report to the Senate Appropriations Committee and advise them on where these tax dollars are going and why."

"Our own government was investigating ... our own government?!" Jake's sudden outburst interrupted his father's recounting of the meeting with the NSC security specialist.

"Unreconciled funds? ... Spent annually?" Jake continued as he connected the dots. "I bet this D'Amato tool was talking about the unaccounted trillions that get diverted into black budgets every year."

"Perhaps," Jake's father said, "but there was nothing I could tell him that he didn't already know. I must admit, I was stunned by his admission of a black government acting behind the scenes."

Jesse expression softened. "At the same time, there was something monumental about that meeting. There I was, sitting in that secure underground meeting room, and across the table a government official was confirming that everything your grandfather saw, that what I'd held in my hands as a boy, along with the cover-up that followed, was real."

Jake was thunderstruck. He felt the truth come crashing down around him. It was as if his father's recollection, in his own words, had unexpectedly led him through a threshold he had always resisted crossing. Jake Marcel knew from that moment he would no longer speculate or believe in a possible ET presence: he had accepted it as fact.

All these years, I never wanted to believe.

When he spoke, Jake's words were barely a whisper: "You never told me about this until now?"

It was as if the words were physically painful for his father to say. "The entire family had to live with what we knew, about what your grandfather found in the desert. They silenced him. It slowly ate at him for the rest of his days. He made your mother and I promise that we would never speak a word about any of it until after he passed. God rest his soul."

"And you never wanted to know, son." His father's eyes looked like they would well up with tears at any moment. "I knew you were conflicted about the subject. I used to see your face when you came home from school; clearly you had been harassed about something. But you never wanted to talk about it. Then you'd freeze up if the topic of UFOs or if your grandfather was mentioned. Although you never said anything, I knew what was going on. I knew people were giving you a hard time about it, about our family's history."

Jake was speechless.

His father's words resonated with the protectiveness of a devoted parent: "So I just let you be."

The words sent Jake's emotions reeling. Again he opened his mouth to speak, but still couldn't respond.

Jesse sensed he had unleashed deep-seated turmoil hidden within his son. He could read from the boy's horrific expression that he was reliving his younger years spent running away from anything that had to do with what his grandfather had retrieved from the desert, denying it was true. Jesse moved to change the topic and bring his son back to the present.

With a soft but concerned smile, he said, "For a long time I never told anyone about the meeting we had that day under the Capitol Building. The NSC official had felt strongly that discretion would be the better part of valor, and due to the sensitivity of what we discussed, I agreed with him. There was one thing I did ask him though."

Jake's curiosity jolted him from his painful memories. "What did you ask?"

"I asked him when the government would release the truth about our interstellar visitors."

Jake's eyes went wide. "What did he say?"

The retired colonel paused, locking eyes with his son.

"That if it were up to him, the truth would have been disclosed years before. He said it was the government within the government that controlled the information and, for reasons of their own, they had kept the secret and continued to do so."

"So Grandpa really did bring home pieces of the crashed UFO?" Jake's voice was full of wonder.

"They're called ETVs nowadays," his father corrected him. "Extraterrestrial vehicles." Jesse flashed a triumphant smile. "They were very real. I held the pieces of one with my own hands."

Jake's eyes shot up at his father. "This scientist was adamant that our family had a piece of the wreckage still in our possession after all these years, even if we didn't immediately know where it was hidden. He said if we did, then he'd be able to help us if other agencies came looking for it."

His father sensed the rumblings of a gathering storm approaching from the distance.

Jake noticed his father's expression turn grim. "Do you think I should trust him, Dad?"

The question hung in the air between them for a long moment while his father carefully weighed his thoughts. "Before I left that meeting under the Capitol Building, D'Amato asked if I'd received any threatening phone calls. I told him I did receive the odd anonymous hang-up, but nothing that would qualify as a threat."

Jake shifted uncomfortably.

"He ripped a piece of paper," his father continued, "wrote down all his contact information—and I mean all of it—and told me that if I were ever threatened, I was to contact him immediately."

Jake's voice caught. "Did you ever need to call him?"

"No. But my point is," Jesse added, "this government official was not only conducting an internal investigation, but also offered me protection if I needed it. Perhaps there are others within the government who don't agree with how this ET secret is being maintained. If you do decide to listen to this Dr. Reilly, tread carefully."

The words echoed in Jake's mind.

Perhaps he is who he claims to be, Jake thought.

"And to answer your other question, son,"—Jake sensed an unexpected glimmer of contentment in his father's eyes as he spoke—"whatever secrets your grandfather kept, he took them to his grave."

CHAPTER 29

Sitting silently in a white sedan, two agents observed a motorcycle approach. Parked four houses away from Jake's home, the agents watched as the motorcycle slowed to turn into Jake's driveway.

The rider dismounted then approached the house without removing his helmet. Unlocking the front door, he let himself in.

⁓

Jake shuffled into his bedroom, heavy with the weight of what he had learned from his father. He slumped onto his bed and dropped his helmet on the floor beside him. Staring at the ceiling for a long moment, he was stuck somewhere between drained and unsettled. His father was no longer the only Marcel in the family to have been approached by government agents. Jake sensed that, for the first time, it was a very real possibility that he was being watched.

Rolling to his side, he reached under his bed. He retrieved a gadget that was a little bigger than an iPod.

It had earphones, but it also had a set of sunglasses that plugged into the gadget. Jake could not see through these sunglasses, however. Instead each lens held a small matrix of LED lights fixed to the inside of the opaque glasses that sat in front of the eyes.

The gadget was a mind machine. He put on the earphones, placed the opaque glasses over his eyes, selected a program, and pressed the start button. Exhaling slowly, he allowed himself to relax as the LEDs pulsed in front of his closed eyelids.

The effect was the feeling of being wrapped in a hypnotic symphony of colors. The strobing flashes accompany sounds and tones specifically set to the same alpha frequencies the human brain experiences when dreaming. Buddhist monks could spend a lifetime training in a meditative state to reach such levels of consciousness. Volumes had been written by monks on the benefits of experiencing states of consciousness beyond alpha, such as the super-conscious state of theta, the mind's frequency when in a deep sleep.

By exposing the mind's senses to these specific frequencies, Jake's mind machine allowed a shortcut to a deep meditative state.

The trick is to let go, Jake reminded himself has he relaxed.

Jake felt his consciousness begin to slide into an ocean of hypnotic colors. It was liberating to kick-start the mind into its dream state while remaining awake. As he let go of his thoughts, careful not to fall asleep, Jake felt as if his body were slowly accelerate upward. He often used his mind device to float in the alpha state while reflecting on his problems. He found his logical mind became dormant, while allowing his creative mind, the part that was highly active during dreaming, to find solutions he would never have thought of otherwise. It was his secret problem-solver.

Images of his father flashed before him; their conversation replayed in his mind. His father's words ricocheted around him. "Whatever secrets your grandfather kept, he took them to his grave."

Now passing the edge of consciousness, Jake felt his muscles melt away; he was floating somewhere between wakefulness and a dream state.

What should I do? he thought, as if willing the universe to guide him to an answer.

He felt his mind drift further away from consciousness. Images of his conversation with Dr. Reilly layered over what he had learned from his father.

Then an unexpected image appeared in his mind—a plateau being cleared; a semitropical forest surrounded by lakes and opulent vegetation. The sky was filled with large prehistoric-looking birds. Thousands of workers dressed in white kilts and shoulder-length cloth hats labored to remove stones from timber platforms suspended from a large cigar-shaped craft.

Jake felt himself being drawn into the vision, as if drifting into a dream.

Is that an airship? Jake asked himself, trying to figure out how the colossal, charcoal-colored craft was being powered. The scene was reminiscent of helicopter transports flying heavy machinery to a massive building site.

In the distance, three more cigar-shaped craft approached, carrying a series of suspended platforms, each cradling huge stone blocks. The prehistoric birds scattered as the craft came closer and slowed to a halt. The huge stone blocks were the color of sand; engraved on their sides were what looked to Jake like hieroglyphics.

In the distance, beneath the newly arrived airships, two more building sites bustled with activity. Armies of workers hauled huge stone blocks into place. Jake realized that whatever the men were building was going to be massive in scale. The shape looked eerily familiar to him. Although construction had only commenced recently, the structures resembled the base of two pyramids.

The construction of the Great Pyramids of Giza?

The revelation jolted Jake upright. He ripped the flashing glasses and earphones from his head and fished in his pocket to retrieve the plain business card. He reached for his phone and dialed the number.

Charles Reilly's raspy voice answered. "Jake. I'm glad you decided to call."

Jake's tone was unwavering. "I want to know everything!"

CHAPTER 30

33 Days before the Building Collapse

"Where would you like me to start?" Dr. Charles Reilly asked.

Charles had arranged to meet Jake at another public place, but this time one Jake was more familiar with. It was the middle of the afternoon under a clear blue sky as they found a bench seat in the park near Natasha's house. Jake, however, had suspected that the scientist most likely already knew who his girlfriend was, and where she lived.

The scientist obviously had volumes to share with the younger man. Jake pondered quietly a long moment before asking his first question. "Tell me about my grandfather."

Charles collected his thoughts. "Your grandfather was a good man, a true patriot. Your father also served, and I know about the injuries he sustained, and that he even came out of retirement to serve in Iraq when his country called on him. He's a good man, too, like his father … The very definition of a true American hero. You come from a fine family, Jake."

Charles recounted to Jake that on Sunday, July 6, 1947, the intelligence office at the Roswell Army Air Field received a call from the Chaves County Sheriff's Office reporting that a local rancher had presented some strange pieces of wreckage. Jesse Marcel, who at the time held the rank of major, drove to the sheriff's office to inspect the strange materials. Puzzled with what had been found, he reported it to his commanding officer, Colonel William Blanchard.

Blanchard then immediately ordered Major Marcel to be accompanied by someone from the Counter Intelligence Corps to collect as much of the strange debris as possible and return to the airbase. Jesse complied.

While Major Jesse Marcel and Captain Sheridan Cavitt of the Counter Intelligence Corps were in transit to the crash site, military police stormed the sheriff's office on the orders of Blanchard to take possession of the debris samples left behind and deliver them directly to Blanchard's office. The samples were then flown to Blanchard's commanding officer, General Roger Ramey of the Eighth Air Force headquarters in Fort Worth, who took control of them.

On Tuesday, July 8, 1947, the *Roswell Daily Record* ran the headline "RAAF Captures Flying Saucer on Ranch in Roswell Region." The article explained that the information had been released under the authority of Major Jesse Marcel. General McMullen called Ramey's office from Washington DC ordering that some of the recovered material be sent to him immediately. McMullen also ordered Ramey to create a believable cover story and quash any stories about the army recovering a crashed flying saucer.

Officers wrapped the material in plastic and placed in a case that was attached to the wrist of Fort Worth base commander Colonel Al Clarke, who personally rushed the samples directly to Washington, D.C., on the direct orders of General Clements McMullen.

Once Washington realized they were dealing with exotic materials beyond their understanding, the General quickly launched a mission to recover all of it. General McMullen wanted to learn as much as he could about it. But, more importantly, he needed to be certain the materials did not fall into private hands or, worse still, into the hands of their enemies. An aerial survey located a second crash site containing the main body of the craft a few miles from the debris field Marcel was still investigating. This was also the site that a group of civilian archaeologists had stumbled on and reported to the Chaves County sheriff the same morning the reconnaissance mission was launched.

A third crash site was found within a few miles of the second. Military scouts found a small, crashed pod with several humanoid bodies about the size of children. Army intelligence faced the shocking reality that the crew and their vehicles were non-terrestrial. The army's mission instantly changed from that of reconnaissance and debris clean-up to securing and recovering bodies and technology from unknown origins.

Meanwhile, Marcel and Cavitt returned to Roswell Army Air Field carrying two carloads of the exotic materials and debris.

Following orders, General Ramey formulated a story to cover up the army's find. To accomplish this, his staff found an object that looked damaged enough to be passed off to the press as nothing more than the remains of a radar reflector.

"The weather balloon!" Jake scowled.

"That's right," Reilly said. "Ramey invited the press to the base and announced that what had been spread over a square mile on the ranch was just a radar reflector from a downed weather balloon. The media reported that the weather balloon had been misidentified by both the rancher and the military personnel who first recovered it."

Jake shook his head. "I remember the photograph in the paper; my grandfather was kneeling next to bits and pieces of a weather balloon. Didn't anyone ask how the hell a flimsy, little, kite-like weather balloon could spread itself out over that area? Not to mention that they don't exactly come rocketing down like spacecraft entering the atmosphere. It's a balloon! They only fall when they develop a leak, and then they slowly float down as the helium escapes."

"Believe me," the scientist agreed, "your grandfather was not happy about being ordered to go along with the story. He detested the very notion of a senior intelligence officer stationed at the only atomic bomb group in the world at the time, where only top-tier personnel served, having his capabilities as a ranking officer brought into question ... not to mention his reputation."

"They made him face the world," Jake said, "as the fool who couldn't tell the difference between an ET craft and a weather balloon. Either that or one of the qualifications of becoming the head of our elite top secret atomic bomb program was to be a complete idiot!" He was fuming.

Reilly was nodding. "And you can see it on the expression in his face; it's unmistakable in that famous photo. He's saying, "You've got to be kidding me!" That was the day that heralded military intelligence's truth embargo on the entire ET subject."

The words seemed to hang in the air before they fully registered in Jake's mind. "But why the big secret? The question of whether we were alone in the universe had been answered once and for all."

Dr. Reilly had known the question was coming; he wondered for a moment how much he would have to reveal to Jake.

"That's a bigger question than you think, with many intertwining layers." The scientist's tone was pensive.

Looking up, Charles drew in a deep ominous breath. "There are billions and billions of potential "Earths" out there based on what we've learned from the Kepler probe, and the number is only going to get bigger as we learn more. On those potential Earths live thousands of civilizations. It would be the height of arrogance to assume that humans are the only sentient life in the universe."

Charles lowered his eyes to meet with Jake's. "But the

primary reason for the secrecy was the Cold War. That's the plain and simple answer."

Jake looked confused.

Reilly continued. "The rise of unexplained sightings occurred in the 1940s; it was no accident that it coincided with the beginning of what could have turned out to be a hot war—a third world war fought with nuclear weaponry. At the time, there was a massive stand-off between the superpowers. It was before your time, but each side was building up stockpiles of nukes. And we had thousands of warheads pointed at each other ready to launch at short notice."

Jake exhaled, sensing a darker possible outcome. "If a third world war was triggered, none of us would be here now."

"That's right," Reilly agreed. "So you can understand that introducing the ET presence into the mix would potentially disturb an already very fragile political climate. The risk was far too great. If one side were to launch a strike because of the fear of being overpowered by ET technology …"

Jake glimpsed an unimaginable web of connections materializing before him. "It could have triggered World War III."

The scientist's expression was uncertain. "Well, there were too many scenarios to contemplate, let alone predict. And none of them ended well for either side."

"So back then," Reilly went on, "some very clever people, the people who ended the Second World War, people a cut above the ones running things now, decided that it was best to keep the arrival of the visitors a national secret until we understood more about who these off-world visitors were—where they were coming from, why they were here, what their technology could do, and what Stalin's plans were."

Jake looked skeptical.

Charles's tone was resolute. "If you understand the political climate in which that decision was made, then you will also understand that they did make the right decision at the time. I still believe that."

Jake narrowed his eyes. "So what happened when the Cold War ended?"

"An excellent question." Charles was pleased that Jake was now following. "The Cold War lasted 44 years, till 1991, when the Soviet Union was dissolved. But in that time the national secret, the truth embargo if you will, had become institutionalized. We'd had over four decades to study ET technology in complete secrecy, and during that time, we'd created some pretty nifty toys. We developed technologies centuries ahead of anything our enemies possessed."

Reilly hesitated a moment. "Most of the clever people who had made the right decision more than 65 years ago are no longer with us. However, the new people running the show aren't yet ready to deinstitutionalize the national secret."

Shifting uncomfortably, Jake asked, "But what about the new technologies, the new toys? Let me guess, they want to keep them to themselves."

The scientist's tone darkened. "That's one way to look at it. They're of the opinion that the few so-called toys they have let filter through to the mainstream is enough for now: integrated circuitry, fiber optics, stealth metamaterials, laser technologies. All reverse-engineered from what your grandfather found near Corona. I'm not the first to confirm it; numerous books have been written on the subject if you know where to look. But to deinstitutionalize the national secret is also to open Pandora's Box."

Jake's gaze focused into the distance toward the horizon. He was again lost.

"Think about it," Reilly went on. "Admitting that the government lied to its citizens for more than 65 years means revealing we have had technologies that could produce clean energy; that we haven't needed to pump oil out of the ground for decades; that we didn't need to go to war to protect Kuwait's oil assets; that we have kept the means to end world poverty and hunger to ourselves; that we have kept our petroleum-based economic system running at the benefit of those selling oil; that trillions in citizens' tax dollars have been sunk into the black budget to develop ET technologies only to benefit those who pull the strings; and that we now have a shadow government run by an elite group that operates without oversight, no matter which party resides in the White House."

Jake couldn't believe what he was hearing. *How can it all be connected?* He thought to himself.

Reilly was still explaining. "And worst of all, that the US Government, even if it was the secret group within our government, did some very, very bad things to its own citizens. All to keep its secret hidden for all those decades. Some very powerful individuals do not want to be held accountable for the bad things that have been done to keep a lid on the ET presence."

Jake's felt his head spinning. Every passing sentence triggered additional questions he wanted to ask. He felt himself disappearing down the rabbit hole fast. *This can't be real!*

Charles could see the increasing trepidation in Jake's expression. "I know it's a lot to take in at once, and believe me, I've barely scratched the surface."

Jake was uncertain how to respond. "Okay … If what you've said is true, then why hold on to all these new technologies if they can solve so many problems? I get that the government needs to cover its ass for what had to be done in the early days, but the benefits have to outweigh the questionable things that had been done. Why are they suppressing everything?"

"That's the pivotal question: why?" Dr. Reilly turned to meet Jake's gaze. "How they did it doesn't even compare. It distracts us from asking the most important questions: Why was the crash really covered up? Who has the power to maintain that secret for so long? And who has been benefiting all this time?"

Dr. Reilly could again see Jake's eyes cloud over. "The day that General Ramey ordered Commander Blanchard to change the army's story of a downed ET disk to a mistaken weather balloon marked the commencement of the truth embargo."

Jake again shifted uncomfortably.

"After they found the crashed disk," Charles explained, "President Truman would have been negligent if he didn't authorize the assembly of a special group to find out as much as possible about what came down and to keep it under wraps until they worked out if it, or they, were a threat. Nobody travels light years, or traverses dimensions, without an agenda. That special group tasked with the mission to investigate would be responsible for managing the secret and any consequential problems that result."

Charles winced as he repositioned himself upright, a flash of pain momentarily crossing his face.

Jake pretended not to notice as the scientist continued.

"Now rewind a few years to when President Eisenhower was a general during World War II. He once met with Churchill to discuss something photographed by a Royal Air Force reconnaissance plane over the east coast of England. The plane captured a detailed photo of a silver, metallic object that matched the plane's speed and heading for quite a while before it accelerated away at an impossible rate and disappeared. Something in that photo made Churchill more concerned with the social impact than the threat of advanced technology from unknown origins to national, or even global, security. He immediately ordered that the photos be classified top secret."

Dr. Reilly paused to emphasize his point. "He made the photo secret because he feared it would cause mass panic among the global population and cause social disintegration, let alone threaten the religious beliefs of billions."

Jake's eyes sprang to life. "Fair enough. But that was a much simpler time, and the Cold War ended years ago."

"That it has," Reilly agreed. "But there are a myriad of moving parts to the story. The issues are now so big, with implications so widespread, that it touches every person on Earth. The more that special group learned from their deep black programs studying the ETs and their technology, the more reasons they had to continue to hide what they had learned."

Jake's next question arose instantly: "What did they learn?"

CHAPTER 31

Jake's words rattled around in Charles's head: "What did they learn?"

If only our planet's population knew the true history of our species' evolution, Charles thought.

Sensing that Jake was overwhelmed, he wondered how much detail he should share about the true history underlying humanity's origins.

He decided not to divulge that the human race is essentially a hybrid—genetically engineered approximately 275,000 years ago into *Homo sapiens*—which explains the absence of a smooth evolutionary transition between us and our closest known ancestors, *Homo erectus*. The cause of this monumental jump between the two genetic sequences has remained an age-old mystery among mainstream paleontologists.

Reilly's Special Access Projects group was tasked with studying the ETs and their technology, during which time, they learned an uncomfortable truth. In the distant past our interstellar neighbors had bioengineered *Homo sapiens* by introducing elements of their own genetic material to terrestrial primate DNA. It added intelligence and agility to mankind's ancestors; after several iterations, the resulting species eventually was catalogued by scientists as *Homo sapiens*, otherwise known as human.

The missing link between the two species isn't actually missing, because the advanced latter wasn't the result of Darwin's evolution. It's the product of very advanced genetic engineering.

Over the next 125,000 to 150,000 years, the *Homo sapiens* population flourished across the Earth. Over time, however, a flaw in the genetic code became increasingly evident. Humans were still too aggressive, obsessively territorial, and they lacked the ability to develop spiritual awareness.

The interstellar visitors returned to Earth to implement a mass genetic upgrade. This time anthropologists named the resulting species *Homo sapiens sapiens*, also known as modern man.

The following 125,000 years witnessed the modern human population develop into organized groups; new civilizations emerged as humans developed and an increasing spiritual awareness and understanding.

As Homo sapiens sapiens, we then reached the limit of our genetic potential when our technology and materialistic values far surpassed our spiritual and moral development. This occurred when mankind entered the nuclear age.

As Earth's civilization enters its twenty-first century, the human population is again exhibiting flaws in its genetic coding, and once again we've attracted increasing attention from our interstellar neighbors. Humans have become an immature, warring race that plays with dangerously powerful nuclear technologies we don't fully comprehend. By reaching this point in our history while simultaneously developing space orbital capabilities, it should be no surprise that mankind has triggered other civilizations to act in their vested interest in where humans will travel next as we venture into space with our new-found nuclear toys.

Humans embrace technology that destroys the natural environment, we fight over land, and, worse still, have used atomic weaponry against ourselves. It's this disruptive nature that has drawn our cosmic neighbors to further modify, or improve, our genetic code. Interventions have been ongoing in recent history via visits to certain people within the population, borrowing samples of their reproductive material so that genetic upgrading can be performed again. They then return the reproductive material to the individual and follow their family over the course of generations to monitor evolutionary growth.

The individuals have no recollection of the abduction event, but would go on to produce naturally gifted children. Being more intelligent than their peers, and in some cases possessing hints of advanced cognitive capabilities, some people mistakenly conclude that these children have psychic abilities. They also naturally hold a cosmic perspective of geopolitics and possess heightened spiritual awareness.

These gifted offspring think differently than other children and have abilities that can seem supernatural to the general population. Some genetically upgraded children process information and arrive at conclusions in ways that don't follow traditional mental constructs, continually frustrating their teachers with unorthodox ways of thinking.

These special children possess an intuitive understanding of nature's forces and phenomena not yet explainable by *Homo sapiens sapiens*'s grasp of physics. Yet they also hold an affinity for their fellow humans, and they care just as much about atrocities happening around the world as they would for their friends at the local playground.

When they eventually reach adulthood, these gifted children have families of their own, cross-pollinating the next evolution of the upgraded genome within the global population's gene pool.

Dr. Reilly couldn't help but wonder, *What will future anthropologists call this next evolution of human species now walking among us? History can only decide.*

CHAPTER 32

A comfortable silence had grown between Charles and Jake as they both stared across the park.

Jake's voice jarred Charles from his thoughts. "You haven't answered the question."

"Sorry?"

"What did they learn?" Jake repeated.

Charles leaned back on the bench in thought for a moment. He felt it was too soon to take Jake down the road of human evolution and the role played by external influences.

Perhaps we'll leave that one alone for now.

"We learned that we were not under attack." Charles hesitated, as if searching for the words. "We are, however, under observation."

The scientist watched as Jake wrestled with the idea before turning back to Charles. "Why are they keeping themselves hidden?"

The scientist gave a soft smile. "Find some night vision

binoculars and look up; they're not trying to hide themselves at all."

Jake looked skeptical, raising his eyes skyward.

"One of the first visiting interstellar groups had told some individuals that they would appear over our nation's capital on July 19, 1952 then again a week later, on the 26th. They made it very clear to these contacts that it would be a benevolent show of force. But more importantly, it was a peaceful display of their presence. There was a mass flyover of the White House seen by millions and captured on film. But then it was as if the incident, all of a sudden, hadn't happened."

Images of old news footage showing small metallic craft flying over Washington flashed through Jake's mind. He still felt unsure, but sensed in Reilly's patient smile that he was telling the truth.

"And because of bureaucratic red tape, it took two years for the visitors to be permitted to land at Edward Air Force base in 1954. That was the day they met with President Eisenhower for the first time. That was the first official contact with the government of the United States."

Jake was dead silent, staring in mute astonishment.

"Their ships landed on the tarmac at Edward right before government officials," the scientist added, his tone conclusive.

"In broad daylight?" Jake finally blurted out.

"In broad daylight," Charles said. "They approached the President and, in the interest of peace, offered the government and all the residents of our planet, technologies that would help us make the transition from an oil-addicted race to a clean energy-based civilization. But there was a condition."

Jake's eyes were wide with a mix of excitement and skepticism.

"They would share the technology with us provided that it would be made freely available to the entire population—4.8 billion people at the time—and not be kept by only one nation or kept secret by a select few."

Jake's felt a fresh wave of disbelief engulfing him. "This really happened? Why don't we know about this?!"

"There is archive footage of the event. Now remember, this was seven years after your grandfather was called out to see what crashed in the desert, so we'd already had a head start on reverse-engineering their off-world tech, not to mention, it was during the height of the Cold War. Our government ..." Charles paused, attempting to hide his embarrassment. "Well, the controlling government group within our government, the ones that created the weather balloon story for your grandfather, had national security issues with the visitors' offer. So they turned them down."

"What?!" stammered Jake. He felt himself grip the seat beneath him. Jake could not believe what he was hearing.

"Wait, it gets better. Soon after they turned down the visitor's offer, another ET group now known as the 'Grays' appeared on the scene. They too made an offer; they were willing to give us working versions of off-world technologies that we already had in our possession but couldn't back engineer because we didn't understand how it worked."

"The crashed disk?"

"The crashed disk," Charles said, nodding. "The very same one your grandfather held bits and pieces of. In return, all the Grays wanted was to be permitted to study our race unhindered and to come and go as they required. They didn't even mind if our government wanted to keep this deal a secret; in fact, it actually suited them."

"We took the deal with the Grays." Jake's realization was a whisper. The pieces of the puzzle were falling into place. It was the height of the Cold War; the shadow government group managing the dealings with the second ET race wanted their advanced tech to gain an advantage over the Soviets as well as anyone else who would threaten the United States.

As the bigger picture of the cover up became clear, Jake felt a cold chill. In exchange for ET technologies, the US Government allowed the second ET group to study humans. More to the point, they would turn a blind eye to it.

They were allowing abductions!

"So all those stories about people being abducted by gray aliens with large heads and black eyes ..." Jake trailed off in a fearful whisper.

Dr. Reilly didn't know how to respond at first; even to him it sounded unbelievable. He finally spoke, as if gently nudging the truth in Jake's direction. "It was the price our government was willing to pay to get our hands on their advanced technology. For reasons of their own, the Grays had a keen interest in our genetic makeup. If they were to study us, they would indeed need samples. So every now and then, they would take one of us."

Jake was speechless; he could barely get his mind around what he was being told.

Charles sensed Jake was struggling with the idea. "Now

you understand what would happen if all this came out. The population's reaction to decisions made by our government, regarding the access to technologies that promised to solve all the world's energy and pollution problems, but never shared … Well, it could be catastrophic. Have you any idea how many federal laws the government has broken since?"

As Jake began to fully comprehend the ramifications of what he was hearing, he felt the world he once knew teetering on the brink of unprecedented change.

Oh my God, this can't be happening!

They were still for a long moment, silent in their own thoughts. More people had entered the park since they'd first sat to talk. A mother had laid out a picnic blanket and was playing with her infant child. A group of children were kicking a soccer ball and arguing among themselves about whose turn it was. The rest of the world seemed to continue, blissfully unaware of the realities beyond our own atmosphere.

Charles attempted to lighten the tone, taking a philosophical left turn. "Now, if it were humans that had discovered another civilization somewhere, wouldn't you want to study them for a while? And if that civilization had a history of violence, was culturally fragile, possessed nuclear weaponry, and were active in hundreds of tribal wars among themselves at any one time, would you want to rush in and potentially cause global mass panic? Do you think that would end well? Or would you let that civilization learn for themselves, in their own time, that they may not be the only life in the universe?"

Jake found his voice. "I would probably leave them a few clues, some signs."

"That's exactly what they've done." Dr. Reilly's face showed a hint of a smile. "We were directly contacted in a more public manner in 2001, but you will never hear about it on the six o'clock news because it was much too shocking. They replied to a message we had once sent, and they even attached a mug shot!"

Jake looked confused.

"In 1972," the scientist explained, "we sent a message in binary code from the Arecibo Radio telescope. It gave a description of who we were, our DNA, which planet in the solar system we live on, and what type of technology we used to send the signal. Imagine the shock and surprise when we received a reply in exactly the same format laid out in two crop circles formed in a field adjacent to a SETI radio telescope that was listening for signs of life. Their reply explained that they were carbon-silica based, had an additional DNA strand, and lived on three out of the four planets in their solar system; the message was accompanied by an image of what they looked like and a low-resolution image of the technology they used to send their reply."

Once again, Jake could only stare.

"As it turns out, in the same field a year to the day earlier, a crop circle was found that resembled the technology they used to send their reply, but in more detail. Then a year after the Arecibo reply, again to the day, in the exact same location, was an enormous crop circle with a detailed image of a nonhuman entity holding a disk, or CD, printed with a binary code. The crop circle was so detailed that we could read the disk right off the ground, as if they had burned a CD and delivered it in person. Printed on that disk was a warning."

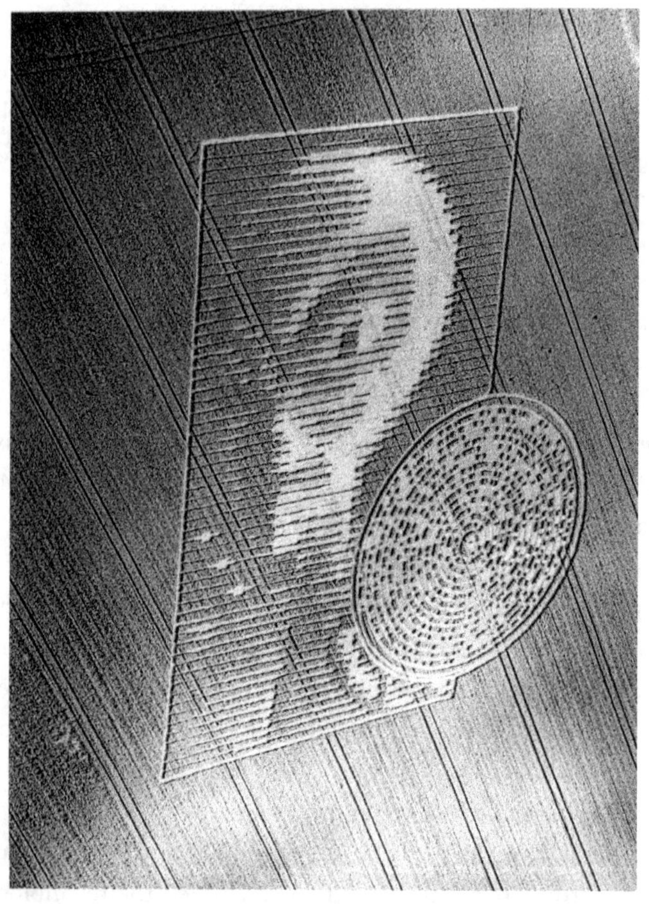

"And … What did it say?"

The scientist cocked his head slightly, as if reading the translation off a memorized image. "Be aware of false gifts, their broken promises. Much pain, but still time. Believe, there is good out there. We oppose deception."

"What does it mean?"

Dr. Reilly's gaze sharpened. "It's a message of hope."

Jake lowered his eyes in contemplation, trying to process what possible meaning the message could hold.

"Be aware of false gifts, their broken promises." The words left his lips as a whisper as he tried to connect the dots. Jake's eyes shot back up in realization. "But it's also a warning; there's more than one ET race. It's talking about the Gray's technology."

Charles sat back looking impressed. "Indeed there are. At last count, we have recorded contact with 63 races since the early 1930s. Some were good, for example, those who met with the likes of Barney and Betty Hill. Unfortunately, other contactees, such as Travis Walton had, well, negative experiences. It's why Stephen Hawking once said we shouldn't be calling attention to ourselves until we truly understand what, or who, is out there."

The scientist waited a moment while his young companion considered the significance of this last revelation.

Jake's mind exploded with myriad questions: *Why are they here? What do they want from us? How long have they been visiting us? What is their technology like? How far ahead of us are they? What is their world like? Do they have a system of government? Do they believe in God?*

His thoughts were a collage of interrelated ideas that seemed to make no sense. Jake flashed on the agent who had approached his father years ago, and one pivotal question stood out. "Someone like you once approached my father. What did he want?"

"He was in fact looking for me." The scientist's tone was calm, but resolute. "Well, more to the point, he had been searching for my employer and the facility where we conduct our research. Mistakenly, he asked your father if he knew where the recovered disk was."

Jake shot him a surprised look.

"Remember, in the military intelligence community there is little we don't know. Despite his best efforts, Mr. D'Amato never did find us. But other countries could have come forward and decided it was time to disclose these realities before our government officials reached an agreement with the shadow government, the secret keepers."

Meeting the scientist's gaze, Jake felt unsure where Reilly was going with this.

"China, the Soviet Union as it was known back then, Brazil … Any one of those countries could have come forward to disclose what they knew to the public. Our President should have worked out a deal with the military intelligence community, learned what they wanted, and formed an agreement for disclosure that absolved the secret keepers of felonies committed during the course of the cover-up. Together, they could have brought forth the most profound event by any political party in all of recorded history."

Trying to follow, Jake said nothing.

"The most important issue in history has been under the President's nose for 70 years, and for 45 of them, he couldn't do a thing because the US had this little problem of 80,000 stockpiled nukes ready to launch against other nations. So, his hands were tied until 1991."

Dr. Reilly sensed his young friend was struggling to keep up. He paused a long moment, as if to emphasize the importance of what he was about to share.

CHAPTER 33

"The initial reason for the cover-up has long since passed. We've had ample time to prepare the public for what is to come. We now know a great deal about these off-world visitations and why our visitors are here."

Jake was still staring in disbelief.

For the last hour, Dr. Charles Reilly's revelations had transformed Jake's perception of the universe and the world he lived in. Sitting on that park bench, Charles had walked him through the answers to all the questions he wanted to ask. The reality of day-to-day life was now morphing into a tiny sliver of a much greater universal reality far beyond the comprehension of human civilization.

Jake's heart was pounding. The implications of what he was learning seemed as unbelievable and awesome as they were terrifying.

"This is the most important issue in the history of the human race," Reilly continued. "And yet, anyone under the age of 70 has lived every day of their life under a truth embargo. The secret keepers have done such a great job. Have you ever heard the terms Fastwalkers, ETVs, or ISEs?"

Jake returned a puzzled look.

"Well, that's how good a job we've done for nearly three-quarters of a century. A fair degree of social engineering of the populous has been ongoing since the forties. There is a vital reason why no congressman or senator will speak out on the subject of ET visitations."

Charles counted on his fingers as he explained: "Universities won't teach it, the government won't acknowledge it, and the mass media won't report on it let alone investigate it."

Jake nodded has he followed.

"When a credible citizen has come forward about a possible ET sighting, the key for the secret keepers to maintain the status quo has been to make the claim unsupportable so there could be no way to verify, or confirm, the sighting. Nowadays, you could show the average citizen footage of the famous 1952 Washington UFO flyover or photos of the crop circle warnings I spoke of, and they *still* will think that themselves are crazy to believe their own eyes."

Jake pictured images of crop circles and old UFO footage, shaky and half out of focus, as Charles spoke. "The education system, government institutions, and the press have made the subject of extraterrestrial intelligence a topic reserved for the disturbed, the crazy, and the weak-minded."

The scientist paused then continued in a lower tone. "But we now live in a different time. The public still has a right to know about issues that affect the whole planet, no matter how reality-shattering the truth is. Our entire population has to deal with it, not just an elite few."

Charles wondered if his young friend knew that 90 percent of Americans already believed life exists elsewhere in the universe or that 40 percent of US citizens accepted that ET visitations were occurring.

Jake spoke, his personal experience of facing ridicule surfacing. "But until something changes, anyone who comes forward with a credible sighting will be labeled a liar. The government will make up an explanation for it, saying it was just swamp gas, Project Mogul, or crash test dummies!"

Feeling his anger build, Jake continued. "You were one of them. Can't you do something?"

Charles's voice was soft, and yet there was resolve in his tone. "I agree, we have to end the government's policy of suppressing the ET presence."

He chose his words carefully. "Jake, my intent is to release information to the public and bring on global disclosure. I'm convinced that the reality of the ET presence is far too important to be held in the hands of the elite organizations. Their only interest is to re-engineer exotic off-world technologies and apply them for military supremacy or commercial gain, no matter how noble their agenda may seem."

Jake's expression turned from one of anger to astonishment as he met eyes with Reilly.

"Ironic, I know, coming from an individual who was once part of the military industrial complex charged with keeping the ET presence a secret," Charles said, a smile growing across his face.

A new realization propelled Jake's head into another

spin. *He's somehow become a sympathizer; that's the reason for his defection.*

Scrutinizing the scientist sitting with him on the park bench, Jake asked, "Who are the keepers of the secret?"

It was a question Reilly knew was coming. He hesitated a moment as if searching for the right words. "Let me answer that by saying there are many organizations that have noble intentions who promote particular agendas to their employees, government, and media. But at the same time other agendas are kept secret, and only the organization's central core is privy to the truth. Their outer layers are only window dressing to cover up their real purpose."

Jake nodded, his gaze riveted on the scientist.

"The International Monetary Fund, World Bank, Federal Reserve Bank, NSA, KGB and the CIA are all examples. Their inner cores are interlaced together to form an elitist, super-secret society with their own culture and economy." He again counted with his fingers as he ran through a list: "Oil, gold, gas, diamonds, platinum and so on. These organizations are powerful, wealthy, and their single intent is to manipulate the world's economic, political and social systems to control this planet's vital resources. These are the elite. And deep within their inner circles are the keepers of the secret."

There was a long silence. Jake breathed deeply as if to absorb the unsettling truth.

How can it all be true? How could one person, or even one country, hope to change all this? Jake wondered.

They both watched a group of families walk past their park bench.

"Jake, think of the global population for one moment;

we live for money, we fight for land then divide the land, represented by different flags, and establish different currencies. The governments chosen to lead us are rife with corruption, and at any given time, one or more will be at war with another. Despite knowing that we are damaging the environment that sustains us, we continue to pollute our land, skies, and oceans."

Jake knew the scientist was right. He pictured a handful of atrocities that had happened in recent history; the invention of the atomic bomb, the assassination of John F. Kennedy, the Gulf War.

Jake listened as the scientist elaborated. "The system that supports life on this planet is under attack. More than three billion tons of coal is burned daily. And it's not only the volume of fossil fuels we burn; it's the rate at which we burn them that is significant."

The scientist explained that 50 percent of all the carbon dioxide that has been released into the atmosphere over human civilization's entire history had happened over the last 40 years. Life cannot be sustained with excessive carbon dioxide levels in the air. The amount of energy used daily has tripled in the last 30 years, and in the last decade human use of electricity has increased by 60 percent. Over the same period, global production of coal has increased by over 25 percent, natural gas by 40 percent, and carbon dioxide levels have risen by 25 percent.

Fuel consumption and oil prices continue to spiral upward. In 1950, one-quarter of the globe's land surface was native forest; now it's less than one-fifth. The oceans cannot soak up all the excess atmospheric carbon dioxide that the shrinking forests don't absorb.

The inhabitants of Earth are literally industrializing themselves out of existence! Reilly thought.

Dr. Reilly's demeanor turned frosty. "I feel strongly about our destruction of this planet. We don't seem to realize that the next generation will inherit an endangered Earth. Humans do not understand how unique this world is. It has a complex range of ecosystems. Its natural resources are plentiful, and it supports countless forms of life with an immense genetic library."

"If you think about it," Charles said, "despite our technological achievements, we really are an infant race. Einstein hit the nail on the head when he said, 'Our technology has surpassed our humanity.' We can only hope one day our humanity can surpass our technology."

The scientist could sense his young companion was struggling with the idea.

"Jake, you ask 'why the secret?' The group managing the secret, my former employer, recognized that the inhabitants have treated this planet poorly. They deemed our civilization not yet ready for something bigger than themselves. Now think of what would happen to the political system if the populous thought their elected governments were no longer in control."

"There would be mass panic," Jake concluded.

"Is it that we can't trust the rest of the population to accept this cosmic reality? Or is it that if we disclose that one person in five thousand are being abducted, then it would be political suicide?" Reilly's tone was ominous.

A cold silence hung between them. Reilly watched as an expression of shock grew across his companion's face.

"That's right," Charles reiterated. "And what would

happen to our economic system? What would happen to the religious institutions? How will they explain it?”

“But doesn’t the government have its own scientific program searching for ET life, the SETI program?” asked Jake.

The scientist considered the question a long moment. “The technology of the ETs allows them to travel thousands of light years while we still use radio waves to communicate. SETI, the Search for Extraterrestrial Intelligence, sweeps the sky for distant radio waves. It’s analogous to you and I searching for a sailing ship transporting a message in a bottle for proof of human existence, while all this time the same people we are looking for are bouncing signals off satellites. The SETI scientists won’t find anything, and that will be the accepted scientific conclusion. Again, the misinformation machine is working.”

Charles now leaned closer to Jake and smiled, as if to stress his next point. “If they want to find something, they should be looking around, not up in the sky.”

“Like on Earth?” Jake was puzzled.

“They should be looking for something almost unearthly. Something we still find difficult to explain. Something we couldn’t duplicate even if we tried.”

Charles waited a moment while Jake collected his thoughts.

Jake’s mind churned as he stared at the ground, trying to connect the dots. He slowly looked up at the scientist, his eyes filling with realization. “Giza!”

“Giza,” Charles repeated, almost impressed, a broad smile crossing his face.

The scientist wondered if Jake knew it was no

coincidence that the pyramids' alignment across the Giza plateau mirrored that of Orion's Belt across the sky. Or that the size of the pyramids correlated to the brightness of the stars in Orion's Belt. Not many people knew that the Giza monuments were set out on the ground in an exact image of how the Egyptian night sky looked during 10,500 BC.

With the pyramids' bases perfectly aligned to magnetic north, as opposed to geographic north, something mankind has only been able to accurately measure in the last four decades, it should be no surprise to the population that we had a little outside help building them. Mankind simply did not possess the technology to delicately maneuver massive limestone blocks around the sand. But mainstream scientists and historians have been too afraid to face the big question.

"You were on the inside," Jake blurted. "You had access to ET tech. Can't you expose this group controlling the government? Can't you get them to share their technology?"

Reilly had known the question was coming. He slumped back on the bench looking troubled. "Imagine a signed affidavit from former Secretary of State Colin Powell about the ET presence, to be opened only after his death. Or one from George H. W. Bush, or even Bill Clinton. In fact, we have one from the man who issued the military press release about the Roswell crash in 1947. It doesn't get closer to the truth than that. But no-one took notice. It didn't shake the media."

Jake had no idea where this was headed.

"Apollo 14 Astronaut Dr. Edgar Mitchell," Reilly said, "has a PhD from MIT and was the fifth man to walk on the moon, declared that the ET presence was real. His statements should have held significant weight on the question of the ET presence. But again, it has since gone relatively unreported by the mass media. The walls of secrecy are never going to be smashed from above. It has to come from a grassroots level."

"But decades have passed," Jake finally managed. "You should be able to finally release the ET-derived energy technologies you've been working on over the last seven decades. It would benefit everyone."

Charles was nodding, a wide smile crossing his face. "That I agree with. But disclosure must be triggered by the people, not by the leaders keeping the secrets."

The scientist now sensed a rising eagerness within Jake. He turned to lock his gaze on the younger man. "We need a piece of evidence, something not in the government's control, to be scrutinized in the public domain. It has to be undeniable proof of nonhuman technologies that cannot be explained away by government scientists."

"Now that sounds like science fiction." Jake was looking skeptical.

For the first time Charles's tone was intense. "Be that as it may," he said, "but the secret itself has been deemed to be a threat to national security, social order, and economic stability."

"I've been listening to you, but it sounds so ... so surreal." Jake shook his head. "I'd always had my suspicions, but the big picture is ... it's so profound. The problem is so big, so complicated. I mean the implications ... It will affect every single person on the globe. And I still can't believe this has been happening on the same planet I live on!"

Charles drew a tired breath. "Contingency plans for misinformation campaigns to target the public, media, government, intelligence, and foreign relations have all been developed. They're ready to be deployed should 'Project Disclosure' unfold sooner than they would like. I think you may have the ability to short circuit the entire event."

Jake looked startled. "How?"

"It has to start at the UN then unfold from there." Charles was unwavering.

"But everything you've said … you have firsthand experience with ET tech because of your work with the government. If you're on the inside, don't you have the power to bring it to the surface? Couldn't you find a journalist who would want to get this story out? Couldn't you give them some proof?"

"You don't understand, Jake. Everything I have shared thus far will sound implausible. Everything I know comes from sources outside the public domain. So anything I disclose, any proof I present, could never be corroborated. It could never be verified. And that's the problem, that's how the misinformation campaigns work. It has to come from the outside. It has to happen independent of government agencies, outside their control. And it has to start with the United Nations."

Jake was silent now, fully engrossed.

"There needs to be a triggering event so undeniable that it shifts the momentum from secrecy to openness. When that happens, there will be an avalanche that will change the day-to-day reality for every single person on this planet."

Charles drew a deep breath. "Jake, you come from a

family that had contact with the Corona crash site. Almost 70 years later, a member of the same family produces, or is involved with, the application of ET geometry in a commercial building. It's more than a coincidence. I am willing to bet your family has in their possession a piece of the crash debris kept hidden from society all these years. Jake, I think you have the potential to start a chain reaction … if given the right direction. And with the right evidence."

Jake paused, looking conflicted. "But I don't think we have anything that can be used as proof."

Charles's eyes illuminated with anticipation. "I know that you *don't think* you have anything in your possession at the moment."

Jake's gaze swung back over the park. *What does he mean? Did he know something that I didn't? Was he implying that Grandpa may have kept something hidden all this time?*

Charles sensed Jake connecting the dots. "Ask the question, Jake."

"How do we stop them?" Jake said, feeling his admiration for the scientist now growing with each passing moment.

A warm smile crossed Charles's face. "Both your father and grandfather once let something slip through their hands that could have changed everything. Our hopes, our beliefs … even what it means to be a member of the human race."

Dr. Reilly's expression now turned serious. "How do we stop them, you ask? Listen very carefully, because I'm going to dare you to do better."

CHAPTER 34

Parked across the road from the park, in a black sedan and out of view of Jake and Dr. Reilly were two agents in dark suits. One held a digital SLR camera fitted with a telephoto zoom lens. Its shutter thrashed wildly, capturing images as the agent watched Jake and the scientist through the viewfinder.

Three hundred feet away from the car, the shutter of another digital SLR clicked in sporadic bursts. This one, however, was trained on the two agents. Unseen and out of view, Mark had climbed one of the park's trees and sat clicking shots of the agents who photographed the meeting between Jake and the scientist.

CHAPTER 35

"Is that what Men in Black look like?" Mark studied the images he had taken from the tree earlier while Jake met with Dr. Charles Reilly in the park.

Mark and Jake were back in Mark's home office clicking through digital images of Reilly and the two inconspicuous men parked across the road. They both cocked their heads to the side as Mark zoomed in with the mouse.

"They kinda look … well, nerdy!" Mark sounded surprised.

After clicking through a dozen more shots, he turned to face Jake. "Well, they've definitely got you under surveillance. That's for damn sure."

"Dr. Reilly did say they'd be watching. That's one thing that checks out," Jake said, his voice trailing off as if in deep thought.

Mark looked dubious. "Do you think you can trust him?"

Jake's eyes shot toward Mark's; a heavy silence settled around them for a number of heart beats.

Finally Jake spoke: "My instincts tell me I can. But everything I know about the military and their government agencies tells me to stay clear."

Mark's face filled with confusion, and he searched Jake's eyes for clarity. Although he opened his mouth to speak, nothing came out.

"I know … But I think he might be right. Dad said something the other day that's been rattling around my head: 'Your grandfather took his secret to the grave.'"

Mark's expression became even more confused as he considered it.

"And today," Jake said, "this ex-black government scientist tells me he is adamant that our family has possession of something that does not belong to …"

Jake stopped mid-sentence as a sudden realization washed over him. He turned to Mark, his voice resonating with excitement. "I think I know where a piece of the crash is!"

He spun to rush for the door. Mark lunged off his chair, instantly forcing himself between Jake and the home office doorway.

"I know that look! Whatever you're planning to do, remember,"—Mark pointed to the image of the agents' car on his screen—"they're tracking you. You're going to need help."

CHAPTER 36

21 Days before the Building Collapse

The line to the front entrance of Capitalism nightclub stretched down the sidewalk of the bustling inner city street. A popular night spot in downtown Las Vegas, the club was known not only for the leggy beauties that frequented the venue, but also for being a safe stronghold for celebrities wanting to avoid the flashes of paparazzi cameras. But there was another peculiarity that differentiated it from other, similar nightclubs—its second entrance.

Riding in formation, five fierce-looking motorcycles approached the busy night spot. Their engines resonated with a deep hum felt by the young patrons lined up at the venue's front entrance. They rolled past the front line to turn into a small side alley.

The second entrance to the venue faced the alley. Two mammoth guards flanked the wide entry; one held a clipboard, the other clasped a handheld RF chip reader. Similar to the security screeners at retail stores, the device was waved at the first approaching motorcycle. The man who wielded it gestured to the motorcycle's rider to stop.

The device chirped as he waved it over a necklace pendant worn by the rider. Information flashed on the device's small screen:

Member: Jake Marcel. Age: 28.

The guard's gaze then flashed up to study the rider's passenger. He was met with a striking pair of female eyes that smiled back at him through her helmet.

He spoke after a short pause. "Go through."

Jake eased the throttle to gently roll through the entry. Inside, another guard directed him toward a metal ramp that led to a catwalk suspended over the side of the main dance floor. Behind him, the mammoth guard was now checking Mark's ID necklace.

On the catwalk, the rumble of Jake's engine was swallowed by the booming dance track that filled the venue. Capitalism was a chaotic explosion of sound and light. Another unique feature of the club was how it encouraged its members who rode motorcycles to park them on the suspended catwalks that circled the main dance floor.

Jake dismounted, and Mark took the next adjacent space overlooking the bar and dance floor. Behind him followed Chris, Paul, and TJ. Natasha was the first to shed her riding jacket, helmet, and gloves. She used the Ducati's mirrors to touch up her hair and makeup while the others took their helmets off.

She turned and spoke to Jake, her voice barely audible. "Let's find Jackie."

❧

After collecting Jackie, the group ordered drinks and claimed a small area to stand and mingle near one of the numerous bars within the club. The girls chatted while the guys engaged in their usual banter.

Mark had noticed TJ's fixation on Jackie since they'd met up. He struggled to converse with TJ above the music. "How the hell do you think you're going to score with that?" Mark nodded toward Jackie's direction.

The question jolted TJ from his daydream. His response was a boastful retort: "Shock and awe."

Listening in, Chris's rebuttal was instantaneous. "More like smoke and mirrors!"

Shooting a seething glare at Chris, TJ took an ominous step toward Jackie in a valiant attempt to defend his manhood.

Jackie sensed TJ's bulky frame looming behind her, but before she could react, he was already upon her.

He wrapped his powerful arms around Jackie, embracing her in a tight hug. "Don't fight it; you know we've both been thinking about this."

Struggling to loosen his grip, she said, "You couldn't be any more wrong, you eff'ing Wookie!"

There was a collective reaction from Natasha and the rest of the boys: "Ooohhh!"

Jake couldn't help but chuckle to himself. *"Eff'ing?* Interesting use of the vernacular."

After watching Jackie struggle against the largest of the boys, Jake's smirk was promptly wiped off by Natasha's elbow jamming into his side.

"Jake, do something!"

Jake's focus never left the sparring pair. "She needs to learn how to handle rough guys on her own."

"Really? Does he need to be so rough? Come on!" Her annoyance at TJ was now being redirected toward Jake.

He flashed his mischievous eyes accompanied by a lop-sided smirk at Natasha before approaching Jackie. She was still struggling against TJ, whose forceful embrace could not be shaken.

"Jack!" Jake's voice boomed over the music.

Instantly, she stopped struggling and whipped her head in the direction of his voice. Her expression was somewhere between annoyance and anger.

"He's three times your size," Jake began. "You don't stand a chance. Instead, hold onto him and take a step forward. Shift him off his balance."

She immediately complied. With what little leverage she had, Jackie gripped his muscular forearms and stepped forward. TJ leaned forward, still gripping her in a bear hug, but awkwardly and off-center.

Stepping closer, Jake spoke directly in Jackie's ear, lowering his voice a notch: "Scrape the heel of your stiletto down the length of his shin. The rush of pain will make him loosen his grip for just a second. When he does, you'll have just enough room to slam your elbow into his chest; aim to hit just under his sternum. It'll make him buckle over, which will give you a little more room to shift your shoulder under his. He'll be off balance, and if you time it right, you'll be able lift him with your legs. Use your upper body to throw him over your shoulder. Size has nothing to do this, it's all about balance, timing, and surprise."

Jake stepped back to give himself room to watch. Jackie

shot him an uncertain glance, which was met with a reassuring nod, as if Jake were saying, *you can do it*.

At that moment, TJ understood. His eyes went wide, but it was too late.

A searing bolt of white hot pain shot down the front of TJ's shin bone. He then felt the air driven violently from his lungs as he buckled forward, an involuntary reflex resulting from Jackie's blow to his solar plexus. In the next half-second the sensation of being airborne shifted his focus from his burning shin and loss of breath. TJ was now a passenger; Jackie's upward thrust into his armpit had thrown his weight forward. Travelling through the air, he was flipped over Jackie's shoulder. His impact on the ground was met with a cheer and round of applause from the surrounding group.

As he lay on his back, the floating stars in TJ's vision slowly cleared as he blinked until he could focus again. Jackie stared down at him, her hands covering her mouth in an expression of shocked surprise.

Recomposing herself as if the defense maneuver had been planned all along, she took a confident stride toward her fallen opponent. "There's your shock and awe … freak!"

The men reacted with a triumphant cheer for Jackie.

Not believing what she had just witnessed, Natasha's hands covered her mouth. She watched in amazement as TJ picked himself up off the floor to tower over Jackie.

Looking lost for words, he smiled down at her. "Impressive."

TJ stepped toward a nearby half-circle booth to take a seat, his movements the slow, delicate actions of a wounded animal retreating to a corner. The amused group followed his lead, everyone jamming into the booth to fill the seats around him.

Chris considered TJ's bruised ego. "Dry your eyes, princess, you've taken a hell of a lot more beatings than that."

Turning to Jake, Chris's face changed to one of quizzical concern. "Mark mentioned you need a hand to collect something."

"Yeah, I heard some aliens left their anal probe inside Mark!" TJ was chuckling.

Everyone except for Mark burst into another fit of laughter.

"That's right, TJ!" Mark snapped. "They crossed trillions and trillions of miles to stick a probe up my ass. Tell me, what could possibly be lodged up there that eff'ing interesting? Huh?"

The friends erupted with hysterical laughter. Around them, curious faces turned to look at the group.

"I don't know, Mark, you've always been a creative guy!" TJ managed to say between fits of laughter.

Paul waited for the jovial waves to dissipate before pressing the question with Jake. "But seriously, what do you need?"

Jake shot a disconcerted look at Mark before drawing a deep breath. "Look, it's serious stuff. We know that I'm now being watched, so it may not be entirely safe for you guys."

"Watched? What do you mean? By who?" Natasha's face clouded with worry.

Jake offered his best reassuring smile. "I don't know, NSA maybe?"

"Shit! You're kidding, right?" Chris spat with a surprised look.

Jake didn't answer. He held Chris's gaze long enough for him to get the message that he wasn't joking.

Jake paused as if his words were physically hard to say. "Look, I never talk about it, but it has to do with something my grandfather found when he was an intelligence officer in the army. But I don't know," Jake said, shooting a grim look at Mark. "I don't feel comfortable asking you guys for help. This is no joke. It could end up being dangerous."

Jake could see the expressions of disbelief and apprehension filling his friends' faces. Natasha's haunting blue eyes flashed with fear.

Jake continued. "I don't want any of you to get caught up in any of this shit my family has been carrying around from when my old man was a boy."

The table fell silent for a long moment as concerned looks were exchanged around the booth.

It was TJ who spoke first. "Look, Jake, I don't know anything about little green men or shit like that. All I know is if you're in trouble, no matter what it is, and someone's watching you, then us getting mixed up in it isn't your decision to make. It's ours."

"Yeah, whatever it is," Paul said, "I'm in."

Chris nodded. "I agree; when do we start?"

Jake leaned back, contemplating their responses silently. As he looked around the table, he was filled with an unexpected surge of confidence. He couldn't help but smile; Their banter and cheap shots at one another had been polished into a fine art over the years. And yet, if one of them were ever to find themselves in trouble, the entire group would step in to help. No questions asked, no matter the situation.

A passing bouncer caught Mark's attention. Jake followed Mark's gaze; he was watching as the bouncer work a concealed radio. The microphone was a sensor fixed against to his voice box, no doubt preferred over traditional microphones because of the loud music.

Mark was fixated on the bouncer. "I think we're going to need a few of those fancy comm units."

With that, Mark promptly slid out of the booth and disappeared into the crowd to rush after the bouncer.

Turning to Natasha, Jackie's eyes remained on Mark. "There is something wrong with that one!"

Jake recaptured the table's attention. "Okay then, it's settled. The rest of you listen very carefully; this is what I need to help pull this off."

CHAPTER 37

10 Days before the Building Collapse

Jake stood over the grave of his grandfather. Glancing up, he noticed a family gathering around their deceased loved one nearby. An elderly priest preformed the burial ceremony as the soft sound of their collective sobbing carried across the sea of tombstones.

Pausing to allow the family to reflect, the priest raised his eyes to look in Jake's direction. Jake held his gaze for a short moment then turned his attention to his grandfather's tombstone.

Something his father mentioned kept echoing in his mind: *"Your grandfather took his secret with him."*

What did that mean? Jake asked himself. *Did he die without sharing his secret?*

"So it would seem that your time in the 509th is still making waves, Grandpa." Jake held a crooked smirk as spoke to his grandfather.

He shook his head. "I know, I know … you would

have wanted me to walk in your footsteps, just like Dad. But I remember what they did to you … to us. We all had to keep our mouths shut about what you found."

Jake drew in a delicate breath, feeling tears beginning to brim. "Did you know they used to tease me in school about you? They used to say our family was crazy for believing you. But we weren't allowed to talk about it, so we just had to agree with them."

Glancing back at the nearby burial ceremony, Jake wiped away an escaping tear. A young boy held his father's hand as the priest spoke. Jake felt a rising anxiety at the painfully reminiscent scene.

For an instant, he was seven years old again. An honorary line of soldiers flanked his grandfather's coffin. Jake didn't know many of the faces of the men gathered at the cemetery; only a few were familiar to him, older men in full military uniform, friends of both his grandfather and father. In the background stood men in dark suits, their eyes hidden behind dark sunglasses.

A large flag emblazoned with stars and stripes draped the coffin. Sobbing softly, Jake watched as one of the soldiers folded the flag into a tight triangle with crisp, military precision. Then in sharp, precise movements a soldier marched to his father. With both hands, the soldier presented the folded flag to his father, who accepted it with a salute.

Jesse looked down at his young son, who had been clutching his leg. His eyes were sad, but warm and proud. "Your grandfather would have wanted you to have this."

With tears sliding down the sides of his checks, Jake held out his hands to accept his grandfather's folded flag.

On top of the flag rested his grandfather's ID tags. Little Jake watched as his father gently took the tags, and with a reassuring smile, draped the chain around Jake's neck. His tears were now streaming as he held his grandfather's ID tags in his small hands.

"I hated how I couldn't defend you. That I couldn't defend us," Jake said, returning to the present and not realizing he now clutched his grandfather's ID tags still hanging from his neck. He would never ride his motorcycle without his grandfather's dog tags; they had become his lucky charm.

"In the end I started believing them, and I hate myself for it." He wiped the tears that had strayed down the side of his face, and he couldn't help but give a lopsided smile. "And yeah, okay … I still miss you."

He paused a moment to compose himself. "Now I have this scientist visiting me, telling me things I don't think I want to know. They had visited you, they used to visit Dad, and now they're on my back! I don't know what to believe anymore, but according to this guy we have something that can prove what you and Dad saw was the real deal."

His eyes dropped to contemplate the inscribed plaque that lay at the foot of the tombstone:

AND YE SHALL KNOW THE TRUTH, AND THE TRUTH SHALL MAKE YOU FREE.

"So, what is the truth? Dad said you took it to your grave. Well … here I am!"

Crouching down now, he inspected the gravestone more closely. The marble headstone was engraved with his grandfather's name; it looked no different from any other. Placed at the foot of the grave, on the front face of the gravestone, was a large flat piece of polished marble that held the inscribed metal plaque. It was also like the surrounding gravestones. There didn't seem to be anything out of the ordinary.

"So what do I do?"

Jake found himself becoming fixated on the metal plaque. The size of a small pencil case, the plaque was polished and firmly fixed to the polished marble by small metal screws.

"He took his secret with him," he slowly repeated to himself.

Jake gripped the metal plaque. Cocking his head to the side, he considered the screws.

He retrieved his keys from his pocket then used one to scrape along the edges of the plaque, trying to pry it from the stone. It wouldn't budge. He looked around to see if anyone was watching him before giving it another try. Careful not to damage his key he tried again, this time with more force.

Then it happened.

The plaque moved ever so slightly.

It can be removed, Jake thought.

Again he looked around to see if anyone was paying attention then gave it another try. This time he kicked the plaque with his heavy motorcycle boot.

It dislodged a little bit more.

He kicked it again with a firm controlled blow. The plaque broke loose.

Breathless, Jake froze for a handful of heavy heartbeats, staring at the loosened plaque. It had rotated on one side to reveal a hollow compartment beneath.

Crouching now, he worked the metal plaque to rotate it a little farther, trying to expose the concealed compartment.

No good.

Using one of his thinner keys, he pried loose the last screw that seemed determined not to reveal the last legacy of Colonel Jesse Marcel. Jake worked the screw gently, persuading it to loosen. The compartment was small enough to be hidden by the plaque but large enough to house what seemed to be a small cylinder about 12 inches long and slightly less than an inch in diameter.

Using the key to pry the tube free, Jake flicked off the dirt and dust that had accumulated over the years. It was made of old cardboard and reminded Jake of the tubes sometimes used by couriers to transport drawings or rolled-up documents. It felt light in his hands, possibly empty.

Jake twisted off the lid without hesitation. The years had rendered useless the adhesive tape wrapped around the lid, which twisted off with the slightest effort.

Peering inside the cylinder, Jake's heart rate climbed; he could see that in fact something had been hidden inside. As his eyes gazed upon the contents, he knew in an instant what it was. It felt as if the earth shifted beneath him.

In a moment of compelling realization, Jake knew he had completely crossed over. He had not only become a recent believer, but he was now holding definitive proof.

CHAPTER 38

"Can I be of assistance, my son?"

Startled, Jake instantly slipped the cylinder-shaped container into his jacket. He spun around to find a priest standing behind him, Bible in hand. It was the priest who had been presiding over the nearby burial when Jake had arrived at the cemetery. Their eyes met for a few seconds before Jake responded.

Jake detected a deep reservoir of authority beneath the priest's courtesy. He found humility and warmth in the older man's soft eyes. But there was also something in his expression that echoed suspicion at Jake's presence.

He opened his mouth to speak, but his words failed him.

Oh my God, it's real!

Overwhelmed by the object in his jacket, the gravity of its existence hit him in waves. There were no words. He felt the breath leave his lungs as the revelation struck him again. In that instant, the truth finally solidified. He went numb at the impossible reality that had stared back at him from inside the cylinder.

Jake managed to summon a semi-polite smile, fighting hard not to show the explosive revelations detonating inside him. He took off for the cemetery gates in a sprint, leaving the priest standing beside his grandfather's grave.

❧

Across the memorial park, two dark-suited agents stood in the shade of a large tree among another group of mourners who were committing their loved one to rest. If not for the cups of coffee in their hands and the high-powered binoculars in their possession, they could have blended into the surroundings.

The senior agent tracked Jake as he left the cemetery in a rush. He watched as Jake crossed the road to join a group of youths huddled on their motorcycles. The group seemed to have been waiting for him.

He activated a microphone hidden within the lapel of his suit. "The target is leaving the cemetery."

❧

"Did you find what you were looking for?" Chris asked as Jake approached the group leaning on their machines.

Mark mounted his motorcycle and was about to fire up his engine. "We've got some familiar friends hanging around in the cemetery. They kinda look interested in us."

Jake didn't hear them; he was in another world. Mark noticed the unmistakable expression on Jake's face as the group gathered around him. His eyes were ablaze with a mischievous determination—he was almost glowing.

Mark immediately understood. *He found something!*

⁂

After a few pensive moments spent watching the young man hurry away, the priest turned his attention to the tomb. He had spotted Jake earlier, but had waited till the end of the burial ceremony before approaching to investigate what the young man was doing at the retired colonel's gravestone.

Still holding his Bible firmly against his chest, the priests gaze found the grave's metal plaque. A wave of shock rolled over him as he realized that the commemorative plaque commonly placed at the foot of most gravestones had been disturbed. The plaque hung askew, held in place by only a single screw.

Beneath the plaque had been a hidden compartment. The compartment, the priest realized, was now empty.

CHAPTER 39

In the middle of the road in front of the cemetery entrance gate, Jake's friends now circled him on their motorcycles. They all leaned in as Jake reached into his jacket to retrieve what had been concealed.

The young men exchanged curious looks, their excitement growing as they all dismounted to gather around Jake. Each felt a tremor of apprehension as they watched him twist off the lid. When he revealed its forbidden contents, they drew audible breaths.

In a breathtaking reveal, he pulled it from the cylinder for the entire world to see. Speechless, the group stared at the shiny object that slid from the tube into Jake's hand.

The object glistened with a reflective purplish hue across the group's faces as Jake rotated it in the sunlight, inspecting it closely. Jake knew in an instant that it was the object spoken of during childhood bedtime stories. It was the small I-beam his father had once held as a boy. Surprisingly, it reminded Jake of the countless terrestrial, and far less sensational, steel I-beams he often specified when designing buildings. But this small piece felt as if it were lighter than air. It was three-eighths of an inch wide and just under an inch deep—about the length of a student's desk ruler. Each end was fractured, suggesting it had been part of a much longer beam.

As he turned it, the light caught what resembled small hieroglyphic symbols, similar to Egyptian, Sumerian or Mayan hieroglyphics along its length. Some symbols also consisted of geometric shapes: circles, pyramids, crescent-shaped arcs and squares.

Jake noticed a ridge along its top and bottom flanges. When he looked at the broken I-beam's end in cross-section, he noticed the flanges got wider in the middle and resembled long, thin diamond shapes. It was exactly how Jake remembered his father describing it, and not too far off Jake's own attempt at manufacturing a terrestrial version.

Not exactly like the one I sketched, but the engineering principles were similar, he thought.

Jake passed the I-beam around for his friends to look at and watched the amazement register in their eyes. He noticed that the hieroglyphics symbols were not imprinted or engraved but solid, as if the I-beam were somehow cast together in a three-dimensional mold. Thus, the circles were in fact semi-spheres, and the pyramids were truncated and three dimensional.

Jake struggled to think of a manufacturing process that could produce an I-beam with such raised symbols, but knew of none. Milling machines used to make I-beams extruded and rolled hot tempered steel into shape; they could not produce raised symbols or shapes.

He cast his mind back to old engineering lectures on

materials. The I-beam's sharp angles, the thinness of its web and flanges, as well as the fine detailed definitions in the raised hieroglyphics, could only be produced with a very high density metal, if it had indeed been molded.

But it's impossible; it weighs next to nothing!

The highly reflective appearance of the I-beam's surface and the crystalline nature of the fractured ends pointed to a metal with an extremely fine crystalline structure. Jake was certain that this kind of metal or alloy couldn't be molded.

The color of the solid hieroglyphics differed somewhat from that of the rest of the beam. They were a shiny, metallic violet against the beam's overall dull, metallic gray. The brightness of its purplish hue changed depending on how Jake held it in the sunlight.

The color combination was unlike any steel, aluminum, or alloy Jake knew of. *It's definitely not of Earth*, he thought.

"This thing won't budge, but it's light as a feather!" TJ strained as he tried to bend the metal piece Jake passed around.

His friends exchanged wide-eyed looks. Nobody needed to verbalize the collective thought racing through their minds: None of them had ever seen anything like this before.

In that moment Jake realized how historically profound the object was. Its implications would change the way every single human would see the night sky.

He locked eyes with Mark, who was now glowing with excitement. Each knew what the other was thinking.

Mark was the first to speak. His words added to the nervous energy building within him. "What are you going to do?"

Jake looked back down at the object that had been returned to him. The little I-beam had brought him clarity unlike anything he had ever felt. He held definitive proof that the extraterrestrial crash his grandfather investigated over half a century ago actually happen. But more profoundly, Jake Marcel cradled in his hands the answer to the question, are we alone in the universe? He held something that had been manufactured somewhere other than on Earth.

Jake felt his mind open to the thrill of unthinkable possibilities. This object would prove that the government had been lying all along, and that his grandfather was not mistaken about what he had found in the summer of 1947. That there was a reason our technology seems to accelerate with every passing year, that perhaps a clean energy source existed that could break our dependence on oil, that the government had been complicit in the abduction of its citizens.

Mark read Jake's mind. "It's you against them now!"

Mark was right. Jake knew he was now at a defining crossroad.

He could either let it go and continue to live the life he had always led. A life far from the US military, removed from government secrets, having nothing to do with its resistance to the disclosure of the ET existence.

Or I could …

Mark's eyes never wavered from Jake's. "It's now or never, buddy. They're watching."

Jake's hazel eyes seemed to blaze with a new fire. Right then and there, he made his decision.

CHAPTER 40

"I'll text Tash; you give us a smoke screen!" Jake's resolve was unwavering.

A huge smile crept across Mark's face.

⤎

From across the cemetery, the agents tracking Jake watched as the group of youths started to mount their motorcycles. One of them throttled his machine, blasting engine noise in all directions.

The senior agent's demeanor turned serious. *What the hell do they think they're doing?*

"Typical punks." The other agent wasn't impressed.

"Idiots!" the senior agent spat.

⤎

Mark quickly distributed small two-way radios he had procured from the nightclub to the others. After checking they could all hear one other, he fired up his own two-wheeled beast.

Jake spotted the two large men in dark suits standing under the tree looking their way.

That's not cliché at all! Two men in dark suits, with sunglasses and short, neat haircuts not talking to each other. Why not carry a sign!

Chris, Paul, and TJ had mounted their motorcycles and were revving their engines. Jake gestured the agents' location to Mark as the collective engine noises started to rise and echo down the street.

Mark maneuvered to position his front wheel so that he faced away from the agents. He turned to look at Jake. No words needed to be spoken—Mark could read the other's face; they had company and they had to lose them fast.

Mark's motorcycle suddenly vaulted forward a few feet before coming to a complete stop. Squeezing as hard as possible on the front brakes, he kicked the motorcycle into first gear, completely opened the throttle, and slowly released the clutch. The machine reacted with a furious roar and shuddered as his rear wheel spun wildly, spewing white smoke in the direction of Jake and the rest of the group.

It only took a couple of seconds for the other three to understand. They followed suit. White smoke now spewed from four motorcycles in all directions. A dense white cloud grew to surround and completely engulf the stationary group of motorcycles.

❧

The agents watched in dismay. The burial ceremony they were pretending to take part in was abruptly halted, disturbed by an angry symphony of throttling engines.

The senior agent dropped his binoculars. "What the hell are they trying to prove?"

"It's a funeral for crying out loud. No respect!" the other agreed.

White smoke now engulfed the street in front of the cemetery entry gates.

"Shit!" It suddenly dawned on the senior agent that something was not right. He dropped his coffee to the ground as he hurried toward the late colonel's grave.

As the density of the white smoke increased, his brisk walk morphed into a jog, then a run, and then a panicked sprint. The second agent struggled to keep up.

They crossed paths with the priest, who himself seemed to be in a hurry, heading in the direction of the cemetery's chapel. They arrived at the late colonel's grave gasping for air.

The senior agent glanced in the direction of the gates to see smoke continuing to fill the street. Its density made it impossible to view the cars parked on the other side of the road.

Wiping the sweat from his brow, the senior agent surveyed the grave and headstone, looking for anything out of place. When his eyes fell upon the dislodged plaque he immediately crouched down to inspect it closer. Swiveling the plaque about its single remaining screw, he realized that it revealed a void that had been previously concealed. Large enough to hide two or three cell phones end on end, it was now empty.

Something had been removed!

The agents heard the motorcycle engines scream off into the distance. Jumping up suddenly, the senior agent spun in the direction of the fading engines. When the smoke dissipated, all the motorcycles had disappeared.

Exchanging a shocked look, the agents understood. The purpose of the smoke was to hide the direction of their escape.

The second agent quickly fumbled to activate his microphone. "We have lost visual on the target."

⁂

In a scream of rubber, the front wheel of Jake's motorcycle lifted slightly as he accelerated out of the white smoke. The motorcycles shot through the smoke screen that had given them the few precious seconds' head start they needed to escape.

By the time the agents got back to their vehicle, the motorcycles were nowhere to be seen. The group sped away from the cemetery before turning into a side lane, crossing over both sides of the road in wide, high-speed turns, a textbook racing maneuver used by superbike racers.

Jake pushed his machine hard through the suburban streets and led the pack until he was certain that no more inquisitive, dark-suited men were tailing them. The others followed in tight formation. They whipped by pedestrians who stopped to watch the pack thunder past at speeds well above the enforced limits. Their exhaust note was loud, startling onlookers as they raced past.

⁂

Jake peered behind him as he overtook two cars in rapid succession. They seemed to be clear of any tails. He slowed his motorcycle, bringing the group back down to the speed limit so they wouldn't draw any unnecessary attention, especially from local authorities.

After passing through two more neighborhoods, Jake

felt it was safe enough to pull over on a street lined by houses on both sides. Nobody was following them.

He removed his helmet and adjusted the ear piece attached to the radio he had rushed to clip to his belt before shooting off from the cemetery. It was one of five so-called gifts that Mark had requisitioned from the nightclub.

"Is this thing working?" Jake said, fiddling to find the right button on his unit. It felt strange talking into a microphone strapped to his neck that picked up sound directly from his vocal chords.

Chris winced. "If by working you mean loud as possible in my ear canal, then yes."

"Volume control, Chris, it's on the side." Paul's injection of sarcasm wasn't hard to detect.

"I wish you had volume control!" Chris fired back smirking.

Mark's earpiece and microphone were comfortably adjusted. "How long do you think it'll take them to figure out where we're …"

Mark didn't get a chance to finish his sentence. The whine of an oddly shaped helicopter shattered the air as it thundered low overhead. It banked hard, hugging the rooftops. It had no insignia or identification markings of any kind; it was matte black from tip to tail.

"Oooooh, I'd say right about now," Chris said and watched as the helicopter barely cleared the surrounding houses, slicing an elongated arc in the direction they were headed.

"Just great!" Mark felt a rush of anxiety. "What do we do now, Jake?"

Jake considered for a moment. "Don't know. Just follow my lead … I'll think of something."

The group strapped their helmets back on.

"Why does that make me feel even more nervous?" Mark muttered to himself.

But there was nobody left to offer him any reassurance; the rest of the pack had already sped off, the bellowing roar of their engines trailing off in their wake.

Mr. Sabre glimpsed the group of riders from the copilot's seat of the Sikorsky S-97 Raider. He quietly smirked to himself as the next-generation helicopter banked low, nearly kissing the rooftops. The maneuverability of the Sikorsky felt as crisp and immediate as an F-16—a fighter jet renowned for its dog-fighting capabilities.

The S-97's design objectives were to cross the bridge between traditional fixed wing and hoverable aircraft. The result was a revolutionary helicopter design, despite its unconventional appearance. With its twin overhead counter rotors and additional thrust propeller at the rear, the Sikorsky doubled the top speed that a helicopter could theoretically achieve.

"We have a visual on the targets," the pilot reported then gave a detailed description of their location and direction in a robotic tone void of emotion.

Unbeknownst to the group, an SUV with dark-tinted windows and no distinguishing markings on its matte-black exterior bounded into the street behind them. Soon after, an identical second then third joined the pursuit as the group passed through several intersections.

It wasn't until the SUVs clustered together in traffic that Mark spotted them in his side mirror. When he and his friends came to a stop at the next set of lights, he pulled up next to Jake.

"Now it looks like we have a *new* set of friends!" Mark gestured behind, his eyes flashing fear.

Jake looked back and spotted the three identical vehicles.

The traffic light turned green. Chris, TJ, and Paul also checked their mirrors to see what had caught the other two's attention before the group again took off.

The pack turned onto a main road with wide lanes and big intersections. The black SUVs followed.

Mark's stressed voice came through over the radio. "Wasn't expecting a helicopter chase! A couple of undercover agents in an unmarked car maybe … but not this!"

Two intersections later, Jake spotted something at the approaching light that would, under normal circumstances, cause the group to ride more conservatively: two police cars. They were stopped at the light on the cross street.

"Do you want the good news or bad news?" Jake asked.

"I know the bad news!" Mark was incredulous. "How could there be good news?"

Jake said nothing.

"Well?" Mark exclaimed. "Is there good news?"

"I'm still thinking," Jake said, his tone firm.

It was then that Jake was struck with an idea. If he could somehow force the patrol cars between them and the SUVs, the police vehicles would be enough of a distraction to slow the SUVs down, giving the group time to split up unseen. But he needed to somehow attract the patrol cars' attention first.

Then there was also that little issue of the overhead chopper to deal with.

One problem at a time, Jake told himself.

Having almost reached the next intersection, and sensing the lights were about to change, Jake slowed to get his timing just right. He watched for the green light to turn yellow, and the rest of the pack matched his speed.

Then the lights changed.

Now or never!

Jake shot a look at Chris, as if to send a clear message: "Copy me!" He tore down through the lower gears and opened his throttle fully. The mechanical scream of his engine blasted across the street. The motorcycle catapulted, his front wheel slowly lifting off the ground as he accelerated toward the intersection.

Trailing last, Mark not only heard but felt Jake's motorcycle redline. He watched in amazement as Jake, knowing the lights were about to turn red, lifted his front wheel off the ground despite being in plain view of two patrol cars and two pedestrians crossing the street!

Then, one by one, the three motorcycles in front of Mark geared down and hit their throttles in succession. Mark stared in disbelief as the front wheels of all three motorcycles lifted, one after the other, as if in a synchronized dance.

"I'm going to die!" Mark stammered, talking more to himself than the others.

Drawing a deep breath, he geared down to open his

throttle so he would not be left behind. As if saluting to the other motorcycles, his front wheel lifted from the ground and headed for the sky.

By the time the lights turned red, all five motorcycles had screamed into the intersection balanced on their rear wheels, front wheels raised.

CHAPTER 41

The traffic light in front of the police cars turned green. The cars slowly entered the intersection.

In front of them, front wheels in the air, five motorcycles tore through the intersection. The symphony of engine screams would have lifted the hairs on the back of any motorcycle enthusiast's neck. The spectacle was more than enough to grab the attention of the police officers, as well as everyone else with a line of sight to the intersection.

The first patrol car screeched to an unexpected stop less than a second after the light turned green. The two police officers in the front car glared after the motorcycles in amazement.

Crossing the road directly ahead of the speeding motorcycles were two young girls, about seven and thirteen years old, walking hand in hand. They froze in place at the sight of five motorcycles hurtling toward them, front wheels in the air.

The officers gasped as the motorcycles tore past either

side of the girls in successive blurs, leaving the young bewildered pair startled but untouched.

"We've got ourselves a pack of smartasses!" the driver of the first police car spat to his partner and slammed his foot on the accelerator.

The police car hurtled forward, its rear wheels laying down two dark rubber lines on the road. The car's rear end fishtailed as it drifted, rear wheels spinning, around the two startled girls who hadn't dared to move. The driver's partner strained to hold onto his seat; it was not customary for patrols to negotiate corners travelling sideways.

The second patrol car followed with lights and sirens blazing. Dark lines of rubber crossed over skid marks laid down by the first patrol car. It swung wide around the two girls, who were still holding hands, frozen in place. The officer in the passenger seat could only lock eyes with the younger of the two girls and watch as the car drifted wide, seemingly in slow motion, around her. Her expression was blank, her mouth agape. Once clear of the intersection, the passenger officer grabbed the radio to report the situation, their location, and the direction of pursuit.

After dropping his front wheel, Jake searched his mirrors for the resulting fallout from his stunt.

He was relieved to see that the two young girls were fine. Not only did all the guys do a good job missing them with ample room, but the girls did exactly what he had expected—they froze in place from the surprise and didn't move a muscle.

The two police cars had taken the bait and were in pursuit. Their lights and wailing sirens caused the surrounding traffic to come to a halt, effectively locking up the intersection behind them. Beyond that, the commotion had caused the SUVs to skid to a stop. The halted traffic blocking the intersection would mean there was no way for the SUVs to get through until traffic cleared.

The motorcycles were all accounted for, still in formation, and had their wheels back on the ground. Jake allowed himself a brief smirk of relief.

Mark even made it through in one piece and was keeping up.

⁓

From the Sikorsky's overhead vantage point, it was clear to Sabre that the developing police pursuit would interfere with the attempts by the agents on the ground to intercept the motorcycle group.

Cute trick, Sabre thought.

Sitting behind the pilot in the passenger's hold, a support agent sat fixated on his laptop screen. He was monitoring the video stream from a camera mounted to the underside of the helicopter. His screen showed a zoomed bird's-eye view of Jake with an overlay of artificial colors that scanned the images for predefined material types.

The support agent sat with four hulking figures in black military fatigues. The uniforms displayed no stripes, name tags or insignia whatsoever. They were Sabre's hand-picked security detachment that provides ongoing security at Section 4.

These ultra-elite soldiers never used names; they were referred to by only their service numbers. In the interest of efficiency, the team leader of any given detachment was designated Alpha, his second was Bravo, then Charlie,

Delta, and so on according to rank. Alpha was 45851, and he sat across from the support agent. Currently Alpha's team accompanied Mr. Sabre to provide security as needed and carry out any other auxiliary tasks for Mr. Sabre.

The support agent spoke into his helmet-mounted microphone. "Sir, there is nothing to suggest any of them are carrying anything."

"Do they have exotic materials with them or not?" Mr. Sabre growled back.

"If they do, sir, they've no doubt got it concealed."

The agent looked to his superior. Mr. Sabre pursed his lips together tight, unimpressed.

&

"Are you okay, Mark?"

"I can't believe you just did that!" Mark spluttered.

"You mean *we* did that," whooped Paul. "Well done, Mark, you lived!"

"Wooooooooooooyeeeee! What a *rush*! Let's go again!" TJ was oblivious to Mark's stress.

The group weaved through the busy traffic cramming the multilane road. Relative to the speeding motorcycles, the traffic seemed stationary. The patrol cars had the disadvantage of having to navigate the busy lanes, which is not always an effective feat mid-chase when the public was sometimes slow to get out of their way, an unfortunate fact of life that Jake had been counting on.

The radio crackled with Chris's voice. "I'm not imagining that funny looking chopper on our asses, am I?"

Jake paused. "No, it's definitely trailing us. But I have an idea … You remember that game where you shuffle a ball under three cups, then you have to pick the cup hiding the ball?"

Mark felt a rising uneasiness. He was almost afraid to ask. "We've got this space-age helicopter following us … that no one has ever seen before … not to mention it looks like it just flew out of the movie *Tron*! And *you* want to talk about games?"

Jake knew Mark would get it in a few seconds. He slipped a hand under his jacket to retrieve the cylinder. He waited a moment to time the next opening between cars then swung over a lane to position his machine inches away from Chris, so close that their knees touched. Not an easy stunt at speed.

"Here!" Jake passed the cylinder to Chris, who reacted instantly and shoved it into his jacket to avoid letting go of the handlebar for more than a millisecond.

Their eyes met again for an instant. Chris nodded in acknowledgment. He understood perfectly.

∾

"Sir! The target just handed an object to the rider on the second motorcycle."

The support agent's handheld touchscreen showed a zoomed image of the two lead motorcycles coming together. From their elevated angle over Jake's shoulder, the footage showed that his right hand momentarily let go of the handlebars and reached toward the other rider after a short pause. The second motorcycle then fell back to meet the third, but this time the object was clearly visible in the rider's hand.

The agent felt a pulse of exuberance and zoomed in

on the image to fill his screen with the foreign object. "It appears to be … a dirty-looking … cylinder?"

"That's it! Stay on it!" Like a hawk locking onto its unsuspecting prey, Sabre trained his eyes on the object that was now being passed from motorcycle to motorcycle.

"Hang on a sec." The support agent's voice went up an octave. "There are two objects!"

The agent's brow furrowed as he watched the second to last rider pass the object to the last rider. Then he seemingly passed another object back to the motorcycle in front. With a frantic swipe, the agent zoomed out to get a better overall view. The motorcycles looked as if they were coming together at random, sporadically pairing up to bump into one another up and down the formation, only to switch positions again and pair up with someone else.

There are more objects? Or are they faking it? thought the support agent.

The support agent felt as if he were trying to keep his eye on a playing card while someone shuffled the deck.

Sabre's jaw tightened, his words being squeezed through clenched teeth: "Keep an eye on it!"

Although the traffic had thinned out to allow the motorcycle formation to spread out, the chase was starting to get dangerous. So far, they had run two sets of traffic lights and weaved passed dozens of cars. With two police cars, three SUVs, and the helicopter on their tail, it didn't look like they would lose their pursuers any time soon.

A mile ahead of them loomed an eight-way intersection; from the sky the intersection looked like a giant asterisk, and was infamous for peak rush hour traffic delays when each direction competed for a green light.

Checking his mirrors again, Jake saw that the SUVs had caught up to the two police cars, and it looked as if they were trying to muscle the police out of their way.

"Time to split," Jake's voice crackled through the radio.

"Great place to do it. You sure you can't find anything a little more dangerous?" Chris's words dripped with sarcasm through the radio.

Jake was confident. "All we need to do is make a spectacle; the other drivers will see us and get out of our way. Nobody wants their car messed up."

TJ was skeptical. "Are you really sure about that?"

There wasn't time for banter. Jake continued, "Paul, you go hard right … Chris, hard left … TJ, to the right … I'll veer to the left toward the hills, and Mark …"

"Let me guess,"—Mark cut in, finishing the sentence—"straight up the middle."

"All make sense?" Jake asked.

Paul said, "Yeah, we got it. Do what you gotta do—we'll lose the tails."

"It's been nice knowing ya, buddy." Mark wasn't convinced.

"All you need to do is visualize the opening in the traffic; you can do it, Mark. Just tell us when to break." Jake tried to sound as calm as possible, despite feeling the pressure of time running out.

"Seriously, Jake, don't be sad, it's been a privilege … Really!"

"Mark, trust me. You can do it. Visualize the traffic opening."

Then it happened.

Mark's eyes rocketed wide as if he had just been punched. The rapidly approaching cars before him decelerated as if they were all in slow motion and moving through water. He watched as an opening in the traffic materialized. What followed next felt like a daydream. Mark watched himself punch through the traffic opening to reach the other side safely, it was as if he had left his own body, so he could see himself and find the safest path through.

"*Mark!*" Jake barked through the radio, jolting Mark back into his body.

The traffic opening then appeared, just as it had in his premonition.

"Break *now!*" Mark yelled.

The group's reactions were instantaneous. Paul and Chris sliced across the front of Mark from opposite directions in a blur, narrowly missing each other. Jake and TJ followed instantly as they cut across the nose of Mark's motorcycle in successive blurs, again narrowly missing each other. Before the four motorcycles had a chance to clear their path, Mark had already gunned his engine, the punch of acceleration kicked up his front wheel in reaction.

Mr. Sabre could not believe the sheer audacity of the group.

From above, their little stunt resembled a well-choreographed fighter pilot maneuver. It was as if he were watching stunt jets cross each other's paths as they broke formation in different directions to form the shape of a star, their exhaust leaving a growing trail that extended in each direction of a compass.

Each rider sped off in a different direction as the

motorcycles left behind a scene of chaos. The cross traffic had screeched to a disorganized halt to miss the hooligans who had run the red light and clearly had no respect for public safety.

The police cars were the first to run into grief; the first patrol car was sideswiped by diagonally crossing traffic trying to enter the intersection. The second patrol car swung around the collision only to be rammed by cross traffic from another direction. The two incidents set off a cascade of smaller collisions from vehicles trying to escape the anarchy. The entire intersection transformed into an auto-body repairman's payday.

Two of the black SUVs were forced into a skidding stop. The third managed to swerve onto the sidewalk to maneuver its way to the other side of the intersection.

Shaking his head, Mr. Sabre peered down at the crash site, the right side of his lip curling in disgust. Two of the three SUVs sat motionless.

"Goddamn FBI! Couldn't track an elephant through snow ... Even if it was bleeding!" Mr. Sabre's retort was thick with disdain.

He switched his radio over to the band used by the SUVs. "Stay on the best friend; he's the last in the procession, the one that went straight through. If it's not too much trouble for you!"

⤚

After successfully finding his opening through the cross traffic, Mark did his best to weave through the cars on the other side.

He was electric with adrenalin. *Did I just do that?*

Always the conservative rider, Mark would never have

dreamt of attempting stupid stunts like that, and now after completing two for two he didn't want to push his luck too hard on a third.

Behind him, his mirrors showed that a single black SUV was gaining on him. The traffic ahead was getting crowded, too heavy to speed through.

I need to find a way out!

Sweeping to the left and right, he passed inside and outside the traffic, wherever he could fit, trying to stretch out the distance between himself and his pursuer.

Then it happened without warning.

A car rushed out of a small side street without the driver seeing the approaching motorcycle. When the rapidly approaching silhouette appeared in the driver's peripheral vision, he instinctively slammed on his brakes hard. He brought the car to a complete stop and inadvertently blocked most of the road ahead of Mark.

Time slowed as Mark weighed his options. Swerving to the left would mean hitting the gutter and flying into the air and impacting a bus stop sign ahead. Another option was to swerve right, but he would most likely topple over and slide with one leg trapped beneath his machine, grinding the skin off his pinned leg.

There was one last choice, something he had never attempted. He lifted himself to raise his center of gravity as far back as he could and crunched the front brakes hard. The front wheel locked, sending him skidding toward the stationary car while his rear wheel lifted off the ground.

Locking the front wheel was a dangerous move, as it caused most riders to lose control. Mark knew this only too well as he fought to keep his balance, as well as keep his center of mass as far back as possible so he would not be flung over his front wheel.

The motorcycle slowed as it skidded, its front wheel smoking and rear wheel raised. He brought the motorcycle to a stop by impacting the car with a light thud, denting its side door.

The collision was relatively minor. A moment had passed before he realized he was still upright, now with both wheels and feet firmly planted on the road, and staring directly at the petrified driver.

I did it!

He checked himself to make sure everything was in the right place and that he was not hurt. But by the time he dismounted, Mark found himself surrounded by hefty, armed soldiers with aggressive looking assault rifles levelled at him. He was astonished by how many there were, or more to the point, how many of these burly figures could have been packed in a single SUV.

"Raise your hands and step away from your vehicle," he heard one of them bark.

He collected himself mentally, put the motorcycle on its kickstand, dismounted, and then raised his hands. Mark was not only astonished at how many machine guns were aimed at him, but also at how many guns were still holstered. He'd never seen so many weapons carried by so few.

As he gazed at the sea of armament, Mark took off his helmet and scratched his head. "Are you sure you brought *all* the guns?"

⤜

The density of the inner-city buildings had thinned out into suburban neighborhoods now that Jake had put some distance between himself and the wide, eight-way intersection. He was now flying through a residential area spread over small hills with long winding roads.

He downshifted to pass over the next crest. The road ahead dropped away to reveal a long steep hill that meandered into a long, sweeping bend to the valley below then continued to curve up the next hill on the horizon. A river cut its way through the valley; gentle parklands cushioned its banks on both sides. The water glistened in the sunlight as a rowboat approached a bridge. Sporadically clustered groups of locals were out by the river enjoying the sunny afternoon, either spending their time sunbathing, fishing, or jogging—until Jake's thundering machine disturbed the tranquil scene.

❧

The unit's team leader completely disregarded Mark's remark and stepped toward him.

"Hey!" Mark shrieked as he was whirled around and pushed against an adjacent wall with a force that was more than required.

"I'm no lawyer, but isn't there something you need to read to me before you can do this?"

"Shut up!" The soldier forced Mark's arms and legs out wide before searching him. Mark's entire body jolted with every forceful pat-down. While the soldier searched him, Mark noticed that all the soldiers were dressed head to toe in black.

The soldier found the old cylinder tucked down the front of Mark's jacket. Peering down the lidless tube, he could see it was empty.

❧

The last remaining ground unit's report came through Mr. Sabre's headset: "Sir, the subject is clean."

Sabre looked at the pilot and motioned in the direction Jake took. "Catch up to Marcel!"

The sun shimmered off the exotic-looking helicopter as it turned. The nose dipped in the direction Jake had taken and accelerated away.

❧

When Jake was almost at the bridge, he banked his motorcycle low to negotiate the elongated bend leading up to it. A familiar silhouette shot overhead, appearing abruptly over the crest behind Jake. It overtook him to fly in a wide arc over the valley, then turned to face him. It reduced its speed and approached the bridge from the far side. The whine of its turbines added another layer of disruption to the peaceful riverside setting being enjoyed by the locals only moments earlier.

The aircraft landed gracefully at the end of the straight stretch of road that led to the bridge from the far side. Its double counter-rotating blades slowed as its turbines wound down.

Jake crossed the bridge and approached the helicopter. He slammed on his rear brake, an ineffective method of slowing the motorcycle because it sent the motorcycle skidding in a straight line toward the helicopter. But that was Jake's intent. He kept sliding in a perfectly straight line, rear wheel screeching to slowing his approach, to get a better view of the now stationary aircraft.

There were two main characteristics that gave the

helicopter an odd appearance, or a sense of being unconventional. It had two layers of rotary blades, one above the other, which spun in opposite directions. It also didn't have the smaller rear rotary at 90 degrees to the axis of the main rotary blades, which served to stabilize conventional helicopters.

Coming from a military family whose jobs involved being in aviation, Jake was familiar with most types of operating aircraft. But he had never seen the likes or configuration of the sleek helicopter before him.

Whichever military branch these guys are from, they are obviously very well funded.

Three men leaped out of the helicopter. Two were mountainous soldiers and heavily armed. Ahead of them walked a suited man who carried an air of unquestionable authority.

With a delicate touch, Jake used his front brakes to bring the motorcycle to a sliding halt, stopping his front wheel barely inches short of the dark-suited man who was lighting a cigarette. The trio didn't seem intimidated in the slightest by Jake's skidding stop.

So much for making an impression, Jake thought.

CHAPTER 42

The suited man in command took a drag from his cigarette. He studied Jake intently as he remained seated on his motorcycle.

Jake felt a rising sense of uneasiness. The fitted black suit worn by the man did nothing to hide his broad chest and shoulders, suggestive of a man that had seen combat. Jake could feel his intense eyes boring into him. The man's powerful presence gave Jake the distinct impression that, in terms of military units, this group was at the top of the food chain.

The man blew smoke in Jake's direction while maintaining his piercing stare a few moments longer.

Finally, the man spoke. "Jake Marcel, I think you may have something in your possession that does not belong to you."

Jake's heart skipped a beat.

He knows my name.

One of the armed soldiers lifted Jake off his

motorcycle with ease then forced his hands on his head while he searched Jake's pockets and patted him down.

The suited man nodded toward the road behind Jake, motioning for the second soldier to investigate the bridge.

Jake thought his body search was unnecessarily rough, but also thought it was best to not say a word. It was then that he noticed a fourth figure, also armed, who looked like he was holding position to guard the helicopter.

Patiently waiting while a soldier aggressively searched Jake, the dark-suited man looked up at the surrounding hillsides, savoring his cigarette. He was taking it all in: the winding road down the little hill, the bridge over the river, even the little rowboat heading downstream on this sunny afternoon.

❧

Two girls wearing bikinis had their beach towels spread out on the river bank by the bridge. Natasha was sunbathing, her MP3 player blaring in her ears. Jackie had just returned from the river and was dripping wet from a refreshing swim.

As Jackie bent down to pick up her towel, she was startled by a mountainous shadow that suddenly stretched over her and her friend.

She instantly spun to face the intruder, covering herself with the towel. "Do you mind?"

Jackie had not expected to find a heavily armed figure towering over her. The man looked like a weight lifter carrying an assault rifle. The soldier looked her up and down intently then focused on Natasha and the area around their towels.

Jackie had yet to meet a man who could intimidate her. "*Hellllo?* Did you lose something?"

The soldier ignored her. His bulky frame slowly moved past her. He studied the scantily clad girls and their surroundings then sized up the old man causally rowing his boat away downstream. Jackie felt like a life raft being passed by a super oil tanker.

Natasha used half of her towel to cover herself from the enormous figure's prying eyes.

Jackie had had enough. "Obviously, you don't speak English. Do you have a term for *personal space* where you come from? Or how about *pervert?*"

The large soldier reacted instantly. Spinning to face her, he was visibly annoyed by her condescending insinuation. He fixed her with a gaze clearly intended to intimidate. Jackie didn't flinch. With a deep grunt, the armed soldier turned and walked back up the bank toward the road.

§

Jake had tried not to look anxious when the second soldier headed for the bridge, but he felt a wave of relief when he heard the first soldier's radio crackle to life. "The bridge is clean, sir. Heading back."

The suited man raised his chin to draw heavily on his cigarette then tossed it on the ground and extinguished it under his shoe. "Mr. Marcel, tell me where your little object is, and I might forget that you broke the speed limit, drove recklessly, ran numerous red lights, caused a road accident, and possibly even breeched the United States National Secrets Act all in less than 20 minutes."

Jake stood beside his motorcycle deshiveled. He opened his mouth to speak, but the words stalled in his chest. The second soldier had returned; the three men waited for him to respond. All Jake could muster was a shrug of his shoulders; he shook his head to indicate he had nothing.

The man in charge gave Jake a soul-chilling glare, his piercing eyes seeming to see straight through the younger man. He looked as if he had reached the end of his patience. Jake felt a ball of anxiety gaining mass inside him.

The man stepped toward Jake. He whispered coldly in his ear, "You could not possibly fathom the power of the organization you are trying to compromise."

Jake almost fell over.

Those few words revealed the true gravity of what he may be getting himself into. He had heard rumors about men in black, secret government departments and limitless black budgets, but for the first time it was real, standing right before him. For the first time, Jake felt a flash of gut-wrenching fear. He struggled to maintain an expression of indifference and to control his body language to avoid revealing his trepidation.

The man dressed in black held Jake's gaze a moment longer before turning to his men. "There's nothing here. Let's go."

Jake watched motionless as they boarded the helicopter and took off. The heavily armed soldiers in black were real. The strange-looking helicopter was real. The little exotic I-beam his grandfather found was real. There was no turning back now.

His only relief was that he'd had the presence of mind to think fast earlier.

Back at the cemetery, Jake had sent a text message to Natasha after asking Mark to organize the smoke screen. His text to Natasha had asked the girls to wait for him under the bridge and for them to bring Dr. Reilly because Jake had something the scientist might be interested in "fishing" out of the river.

Before Jake passed the cylinder to Chris as they rode side by side, he used his thumb to pop open the lid then let the small I-beam slide under his jacket just before handing over the empty cylinder to his friend. Realizing they were passing an empty cylinder, his friends then improvised by pretending to pass around multiple objects.

As Jake sped over the bridge, he slid the metal I-beam out of his jacket and tossed it over the bridge railing into the water, just as the black helicopter approached from the far side to land in the middle of the road.

The exotic fragment made a little splash as it hit the water. Natasha was already in the river swimming under the bridge, waiting for the splash to signal where to dive. She instantly retrieved the metallic object.

By the time she had surfaced for air, a small rowboat had reached the bridge and was heading downstream. She tossed the fragment into the boat as it drifted past. Dr. Reilly didn't say anything. He didn't even pick up the metal fragment after it bounced at his feet inside the boat. He just smiled at Natasha and kept rowing.

The only thing Jake hadn't anticipated was personally coming face-to-face with an unnamed government agency so soon, who also knew far too much about Jake's movements for his liking.

&

On approach to Section 4, Sabre reflected on the debriefing he would have to give Thirty-Three. He would have to report that he had revealed himself to the target and that the target knew that he was under surveillance. This was a move Mr. Sabre wouldn't want to make without yielding information that would secure the object he had been assigned to retrieve. Perhaps startling Marcel would cause him, and any exotic materials he may have in his possession, to go deeper into hiding. Such a turn of events would not be too concerning he thought. With almost unlimited resources at his disposal, the thought of a decent chase gave Mr. Sabre something to look forward to.

CHAPTER 43

After traveling twenty minutes downstream from the bridge, Dr. Charles Reilly slowly rowed his boat in the direction of a small fishing pier. He allowed the current to carry him alongside the pier's waterside edge.

With the metal object wrapped in a towel and gripped in one hand, he reached for the boat's mooring rope and struggled to pull himself up. He stood in the boat and found himself gliding toward an outreached arm.

The arm belonged to a bulky figure carrying an assault rifle over his shoulder. The soldier was outfitted in black fatigues void of any military branch insignia. He took the mooring rope and secured the boat before again extending a helpful hand. Reilly took hold of the man's powerful arm and was gently heaved off the boat onto the old wooden pier.

"A pleasure to once again see you, sir. Dr. Primakov felt a full security detail was more befitting to bring in the legend himself." The soldier smiled.

Behind the soldier, Reilly saw a full detachment of

soldiers that flanked four identical DHL vans parked nose to tail on the nearby road. One member of the detachment approached with a wheelchair fitted with an attached oxygen tank.

"How is the old man?" Reilly fixed him a nostalgic smile.

The soldier guided Reilly to the wheelchair and delicately helped him in. Reilly gripped the wrapped metal fragment firmly under his arm.

The soldier took hold of the wheelchair and pushed Reilly toward the four waiting vans. "Sir, still very much active. He'll never retire."

Allowing himself to relax now that he was in the hands of his assigned security detachment, Reilly placed the wheelchair's oxygen mask over his mouth and inhaled deeply as he rode toward the nearest of the DHL vans. After he'd been helped into the van's rear storage hold, the large soldier climbed into the front passenger seat beside the driver. The remaining soldiers climbed into the three remaining vans in equal numbers.

The vans left the pier in succession. They made their way onto a nearby highway, shuffling lanes as they passed under a number of road bridges. After reaching the first major intersection, the four vans split up, each heading in a different direction.

✍

The sun was on its way down, a big red sphere sliding toward an outcrop of scattered industrial buildings, when the DHL van approached one of the National Reconnaissance Office's research and data harvesting installations, located in the middle of its own block with open space surrounding the building for parking. The van cleared the security gates and approached the short road that led to the mid-rise building.

The van passed through the parking areas surrounding the structure then circled around to the facility's basement entry ramp. The parking spaces here were empty and its loading dock deserted except for a single figure who was slowly descending the stairs that extended from the dock.

By the time the van was parked, the gentleman was waiting patiently before the vehicle. He watched as one of the soldiers helped Dr. Reilly down from the rear of the van then approached with an armed escort.

It was Dr. Primakov who spoke first. "When you contacted me, I thought a ghost was playing tricks!"

"I'm not dead yet, Vlad." Reilly smiled at his old friend.

Only six years Charles's senior, Dr. Vladik Primakov was in remarkably good shape for a man of his vintage. Adorned with a head of silver hair, his insightful gaze exuded the confidence of a man who wielded an awesome intellect.

When Primakov spoke, his tone had the precision of a finely tuned musical instrument. "It gives me great pleasure to see you up and about. Your welcoming party wasn't too much I trust?"

The two men exchanged a warm handshake.

"A little over the top, but functional," Reilly joked.

Primakov looked at the escorting soldier. "Thank you, please leave us."

"Sir," the soldier said then nodded and turned to the waiting van, which still idled. The scientist and the physicist watched in silence as the van took off.

After the van had exited the building's basement, Primakov turned to Reilly, looking at the wrapped object held firmly under Reilly's arm. "So, there's a specimen out in the open?"

Reilly unwrapped the object and held the small I-beam up to the light for them both to study then handed it to the physicist. As Primakov inspected the objet, Reilly's mind flashed back to his conversation with Dr. Steven Greer. The hieroglyphs along its side looked consistent with the style of symbols Greer had showed him.

"We are living in a time when there is a tremendous disconnect between what is supposed to exist,"—Primakov looked intently at the metal specimen he was now holding—"and what is *not* supposed to exist."

"Are you running the analysis in-house?" Reilly asked.

Primakov's eyes shot up. "Of course not! What was the point of going to extreme lengths to flush this out only to bury it again?"

CHAPTER 44

9 Days before the Building Collapse

"Reilly!" Sabre was seething.

His words ricocheted off the walls of his Section 4 office.

One wall had transformed into a satellite image. Across it blazed a zoomed semi-holographic pictorial of a river crossing. To one side of the bridge sat a black helicopter in the middle of the road. On the bridge stood two figures next to a red motorcycle. A third figure faced away from the other two while smoking. A fourth figure approached the bridge with a rifle in hand.

Sabre studied the small rowboat that slowly drifted toward the ceiling inside his office. Behind Sabre stood his detachment commander and the commander's second, Alpha and Bravo. The timing of the boat's passing under the bridge had seemed too coincidental to Sabre. His instinct told him there was no such thing as coincidences.

"Skip ahead again and center the image on the rowboat," Sabre said to the wall.

The bird's-eye image followed the boat in fast motion as it proceeded to the pier then showed the man who was helped onto the small wooden pier.

"Stop. Play it back in real time," Sabre barked.

The video tracked the man being pushed in a wheelchair toward a group of armed men flanking four yellow vans.

Sabre's visage turned ice cold, an eerie transformation. "Reilly has been helping him. He has the specimen."

Sabre's jaw tightened as he bounded to his desk. His fingers jabbing the buttons of the desk phone, he dialed Thirty-Three's office.

A female voice answered. "Yes, Mr. Sabre."

"Give me Thirty-Three."

"He is unavailable," the voice replied, polite yet insincere.

Sabre spoke through clenched teeth. "I understand. Regardless, can you please patch me through, wherever he is."

The female voice was still polite. "By unavailable, I mean he is uncontactable. By anyone. He is meeting with the Group."

If he's with the Group, Sabre thought, *I'll have to go there myself.*

"Thank you." Sabre hung up.

With that, he stormed toward his office door.

❧

Sabre appeared alone in one of the Section 4 hangars. Facing the hangar doors was a terrestrial-looking fighter attended by an engineering crew.

Wearing a flight suit, he approached the modified F35B-A Lightning III while it was prepped for takeoff. The Lightning's waiting pilot handed Sabre a flight helmet. In exchange, Sabre handed him a thin screened tablet that listed the details of the flight.

The pilot scanned the flight time and details of the trip's refueling requirements. His eyes went wide when he read the destination coordinates.

&

A rectangular patch of mountainside that faced Papoose Lake opened up to reveal one of Section 4's hidden hangars. The F35B-A taxied into the middle of the dry lake bed before turning to face north, parallel with the length of the lake.

The plane's sleek lines shuddered as its single afterburner ignited in a pale blue roar. Developed by Lockheed Martin and derived from a constellation of three F35 variants, the first letter *B* in its designation signified its short takeoff and vertical landing capability, and the *A* and *C* classes indicated conventional and carrier variants respectfully.

After a short sprint across the dry lake bed, the F35B-A's nose flicked skyward. It leaped off Papoose Lake to bank toward the Group's secret meeting location.

CHAPTER 45

The magnetic north pole, as opposed to the geographic North Pole, is one of only two locations known to man to be a natural Faraday cage. It's the only place on earth where the convergence of the planet's magnetosphere disrupts all electronic communication, making any attempt at surveillance impossible from both terrestrial or off-world origins.

The fighter's undercarriage opened to reveal a mid-mounted, vertical jet turbine as the pilot slowed the F35B-A to hover 60 feet above the Arctic's rolling surface. Rechecking his location, the pilot glanced around. In the distance, all that could be seen was barren ocean stretching out to meet the curvature of the Earth. There was no land or vessels in any direction.

Now hovering, the aircraft slowly descended. What sets the F35B-A apart from the constellation of three F35 configurations is the additional *A* designation. Specially developed for Section 4's exclusive use, the *A* signified the F35B's aquatic conversion.

The fighter's jet turbines shut down the instant its undercarriage kissed the ocean's surface. Buoyancy tanks both inside its weapons hold and under both wings kept the aircraft afloat.

Sabre felt the plane rise and fall as long, drawn-out waves passed beneath. His eyes traced the raising waterline climbing the canopy as the buoyancy tanks slowly took in water. The pilot had shut down the engine and switched the avionics to submariner mode. Thin propellers, previously concealed by the fighter plane's wingtips and tail wings, extended and engaged to guide the aircraft as it sank. Within moments the aircraft was completely submerged, swallowed by the Arctic Ocean and descending toward the dark, gaping abyss below.

In complete darkness, Sabre watched the fathometer reading on a display before him, its number increasing as it measured their depth. Below them, a mammoth form materialized against a backdrop of complete darkness. Ominous and ghostly, the form dwarfed the fighter as it approached.

As the fighter maneuvered to descend over the colossal shadow, lights along its length blazed to life, revealing the outline of an Ohio-class submarine. Like a submerged runway landing, the parallel lights guided the fighter toward a docking compartment that opened on approach, allowing the fighter to dock inside the submarine.

Once the hatch slid closed to seal the fighter inside, the docking platform lit up to show the water level now had dropped around the aircraft. Thirty seconds later, the dripping aircraft was resting in a dry dock.

⌇

The Group has taken on many names over the years. Born out of necessity by Secret Executive Memorandum

NSC-5511 in 1954, President Eisenhower commissioned the committee to study, oversee, and conduct all covert operations dealing with the extraterrestrial presence.

The committee's original finding on the study of the alien question was that the public could not be told. The committee believed that such an action would most likely lead to global economic collapse, the collapse of the world's religious groups, and incite national panic. Secrecy was therefore mandatory. The committee decided that if the public could not be told, then Congress also could not be briefed. Funding for the committee's projects and research would have to come from outside government sources.

Originally nicknamed Majestic 12, under Eisenhower and Kennedy, the committee was labeled the 5412 Committee or the Special Group. During the Johnson administration, it became the 303 Committee. Under Nixon, Ford, and Carter, it was called the 40 Committee, and under Reagan it became the PI-40 Committee.

Now known as the National Security Council's Special Studies Group, dubbed the Group or SSG-36, it consists of 36 members made up of scientists and high ranking military heavyweights. SSG-1, the head of NSC's Special Studies Group subcommittee, answered to no one, not even the elected president. Over the years, only the committee's name had changed. Its resolve remained unchanged.

SSG-36 met in various confidential locations, including the Battelle Memorial Institute in Columbus, Ohio. When meeting to discuss matters of planetary importance, they have the power to commandeer military assists. In this instance, the US Navy's Ohio-class submarine had been redeployed to the magnetic north pole, ensuring

SSG-36's meeting was hidden from both terrestrial and orbital surveillance.

At the head of the long table in the submarine's situation room sat Thirty-Three, otherwise known as SSG-1. With his fingers steepled, he listened intently as the merits of trusting the extraterrestrials, or the others as they were sometimes called, was debated over the table.

"Are we to forget the 1975 Dulce incident? We lost two scientists and over 40 of our military personnel. All killed!" SSG-10 scowled.

Across the table, SSG-13 considered it and shook his head. "It was a demonstration of the ET's antimatter reactor. They warned us that the energy discharge would ignite all the munitions in the room. They asked that all bullets and rifles be removed. We didn't understand the technology."

SSG-18 stared at SSG-13 in disbelief. "Even so, when the guards refused, the ensuing commotion escalated to an underground warzone!"

SSG-10's eyes shot back to SSG-1. "They have lied to us more than once. How are we to calm the population when they—"

The sound of Sabre being briskly escorted into the situation room took the members of the meeting by surprise. Flanked by four heavily armed Navy SEALs, Sabre stood at attention, helmet in hand, as if waiting for permission to speak.

Thirty-Three's eyes lit up in surprise then concern. "Mr. Sabre, this is highly unusual. I take it that your unexpected need to join us is a prelude to some pressing developments."

The room fell silent; all eyes were on Sabre.

"Sir, an exotic specimen from the '47 Corona crash

site is out in the open. Marcel is receiving assistance from Reilly." Sabre's tone was robotic.

A wave of hushed murmurs and wide-eyed exchanges went around the room at the mention of Dr. Charles Reilly. Thirty-Three silenced the table with his raised hand.

"When did this occur?" Thirty-Three's eyes were calculating.

"Within the last six hours, sir."

Seated to the right of Thirty-Three, SSG-2's face was grim. "Then it is already too late to send an extraction team. Reilly would already have it back underground, and with his involvement, no doubt having it scrutinized by outsiders."

SSG-4 shook his head. "This is a catastrophic breach! Should it be leaked into the public arena—"

"Agreed!" SSG-10 cut in. "This needs to be contained. If that irrefutable sample of non-terrestrial material, or its analysis, were circulated, it would unravel everything. The greater good must be considered. All knowing parties need to be sanitized; the blowback would be incalculable. This rising threat of premature disclose could be devastating. It must be eliminated. It will bring forward the reveal event 20 years ahead of schedule. It cannot be permitted."

Everyone around the table agreed.

"Then it is unanimous." SSG-2 leveled a fiery stare at Sabre. "Sanitize the situation, Mr. Sabre. Execute extreme prejudice as necessary and return that specimen to the classified arena."

Sabre looked to Thirty-Three. "Sir?"

Thirty-Three paused as if afraid he'd say something he might regret. "It would appear you have your orders."

CHAPTER 46

2 Days before the Building Collapse

The NRO's research and data harvesting building formed a distinctive profile against the darkened horizon of scattered industrial buildings in Dr. Vladik Primakov's rearview mirror. Towering over its neighboring installations, and although now miles away, its blazing office lights outshone the lowest scattered stars against the ink-black sky.

Primakov was excited. He fumbled around in his briefcase for his phone while trying to keep his speeding car within its lane. With eyes darting between the dark road ahead and the keypad, he selected a menu item to place a secure call.

"Vladik?" The voice on the line was Dr. Charles Reilly's.

"It's miraculous!" A chill raked Primakov's flesh.

"Is everything okay? What's happened?"

Vladik spoke in rapid bursts. "It's the metallurgical tests on the specimen. Iron, cobalt, nickel, with large traces of iridium and meteoric iron. Charles, iridium of this nature is normally found only in meteorites!"

Unsurprised, Charles sat up in his bed as he listened.

"The broad-spectrum elemental analysis showed extremely rare elements in this thing; they're exotic, and there's so many of them. Thirty-six different elements in all, two of which we haven't seen before! This is a complex, highly advanced, manufactured alloy built for strength."

Charles nodded, a knowing smirk crossing his face.

"The surface coating is very peculiar," Vladik continued. "It appears to be sensitive to voltage; it emits electromagnetic radiation when charged. The iron ore we mine does not possess these properties. Under its surface, we found layers of carbon nanotubes unlike anything we've seen, and Charles, nature doesn't grow nanotubes!"

Primakov was talking faster now. "It's incredible to witness; the atoms appear to have been coded somehow to self-organize. In over 40 years of working as a physicist, I've never seen anything like it. If you fracture this thing, it self-heals—it reassembles at the atomic level! We're talking about an intelligent material with the ability to repair itself. This is centuries, possibly millennia, beyond any manufacturing processes we have!"

Reilly felt himself being swept up in the physicist's infectious enthusiasm and realized he was also smiling as he listened.

Vladik's excitement was building. "And get this ... this is the real debunker killer: The isotope ratio is off the scale. Its isotope shift is 20 percent; the material has a week's decay with a half-life of about a billion years. They are so far outside the standard percentages that there is no way they could have been formed in our solar system, or even the supernova that created all the heavier elements in our local star cluster. That means that this material came from an area of the galaxy that is ahead of ours by 90 million years or so. Charles, you can't fake this; these isotope shifts are unusual to the extreme. And with atoms that self-organize … how the hell do they do that? When was the last time you broke something and watched it reassemble? It just doesn't happen. How did you get this your hands on it?"

Reilly couldn't help but flash a wide smile at his friend's excitement.

"Charles, the metallurgical testing determined that some of the metals in the specimen not only contain non-terrestrial isotopic ratios, but contain atoms that do not exist in the periodic table. I don't believe any human made this sample. Simply put, whatever you gave me did not come from this Earth."

Primakov's tone intensified. "This sample generated the most significant and most compelling data we have ever seen in support of intelligent life elsewhere in the universe. The impact of this is mind-stretching."

Reilly was still smiling, but spoke with a resolute tone: "Then I don't have to impress upon you the paramount importance of keeping the metallurgical test results away from prying eyes."

"We'll do this just like the old days!" Vladik Primakov's voice still reverberated with excitement. "Only one control copy of the lab report, no electronic copies, so no chance of electronically snatching through firewalls."

Charles nodded as he listened.

"And if I had to make an educated guess on where this thing came from based on the isotopic decay, I'd have to say it came from a place in our galaxy at least 40 light years in the direction of …"

With a sickening crash, the phone connection was severed from Vladik's end.

CHAPTER 47

An unexpected movement had caught Dr. Vladik Primakov's eye on his left side.

The colossal impact from the ramming truck caved in the driver's side of Vladik's car. The energy from the side impact twisted and contorted the car's chassis, wrapping it around the front of the speeding Kenworth truck.

Now airborne, the mangled car spun in the air, its remaining windows and side mirrors exploding as it hit the road and continued to roll end over end ahead of the truck.

The rear wheels of the Kenworth skidded and skipped. Its brakes screeched in protest as the driver attempted to slow the 18-ton beast that trailed only inches from the rolling car. The two vehicles continued along the road, the truck's tires smoking as the car rolled on its side for another 100 feet.

With a final spin, the car slammed to a halt on its roof in the headlights of the huge Kenworth, which screeched to a standstill 15 feet away.

～

"Vladik?" Charles's face was contorted in anguish. "Vladik!"

Slowly he lowered his phone. Mute with terror, Reilly was frozen in disbelief. His lips quivered in a hopeless attempt to speak. His voice was barely a whisper as a soul-chilling realization washed over him: "They have already begun."

◈

A hulking black-clad figure emerged from the cabin of the truck. He approached the mangled wreck in the headlights with an assault rifle held diagonally across his chest, muzzle aimed downwards.

Peering through what was left of the driver's side door, Alpha inspected the disfigured body that was still strapped to the seat. The face had caved in to the blood-soaked cranium. Jellified gray matter seeped through cracks in the physicist's skull.

Alpha thumbed his comm unit, its microphone strapped to his voice box. "The target has been disposed."

CHAPTER 48

1 Day before the Building Collapse

"You'll have to move fast," Charles said ominously to Jake.

Natasha and Mark stood with Jake as Charles explained that they now had definitive, unprecedented proof that the crash debris that Jake found at his grandfather's grave was manufactured somewhere other than on Earth. The form of this evidence was by way of independent and verifiable expert analysis by a nongovernment physicist, a leader in his field who could not be refuted.

They had met just before dawn, gathering under a bridge away from the telescopic lenses of spy satellites. The scientist arrived in a borrowed DHL van, the others in Mark's car.

"So all we have to do is break into the NRO building, a secure government facility, grab the report, and run." Jake looked skeptical.

Dr. Reilly's reply had the soft, controlled patience of a

school teacher. "Jake, I'll give you what you need to get in and out."

Mark was unconvinced. "Sure, sounds easy!"

Natasha stood with arms crossed and looking increasingly uncomfortable.

Reilly was silent for several seconds as he locked eyes with Jake, Natasha, and Mark. "Your friend is right. I can get you in and out. But it will be up to you to deal with whatever surprises get thrown your way."

"And by surprises, you mean big guys in black helicopters," Mark interjected.

Natasha's eyes widened. She could bear it no longer. "Jake, you didn't say anything about a SWAT team or a chopper chasing you last time! And now this!"

"You should have seen the firepower they brought with them," Mark added.

Jake shot a silencing look at Mark and shook his head.

Completely wrong thing to say, Mark!

A terrifying thought gripped Natasha. "Why did those officers need machine guns?"

"They weren't officers, hon," Jake said, feeling himself being dragged into an argument.

A trace of fear laced Natasha's voice. "Then who were they?"

Jake had been wondering the same thing. A heavy silence descended around them as they all turned to Reilly.

"Who's the guy in the suit?" Jake finally asked.

Charles took a deep breath. "Natasha is right to be scared. They are tracking us. It's only a question of time before they—"

Jake's tone intensified as he interrupted mid-sentence: "Who's the guy in the suit, the one that smokes?"

The scientist considered the question a long moment. He turned to stand next to the van and leaned on it for support before continuing.

"For the sake of argument," Charles paused, "let's just say for a moment that there exists a classified group whose sole purpose is to study and handle off-world technology. Let's also assume that the crash your grandfather was called out to investigate was retrieved and delivered to this special group. They would then have in their position exotic, off-world tech. Now let's also say this group has access to black budget funding in large amounts, which grants them the means to employ genius scientists to study and understand the off-world tech under absolute secrecy deep within the classified world. They'd have no outside influences, so they could take all the time they needed to understand the non-terrestrial technology enough to gain a working knowledge of its science and principles."

Jake remained silent, wondering where the scientist was headed now.

Charles shifted before continuing, as if he felt some internal pain. "It would then be safe to assume that after the scientists spend years studying this stuff, they make one or two scientific breakthroughs in their understanding, some of which leads to profitable licensing of patents: lasers, integrated circuits, night vision, nano-carbon fibers, or even fiber optics. So, now their research has yielded unprecedented, leading-edge technologies, which also double as income-producing investment opportunities. Do you think this would give the group more or less incentive to reveal their secret?"

Jake cocked his head. "Less, obviously."

"Let's go one step further," Charles continued. "Let's pretend they make breakthroughs that are even more significant, like antigravity, zero-point energy, field propulsion, or a new source of energy that was clean and freely available. That is when their superiors would decide not to share these discoveries with the mass population."

"But why not?" Mark protested. "They would make millions, maybe billions."

"It's not about what they would make," Charles corrected, "it's about what they would destroy. Yes, they would make billions, but in doing so, they would break down the world's largest industry worth multitrillions: the petroleum industry. So let's say they continue studying these new sciences in secret. They would be ahead of everyone else in the outside world and able to break away from our society to advance on their own. Fast forward three or four decades later, and this small group would create a very different society from the rest of the world. Not only would they have very advanced technology and substantial resources, but their worldview and geopolitical beliefs would significantly differ from that of the rest of us. Their technologies may even allow them to interact with off-world entities before the rest of us; maybe even have the means to travel off-world to have encounters that would revolutionize their own worldview, making them far removed from the rest of civilization by orders of magnitudes."

"When you say the off-world entities, you mean,"—Mark hesitated—"aliens?"

"That term is implicit in evoking ridicule. Let's just refer to them as *off-world visitors* or *the others*. The intelligence community use words like unconventional aircraft, unknown aircraft or extraterrestrial vehicles also called ETVs and are very careful not to use the term UFO or alien."

Jake wanted to get back to the point. "What you're saying is there exists a group that has broken away from mainstream civilization and is independent from government. How is this connected to the guy in the suit?"

An uneasy frown crossed Reilly's face. "And they would possess substantial financial power enabling them to influence governments, even dictate terms to governments if deemed necessary. They would also have their own ultra-elite security force at their disposal. The guy in the suit, as you described him, commands this group's ultra-elite security personnel, his name is Mr. Sabre."

This revelation made Mark gasp, and Natasha looked as if she was going to be sick. Jake's eyes narrowed. He didn't know whether to take the scientist seriously.

This can't be real, Jake thought.

Although he couldn't believe his ears, he sensed in Charles's eyes that the scientist was telling the truth.

"We don't stand a chance," Jake said, his voice barely a whisper.

Charles remembered his friend Dr. Vladik Primakov and felt nausea creeping to the surface. He pushed the thought from his mind. "If there were ever a man who personified a wolf in sheep's clothing, Sabre would be the one … he's a titanium fist in a velvet glove. There are some very powerful interests that don't want the truth to come out. Sabre commands the security force tasked with keeping the world's most dangerous secret."

"You know him?" Jake struggled.

"I know of him … I was one of them … I had the privilege of being able to study their science, learn from the others' technology. Sabre was one of those who was given the privilege of keeping the secret from falling into our enemies' hands. Well, that's what we believed … what I once believed," Reilly said. His voice trailing off.

"We're going to die! All of us!" Mark's voice was heavy with fear.

A gentle smile crossed Charles's face. "Yes, it is dangerous. They are very, very powerful people. But they are just that, people. They do possess an Achilles heel. The one thing they fear the most is the same thing that will guarantee our safety, and that is to get this out in the open. If we can get that report, that one body of evidence that is indisputable, the mass media will be unleashed on this story like it has *never* been unleashed before."

Reilly paused to punctuate his point. "And safety, my friends, is in the masses. The perfect irony is that once it's out, if they move to eliminate any of us, it'll only serve to prove the very thing they are trying to suppress."

Jake, Natasha, and Mark exchanged startled looks.

The scientist waited for them to arrive at the same conclusion. "When my father was born, there were no such things as flying machines. Before he died, man had gone to the moon and back. In your generation, there will be changes just as profound, which this group has been trying to hold back. What if I told you that the former head of Lockheed Martin, Ben Rich, once said that we now have the technology to take ET home? That was back in 1993; just imagine what we can do now."

Mark shot Jake a curious look, hoping the scientist would elaborate.

"The truth embargo is now in its seventh decade," Charles explained. "This isn't the first time our civilization has enforced a worldwide truth embargo. We've been doing it since the fourth century. That's what much of the Crusades were about—gathering and destroying information when the Vatican tried to bury the truth about Christ's bloodline."

He paused. "But we'll save that story for another day. The basic objective remains consistent … to restrict information from the many in order to empower the few."

Charles looked at each of his young companions as he spoke. "If we can retrieve the report and get it out in the open, it'll set off a shockwave in physics and force a disclosure event. And when disclosure happens, it will be a *where-were-you-when-it-happened?* moment. There will be a new dividing line in history. AD will come to be globally accepted to refer to after disclosure. The sum of all modern science will be rendered obsolete; it will bring an end to the age of silicon and change human civilization."

There was a long silence.

Charles continued. "A disclosure event will be more profound than the Kennedy assassination, the moon landing, the shuttle disasters, the Twin Towers collapse, and both world wars all combined."

Reilly stared deep into Jake's eyes, and said solemnly, "This, my friend, is the third prophecy of Fatima. So terrifying that the Vatican would never reveal it because it will also call into question the world's religions. Notwithstanding the fact that the first two prophecies have already come to pass."

Over the next 15 seconds, Jake took several slow breaths,

trying to absorb what the scientist had just shared. Jake felt his senses igniting, a new compulsion rising within him: determination, defiance. Jake knew exactly what he needed to do. His eyes slowly rose to meet Natasha's; her eyes were welling with tears of fear. She fixed Jake with a deep stare that seemed to imply, *you don't have to do this.*

Jake sensed Natasha's apprehension, her anxiety. But there was also understanding there. She understood the paramount importance of retrieving the report, and she also understood Jake's personal yearning to set the record straight about what his grandfather once found in the desert.

With a new determination, Jake turned back to Reilly. "If we do get our hands on it, how do we get it to the public quickly?"

"You leave that one to me," Charles said confidently.

"And what about the little I-beam?" Mark questioned.

"You should find it with the report. Take it back." Charles's face filled with anguish as he thought about his missing friend. "If we can get the report to the media, it'll put a spotlight on the Special Study Group's activities and force their hand in disclosing the rest of the ETVs they have in their possession."

"You really think we can do this?" There was a hint of doubt in Jake's eyes.

Charles's confidence was unwavering. "Perhaps you are capable of much more than you know. All you need to do is create the trigger event then sit back and let the avalanche come. Now listen carefully: this is how you get into a secure NSA building."

CHAPTER 49

Day of the Building Collapse

The dozing security guard jolted awake at the sound of an approaching delivery van. Cursing the early hour, he fumbled for his clipboard and stepped out of the security guard hut at the gates of the NRO research and data mining facility. Checking his list, he found it odd that no deliveries were expected so early.

He stepped toward the approaching vehicle, raising his hand against the glare of the headlights, and peered at the looming van. As the glare subsided, the familiar yellow of a DHL courier van became apparent.

The van slowed to a halt for the guard. He looked at the license plates before stepping to the driver's side window. "You're lucky I recognized the plates. If this vehicle wasn't one of our decoys, you'd be waiting on the street till the delivery dock opened."

Stepping back, the guard waved the van through.

As they drove past the security checkpoint, Mark

realized he was trembling. Dressed in a makeshift uniform that roughly approximated a delivery driver, he turned to Jake and Natasha, who hid in the back of the van among empty computer boxes.

"Where are we supposed to go now?" Mark choked.

Jake didn't share Mark's anxiety, and replied in a calm tone. "Drive past the entrance, let the next guard see the van."

They followed Dr. Charles Reilly's instructions to the letter. Mark drove the yellow van up the road toward the building and pulled into the semi-circular drive in front of the building's entry. He stopped to park haphazardly in the middle courtyard adjoining the building.

❧

"What the hell is this jerk doing?" the reception guard growled, looking up from his morning paper.

The guard watched with contempt as the driver got out then opened the side door of the van and blundered to stack three computer boxes on top of each other. Attempting to balance the swaying boxes, the driver stumbled as he carried his delivery toward the building's entrance.

"Doesn't this idiot own a watch?" the guard said as he pressed the intercom button. "All deliveries must be unloaded at the rear dock. It's too early, and they're not open yet."

Mark spoke into the intercom: "But security at the gate said I could enter."

"He must have meant you can wait out back till the dock opens. Regardless, you can't come through here. Wait by the dock until it opens; then they'll clear you."

With that, Mark struggled to regain his balance as he

turned to carry the boxes back to the van. He released his grip on a small, black USB drive concealed in his hand under the boxes, letting it drop to the ground before staggering back to the vehicle.

The guard watched suspiciously as the clumsy driver reloaded the van and drove away. An indistinct object on the ground outside the door then drew the guard's attention. He discarded his reading material and moved to the entrance for a closer look.

Sitting on the pavement was a small USB drive.

Was that there before? the guard asked himself.

Using his security card to release the entry lock, he ventured outside the entry to retrieve the small object. He looked in the direction of the departing van then down to inspect the object. There were no markings; it was a plain USB drive. He peered again in the direction of the van, which had disappeared behind the building, then pocketed the USB and returned inside.

Back at the reception desk, the guard inspected the USB drive more closely. With a ponderous expression, he inserted the USB into one of the reception computers, clicking on its icon. It was empty.

In that instant, unbeknownst to the guard, a spyware program was executed and began to tunnel through the NRO's firewalls to target the building's electrical and security systems.

⤋

On the other side of the city, Dr. Charles Reilly was sitting in an empty café in front of an open laptop. With his computer screen active, he sat and waited patiently.

Then it happened.

Reilly's computer pinged and a prompt appeared on his screen: CONNECTED.

Several keystrokes later, Reilly gained remote access to the security system and video feeds of the NRO building.

❧

Jake crouched while he waited outside a fire escape door next to a closed roller door that allowed access to the building's delivery dock. Mark and Natasha remained in the van parked close by, which Mark had backed up against the building.

No doubt for a fast getaway, Jake thought.

He adjusted the radio he had worn when leaving the cemetery and squinted at the horizon. The sun was emerging from behind the silhouette of distant warehouses. Jake's heart pounded at the sound of the door's latch. He tested the handle right away.

The door had been unlocked.

Brilliant, Charles!

Jake sprang into action. He sprinted through the doorway and bounded up the stairs. His eyes were trained on the floor numbers on the doors as he passed them. Reilly had told him that the office where he would find the analysis report was on the 35th floor.

❧

The guard at the building entrance settled back in at his desk and returned to his paper. He periodically looked up at the screens in front of him; they displayed a bank of security images that rotated through the myriad of video feeds showing all areas of the building. Other than a slight flicker, as per usual, there was no movement in any of the camera views.

⁂

Eighty seconds later, Jake passed the 34th floor. As he ran up the final flight to level 35 he glanced at an overhead security camera. He plunged his hand into his pocket to retrieve the security card given to him by Dr. Reilly.

His heart was pounding, and his breath caught as he reached out to touch the plain white card against the door sensor. He braced himself for a dangerous result.

No alarm sounded.

He walked quickly through the elevator lobby and a pair of locked doors until he stood in what seemed to be a foyer lined with windows that looked over the surrounding buildings and warehouse. The sun had risen. Jake could see city buildings on the horizon. To his right was the entry into an office area, to his left, an enormous steel door with a sign that read "Armory."

Feeling slightly uneasy now, he took a curious step toward the armory's security pad and tried his card. Jake gasped in astonishment. He didn't expect the mechanism within the door to click upon acceptance of the security card. With a final *clunk* the door was open.

Bursting with curiosity about what he would find, Jake hauled open the heavy door and stepped inside. The walls were lined with smaller, locked doors, each with its own complicated looking touchpad. The rear wall held racks of assault rifles, pistols, grappling guns, and bulletproof vests: everything needed to outfit several SWAT teams. Jake felt himself momentarily fixated on the grappling guns; their quadruple-headed hooks sparkled under the lights.

He was not prepared for what lay deep inside the safe against the rear wall of locked cabinets. A large black case on the floor displayed the words FIM-92 STINGER. Jake felt his mouth fall open as he stepped toward the black case. Then, as if emerging from a trance, he helped himself to a grappling gun and returned to the task at hand.

Just in case, Jake thought.

After charging through a locked entry into the offices, Jake found himself in another foyer that looked out at the horizon; a corridor lined with individual offices on either side was to his right. One by one, he read the names of the occupants on the doors as he rushed past.

His heart pounded harder when he found the name given to him by Reilly.

Dr. Vladik Primakov.

CHAPTER 50

Dr. Primakov's office was furnished like any other. Dominated by a large desk, he had a computer, scattered files, and office supplies. The room was filled with bookshelves and filing cabinets.

Jake scanned the room for a locked drawer or secure cabinet. He felt drawn to the chair behind the desk. The hairs on his neck bristled with anticipation. It took only a few moments before he found a safe in a cabinet behind the desk with an alphanumeric keypad. Jake keyed in the access code Dr. Reilly had given him: ELEMENT115.

The lock released with a *click*.

Jake felt a rush of exhilaration pulse through his nervous system. He opened the metal door and spied a large document-sized drawer and a narrow shelf. He felt his heart beating against his rib cage as he recognized the butt of a pistol on the shelf next to a stack of what appeared to be ammunition clips. A cylindrical canister sat on the shelf as well.

He snatched the cylinder, running his eyes over its

gleaming silver surface. The warning sign printed on its metal label made his nerves tingle. It was the universal pictograph representing a biological hazard.

Regardless, he didn't hesitate to unscrew the cap. Jake thought he heard the hiss of air or gas released from pressure as he unscrewed the top quarter section of the cylinder. Relief flowed through him when he saw the familiar I-shaped object inside. Although it was dark inside the canister, light reflected off the object's metal surface in shimmers of violet.

Returning to the task at hand, he refastened the cylinder's cap and pocketed the canister inside his shirt. He slid out the large drawer to reveal a myriad of files labeled with various levels of security restrictions. One by one, Jake sifted through the files.

Sitting in the van, with the NRO building behind them, Natasha was staring into the distance when a small gray speck appeared over the horizon in the sky. She felt a dreaded chill spread across her flesh. She shot an anxious glance at Mark who sat beside her; it was as if a distant fear were suddenly simmering in her eyes. "This is taking too long!"

Natasha was unsettlingly beautiful, and Mark's words always seemed to get jumbled around her. Mark followed her gaze to the small gray speck on the horizon. That speck was closing in fast and grew into an aggressively streamlined shape.

Marked stared at it for a long, puzzling moment; he felt a knot tightening in his stomach. He eyes flashed at Natasha then snapped his attention back to the incoming object.

Mark shouted into the radio, his face wild with disbelief. "Come on, come on, come on! We gotta GO!"

§

Like a shark hunting its prey, the Raptor circled the NRO building. A live video stream from the F22's point of view was transmitted to NSA's Operation Control.

Buried deep inside one of the NSA's numerous secret metropolitan installations, Operations Control was the nerve center to direct and coordinate tactical field missions and unacknowledged special access programs. Curved rows of computer terminals faced huge wall-sized screens displaying satellite images and video streams from field operations; technicians who monitored the terminals often joked that it seemed they were working at NASA's Mission Control.

Sabre's eyes were trained on the large central screen as the image rotated around the NRO building and a yellow DHL van came into view. The van was positioned with its rear bumper up against the building near the entry to the loading dock.

Commentary from the Raptor's pilot boomed inside the control room. "A single vehicle is parked on site."

Mr. Reilly, so predictable, Sabre thought.

A technician reported on the building's security status. "There's been an entry into the building, but it checks out. The security pass identified him as a site staff member."

"Oh no … Jake is definitely in there. Which means so is the sample."

Sabre's tone turned frosty. "Level the building. We can retrieve the sample from the rubble; it's indestructible."

The technician looked up. "Sir?"

෨

Jake had just found the report hidden in Dr. Primakov's safe when the building shook around him. The sound of the circling fighter jet reverberated through the office corridors, shaking picture frames from the walls.

Instinctively he reached into the safe to retrieve the gun, a Glock 22 based on the label on the side, and a bullet clip from the narrow shelf over the file drawer. Working quickly, he worked out which way to insert the clip into the butt. When the clip snapped into place, time seemed to stand still. Although he could not understand how, images of an F-22 firing on the building streamed into Jake's mind. He saw himself firing a Stinger missile as a way to escape.

There isn't much time!

෨

By the time Jake had retrieved the rocket launcher from the armory and planted himself in front of the windows facing the approaching assault, the Raptor had circled the building twice.

Through the Stinger's gunsight, he observed the fighter circle around to head straight for the building, approaching fast. He released the safety and heard its gyro start to spin, commencing the weapon's warm-up sequence. Seconds later, the weapon started to buzz. This was a sound that Jake recognized; it was the confirmation signal that the Stinger's sensors had picked up a heat source.

Target locked.

Jake's eyes rocketed wide with surprise. His nerves tingled, his pupils dilated to let in more light. In that moment, he felt super-sensitive, as if the atmosphere in the room had changed. His consciousness was like a television tuning into a signal, the sensation of streaming images again overtook his mind; he saw himself escaping a missile strike by jumping through a hole blasted through the building's facade then using the grappling gun to swing back into the building.

Jake shook off the images and abruptly spun 180 degrees, squeezing the trigger.

❧

The F22 pilot approached the front of the building and didn't see the rear wall explode from the inside. The wall erupted outward in an expanding flash of flames and rubble.

An instant later, a figure emerged from the smoke. A man leaped out of the smoldering hole on the 35th floor of the NRO building and into a free-fall dive. On his descent, he fired a grappling gun back into the building.

When the hook gripped, Jake found himself swinging in an arc and accelerating toward the outside wall. He caught a glimpse of the window he approached moments before impact. With barely enough time to curl into a ball for protection, he had more than enough momentum to smash through the second level facade glazing.

Jake felt a bone-shaking thump on impact, which forced the air from his lungs. Glass exploded around him as he burst through the window. He felt the sensation of rolling along the floor, again and again, and struggled not to black out as he catapulted across the second-story office.

Thirty-five floors above him, the missiles from the F22 hit the building.

∽

Natasha was hysterical.

Mark's cries of panic didn't help Natasha's anxiety. It was the shower of broken glass following the earth-trembling explosion that finally triggered him. Debris in various shapes and sizes pelted the van. The shower lasted for only a minute, but to him it felt like hours.

An eerie stillness settled on the scene. Mark couldn't hear the fighter jet any longer.

Mark and Natasha looked at each other, glazed with shock. They frantically tried to catch their breath as their bodies trembled. A few moments passed before their nerves began to calm.

It was over. Everything was quiet again.

Without warning, a tremendous thud on the van's roof sent them both leaping out of their skins. They screamed in fear, instinctively reaching for each other, as if their embrace would protect them from whatever had landed on the van. They watched in dismay as an office chair bounced off the roof and fell to the ground in front of them.

Natasha's anxiety was briefly overshadowed by a wash of confusion. She searched Mark's face for an explanation, some sign of reassurance. But he had nothing. Mark was equally baffled.

A second thump, this time twice as loud as the first, hit hard and dented the roof. The impact sent them reeling a second time; they screamed back into each other's reassuring embrace. They watched, terrified, as a hand appeared from the roof and slapped the windshield.

It was Jake. He attempted to drag himself to the front of the van so that his two petrified friends could see he was still in one piece. He had thrown the office chair through the second-story window to break out of the building. It created the exit he needed before hitting the van's roof and bouncing to the ground below.

As Jake lay on the van's roof, he managed to poke his head down in front of the windshield and gave them a weary half-smile of reassurance. The occupants of the van instantly erupted into a barrage of questions and curses.

"What the hell was that?" Mark yelled.

Natasha screamed over Mark, "Why did they fire at us?!"

Jake rolled onto his back as Mark and Natasha seemed to compete to be heard. They may have been asking if he was okay, but Jake couldn't be sure. With the two of them yelling, neither was comprehensible.

A deep penetrating *clunk* took Jake by surprise. It was as if the noise had come from inside the building.

Then it happened again.

A series of images flashed through Jake's mind. His body tensed, and he saw the damaged structural columns of the building give way under the weight of the upper floors. Waves of anxiety came faster now; he saw images of the building's collapse.

The scenes in his mind were cut short by Natasha's and Mark's yelled questions.

Jake's voice drowned out the other two. "Mark, we gotta go! Drive!"

There was a moment of silence. Mark and Natasha shared an anxious glance.

Jake yelled, "Mark, PUNCH IT … NOW!"

Mark reacted with his right foot, as he fired up the

engine and slammed the accelerator down. Jake held on to the roof as the yellow van rushed back around the building.

Clenching the roof tight, Jake looked behind to see the columns on the 35th floor had given way. Windows blew out as the levels above slammed down into the floor Jake had occupied minutes earlier. The columns on level 34 exploded under the crashing weight. What followed next was a cascading failure of floor after floor; windows at every level blew out in turn as the building imploded.

The van was already racing through the security gate by the time the building had collapsed halfway. Seconds later, a growing dust cloud engulfed the building in an enormous, gray haze that swallowed the block where the building had stood only moments earlier.

CHAPTER 51

"What was that? Play that back and zoom in!" demanded Sabre, pointing at the large central screen that dominated the Operations Control room.

With a frantic burst of button-pressing, the technicians managed to freeze the satellite telemetry of the F22's assault on the Research and Data Mining Facility after a couple of seconds.

The occupants of the room watched with a mix of confusion and astonishment as a figure jumped out a window and was hauled off on the roof of a yellow van seconds before the building imploded.

Sabre's eyes hardened. "What the hell! Pan to the left and play that back."

On the main screen, a gray fighter jet appeared to fly backward in a blur; on playback, the room gasped as the figure appeared to leap out of the building within seconds of the missiles' impact. In that instant, the view was obstructed by the explosion from the Raptor's ordinance.

Sabre glared at the screen. "Can we get another angle?"

Another technician sifted through site security footage before transferring his find to the main screen. They watched again, this time from the vantage point of a fence-mounted security camera: The figure leaped out the side of the building halfway up the structure.

What came next set off murmurs of astonishment around the control room. As the ordinance exploded, the figure fell clear of the blast, fired a cable into the building, and was flung back inside the building on a lower floor, averting certain death from the fall.

"Impossible!" one technician cried.

Another technician agreed: "That's a one-in-a-billion shot!"

"Quiet!" Sabre was seething. "Go back to the other side again, tighten the zoom."

Disbelieving observers saw an office chair bursting out of a window on the side of the building opposite from the impossible free-fall escape. The chair bounced off the van and onto the ground. Then the figure leaped out the smashed window onto the van's roof, holding onto the roof as the van sped away to safety.

"Follow him! Push in closer." Sabre's tone intensified.

The image on the room's main screen snapped back to a satellite view zooming in, the figure riding the van's roof growing. As the video progressed, the figure turned on to his back.

"Freeze that image!" Sabre commanded.

"Did he just …" Sabre's voice then trailed off, his head cocked to the side. He was trying to make sense of what he was viewing. "Back that image up a little and tighten in on the van."

Sabre watched in confusion as the huge image rewound with a splutter of static then zoomed.

"More," Sabre urged.

The van's roof dominated the main screen. The figure was on his back and appeared to be holding up something in its hand.

"That's Jake Marcel!" an agent gasped.

"Can you zoom in on his hand?" Sabre's voice was laced with an undercurrent of enthusiasm.

He can't be, Sabre thought.

As the technicians worked to sharpen the image, Sabre became increasingly aware of the people in the room around him stopping in their tracks to become transfixed on the big screen.

"Is he really …?" a technician whispered.

"No, can't be," another replied.

As the technicians finished sharpening the enlarged image, they looked up to witness what had mesmerized the control room.

With a rare smile, Mr. Sabre looked almost proud. "You've got to admire the balls on that kid!"

Up on the screen, frozen in time, was a three-story high image of Jake looking skyward with a lopsided smile, his middle finger prominently displayed. He was flipping the bird directly at the satellite camera high above in orbit. It was as if Jake not only knew that they were watching, but also knew exactly where in the sky to look.

Sabre stared at the main screen dumbfounded.

No one inexperienced in urban tactical incursions should be that good. Sabre thought.

Mr. Sabre had just watched Jake Marcel, an untrained civilian, execute maneuvers that most of Section 4's hand-picked, elite Navy SEALs would not have the courage to attempt, let alone complete.

It should be no surprise though.

Marcel's grandfather had been a colonel in the US army, and his father was an American hero, recalled to serve on active duty in the Iraq War at the age of 60 after having been retired as a US army colonel. Valor and fearlessness was evidently native to Jake's DNA.

He would have made a fine soldier, Sabre thought.

Something profound must have occurred to make Jake choose a different path in life from his father, and now his two-story high middle finger was sprawled across the wall of the most secretive and powerful agency of the United States. The gesture screamed of defiance against the very government his father and grandfather had once dedicated their lives to.

"Sir, the pilot can get a clean lock on the van. He's asking if he should re-engage," the communication officer said.

"Negative. Let … him … go," Sabre said, stretching his words as he emerged from a thought and contemplated his next move. "He couldn't pull off this stunt without some help. We need to round them up and find out their intention."

CHAPTER 52

"YOU JUMPED OUT OF WHAT!" Natasha exploded.

Jake had just finished explaining to Natasha and Mark how he had found a way out of the building before the missiles hit. They sat in the sterile waiting room of a radiology clinic within the hospital where they were to meet Dr. Reilly. The scientist had instructed them before the mission to go directly to the hospital immediately after they'd retrieved the metallurgical analysis of the extraterrestrial I-beam.

Natasha was way past furious. "YOU could have KILLED YOURSELF!"

Mark was amazed. "Coooooool … I wish I had seen it."

"YOU'RE just as bad as HIM!" she snapped at Mark.

"Honey," Jake explained, "I was targeted by not one but two missiles. My options were kind of limited."

"Well," she said, folding her arms and trying to stay angry. "That's still no excuse!"

"Why did we have to meet him in a hospital?" Mark was oblivious to Natasha's rage.

Before Jake could respond, a door opened behind the reception desk. A mature woman stepped into the room. The lines on her face spoke of years working in healthcare.

She peered at Jake over thin reading glasses. "He's ready to see you now."

✍

Jake, Natasha, and Mark were not prepared for what they saw; they gasped as they stepped into the magnetic resonance imaging room. Pale and ailing, Dr. Charles Reilly sat in a wheelchair beside the MRI apparatus. An intravenous drip connected him to a portable machine that administrated a clear liquid. Dr. Reilly looked as if he had aged 25 years overnight.

"Don't be startled." Charles gave them a strained smile. "I have this treatment every six weeks."

Jake and his companions stared in silence for a long awkward moment.

It was Jake who finally found his vocal chords: "Is that …"

"Chemo. Yes," Charles answered, "but it's not why I asked you all here."

Jake felt a knot suddenly tighten in his chest.

"I asked you to come here because, well, it's not as good as a submarine under the North Pole, but the walls surrounding the MRI here are heavily shielded."

Mark looked lost. Natasha's face filled with compassion.

"It means," Charles elaborated, "that we can speak without any prying ears."

Jake nodded, understanding. His voice was a faint whisper: "I got it."

An exuberant smile materialized across Charles's lips, and suddenly there was color in his face again. "You got it."

Reaching behind him, Jake retrieved the report that had been tucked under his shirt in the small of his back. With both hands, the scientist accepted the offering, handling it delicately as if being handed a rare original, first edition, King James Bible.

"And the specimen?" The scientist's eyes shone with anticipation.

Jake nodded slowly. "It was there. I got it."

Charles's eyes widened, as if to ask where it now was.

Jake gave a broad smile. "I've got it hidden in a safe place."

Relieved, Charles refocused on the report that lay on his lap, almost mesmerized by the document. "Do you know what this is, Jake?"

"I know that they leveled the building trying to stop me." Jake declared.

Natasha shifted uncomfortably.

Charles studied Jake. "Obviously you got away safely?"

Jake considered the question for a long moment. "I saw these images, flashes. I don't know where they came from, but the way out just came to me. It felt like remembering things that hadn't yet happened."

The scientist nodded with the knowing smile. "They are helping you."

Jake paused, not getting his meaning.

Reilly's focus shifted to the report he was clutching

about the exotic metal. His gaze darted across the pages as he flicked through the document.

"Jake," the scientist said pensively, "you may find this hard to accept, but you are capable of more than you know. You now know for yourself that my former employers will destroy their own assets if it means stopping you."

Natasha shifted again, agitated.

There was finality in Reilly's tone. "There is no turning back. They will stop at nothing to …"

"I'm sorry!" Natasha blurted out, cutting the scientist off mid-sentence. She had heard enough.

With her hand cupping her mouth as if to stop herself from objecting to Jake's involvement, she spun and stormed in the direction of the door to the room, her eyes welling with tears. The three men watched in stunned silence as the door closed behind her.

Charles spoke first. "She is right to be scared. These are serious people who were trying to stop you, and they will use deadly force if challenged."

Jake and Mark turned back to Reilly.

"There is a global reality shift coming." Jake noticed the scientist's hands trembled ever so slightly as he continued. "It will change the world in a way second only to the times of Copernicus and Galileo, when we discovered the sun, planets and stars did not revolve around the Earth."

The words hung in the room for a long moment.

Charles's voice softened. "Go to her. And be careful. Keep yourself hidden in plain sight. Staying in public places means they can't make a move on you without being seen."

"And what about you?" Jake's eyes shone with concern.

"I have a flight to New York to catch." The scientist

looked back down at the report. "And I will see that this triggers an undeniable shift in momentum from secrecy to full openness. When it happens, it will bring on an avalanche that will change reality for every person on the globe."

Jake and Mark nodded their goodbyes and turned to the door. Jake followed Mark out toward the radiology's reception, but stopped mid-stride caught by a thought.

Standing in the doorframe, he turned back to the scientist and asked, "What is element 115?"

Charles raised his eyes. The words seemed to hang in the air for some time.

Jake asked again, "The code to the safe the report was in. Element 115. What does it mean?"

A knowing smile slowly materialized across Reilly's face. "It's a code within a code … the key to free energy. It's their energy source, the fuel that drives their vehicles."

CHAPTER 53

Natasha wiped her eyes. "Give me a reason to stay."

Jake had found her alone in a patient waiting room staring out a large window. Jake slowly approached. Although her back was to him, he could see that the makeup on the side of her cheek was streaked.

Jake heaved a heavy sigh. "It's haunted my family for two generations; give me a reason to let this go."

She turned to him in disbelief, gaping at him in shock then betrayal.

"This isn't a game, Jake! This is serious. You got shot at … WITH A MISSILE!" she snapped, fighting her anger.

Tears welled up again in her eyes. "They demolished an entire building trying to get to you!"

Jake moved closer, but her expression darkened. She turned away, unable to meet his gaze.

"But, hon, this is REAL." Jake wondered how much he should tell her. "I'm just the messenger. We have the evidence, we have the proof, and we've got one of them on our side, now all we have to—"

Natasha cut him off mid-sentence, her rebuttal loud and powerful: "DON'T YOU THINK I KNOW THIS IS REAL!"

Her pretty features hardened. When she spoke, her voice was unyielding: "They are real too, that's the problem, and so was that friggin fighter jet!"

Natasha's voice rose as she said, "WHO sends a fighter jet after a civilian? Who the HELL are these people, Jake?"

Her response tore at his emotions, reminding him that whether she liked it or not, she was an unwilling participant along for the ride. There was no comeback. He could feel himself trapped between her logic and his own drive to reveal the truth. Standing there, he felt himself being drawn into her loving yet conflicted eyes.

Natasha couldn't hold back her tears any longer, letting them flow openly. "I love you, and you know I'll stand by your side no matter what."

Her eyes burned with a mixture of fear and anger. "I will always keep your family's secret, but I just want to lead a normal life."

She turned away, wiping her eyes. Jake moved closer, taking her by the hand then drawing her into an embrace. Her slim frame was shaking, as if the floodgates of fear were about to burst wide open.

He felt the fury drain out of her as she held on to him with both arms, searching for comfort in the nape of his neck. Sobbing softly, she whispered, "I don't want to ever lose you ... but I'm really scared about how this all ends."

❧

Dr. Charles Reilly heaved his wheelchair to the

adjoining MRI room. Waiting alone to greet him was Dr. Steven Greer.

Greer's eyes lit up. "Is that the report?"

Reilly nodded and gave the document to Steven.

A torrent of emotions were visible in Greer's face: excitement, gratitude, fear.

"This is incredible!" Greer said, triumph in his voice. "After years of lobbying the UN, we are being granted a brief timeslot to address the assembly at their symposium. And with this, what we are going to present will bring on the last days of official denial and end the age of secrets."

CHAPTER 54

A black SUV with dark-tinted windows slowly pulled up to the curb across the road from a small office building. Its lights and engine were cut, its occupants waiting in silence.

Inside the deserted office building, a single floor remained lit. Although it was well after 11:00 p.m., Dr. Steven Greer sat at his desk typing an email. His fingers punched the keyboard with the excitement and frenzy of someone with profound news to share. He checked his watch; the late hour added to his eagerness to get his message sent.

He typed the last line, signed off, and moved the pointer over the send button on the screen. His finger hovered nervously over the mouse button for several heavy heartbeats. Then with a deep breath, he clicked send.

Twenty seconds later, Greer was shutting down his laptop. He placed the report Dr. Charles Reilly had given him in his briefcase and headed for the door.

Sitting in the SUV, Alpha watched Greer leave the office carrying a briefcase, cross the road, and get into his car. Greer's headlights illuminated the street in front of his vehicle; he pulled into the empty street and drove into the gathering night.

Alpha turned to look at Sabre, who sat in the passenger seat. Sabre gave him a nod— the silent order to move in.

Mr. Sabre watched Alpha exit the vehicle and head toward the office entry. As he strode, he peered down the street after Greer's tail lights disappearing around a corner.

Alpha's muscular bulk blended into the darkness as he crouched down to work the entry's electronic locking mechanism. He took a small near-field radio transceiver from his pocket. It cycled through thousands of proprietary security door frequencies in seconds. An instant later, Alpha was through the door and on his way to Greer's office.

Minutes later Sabre's attention was drawn by an approaching car. He was surprised to recognize the model as identical to Steven Greer's. The glare of the headlights, however, made it impossible to see the driver. He observed silently as the familiar car found a spot on the street. Its driver got out carrying a briefcase that closely resembled the one Greer had carried minutes earlier.

As the driver drew closer to the office, his frame, clothing, and facial features were similar to that of Greer's. Sabre's jaw tightened.

❧

Greer froze in place after unlocking the door and stepping into the Disclosure Project's headquarters. Across the room, he spotted a hulking figure dressed in black fatigues hovering over an open laptop in his private office. The man in black reached for something attached to his belt, then paused, as if he'd had second thoughts. Greer felt an upwelling of dread as the mountainous figure calmly stepped around the desk toward him.

"Can I help you?" Greer's voice wavered; he felt his palms begin to sweat.

The black figure said nothing but stepped closer. Greer noticed the man gripped the butt of a holstered sidearm. Although his clothing and tactical vest were black, there were no military markings to be seen.

Feeling a surge of panic Steven Greer gripped the briefcase tighter. "What do you want?"

The enormous figure's silence sent an icy chill through Greer's flesh. He thought of the report in his briefcase from Dr. Charles Reilly and felt his breath grow short. His alarm at the devastating implications now showed on his face.

"Whatever you do to me," Greer said, hands trembling, "one day YOU will have to answer to a higher power."

Greer hadn't realized he had been slowly inching away from the approaching danger until he felt himself back into something solid. He remembered now that he had not shut the door behind him. Turning in terror, he spun around to find a second solidly built figure standing directly behind him.

"Who are you?" Greer demanded, looking startled.

Sabre's voice sounded icy calm. "A higher power."

Greer stared in horrified silence as Sabre produced a sidearm in a blur of movement. In a freeze frame of disbelief, he felt the muzzle press against the flesh under his chin. With a muffled spit, the top of Steven's head exploded in a mist of crimson. A fine spray of blood with small gray chunks splattered on the ceiling.

Sabre took hold of the briefcase as Dr. Steven Greer fell. Lifeless, the doctor's limp body collapsed into an awkward pile.

Sabre stepped over the body toward his detachment commander.

"You made a tactical error, soldier. You do *not* hesitate. I require efficiency, understood?" Sabre's voice had dropped an octave, filling the office with a chilling resolve.

Alpha stiffened. "*Yes*, sir!"

Alpha followed Sabre to Greer's desk. Sabre lay the briefcase on the desk; the locks held for 30 seconds before Sabre picked the locks. Inside he found a single document.

As Sabre flicked through the pages, Alpha resumed probing the laptop searching through files.

"Within the last 10 minutes, he sent a document to a group of people. Among the recipients are congressmen and UN delegates," Alpha said with military efficiency.

As Sabre studied the document, he was surprised he hadn't connected the dots sooner. Even so, it was becoming evident that his assignment had just increased in complexity.

"Is the circulated document a metallurgical analysis?" Sabre asked, his tone darkening.

"Affirmative. Something to do with an exotic metal," Alpha answered. After a series of mouse clicks, he looked up and turned the laptop for Sabre to see from the opposite side of the desk. "A sample from an ETV crash site."

Sabre studied the screen for a long moment before retrieving a small USB drive from a concealed pocket inside his jacket and handing it to his second-in-command. Alpha jammed it into the port on the side of the laptop; a self-executing program launched from the USB, and the screen erupted in a sequence of opening windows. Data scrolled up the screen before the program displayed the results of its search.

"It would seem that our late friend took the liberty of tripling our workload." Sabre studied the screen, unimpressed. "Reilly has been helping him prepare for an unauthorized announcement."

Listed on the laptop were the personal details of all the contacts that were now in possession of the metallurgical report on the I-beam retrieved from the 1947 extraterrestrial crash site. When Alpha glanced across to lock eyes with his commander, he realized the rules had changed.

Sabre left little room for misinterpretation: "Each of these individuals has just become a risk to national security. Get a Sniffer deployed; we are going to pay each one of them a visit."

Forty minutes later and one hundred and fifty miles away, a small, matte-black quadcopter drone called a Sniffer silently descended from the night sky to hover above the roof of a suburban home. It remotely hacked the firewall of the home's wi-fi router, accessing the householder's private network, making all the connected computers and smart devices susceptible to outside snooping.

The suburban home was the residence of a congressman who was the first contact on Dr. Steven Greer's email list. He was also now in possession of a copy of the metallurgical report on the I-beam retrieved from the 1947 extraterrestrial crash site.

The congressman sat in his living room reading the report on his iPad in astonished amazement. As he read through the details of the analysis, the drone identified the iPad on his private home wi-fi network and streamed details of his emails, calendar entries, and scheduled appointments back to its operator.

The operator of the quadcopter drone scanned the telemetry from the Sniffer as it scrolled up his screen at the NSA's Operations Control under Mr. Sabre's command. On his screen was a diary entry from the iPad for a private charter flight with all but two of the contacts from Greer's email list. The flight was scheduled to leave early the following morning. Its destination was New York City, where the headquarters of the United Nations was located.

CHAPTER 55

The privately charted Gulfstream sat in its hangar with all its underside compartments open, exposing the internal electronics and mechanical components to the small team of maintenance mechanics preparing the aircraft for its morning flight. Each mechanic operated on a different section of the aircraft.

The mechanic working on one of its powerful Rolls Royce engines glanced up to discover a white van emblazoned with the Federal Aviation Administration's insignia pull into the open hangar. The mechanic jumped to his feet and reached for a dirty rag, wiping the grease from his grimy hands. He walked to greet the four men who stepped out of the FAA van.

Three of the burly FAA men carried toolboxes. The fourth man had an equally large frame, wore dark glasses, carried a clipboard, and appeared to be the man in charge. Each of them wore work overalls.

"Good morning!" the man with the sunglasses said with a salesman's smile. "Andrew, isn't it?"

The mechanic was caught off guard by the unidentified man in sunglasses knowing his name. "Umm … Yeah."

Alpha removed his sunglasses. "My name is Robert. We're from the FAA Aviation Safety branch."

Handing the mechanic an ID badge, Alpha continued with his practiced smile. "We're carrying out random safety checks as part of a joint program with the Aircraft Mechanics Fraternal Association and the National Transportation Safety Board."

After scrutinizing the ID badge, the mechanic appeared convinced. As a member of the Aircraft Mechanics Fraternal Association, the mechanic was aware of random checks being an initiative that the AMFA was pushing.

Alpha studied the mechanic. "We understand this aircraft is scheduled for takeoff in less than an hour."

"That's right," the mechanic replied. "We're just about done here."

Alpha maintained his polite tone. "Do you mind if we inspect the aircraft while your boys pack up?"

The mechanic returned the smile and shrugged. "Sure."

As the mechanic's crew finished their maintenance routine and preflight checks, Alpha's consignment fanned out around the aircraft, checking various components and valves.

Two of Alpha's team members climbed the access stairs and entered the cockpit. They retrieved a cordless DeWalt impact driver and other equipment from their toolboxes that they required to remove the cockpit dashboard panels. The panel they removed belonged to a battery of warning indicators, in particular the panel that housed the decompression warning alarms so Alpha's men could alter its internal electronics.

The aircraft mechanics had finished their tasks and were packing their equipment. Alpha focused on the underside of the aircraft, where he held a line of sight to the mechanics. His third man was on top of the aircraft access stairs checking seals around the external cabin door.

As he felt around the door, he inconspicuously checked that no one was looking his way. Most of the mechanics were on the other side of the aircraft. He waited until the last of the mechanics joined the rest of the maintenance crew then removed a small slender device from his toolbox.

The device was pale blue and the size of a pencil. It housed a small microchip with a tiny digital display attached to one end. He pressed a small button on the circuitry, and the microchip blinked to life, revealing a series of numbers that had been preset to automatically count backward.

The display read:
0:40:00
0:39:59
0:39:58
0:39:57

Alpha's third soldier slipped the small device inside a fold in the door seal, jamming it between the rubber and the door itself.

The two soldiers carrying out their checks in the cockpit reappeared and approached Alpha to report that their work had been completed. Alpha's third soldier did a final check that the device could not be seen before regrouping with the others.

With his team's objective accomplished, Alpha returned to the head mechanic and again flashed his salesman's smile. "Well, Andrew, we're done here."

With that, he handed the mechanic a piece of paper. "This is a duplicate of our safety report; it's your record that we've conducted our inspection."

⤙

A black limousine traversed the runway tarmac to ferry the honorable congressman and his accompanying group of delegates to the stairs of the chartered Gulfstream. By the time the limo arrived, the aircraft had had its maintenance work signed off, and its pilots had almost completed their preflight checklist.

The congressman and accompanying delegates promptly boarded the aircraft. Twelve minutes later, the chartered aircraft taxied out of the hangar to take off.

⤙

At cruising altitude, the flight crew went about their routine business of serving their passengers, who were engaged in discussions about an exotic metal sample found at an unexplained crash site in the 1940s. The pilots confirmed that the aircraft was at the correct speed and altitude before engaging the autopilot. Once all was settled in the cockpit, the flight attendant served the pilots their morning coffee. The flight proceeded as normal as it had previously done with the same congressman dozens of times before.

Until the countdown clock on the small, hidden device reached 00:00:00.

Twenty minutes into the flight, the device jammed in the aircraft door seal silently detonated. Unnoticed by the passengers and flight crew, the micro-explosion was so small, its flash was barely visible from inside the plane.

However, the micro-explosion was, by design, damaging enough to rupture the door seal, allowing air pressure to slowly leak from the breached seal.

Such a breach would normally have triggered the decompression warning alarm, causing the emergency overhead oxygen masks to suddenly drop. But the decompression warning alarm had been modified and failed to activate.

The delegates' discussion soon slowed as they felt increasingly lethargic. One by one, they all fell asleep. In the cockpit, the pilots' eyes also grew heavy; unbeknownst to them, the cabin pressure had gradually dropped. Slowly, the copilot let go of his coffee as he fell asleep, spilling his cup's contents over the instrumentation console.

With the entire passenger complement and crew now unconscious, the Gulfstream continued along its flight path under the guidance of its autopilot.

CHAPTER 56

Two hours had passed since the micro-detonator ruptured the door seal of the chartered Gulfstream when the air traffic controller on duty at JFK International Airport identified the approaching aircraft. Following standard procedure, he worked to slot the aircraft into a landing pattern.

He noticed, however, that the aircraft was still at both cruising speed and altitude.

"Flight FQ442, we have you on approach, please adjust your altitude and heading to commence your descent."

There was no response.

"Flight FQ442, we have you on approach, please adjust your altitude and heading to commence your descent," the air traffic controller repeated.

Again, no response.

That's strange, the controller thought.

The other aircraft already in landing patterns responded to his hails. The controller checked his equipment, but everything was plugged in and appeared to be functioning correctly.

The controller felt his pulse quicken as he tried switching to an emergency frequency. "Flight FQ442, your altitude and heading needs to be adjusted to commence your descent, are you receiving me?"

Still no response.

Protocol dictated the controller's course of action. He called his supervisor then shuffled the other aircraft in holding patterns to allow an uninterrupted corridor for the Gulfstream to safely pass through. That was, of course, assuming that the aircraft would continue to fly at both its current heading and altitude.

The controller jumped out of his chair and dropped his headset as he rushed to the window to look at the unresponsive plane. He caught a glimpse of it as it sailed straight over the airport. He ran to the opposite window, skidding to a stop to watch the plane gently arc and sail out of sight.

Rushing back to his terminal, he checked the plane's flight statistics. He swallowed hard, a visceral fear gripping his insides as he read its fuel tank status. The unresponsive jet's fuel reserves were diminishing to alarming levels.

The controller's heart pounded as he quickly briefed his supervisor on the grim situation. Under these circumstances, protocol dictated that such an incident be immediately reported to the military, which would then take command of the situation.

Without hesitation, the supervisor reached for the emergency phone and pressed the speed dial button labeled Otis Air Force Base.

✍

Within minutes of receiving the report on the unresponsive civilian aircraft, two F18 Hornet fighter jets scrambled to intercept. Emerging through light wispy clouds on a backdrop of turquoise-blue sky, the two Hornets quickly caught up to the unresponsive Gulfstream.

The Hornets dropped into flanking positions on either side of the civilian aircraft's wings.

The flight leader captaining the Hornet on the jet's left side inspected the windows looking for any signs of damage or clues why the aircraft had strayed so far past its destination. But the jet's fuselage was intact, engines were functioning, and everything seemed to be in order.

"This is flight leader Echo One," the captain reported back. "We are in position alongside Flight FQ442. The aircraft is intact. Attempting to obtain a visual on the pilots."

Accelerating slightly, Echo One aligned his fighter with the windows of the Gulfstream's cockpit. If he could see the pilots for himself, he may be able to determine the problem with hand signals.

But that was not going to be the case. The flight leader took a second to process what he was seeing.

CHAPTER 57

Bravo, the second-in-command of Alpha's security detachment, slipped on a pair of skin-colored rubber gloves before exiting his black SUV. He approached a late model black Mercedes parked in the driveway of a suburban home that was peppered with tiny droplets of morning dew.

He approached the vehicle silently, careful to go unnoticed. Surreptitiously, he allowed a small thin aerosol canister to drop into his palm from inside his sleeve. He sprayed a small amount of moisture under the door handle as he passed the driver's side door.

The owner of the car, Senator Peter Bishop, had been the second to last recipient of Dr. Greer's email containing the report on the exotic metal sample. He was finishing his coffee while watching the morning news in his kitchen, unaware of events unfolding in his driveway.

Thirty-five minutes later, the senator was driving his black Mercedes, battling freeway traffic on his daily commute to the office.

Bravo's chosen approach on his target was diabolically simple. He employed a weaponized pathogen, a virus with a short half-life sprayed on a surface he knew his target would touch, in this case the door handle of his target's personal vehicle. It was genetic warfare, the next evolution of chemical warfare. Half as messy as a snipper bullet, but twice as effective; it left no trace after the virus's half-life expired.

The senator felt a sudden unexpected weariness as purple stars began to dance before his eyes. Shortness of breath accompanied an unexpected jolt of searing pain across his chest. His eyes were wide as he fought against blurring vision. The senator's knuckles gripped the steering wheel to keep the car steady in the speeding traffic.

Over 600 miles away, research scientist Leslie Cooper locked the door behind him as he left his inner-city townhouse. He opted to commute to work by motorcycle due to the ease of parking. Setting his backpack down next to his Yamaha R1, he double-checked that its compartments were all secured.

Leslie was a trusted confidant of Dr. Steven Greer and was the final recipient on the circulation list. The email containing the report on the exotic metal sample had reached his inbox the night before, but he hadn't yet opened it.

CHAPTER 58

After accelerating to fly alongside the windows of the Gulfstream's cockpit, Echo One's pilot peered into the windows of the unresponsive Gulfstream.

The cockpit windows appeared to be fogged up from the inside, making it impossible to see through. The only thing discernible through the cockpit windows was diffused light shining through from the cockpit's opposite side windows.

This could only mean one thing.

Gradual aircraft decompression.

The pilot reported back: "This is Echo One; we are in position alongside the cockpit of Flight FQ442. We have a negative visual on the flight crew. All windows are fogged up from the inside. Repeat, all windows are fogged up."

❧

At Otis Air Force Base, home of the recently dispatched F18 Hornets, Colonel Norrish looked over the shoulder of the military flight controller tracking the planes. The terminal screens within the command center flooded them with every quantifiable piece of information possible: air speed, altitude, relative headings, global position coordinates. All in real time and high resolution.

The focal point of the command center was a bank of cinema-sized screens that could be read easily from the myriad multi-level offices that surrounded the main floor area. Three levels of offices overlooked the command center floor, all fitted with full-height windows to provide unimpeded views of the main screens and tiered rows of flight controller terminals below.

Echo One's voice boomed over the command center's speakers: "Autopilot is clearly engaged. It looks like a hull decompression failure. It's possible that the emergency air masks didn't deploy. But it's impossible to tell whether the flight crews are incapacitated, unconscious or deceased."

The controller in front of Norrish looked up to meet the disturbed expression on the colonel's face. He didn't have to explain the situation to the controller; his face conveyed its severity. If the Gulfstream were permitted to continue, it wouldn't matter whether the crew was unconscious or dead; it had already overflown its target destination and was heading toward a densely populated area. Judging by the distance it had already flown, and assuming its tanks had been full on takeoff and that the fuel reading had been correct, the aircraft didn't have much time left before it would run out of fuel. Assuming their computer's predicted point of impact was correct, by the time the Gulfstream was out of reserve fuel, the plane would come down two miles southwest of Boston. That was, of course, if it didn't hit a building on its way down.

The controller double-checked his radar and tracking telemetry. There was no doubt; the civilian aircraft would reach the Boston area before running out of fuel and falling from the sky. He looked back up at the colonel, who had read the same information off the controller's screen.

The true horror of the unfolding situation descended like a bird of prey. Frozen in disbelief, the colonel knew the grave situation of the Gulfstream, and anyone who happened to be within close proximity of its point of impact.

The colonel turned to look up at his commanding officer, a two-star general in command of Otis Air Force Base. He had been following the events from his office, which overlooked the command center. The general would be the one to make the final decision on the actions taken to neutralize the unresponsive plane. The general held the colonel's gaze for several heartbeats before picking up the red phone on his desk.

Without saying a word to any of the controllers, the colonel immediately left the control room floor to rush up the stairs to the overlooking offices. The door to the general's office burst open, the colonel not bothering to knock before entering. In fact, the general didn't even notice the colonel's minor indiscretion.

"I understand, sir," the general said with both precision and conviction before setting down the receiver.

The colonel's tone was ominous: "Sir! That aircraft is going to run out of fuel soon, and when it does, it will be over a densely populated area."

Looking out the window, the colonel checked the real-time satellite projected on the main screen that showed the plane's exact location and heading. "And in about 90 seconds, sir, that aircraft will be over an industrial area."

"We have no way of taking control of the plane?" the general asked.

"No, sir," the colonel said, "and might I add, sir, that if that plane goes down in the middle of a city, it might hit …"

"I know," the general interrupted with a grim look. "We are not going to allow that aircraft to reach Boston. We're authorized to take whatever action is necessary to minimize casualties."

The general took a deep breath. "Colonel, that plane is to be destroyed in the air to reduce the risk to lives on the ground."

"Understood, sir."

⌁

Echo One's radio crackled with the command from the colonel: "Your orders are to neutralize the aircraft with *extreme prejudice*. You are to disintegrate that aircraft over the industrial zone you are about to enter."

Echo One recoiled; he was not prepared for what he'd heard. "Copy that. I understand."

Drawing a startled breath, Echo One realized it was his job to ensure that the aircraft was completely destroyed, leaving as little debris as possible to fall to the ground. His navigation screen indicated that he had a 20-second window to strike the aircraft over a minimally populated zone, which he would reach in 40 seconds. Immediately, Echo One switched his display to targeting mode, which was projected onto his forward windshield.

He instinctively looked to his wingman, though he

couldn't see him because he was on the other side of the Gulfstream. "Echo Two, fall back to the rear of the jet, match my velocity and maintain your altitude."

"Copy that," his wingman immediately responded.

The two planes slowed in unison to take positions behind the Gulfstream. The squadron leader could now see the tail of the doomed aircraft through his front windshield with targeting information projected over it. To totally disintegrate the aircraft, Echo One knew, they would both have to unleash their entire complement of armory.

Echo One's infrared missiles could target the engines, but that wouldn't be enough to break up the aircraft sufficiently. Switching to micro-targeting mode, he toggled his laser-guided missiles through different targeting points on the aircraft to lock his infrared missiles on to the port side engines and his laser-guided missiles to various points along the tail.

Echo Two had also heard the colonel's orders over the radio, but was feeling uneasy. His 12 years of training and experience had prepared him for every conceivable battle scenario. Between the two of them, they had shot down every type of hostile aircraft in flight simulators. But it was the thought of shooting down a civilian aircraft, an American civilian plane, which sent his heart pounding against the inside of his rib cage.

His orders came through the radio, tearing him from his thoughts: "Echo Two, target the starboard wing, forward fuselage, and nose. Fire on my mark."

Instantly, Echo Two engaged his afterburners, pulling his control stick back toward him. With an explosive rumble, he pointed his fighter's nose to the sky to gain altitude, the G-force thrusting him back into the seat.

Although the fighter gaining altitude, the targeting camera remained fixed on the Gulfstream. Echo Two watched his targeting screen; the image of the doomed aircraft slowly rotated as he rose above it, revealing the white outline of the aircraft from a bird's-eye view.

Having reached an altitude where he could hit the front of the plane, Echo Two used his computer to toggle through the different sections of the aircraft. He targeted his laser-guided missiles on the plane's nose and selected points along its midsection and starboard side engines. When the computer confirmed that all the armaments were locked in, he programmed his weapons system to fire all selected targets simultaneously.

"Targets acquired and locked." Echo Two reported.

"Okay ... on my mark." the flight leader replied. He drew in a deep breath and said, "Three ..."

With a flick of his wrist, Echo Two threw his stick to the left and pulled back.

"Two ..."

Echo's Two's fighter flipped upside down then pulled downward to point its nose at the doomed plane, an aerial maneuver executed with precise military precision, enabling the missiles to face the target.

"One ..."

Echo Two flicked the red safety switch off the trigger.

"MARK!"

With an explosive burst, all six missiles accelerated away from the upside-down fighter, leaving thin trails of white smoke streaming behind. In the same instant, all six missiles under the flight leader's wings fired into life and catapulted away, their paths also traced by an increasingly lengthening trail of thin white smoke.

In that moment, the two F18s had unleashed enough firepower to destroy a squadron of 747s, let alone a single, relatively small private jet.

The two groups of missiles converged on a single point in the sky.

❧

The tail of the doomed Gulfstream erupted in an explosive burst of white heat first, the blast ripping the tail from the body of the fuselage. As the plane jolted from the shockwave, a Mont Blanc pen belonging to an unconscious United Nations delegate started to fall from his side table tray.

Milliseconds later, just before the pen hit the floor, the port engine violently erupted. The fuel tanks detonated next in cascading explosions, the force severing the left wing entirely. A few more milliseconds passed before the starboard engine exploded, closely followed by its accompanying fuel tanks in successive white flashes.

A missile then punched through the fuselage into the cabin over the delegate before it detonated inside the aisle between the rows of seats. In a blinding flash, the temperature in the cabin increased to match the surface of the sun. The unconscious passengers perished as flesh and bone were incinerated in an instant.

The blast ripped through the wingless cabin like a volcanic eruption, incinerating all nonmetallic materials. The steel skin of the fuselage ripped open like aluminum foil being torn into tiny fragments. The final missiles hit what was left of the cockpit. Already weakened from the intense blasts, it fractured into small pieces on impact. The pilots were incinerated along with the aircraft.

The inverted F18 rolled upright. The two fighters broke off from their assault as the Gulfstream disintegrated. The multiple explosions consumed the aircraft, almost obliterating it completely. The remaining fragments were torn into smaller pieces and fell over the outskirts of an industrial park, a minimally populated area where factories and warehouses stood, lessening the probability of collateral damage or injuries on the ground.

From below, the explosion dominated the sky, and the blast shockwaves rocked factory windows below. As the assault unfolded, the few people on the ground watched in disbelief as small debris rained down on the roofs of several factory buildings below. Indiscriminate cries for help could be heard as people scattered to avoid the hail of small aircraft fragments still burning from the blast.

CHAPTER 59

In a chilling moment, the Senator felt the last of his oxygen drain from his lungs as he struggled to draw breath. Fear swept across his flesh and took control. His gaze darted around, searching the blurriness for a break in traffic to pull over. Just before the crushing darkness came flooding in, he saw the side of his car rebounding off a sedan travelling in the lane to his right.

The Mercedes slammed into a truck in the process of overtaking him on the left; its front corner caught the Mercedes's midsection, crushing the doors. The airborne car catapulted ahead of the speeding truck, doors flinging open as it rolled in the air then bounced along the road like a spinning top on its side until the fuel tank ruptured.

The blast signaled surrounding traffic to screech to a chaotic halt. White smoke poured from the truck's screaming tires as it skipped and shuddered in the driver's attempt to stop before it hit the spinning fireball.

The Senator was incinerated as his car came rolling to a fiery stop.

❦

After securing his backpack, Leslie Cooper mounted his Yamaha R1 and turned the key to fire the starter motor.

A horrific vision seared the eyes of onlookers across the street. The scientist's body was a silhouette on the backdrop of a blinding explosion as the motorcycle erupted from beneath him.

Motorcycle components flew in all directions as the Yamaha lifted off the ground. Engulfed by the brilliant flash of light, the scientist transformed from man, to silhouette, to disembodied fragments of charred flesh as legs and arms appeared to detach before being swallowed by the expanding eruption. Tires tumbled through the air as cartwheels of fire. The windows of the adjacent townhouses burst inward as the shockwave hit.

CHAPTER 60

"How did he upset you?" Jackie asked, looking somewhere between frightened and concerned.

Natasha DeMorea didn't respond. She stared out the café window at the passing evening traffic, her expression a mix of anxiety and dread.

Jackie searched her eyes. "What did he do?"

Silence.

Natasha's eyes were welling. She looked as if she wanted to speak, but said nothing. Her lip trembled.

"Was he with someone else?" Jackie gasped.

"No!" Natasha recoiled and gave Jackie a dismissive glance. She turned to the thinning traffic and sunk into deep thought.

Her best friend studied her, feeling a rising concern. Jackie's voice was a whisper. "Natasha, what is it?"

Natasha drew a short breath, as if the question had injured her personally. The eerie sight made Jackie swallow hard. Natasha spoke to the window, her words thick with emotion. "You know when things are so unimaginable, so far beyond reality, that you don't know what to believe anymore?"

Jackie looked confused. She hadn't expected the response.

"Sometimes it's hard to know what's the truth or what's real." Natasha's tone was awash with dread as it turned to a whisper. "Sometimes it's even harder just believing."

Slowly turning toward her, Natasha met her friend's puzzled gaze. Jackie stared for a long moment, not saying a word, her concern deepening with each passing breath. She searched Natasha's face for a clue as to what was so troubling.

"Natasha, you know you can tell me. Whatever it is."

Wiping a tear, Natasha again turned back to the window. "I want to."

The girls sat in uncomfortable silence, Natasha returning to her conflicting thoughts, her friend quietly sipping her coffee. Across the café, two large figures observed as the waitress brought the men's orders to their table.

Feeling the weight of prying eyes, Jackie scanned the café. She stole a quick glance at the two large figures who looked on before averting their gaze. Sensing a sudden change in her friend's focus, Natasha turned toward Jackie then followed her line of sight until she also spotted the two large men. With muscular physiques and large frames, they were dressed in similarly dark clothing.

Female intuition was a potent instinct Natasha had learned to trust. Sensing a sudden surge of danger, she snatched her purse and pulled out several dollars to cover the coffees. She left them on the table as she stood.

Natasha's anxiety was intensifying. "We need to go!"

⚬

The girls hailed a passing cab and shuffled into the back seat. After the taxi took off, Natasha glanced back to see if anyone was following.

Jackie probed Natasha with her green eyes. "Who were those two apes?"

Natasha didn't hear the question.

"Where to?" the taxi driver's gruff voice interrupted.

"You were going to Jake's later—you should go there," Jackie offered.

"They'll just follow me there. I need to warn him first," Natasha said, her voice determined.

Jackie shook her head in disbelief. "Warn him about what? You're not making sense. Just call him."

"They'll know. Find out where the guys are."

There was a tense silence as Jackie sent a text message then asked the obvious question. "They'll know? Who are these people? This obviously has to do with what Jake spoke about at the nightclub. Shit, Tash, how much trouble is he in?"

Natasha didn't answer. She was still peering at the traffic following the cab, her eyes trained on a dark-colored SUV two cars behind.

Jackie's phone chimed in response to her text. "It's them; they're playing pool at some club called the Imperial."

Natasha turned to the driver. "The Imperial, you know it?"

"Yeah," the driver said then whispered under his breath, "Finally."

Fifteen minutes later, the girls were getting out of the cab in front of the Imperial and paying the driver. Natasha's eyes were still trained on the dark SUV that had coincidently been headed for the same venue. It had pulled over behind them seconds after the cab had stopped. Two large men, both wearing dark clothing, were getting out.

Natasha grabbed her friend's arm before Jackie had a chance to notice the following pair. She turned her toward the line of people waiting to be granted entry by the bouncers.

Jackie did a double take. "Wow, it's busy tonight."

A monstrous bouncer holding a clipboard was turning away well-dressed hopefuls. Behind him stood another security guard who was armed. Natasha stole one last glance over her shoulder at the approaching figures and recognized their faces. They were the pair from the café.

Jackie forced a provocative smile, her eyes fixed on the bouncer. "Okay, usual routine then."

Both Natasha and Jackie had been fortunate in the genetic lottery. They were graced with attractive features and elegant lines that had sometimes brought an abundance of male attention in social settings. Discovering early in their teens that such gifts could be exploited, they had fine-tuned the art of working their appearance to gain an advantage over males.

Mindful that she had no time to object to Jackie's suggestion, Natasha followed her friend's lead. In that moment, they were Victoria's Secret models strutting a catwalk as they strode past the roped-off line of waiting people and headed directly for the bouncer obstructing the entrance.

The bouncer's eyes bulged at the approaching beauties, who were vibrant with confidence and purpose. There was no question of membership or of the girls' being on the guest list. As if in a trance, the huge bouncer unclipped the red rope blocking the entrance, silently let Natasha and Jackie through the door, and signaled reception to allow the girls in without charge.

Sixty seconds later the bouncer was met with two hulking figures both wearing dark clothing. Shaken from his trance, the bouncer narrowed his eyes at the offensively dressed duo before him. "You boys on the list?"

∾

The club was a dark, cavernous labyrinth; its rooms pulsed and pounded to a myriad of hypnotic rhythms. Paul and Mark were shooting pool in a side room of the venue. Chris chatted as he watched.

It was Paul who first spotted Natasha and Jackie emerging from the mass of bodies.

Frantic, Natasha ran to Chris. Paul abandoned the shot he had lined up to meet the approaching girls.

Natasha arrived breathless. "These two big guys have been following us."

Paul's welcoming smile deteriorated. His eyes slowly rose to find the two Herculean figures part the crowd as they stepped toward the group. Paul instinctively swept Natasha behind him, readying himself as the two large strangers closed in. Jackie hid behind Chris, who fell in line alongside Mark and Paul, forming a defensive line to protect the girls.

Bravo took a menacing step toward Paul, his tone abrasive: "Now listen, kid, I don't want to have to hurt y—"

The soldier didn't get to finish his sentence. He felt his weight suddenly shift as something smashed the side of his face. For an instant, he was airborne. TJ had appeared from the side to unleash a heavy right hook. The unexpected blow sent Bravo stumbling backward.

"That's okay, I didn't feel a thing!" TJ spat.

In a blur of motion, the second soldier produced a gas-operated semiautomatic Desert Eagle and trained it directly at TJ's forehead.

"STAND DOWN!" the soldier holding the gun commanded.

TJ slowly raised his hands. The boys were battle ready in formation behind TJ. Jackie froze where she stood.

Regaining his composure, Bravo shook off the surprise blow to his face. He stepped toward TJ as the second soldier maintained his aim. The crowd was a mix of stunned onlookers and frightened faces.

Bravo growled through clenched teeth to TJ, "Dare to try me, boy! Fortunately for you, we're here for DeMorea."

Chris and Mark exchanged alarmed glances at the mention of Natasha's name. They turned back to the girls with puzzled looks. Jackie, frozen to the spot, recognized the soldier holding the gun to TJ's head as being the same one from the bridge. Natasha was nowhere to be seen.

CHAPTER 61

Natasha was on the move. Snaking through the dense crowd, she glanced back to check if she was being followed. The crowd behind her parted for two mammoth figures plowing through in pursuit. She found the club entrance and rushed to the front lobby.

Standing in the entrance lobby was the armed security guard; ahead of him was the large bouncer obstructing the roped-off entrance and the line of waiting patrons. Composing herself, Natasha slowed to strut toward the security guard.

The guard turned toward the approaching beauty, a smile materializing on his face as she closed in. She gazed at him and forced a cheeky smile. Natasha leaned in close and pursed her lips as if to whisper in his ear.

She placed a hand on his chest. The guard didn't object, but pivoted slightly to offer his ear. As her lips closed in, she reached down to feel his waist. Her hand found his belt and followed it around to his holster to find both the trigger and safety switch on his firearm.

Natasha DeMorea was a force of nature, barely aware of her own actions. With a quick snap, she thumbed off the safety and fired three quick shots into the ground beside the guard's feet. The sudden explosion sent the crowd near the entrance diving for the floor. The mass of panicked bodies behind her formed a roadblock ahead of the pursuing soldiers.

In the confusion, Natasha sprinted for the unobstructed entrance. More panic followed her has a frantic rush of bodies poured out into the street to escape the chaos.

Natasha kept running and left the frenzied crowed behind her as police sirens wailed in the distance. Spotting a taxi, she waved it down and jumped in.

❧

Jake Marcel was floating in a lucid dream, teetering on the edge of consciousness. Lying on the couch in total darkness in his living room, the multi-colored light and sound frequencies of the mind machine had him deeply relaxed.

The living room was a mess: his kendo armor and equipment were spread over an adjacent couch. His motorcycle helmet lay on its side on a nearby coffee table next to his keys.

Jake was mesmerized by the hypnotic rhythm of the strobing flashes pulsing behind his closed eyelids; he felt almost as if he had left his body. In this trance, he achieved clarity of thought far beyond any natural waking state. His thoughts soared through the recent events: the scientist, his grandfather's crash debris, the black-suited agent who confronted him on the bridge, Natasha being caught in the middle of a situation that had been set in motion years before she was born.

The images that played through his mind were intensely visceral, as if he could consciously control his own dream. He stood in the middle of a desert, desolate emptiness under a clear blue sky. Not far from where he stood, a cavernous gorge split the desert toward the horizon, a sheer cliff face was visible on the other side of its gaping depths.

Natasha's elegant form stood before him; her bright arctic blue eyes seemed to luminesce with a deep sorrow. Her eyes, which had always held the answer to his happiness in their depths, were now full of distress. They flashed a warning of approaching danger.

Behind her, a white star glistened in the distance; it slowly descended from the bright clear blue sky.

The image was suddenly ripped from his mind. He saw boots standing on a roof. As the confusing image became clearer, he perceived the outline of a dark figure. It rappelled down the side of a building with the aid of a rope.

Jake awoke with a start. He catapulted to his feet and vaulted over the coffee table to the other couch to seize his shinai. By instinct, he assumed a sword-wielding, battle-ready stance. Moving silently, he approached the window facing the street and pressed his back against the wall beside the window. His senses tingled; something told him there was a presence directly outside, on the other side of the wall behind him.

The window exploded inward as a black figure sailed through, feetfirst like a battering ram. However, there was no way for the intruding figure to know Jake was ready. Within seconds of his entrance, Jake was on him. Jake's initial blow knocked off the intruder's helmet, the energy from the impact shattering the helmet's clip that gripped under the soldier's chin.

Jake's follow-up blow caught the intruder as he freed himself from the rope and leveled his weapon. The intruder's head snapped sideways, the momentum throwing his limp body to the floor.

Maintaining his fighting stance Jake studied his assailant, his shinai pointing at the unconscious body that lay motionless on the ground. The intruder was dressed in black military fatigues; a utility vest held ammunition clips. There were no insignia or military branch patches that Jake could see. Still attached to the downed soldier's head was what looked like a futuristic pair of goggles.

With the tip of his wooden sword, Jake cautiously lifted one side of the goggles. An eerie green glow emanating from inside the headpiece bathed the man's closed eyes.

Night vision, Jake thought.

A creak disturbed the quiet darkness, drawing Jake's attention. His pulse quickened at the thought of another armed soldier in the house.

Jake's back slid against the wall as he silently reached the entrance to the dining room. He felt a slow, spiraling horror as he realized the truth; Sabre's men were closing in. The prospect sent a tremor through him. Why did they need to be so heavily armed and attack with stealth?

He stole a peek through the dining room entrance. On the other side of the table, also adorned in black and wearing night vision goggles, another armed intruder approached.

Jake snapped his head back, again pressing his back against the wall. A fierceness crept into his eyes; he felt his central nervous system electrify as a rush of adrenalin flooded his body. Like a gathering storm, he prepared to advance on the soldier.

With incomprehensible speed, Jake flicked on the lights and charged toward the end of the table. He launched off a chair and landed on top of the table, eyes blazing. In a rush of thunder, he had instantly traversed the length of the table and was almost on top of the soldier.

The soldier recoiled from the blinding light, instinctively flinging the night vision apparatus off his head. In a stunned daze, he strained to refocus on the silhouette jumping on the table and approaching fast.

White knuckled, Jake cut a wide arc through the air; his wooden sword an apocalyptic flash before the intruder's straining eyes. There was a millisecond of blurred vision before a painful burst of white heat was followed by stars. With a sickening *crunch*, the blow rendered the soldier immediately unconscious as Jake came down on him from the table top with all his body weight fueling the attack. The strike crashed down on the soldier's head before he'd had time to raise his weapon, and he dropped to the floor in a limp heap.

Jake landed over his body, kicking the dropped weapon away and holding his sword poised for another strike. But the soldier didn't move.

Jake's heart hammered as he stared at the motionless body. He breathed deeply, as if to absorb the terrifying truth. Sabre's men won't stop until they have him.

The scientist's voice echoed faintly in his mind, sending a chill through Jake's flesh: "Yes, it is dangerous. They are very, very powerful people." The shock lasted only an instant before he heard a faint rustling from upstairs.

Jake was on the move again. He crept far enough up the stairs to peer down the corridor. He saw nothing. Gliding down the corridor without making a sound, Jake caught a glimpse of a faint shadow cast on to an open bedroom door. He leaped into the adjacent room.

With his back pressed against the wall, his nerves tingled as he sensed a presence pass by in the corridor. His breath came in shallow gasps; his blood felt alive with another rush of adrenalin as he stepped into the corridor. He followed the third intruder as he stalked down the corridor toward the upstairs TV room. Jake raised his shinai, his arm flexed ready to attack.

Jake's voice crackled with aggression, "Surprise!"

The intruder turned instantly, his eyes wide with shock. Jake watched as a gun barrel swung around in his direction. Fueled by adrenalin, Jake unleashed his attack. Only barely conscious of his actions, his muscles worked instinctively, his arcs swirling at light speed. He was a blur of kinetic poetry as he slammed the weapon out of the soldier's hand then landed a heavy strike to the backup pistol that the intruder produced in his other hand. The pistol discharged as it catapulted across the room, the bullet slamming into an adjacent wall.

With the vigilance of a trained killer, the soldier produced a knife. His thrusts and counter swings were as precise as they were powerful. But Jake's defense was fluid; with a double-swinging motion he hit the arm gripping the knife and followed up with a powerful blow to the soldier's thigh.

The intruder was still holding on to the knife, but searing pain shot up his leg, and he crumpled to one knee. The soldier drew in a seething breath, clearly preparing to attack again.

With a powerful lunge, the soldier's hulking form raced toward Jake in a blur of rippling muscle. With all the grace of a trained swordsman, Jake managed to block and counter the intruder's attacks. The colossal figure seemed to let the rage pour out of him as he bore down on Jake.

Jake fought his own rising fear as he struggled to focus, waiting for his attacker to provide an opportunity penetrate his muscular defense. When Jake saw it, he lunged, swinging with all his weight. The huge soldier had momentarily left his ribs unguarded as he threw a punch. In a triple-swinging motion, Jake slammed his attacker's ribs, driving the wind from his lungs, knocked the knife from his hand, and land a strike against his aggressor's jaw.

The soldier arched in anguish, the pain exploding through his skull.

Jake's attacks, however, only served to harden the soldier's resolve.

CHAPTER 62

Jake faced his attacker squarely, his wooden sword drawn, ready to fight. The Herculean presence was before him in the upstairs hallway and had so far been stripped of two automatic firearms and a knife.

The soldier charged while Jake readied his defenses. He blocked the soldier's penetrating front kick across his raised forearms, but the momentum from the blow lifted Jake off his feet, throwing him into the closed door of an upstairs bedroom a couple of feet behind him. The door exploded from its hinges; Jake catapulted through then tumbled across the floor of the spare bedroom. He landed hard on his back, the air crushed from his lungs in piercing bolts of pain. His pulse thundered. He waited for the stars to clear from his vision. Reaching out, he swept the floor for his shinai and found his feet, gasping to find his breath as he stood to face his attacker.

As the dark figure emerged through the doorframe with its hinges now missing a door, Jake heard the characteristic click of a gun's safety mechanism being disengaged.

Apparently while Jake was on the floor, his attacker had found his weapon. Blinking hard to clear his vision, Jake again assumed a fighting stance, his sword pointed at the throat of the approaching aggressor. The adrenalin coursing through his veins was muting his pain and sharpening his senses.

"Drop your weapon," the soldier ordered, nodding his head at Jake's sword. "Place both your hands on the back of your head and drop to the floor face down!"

Jake paused. The shinai fell to the floor with a thud. His fingers met at the back of his head. As the soldier stepped closer, Jake felt his stomach tighten. The dim light filtering through the room's windows showed him it was one of the large soldiers from the bridge who now had his gun trained at Jake's head.

"Impressive … but it's over." The hulking figure cocked his head. "You're quick, Flash, I'll give you that! Think you can beat a bullet?"

Jake stiffened but said nothing.

"You still have something that does not belong to you." The soldier's voice intensified. "And there are some people who would like to talk to you. You *will* come with us *now*!"

Jake couldn't help but be distracted. His eyes wandered for a second as he detected a faint but familiar wisp of perfume fill the room.

Is that her *scent?* Jake wondered. He drew in a deep breath through his nose. It was almost imperceptible, but there was no mistake; he knew that signature fragrance. Jake's lopsided smirk stretched into a wide smile. "I won't need to."

The soldier was incredulous. "I cannot imagine what you could possibly have to smile about!"

Jake's eyes narrowed to a soul penetrating gaze. "Hell hath no fury like a woman scorned."

At first the soldier was confused by the remark. Then, with a trickle of realization, he spun to face what was behind him. When he saw it, his blood went cold, and his eyes bulged at the sight of the weapon being leveled at him.

❧

Self-preservation is the first law of nature, second only to the imperative of protecting a loved one. Natasha felt her primal urges blaze through her core as she silently appeared in the doorway. As if in slow motion, she raised the gun she'd picked up downstairs. Bringing her hands together in alignment with her hulking target, her knuckles turned white, her fingers clenching the gun in rage. Closing one eye, Natasha adjusted her head until she could see the huge figure through the gun sight. When everything lined up, she closed both eyes, turned her head away, and discharged her weapon.

❧

Jake dropped to the floor as bullets sailed over his head, covering his head to protect himself.

The soldier didn't have time to re-aim his weapon at Natasha. His arm had made it only halfway around to her before his torso was hit in a hail of bullets. The extended arm holding the pistol burst in a spray of crimson red as bullets sailed through muscle tissue. His hand involuntarily flexed, causing the gun to fire as it swung toward Natasha, sending another stream of bullets across the room. Gunshots roared. Spent shells clinked onto the hardwood floor. Drywall and timber debris ricocheted around the room, engulfing Jake in a haze of dust and splinters.

Most of the bullets that found their mark on the soldier were embedded in his ballistic vest. Nevertheless, the force of the bullets rendered him unconscious before his body hit the floor.

With her eyes still clenched tight, Natasha kept firing, the weapon ticking over even though its magazine was completely empty.

Slowly, the white haze cleared as the dust settled in the room. Jake was still sprawled on the floor, his arms over his head. His clothes had turned to a lighter shade from the dust. Faint light streamed sideways into the room through newly formed holes in the walls. The unconscious intruder lay face down in a twisted heap, his arm pumping out blood. The only sound that could now be heard was that of Natasha's empty weapon clicking over as she kept pulling the trigger.

Realizing it was over, Jake sprang to his feet and leaped over the soldier's body toward Natasha. She dropped the gun as soon as she saw Jake move. He pulled her in, both arms wrapping around her in a tight embrace.

Jake's cheek pressed hard against hers. "Would it be a cliché if I said I'm so happy to see you?"

She didn't respond; Natasha just held on to him.

As Jake's heart rate calmed and his adrenalin subsided, he noticed her cheeks were moist. He kissed her and gazed deep into her eyes. They were watery. Her bottom lip quivered as she pulled back from him.

If a line of reason had ever existed, Natasha had now

crossed it by firing at the soldier. Shocked beyond belief at her own actions, she stood frozen and stared at the bleeding body on the floor. Sensing Natasha's fear, Jake crouched down near the motionless figure and reached to feel a pulse.

"Don't worry," Jake said, feeling around the soldier's chest. "He's got a vest on; he'll be okay. You only got him in the arm."

Natasha's face was bloodless with dread.

Jake stood. "What is it?"

She struggled to find the words. "They came for me too. I got away."

Jake's heart sank, and he suddenly felt short of breath as his chest tightened with fear. Silently he grabbed her, squeezing her tight.

It was then that he felt a low rumble vibrate through the floor.

Their eyes met; Natasha had felt it as well. "An earthquake?"

CHAPTER 63

Silent and unseen, a remotely piloted matte-black drone circled at an altitude of 25,000 feet above Jake's neighborhood. Onboard, its light detection and ranging (LiDAR) technology and computer enhanced imaging (CEI) radar was trained on Jake's upstairs bedroom. The drone's was technology borrowed from F117A stealth fighters; the LiDAR and CEI radar enables its operators to see objects in a house to the resolution of an inch at an altitude of 30,000 feet. It allowed a F117A to track a person walking from room to room and identify the model of sidearm hidden in their jacket. Currently, the drone's surveillance instruments were streaming video and radar telemetry to a dark-colored van stationed on Jake's street.

Alpha stood behind the seated agent who monitored the incursion to apprehend Jake Marcel; the van was a mobile command center packed with computer servers, display monitors and assault rifles. Alpha's eyes flashed concern at the LCD monitor displaying the video stream. He had silently watched as Natasha arrive at the house and now followed her on the monitor as the thermal image of her slender form picked up an object from a motionless operative and slowly advanced toward the room now occupied by Jake and Bravo. The agent was providing support to the assault unit. "Bravo, there's a Tango approaching your six. Respond."

Both Alpha and the support agent were fixated on Natasha's red thermal image closing in on Bravo and Jake. There was no response.

The support agent turned to Alpha and said, "Sir, it's possible that his comms unit was damaged in the altercation."

"She wouldn't dare!" Alpha whispered, seething.

Seconds later, the monitor showed a red thermal image of Bravo holding a surrendered Jake at gunpoint. Natasha's form was raising a weapon.

Alpha exploded into his comms unit. "Shake them out!"

The rear doors of the unmarked van flew open; Alpha was still barking commands as he stormed into the street: "Unit Two, blockade the street! NOBODY LEAVES!"

The side doors of a second van flew open to reveal a strange looking gun mounted on a turret. Larger than a traditionally mounted .50 caliber machine gun, the device was comprised of two large dishes that produced high-intensity, low-frequency sound waves similar to those generated during an earthquake. When focused, the high-energy sound waves were a nonlethal weapon. They cause nausea and disorientation in combatants by saturating the inner ear, which regulates spatial orientation, with high energy sound waves.

When focused on a building, the high-energy beam made structural elements resonate. Cycling the beam through various low frequencies caused a building to continue to tremble when its natural frequency is matched by the sonic weapon. When that happens, the vibration intensified until the building literally shook itself apart.

With a deep rumble, the sonic weapon's hum intensified as it focused on Jake's house. At first, the house only creaked and groaned, as if irritated by the inaudible sound waves being focused on it. As the energy of the beam intensified, the windows started to vibrate. Then the walls began to tremble. Twelve seconds later, the house began to sway back and forth as if under assault by its own private earthquake.

In front of the trembling house, two of Alpha's teams materialized from another parked van to form a roadblock in front of the neighboring properties on each side of Jake's residence. Two soldiers headed for the rear of the house to cover the back door. Another two soldiers remained on the front lawn, readying their weapons.

The agent monitoring the live thermal stream watched as Jake appeared to hold on to the walls and struggled to keep his balance while trying to walk. Natasha held her stomach as she followed, also appearing to have difficulty moving. Jake paused then stumbled into what looked like a bedroom. He retrieved an object from under a desk then rummaged through a couple of drawers. Finding what he was looking for, he wrote something on it then took Natasha's hand and led her down the stairs.

The controller used a joystick to zoom in on the moving couple as they struggled to keep their footing, gripping the walls as they rushed through the house and into the garage.

Outside, the two soldiers holding position on the front lawn exchanged glances at the sound of a motorcycle revving over the trembling sound of the shaking house. After giving confirming hand signals, they repositioned themselves on the driveway in front of the garage doors. They exchanged puzzled looks, but held their positions, as the sound of the motorcycle's revving engine seemed to move from the garage into the house.

Inside the van, the agent's brow furrowed in confusion as he watched the video stream. The heat signatures from Jake and Natasha appeared to have driven into the trembling house. Alpha watched in astonishment as the house's front door exploded outward, smashed through by the raised front wheel of Jake's Ducati.

The waiting formations of soldiers were freeze-frames of confusion and surprise as the motorcycle screamed across the sidewalk, crossed the road, and gunned up a driveway on the opposite side of the road, avoiding both roadblocks and the soldiers waiting on the driveway in front of Jake's garage.

The soldiers turned to follow the sound of the motorcycle, its engine howling as it crashed through a backyard fence to find the parallel street on the other side of the houses.

All eyes turned to Alpha as the scream of Jake's engine faded in the distance.

⌘

Twenty minutes later, Jake was still tearing through deserted suburban streets. He checked the mirrors and the sky but didn't spot anyone in pursuit.

He pulled over in the front of cascading steps that led to the large wooden arched doors of an old church. Beside the church was the cemetery that was his grandfather's final resting place.

"Why are we stopping? We need to get out of here!" Natasha's voice was frantic.

Jake fully understood Natasha's trepidation. The shock of what had occurred back at Jake's place had solidified her worst fear. Natasha's eyes told him what he already knew; that everything had spiraled wildly out of control and now they were on the run.

But was it within the realm of possibility that their lives were now in danger because of what they knew? Or even worse, for what they had in their possession?

Jake dismounted. "They don't only want to kill the messenger, they want to kill the message! Wait here."

Eye's wild with fear, Natasha watched in silence as Jake approached the arched double doors of the church and knocked twice. They heard the creaking of a heavy metal lock turning from the inside. The door moaned as it swung open. In the doorway stood a priest, his expression a mix of concern and annoyance.

The priest hesitated with a flash of recognition in his eyes at the sight of Jake. "Can I help you?"

Jake stared as the words hung in the air. It was the same priest who had approached Jake at the cemetery when he had retrieved the small non-terrestrial crash debris from his grandfather's tomb.

Jake plunged his hand into his jacket to produce a small object wrapped in a T-shirt. He held it out to the priest and said, "I need you to keep something safe for me."

CHAPTER 64

Mr. Sabre stepped through the doorframe where Jake's front door had once hung. As a NSA agent, Sabre had been trained to think on a macroevolutionary level, setting aside any ethical, moral, or legal concerns and focusing on the preservation of the human civilization. Collateral losses in the form of civilian lives had always been justified, outweighed by the need to protect the masses from external nonhuman interests.

Sabre's mandate was to keep the ET truths from touching humanity's delicate consciousness no matter the unfortunate human expense. However, protecting the masses from the secret was effectively protecting the masses from themselves. Or rather, protecting an unready, immature civilization from its own negative reaction resulting from learning the truth. A truth that had the potential to tear the fabric of human society from the inside out.

The house was a frenzy of movement. Downed combatants were having their wounds tended while agents searched through cupboards and drawers.

"Sir, they've fled the premises." Alpha's robotic report came from behind Sabre.

Turning slowly, Mr. Sabre met the emotionless gaze of his second-in-command, who approached from the front door. Sabre stepped out into the early morning light as it appeared above the suburban rooftops.

"What about the road blocks?" Sabre's tone was razor sharp.

"They were ineffective, sir," Alpha said, hesitating, his expression turning to one of confusion. "But our drone is still tracking them. They seem to be heading for the open desert."

Alpha's response was met with an intrigued look from Sabre. The NSA leader seemed to consider it for a moment as his expression darkened.

What the hell *is in the desert?* Enraged now, Sabre pushed past Alpha and stormed toward the closest SUV. "We're going to need air support. Round up everyone."

⁂

Nellis Air Force Base occupies over 4,000 hectares of the Las Vegas Valley in Nevada and is home to more aircraft squadrons than any other military installation in the United States. Located at the northeast tip of downtown Las Vegas, it's approximately 290 miles from Los Angeles and 288 miles from the Grand Canyon National Park.

Four black SUVs converged on the multilane entrance to Nellis, storming toward the security checkpoint. Two armored guards materialized from their security hut to meet the approaching convoy, halting in surprise as the vehicles tore past without stopping.

Inside the base's Combined Air and Space Operations

Center, the Air Force Chief of Staff, General John Archer, was midway through a phone conversation with the Secretary of Defense of the National Security Council. His eyes darted between the 10-foot high wall screens that overlooked the Operations Room and his internal security officers now amassing at the room's entrance.

The disturbance at the entrance to the operations room drew the general's attention. Contingents of armed soldiers in black fatigues were muscling their way past base security, led by a black-suited figure.

"Yes, sir." the general replied into the phone, his eyes trained on his security officers now threatening to draw their weapons on the intruding detachment.

Before one of the security officers could raise his gun, he found himself being flipped over the shoulder of one of the intruders. Seconds later, the three remaining security personnel met with overwhelming firepower, the nozzles of FN SCAR assault rifles directed at their faces. With the line of defense now nullified and dropping to their knees, the man in the black suit approached the general.

General Archer put the phone down. "Are you the one they call Sabre?"

A tense silence filled the room. Sabre continued to approach the general without responding.

The general continued. "You have no right to storm in by force, despite your clearance with the NSC!"

"Actually, I have every right," Mr. Sabre said, his voice eerily calm. "Cosmic Clearance, Top Secret UMBRA, National Security—pick one. I have an enemy of the state on the move and only a short window in which to apprehend him. I'm going to need to requisition all available helicraft."

"Sir?" A controller attending one of the 500 flat-screen monitors in the command facility looked up from his terminal. "There's a call for Mr. Sabre coming through on the priority line; it's from NORAD."

The general glared at Sabre. "You're having your calls directed here too?"

Archer read between the lines. The North American Aerospace Defense Command, NORAD, is a defense surveillance and aerospace warning facility servicing the North American region. Housed inside Cheyenne Mountain in Colorado, NORAD provides tactical missile warning and attack assessment to the governments of Canada and the United States, as well as tracking both domestic and foreign satellites. If Sabre was taking calls from NORAD, the general suspected the information would be classified above his own clearance.

"Put it on loud speaker." Archer commanded.

"Go ahead, you're on with Mr. Sabre," the controller's voice boomed over the speakers feeding the command center.

"Sir, we're tracking a Fastwalker on approach to the western coast."

The general was glaring at Sabre. "What the hell is a Fastwalker?"

The booming voice went on. "On its current trajectory, it's going to enter the upper atmosphere in 22 minutes at a speed of Mach 28."

The general did the calculation in his head. "The space shuttle never reached that speed. What is that thing?"

Sabre ignored the question, instead turning toward the controller managing the call. "Can you patch their telemetry onto your screens?"

Looking almost scared, the controller looked to the general as if to ask permission. With a dismissive wave, Archer silently agreed. After clicking through several windows on his screen, the controller looked up at the main screens that were the focal point of the command center.

The screen's current radar map tracking local air traffic dissolved into an image of the United States. A thin, yellow line representing the object's path extended from offscreen and slowly lengthened over the North Pacific Ocean toward the US's western coastline. A gray dashed line extended from the moving object's current position to predict its direction. The dashed, gray line stopped in the Nevada desert region, based on the object's speed and rate of descent.

"Sir." Alpha was handing Sabre a small tablet screen. "Telemetry from the drone tracking the target."

Sabre took hold of the tablet, studying the bird's-eye view of Jake and Natasha tearing across a road that appeared to cut through an unpopulated arid region. He zoomed out and swiped to a screen that plotted the motorcycle's location over a larger map. Jake was outside the city limits, headed for open desert.

In a shocking moment of realization, Sabre slowly raised his eyes to the screen that showed the object's path. It looked as if the incoming object was headed for the same region. His years with the NSA had taught him there was no such thing as coincidence. Sabre felt an anger welling deep within him. He glared at the general. "I'm going to need a couple of interceptors in the air right now!"

Archer stared at Sabre like he was crazy. "All our fighters are on Red Flag maneuvers out at Elmendorf, Alaska." Red Flag is an advanced, 10-day aerial combat training exercise held up to four times a year. The realistic exercises are hosted by either Nellis Air Force Base in Nevada or Elmendorf Air Force Base in Alaska. "Even if I was willing to give you a pair of fighters," General Archer declared, anger simmering in his eyes, "shouldn't the president be informed first?"

"The president doesn't have a high enough clearance," Sabre seethed.

The general was caught off guard by the comment. "The closest squadrons are either at Edward or Creech, but we don't possess anything that can catch up to whatever that Fastwalker is."

Retrieving his phone, Sabre considered the remark for a moment then selected a speed dial number. His eyes narrowed as he allowed himself a brief smile.

Actually, General, we do.

CHAPTER 65

A clear morning sky stretched over the desert basin at Groom Lake, the original home of the retired SR71 Blackbird and the testing ground for the F117A stealth fighter. The runway lit up for the next generation of classified military craft. Sleek and angular, the Aurora looked more like the genetic offspring of the space shuttle than an advanced fighter jet. Powered by a battery pulse detonation wave engine fueled by liquid methane, the Aurora can reach speeds well in excess of eight times the speed of sound.

The worst kept secret in US military history, initially the SR-91 Aurora Project was managed by Lockheed Martin's Advanced Development Programs, and their engineers had set out to achieve the holy grail of space flight: single stage to orbit launch capability. Its loud, deep, and rumbling engines were reminiscent of heavy-lift rockets and left a signature contrail that resembled smoke rings on a rope.

Twenty-six miles east of Groom Lake, perched on a

mountain, two UFO enthusiasts were packing up camp at the last legal location with a view of Area 51, known as Tikaboo Peak.

Enthusiasts camp out at night because of daytime atmospheric-heat distortions emanating from the desert floor, which makes it difficult to differentiate hangars from the desert surface. For this reason, night has always been the best time to witness advanced aircraft and test vehicles glide in and out of the restricted area.

This time, however, would be the exception. The clear morning had brought with it cool conditions with none of the atmospheric heat distortions that usually made observing from a distance difficult.

Alerted by the deep rumble of the Aurora's engines, the campers fumbled to find their binoculars and camera to steal a glimpse of the ultra-secret aircraft in the morning sunlight.

They watched in silent wonder as its afterburner jets parted ways with Groom Lake's four-mile long runway. They followed the top-secret aircraft until it was a speck in the sky. It was then that they felt the ground tremble; their chests vibrated with the fabled skyquake as the Aurora tore through the upper atmosphere.

CHAPTER 66

Jake hit the brakes and brought the motorcycle to a skidding stop.

Jake and Natasha were in the middle of the desert now, having left Las Vegas miles earlier. He got off but left the engine running and took several steps in their intended direction to survey the landscape. They had stopped a couple of miles short of a deep canyon that cut across their path. He looked left and right; the sunburned canyons, crisscrossed by jagged ridges and sheer cliff faces, stretched out to the horizon as far as he could see.

But there was something else. Jake felt a familiarity about the location. He didn't know how, but he felt as if he knew the area. As if he had been there before.

It was when he turned back toward Natasha that it hit him.

I dreamt about this place. Was I supposed to find it?

He could make out a number of dark vehicles on the horizon in the distance. Plumes of sand and dust were being kicked up in their wake. Above the vehicles flew a contingent of helicopters.

He walked a short distance parallel to the cliff face; there was no way to get to the other side of the canyon. The realization crashed over him like a wave—there was nowhere to run. Slowly, Jake turned to face Natasha, his eyes lifting to meet hers. "This has gone on long enough."

Natasha had dismounted and was still shaken by the events that had transpired back at Jake's house. Leaning on the motorcycle for support, she patted dust off one of her boots. "When they catch up to us, do you think we'll be okay?"

Jake did not answer. Behind Natasha, something had drawn his attention. When he saw the object in the distance, all the pieces fell into place. On the horizon, a small, white glowing disk, as bright as a flare, was slowly descending from the sky. Jake stood stunned. He followed the path of the object until it disappeared from view into the distant ridge.

His tone turned pensive. "Hon … remember when you asked me what I believe?"

"Yeah," she said, working the sand and dust off her other boot.

"Well … what do you believe?"

Natasha stood upright and gazed at him with loving eyes. "I believe in you."

The answer caught him completely off guard. Her words seemed to penetrate deep inside him, shaking him from his fixated trance.

Jake stared; he was captivated by her beautiful

vulnerability. She was magnificent; a vision of beauty on a backdrop of desolate emptiness.

Glancing over her shoulder, Natasha tried to find what had captivated his attention, but saw nothing. The glowing object had disappeared into the canyon below. Her hair seemed to dance on her shoulders as her warm eyes met his. A quizzical expression crept across her face, but behind it, all Jake could see was absolute devotion. He felt himself momentarily lost in her strong gaze. In that moment, it all made sense: him, her, and why they were there.

Jake had always stopped to appreciate life's perfect moments. They were very rare; at any given time, he would be able to recall only a handful: riding his motorcycle for the first time, his first kiss, his first stolen embrace with Natasha. But whenever it happened, it was a moment in time he wished could last forever. As he got older, he went on to believe that life's purpose was to experience as many perfect moments as the universe would permit. Feeling his heart grow heavy, he realized that this was one of those times. Jake knew this was the woman he wanted to spend the rest of his life with.

"You would follow me to the end of the world … and you have."

He stepped toward her. Her quizzical look had turned to confusion.

"What are you talking about, sweetheart?" she said with a soft smile.

Natasha had already been through so much—far more than any partner should be expected to endure. It was for that reason he could no longer drag her along his path.

The black vehicles were getting closer. Jake's ears

pounded rhythmically along with the deep pulsing of the approaching chopper turbines. There was nowhere to run. If he was going to find answers, he could not take Natasha where he needed to go. He pulled her into a tight embrace and slowly kissed her. At the same time, and without her noticing, he plucked the dog tags from around his neck.

The military vehicles were getting closer.

His arms circled her waist, and Jake slipped Reilly's business card into Natasha's back pocket. Taking her by both hands, he took a step back. "*You* will be fine."

Although confused, Natasha smiled and said, "You're not making any sense, sweetheart."

The deep throbbing of the helicopter blades grew louder; their vibration could now be felt through the ground.

Jake felt there was so much he wanted to say: that he loved her, that he was lucky to have her in his life, that he didn't ever want to leave her. But the words caught in his chest.

It was in that moment that she noticed the small object he had placed in her hand. Looking down, she opened her hand to find Jake's dog tags, the ID tags that had once belonged to his grandfather. It was something, she knew, he never parted with. They were his good luck charm when he rode.

Her smile slowly evaporated.

The helicopters were nearly upon them.

Jake let go of Natasha's other hand and took a hesitant step back toward the idling motorcycle. Struck with confusion, she slowly looked up at him, eyes welling, searching his eyes for an explanation. She looked back at what was approaching, and a flash of realization raked her flesh. She felt a knot tighten in her stomach.

The canyon?!

The outlines of the fast-approaching ground vehicles were now evident. They were the same black SUVs that had pursued Jake before. The sky overhead roared; two choppers had reached them and were hovering low, the downdraft whipping the loose sand around them into a frenzy.

Jake took another step back and shook his head. His eyes, too, were glazed with tears. Natasha got the terrifying message.

Her confusion turned into desperate panic. The tears overflowed, creeping down her cheek. Focused on Jake, Natasha didn't register that the helicopters were directly above them whipping up a dust storm.

"Jake …" she said desperately, "what are you doing?"

Jake took a last long look at her. He wanted to remember her in every detail. A deep emotion arose within him; he realized she had brought him happiness beyond measure.

"Jaaaake …?" Her voice was inaudible now above the sound of the thundering helicopter rotors. A rappelling rope dropped down between them from one of the helicopters above.

Natasha stepped toward Jake, consumed by panic, moving as if in a dream. She didn't notice that the rope from the chopper had brushed against her.

Natasha's lips were moving. "What are you doing?!"

Black-clad figures poured out in synchronized motion from each side of the helicopter hovering directly above. Ropes dropped from a second helicopter nearby. Two more helicopters were closing in. The ground vehicles tore up dust and sand, spreading out as they drew closer. But Natasha was oblivious to the chaos around them.

He watched her lips again moving, muted by the thundering helicopter turbine: "JAAAAKE?!"

Jake gave his signature half-smile. He could have stood there forever with her.

She felt her chest sink. There was no way to hear him over the thundering drone of the helicopters above.

Jake's four words ripped through her soul as she read his lips: "I have to know."

The bulky figures had now rappelled most of the way down the ropes.

Out of time, Jake thought.

Jake spun around and lunged for the motorcycle.

The first soldier to touch down leaped for Natasha, restrained her from behind, and pinned her arms back.

"JAAAAAAAAAAAAAAAAAAAAKE!" Her scream was primal to the core and, this time, audible above the thundering turbines.

Jake managed to jump clear of the second soldier touching down. Thrusting himself on the Ducati, he set it in motion. The rear wheel spun, and he pivoted until he was aimed directly for his target. He let the throttle open full; the tires howled then clawed at the loose earth. The motorcycle threw up a cloud of sand and dirt as it shot away with a high-pitched scream.

Beside him, the desert floor tore by in a blur as he catapulted away from the aggressor's hopeless efforts to neutralize him.

The armada of SUVs had reached Natasha,

shooting past her as they fanned out in pursuit of the speeding motorcycle.

"NOOOOOOOOOOOOOOOOOOO!" Natasha guttural cry was bone chilling.

Panicking, she struggled to free herself from the soldier who held her in the grip of his tightening bear hug. A dusty haze kicked up by the passing SUVs made it difficult for her to see Jake disappear into the distance.

Two more helicopters flew overhead. The chase was on for the motorcycle that raced toward the ridge. Beyond that was a 130-foot sheer drop to the base of the canyon below.

CHAPTER 67

The motorcycle's tachometer needle swung passed 8,000 RPM. Jake strained for more speed as his engine's shriek changed pitch from a bellowing roar to a mechanical scream as the needle entered the red zone. Before shifting into second gear, he was already travelling at over 60 miles per hour.

※

From the helicopter flying over Natasha's location, Mr. Sabre watched the motorcycle accelerate toward the cliff in the distance, kicking up a line of sand that marked his path. In close pursuit was the formation of black SUVs.

Then something drew Sabre's attention to his far right.

A brilliant bright light emanated from deep within the canyon. Despite his altitude, he didn't have a clear line of sight to identify the object. Yet, whatever it was, it illuminated the canyon walls from below and was approaching fast.

Focusing back on the motorcycle, he could see that

Jake would reach the canyon's edge in only moments. And at his current speed, it appeared that the bright light would reach the canyon's edge at the same time.

Sabre instantly connected the dots. Furious, he flicked the radio to an open channel.

With an injection of spite, he ordered, "Drop the bike before it reaches the edge."

A voice responded, "Sir, at that speed a shot at the target would mean instant—"

Sabre cut off the voice mid-sentence, intensifying his resolve. "Drop THAT bike before it reaches the edge. BRING ME MARCEL'S BODY!"

Sabre's order echoed inside the lead SUV in close pursuit of Jake. Alpha looked back at his third in command, Charlie. Words weren't necessary.

With robotic precision, Charlie switched off the safety on his assault rifle, lowered his window, and hung halfway out of the SUV to take aim.

Jake shot a glance down at the speedometer: 85 miles per hour.

Packets of sand exploded just behind his rear wheel from gunfire, Jake didn't notice. The edge of the cliff was getting closer.

Three gears to go.

100 miles per hour.

110.

The desert floor was a blur. He was oblivious to the

rifle rounds that were zinging past his head, missing by barely inches.

120.

Bullets buried themselves close behind his back wheel. His side mirror exploded in a mist of shards. The motorcycle's engine screamed in protest as he urged it faster toward the cliff. Jake was too focused at gaining speed to notice his arms and upper body had started trembling.

135.

150.

The deep ridge that cut through the desert approached. He had no idea how far the drop was to the bottom; all he could see was the cliff face on the other side of the gaping abyss.

To his right, something was illuminating the ridge walls from below. It was out of view, but Jake knew exactly what it was. It was the bright object he'd seen descend into the canyon, and it was closing in on his location. He didn't understand how, but something inside beckoned him to race toward the cliff and intercept that bright light. It was the same voice from within that reassured him he would be safe.

❧

The driver of the lead SUV shot Alpha an ominous look; he realized with fearful clarity that they would never catch the motorcycle in time before it reached the cliff's edge. If they didn't start braking soon, they'd be following Jake Marcel over the edge into the canyon.

Alpha acknowledged the unspoken request. Charlie ceased firing and sat back inside the speeding vehicle. The occupants of the lead SUV braced as the driver braked. The trailing SUVs all braked in response.

Alpha watched what followed in disbelief.

⁂

Jake knew what he was attempting was nothing less than suicidal, but for some reason he trusted the reassuring voice inside him.

160.

170.

180.

As Jake Marcel broke over the crest of the cliff, he leaped as hard as he could, propelling himself into the air. Both Jake and the motorcycle shot over the edge.

As he catapulted through the air with both arms reaching in front of him, time seemed to slow down. It was then that he caught his first glimpse of what his grandfather knew to be real all along. The resplendent approaching object hugging the canyon floor was a disk, its diameter the length of two school buses. Its sleek silvery skin seemed to glow brilliant white from the inside out. An unexpected feeling of contentment and peace enveloped him, penetrating every cell of his body.

Jake had always thought that the expression of having your life flash before your eyes was just that, an expression. But in that moment, he felt himself reel back in time. In his last seconds of consciousness, he saw images from his life stream through his mind:

Playing as a young boy, laughing with his father, attending his grandfather's funeral, watching his grandfather being lowered in the ground, holding his grandfather's service tags, sitting next to Mark at school, sharing meals with his parents, meeting Natasha for the first time, riding his motorcycle with his friends, looking at the stars with Natasha, their first stolen embrace, her smile, and her touch.

The images flashed past faster and faster: Meeting Dr. Reilly, the motorcycle chase, Natasha standing by the motorcycle and smiling, her sparkling blue eyes.

The images turned to the future, to what could have been: Standing in a church, dressed in a suit before a priest, looking back to see Natasha in a radiant white wedding dress.

Then he was totally engulfed by an all-encompassing, brilliant, white light.

✍

"Drop THAT bike before it reaches the edge. BRING ME MARCEL'S BODY!"

The order was relayed to the pilot of the Aurora.

The pilot's emotionless acknowledgment was automatic. "Copy that. Engaging."

The strange-looking aircraft was decelerating as it approached the canyon. The heat tiles along the leading edges of the craft's nose and wings still glowed red from heat generated by friction as it entered Earth's lower atmosphere.

The cockpit targeting screens showed zoomed images of the motorcycle hurtling toward the canyon. Another screen had locked onto a spherical objected that glowed white, tracking it as it hugged the canyon floor at an unearthly velocity toward the speeding motorcycle.

The copilot refocused his targeting computer at the fast-moving motorcycle in an attempt to lock on to the target.

The Aurora's undercarriage slid open to reveal a battery of AGM-116 Hellfire missiles that lowered into position.

A green square tracking the motorcycle on the copilot's targeting screen turned red, indicating the system had locked on the target.

❧

The radio on board Sabre's helicopter chirped. "Commander, we have a priority connection to patch through."

Sabre heard a series of clicks, and then the voice of the Aurora copilot: "Commander, we have a visual on the ETV, permission to engage."

Mr. Sabre paused for a second, almost reluctant. "Light 'em up!"

CHAPTER 68

The copilot of the Aurora heard Mr. Sabre loud and clear.

"Roger that," he answered.

Without hesitation, the copilot redirected his aim at the glowing disk and squeezed his trigger.

A volley of Hellfire missiles snapped to life and hurtled toward the target. The copilot remained focused on his targeting screen in expectation of the second phase of the launch sequence. One by one, the nose of each missile broke away to reveal a cluster of smaller missiles, each carrying their own deadly payloads.

✦

Sabre watched intently as Jake went over the edge; his screen was also tracking the motorcycle, recording the horrifying act of defiance as Jake went over.

Shocked beyond belief, Sabre tried to comprehend what he was witnessing. The brilliant white craft intercepted Jake mid-flight. The glare emanating from the craft swallowed both him and the motorcycle. Milliseconds later a midair explosion erupted, the result of the motorcycle impacting the craft. In a blur the craft then accelerated away, continuing its path along the bottom of the canyon at an impossible speed, barely perceptible by human eyes.

∽

The AGM-116 Hellfire is the next generation of air-to-surface missile systems. Developed by Lockheed Martin, the weapons system has not yet been released to the US Defense Forces. This generation of Hellfire had multi-mission, multi-target, precision-strike capabilities effective against tanks, bunkers, and all manner of armored fighting vehicles in motion. Halfway toward their target, each of the four rocketing AGM-116 Hellfires launched eight of their own smaller missiles mid-flight, sending a spread of warheads designed to engulf a moving target, guaranteeing a kill.

The targeting system was now locked onto the extraterrestrial vehicle as the motorcycle catapulted off the edge of the cliff to slowly drop away from its rider, who had also been propelled into the canyon.

The copilot was then alerted by his targeting screen. An error message appeared.

An unseen force divided the spread of missiles; half diverted to the left, vectoring toward the cliff's edge. The other half diverted to the right, each missile deflected randomly, all redirected toward the canyon floor.

The copilot watched in disbelief as both the rider and motorcycle were intercepted midair by the glowing disk. The motorcycle exploded as it collided with the luminous craft, but the spread of missiles completely missed its target. Then suddenly, the glowing object was gone.

❧

Alpha watched Jake leap into the air as he went over, then drop out of sight beneath the edge of the ridge. An explosion erupted an instant later, followed by a hail of missiles that rained down from the sky. It was unusual for the surprised soldier not to notice incoming fighter support; the resulting missile impact birthed a wall of fire that shot along the cliff's edge, engulfing Alpha's full field of vision.

Poor kid; nothing could survive that.

❧

"Drop THAT bike before it reaches the edge. BRING ME MARCEL'S BODY!" The order was barked from the personal radio strapped to the soldier who had restrained Natasha.

Natasha had once read that raw terror was paralyzing. She now knew this was not true. She kicked against the soldier with a single thought in her mind.

Jake!

"NOOOOOOOOOOO!" her soul cried out in anguish as she struggled against her captor.

Her adrenalin surged, pulsing through her body.

She felt instinct take over. With her right foot, she stumped down hard, scraping the length of the soldier's shin before stabbing her heel into his foot, using the maneuver Jake had taught Jackie.

The sudden shock of white hot pain gripped the soldier and took him by surprise, causing his hold on Natasha to loosen.

That was all she needed.

She tucked her right shoulder under his, and with the force of someone three times her strength, Natasha lifted the soldier off his feet and sent him flying over her shoulder. His shoulder almost ripped from its socket from her adrenalin-fueled strength. When he landed, he slammed down hard on his back.

In frantic desperation, she was in motion, catapulting herself toward the cliff, screaming for them to let him go. The nearby soldiers let her run; there was nothing she could do that could help Jake now. Tears streaming, she ran as fast as her body would take her.

The SUVs hit their brakes one by one; the soldiers watched on in terror. Jake didn't stop.

She watched as if in a dream.

This can't be happening!

The horror was instantaneous. Natasha's soul cried out in agony as she witnessed her world disappear over the edge. She brought her hand to her mouth and muffled a scream. She saw an explosion then a wall of fire like nothing she had ever seen. Suddenly she couldn't breathe. Her tear-streaked face contorted in anguish and disbelief.

Sabre watched the events unfold from above.

After the spread of missiles exploded, he noticed that the girl had been let loose and was foolishly running toward the canyon; then she stopped and collapsed to her knees.

One of the soldiers caught up to her and attempted to assist. The girl just stared toward the canyon, motionless.

CHAPTER 69

At the bottom of the canyon, a field team was surveying the area of Jake's motorcycle wreckage.

They observed no impact or burn marks on the canyon floor. The motorcycle had mostly disintegrated in the air. A senior field officer reported to Sabre. "Sir, there isn't much left of the motorcycle, only charred fragments scattered over 160 square feet."

Sabre listened intently through his earpiece, stopping mid-sentence during his debriefing with Alpha and his team who had encircled him. Sabre had landed at the top of the cliff, along with the rest of the air support. A second team had been sent down to investigate the wreckage at the bottom of the canyon.

The earpiece squawked again: "There also aren't any signs of human remains at all … Either he completely disintegrated, or … he just isn't here."

❦

Two dark-suited agents had helped Natasha stagger toward

the back of one of their SUVs, which was now parked alongside the unmarked military vehicles now amassed close to where Jake had taken off. She was still clutching Jake's dog tag necklace, her haunted eyes brimming with tears. She was short of breath as they sat her down. Witnessing Jake disappear over the edge of the cliff had left her catatonic. She sat silently in a paralytic haze. Natasha was in shock.

Soldiers and NSA agents bustled around her. She didn't hear their questions or offers of aid. Her gaze was fixed on the single tire track that was left by Jake's motorcycle, stretching out to the cliff face.

The image of Jake going over the cliff replayed in her mind.

Is he really gone? Natasha could not stop trembling.

A feeling of emptiness and despair was intensifying deep within her, somehow restricting her breathing. She didn't bother wiping the tears that were trailing down the sides of her face. Another helicopter landed nearby, but Natasha was oblivious to all around her.

Jake's grandfather's ID dog tags were still tightly clenched in her hand.

"You know I never ride without them," she remembered him saying.

What the hell was he thinking!

A commanding figure in a dark suit approached Natasha, his icy gaze parting the crowd before him as he stepped toward her.

Drawing on his cigarette, he unapologetically spat out, "Where is your boyfriend?"

The words hit her like a thunderclap, shattering her

trance and allowing reality to rush back in. Natasha tried to speak, but found that she still could not even breathe. She looked away, unable to meet his gaze.

The black-suited man repeated, "WHERE IS JAKE MARCEL?"

Natasha slowly looked up. A strange glint of hope flickered across her face. She needed only a moment for the meaning to register.

CHAPTER 70

Jake slowly floated back from the edge of nothingness.

It was peaceful.

It was quiet.

His mind seemed to hover in an endless dark abyss.

Is this death?

Off in the distance, he felt something familiar. A vague memory, or rather, a sensation. The feeling wasn't totally clear, but he remembered being weightless.

Skirting the edges of consciousness, an awareness of his physical body returned to him as feeling came back into his hands and feet. Pale, colorless light crept through the slits of his eyes, but all he could see was a blurry haze. The air around him seemed still, dead. There was no sound, no echoes, only silence.

Jake became aware that he was lying on his back with his arms by his sides. As the mental fog lifted, he remembered the sensation of acceleration, of flying. No, of being catapulted through the air.

Had time slowed down? Is this what it's like to be dead? Am I still flying over the cliff?

He felt that the hairs on his body were raised under his clothes. It was also odd that he couldn't feel the bed beneath him, or whatever it was that he was lying on. Despite the pounding now in his head, and with what little strength that had returned, he opened the palm of his hand in an attempt to feel what he was lying on.

There was nothing. The space beneath him was empty air.

Lowering his arm a little further, he felt around.

Still nothing.

Jake was floating!

He felt a surge of panic. The adrenalin brought a little more strength to his arms and legs, allowing him to awkwardly thrash around while suspended in midair, as if learning how to swim for the first time. The sensation was both unnerving and disorientating; he could feel his heart racing, almost leaping out of his chest. He couldn't tell if he was balanced, floating, falling or all three!

There was no way for Jake to know that a slender, spherical ring surrounded his body. Floating midair parallel to the floor, the ring was silver and suspended precisely in the center of a circular room. A strong electromagnetic field that emanated from it held Jake in place above the metallic floor.

As if sensing that the ring's captive was in distress, it slowly descended toward the floor, lowering the captured human. Directly under Jake, the metallic floor liquefied to restructure itself, flowing upward beneath him to form a bench.

With his frantic attempts to balance himself in midair, Jake could not perceive that he was slowly being lowered. But then he felt the bench raise up to support him. Feeling the cold metal surface with his arms and legs helped calm his panic a fraction; he stopped thrashing about and lowered both hands to feel the bench rise until it made contact with his back.

He tried to relax and catch his breath. Three small, chalky-gray figures observed as the large ring continued to descend past Jake down the height of the bench until it touched the floor; it slowly liquefied to remold itself into the floor, completely disappearing as if its molecular structure became one with the floor's surface.

Feeling a little stronger, Jake tried to look around, but the movement of his head sent a jolt of pain radiating through his skull. His eyes were open, but he couldn't make out any details in the room. The environment was warm and humid, and seemed sterile, like that of a hospital. The room was brightly lit, but there were no obvious signs of light sources. He did detect the faint scent of ozone.

Am I in a hospital?

He fought off the searing throb in his head, but his near vision remained clouded. Above him on the ceiling were what seemed to be two large, black windows. The windows were almond-shaped and elongated at their opposite ends.

The grogginess pulled harder at him, and a stream of images flashed through his mind. He saw himself racing toward the cliff, going over the edge, and approaching the silver disk in the canyon.

There was something foreign about these memories, as if someone else was guiding him through the images.

Battling weakness, Jake tried to blink the deep black windows into focus.

In that instant, a sharp panic gripped him as his reality

shattered. They weren't windows. They were a pair of large, deep, black eyes.

One of the small gray figures was over him, its face immediately in front of Jake's, scanning his memories. It was as if the creature were walking through his thoughts, forcing him to remember.

Jake was overcome by a fierce terror. Panic and instinct overruled the searing aching in his head. With what little strength he could summon he pushed the figure off him, sending it across the room.

Is this real?

Jake's body felt like it weighed several hundred pounds as he rolled onto his side to sit up. The remaining small figures moved with efficiency and impossible speed as they shifted out of Jake's reach.

With fascinated horror, Jake searched the room. But all he could perceive were gray and silver blurs.

Then without reason, his panic subsided as he felt a distinctive presence suddenly manifest within the room. It was powerful, warm, and seemed to radiate an energy that saturated every cell of his body. It was unlike anything Jake had ever felt; it enveloped him with a sense of calm and reassurance, and somehow told him that he was safe, that there was nothing to fear.

As the room came into sharper focus, Jake stood and turned toward the source of energy. He lifted his head slowly. His breath caught as he felt the collision of excitement, privilege, and mortal fear when, for the first time, he saw it with his own eyes.

CHAPTER 71

The sun was beginning to dip below the suburbs surrounding Natasha's house. Being of no further use to Mr. Sabre, she'd been permitted to leave the site where she'd watched Jake ride over the cliff's edge.

Natasha had barely registered being driven home in one of the dark SUVs. She felt detached as two NSA agents escorted her to the front door. Filled with an overwhelming dread, she let herself in.

Natasha couldn't push the image of Jake disappearing over the edge from her mind. A suffocating loneliness pressed down around her as she held the walls to steady herself on the way to the bathroom.

She stood paralyzed in front of the mirror. The image that greeted her was a mask of desperation, her face pale and dirty from the desert ride. The prospect of life without Jake sent a crushing tremor of loss through her.

She removed her top, and turned on the shower to let the water warm up. Her heart sank when she emptied her pants pocket to find Jake's dog tag necklace.

She was gripped by a fear she had never known. *Will I ever see him again?*

Her eyes welling now with emotion, she gently placed the ID tags on the sink and emptied her other pockets.

From her back pocket, she retrieved a card she had not remembered carrying. She felt confused as she studied the single word handwritten on the card in red, *Shift*.

Turning the card over, she studied the mobile number that was printed on it; there was no accompanying name or address. Above the number was another handwritten inscription in Jake's handwriting: *Find Reilly*.

Natasha's eyes went wide.

❦

Mark's motorcycle maneuvered around the boom gate at McCarran International Airport's security checkpoint with surgical precision. His engine's mechanical scream drowned out protests yelled by the stationed security guards as he accelerated toward the busy runway strips that greeted commercial aircraft visiting Las Vegas.

Unaware that he had just triggered a homeland security response, Mark thundered toward Dr. Reilly's A380, which was taxiing to its designated runway for takeoff.

In an effort to intercept the scientist before his flight to New York departed, and having been unable to reach Dr. Reilly because his phone was switched off, Mark tore down the length of the runway to meet the huge aircraft head on. Behind him, a fleet of security vehicles were in pursuit with sirens blazing.

The gigantic aircraft lurched to a halt immediately after commencing its takeoff acceleration. Mark felt dwarfed as he dismounted his motorcycle while the enormous A380 buckled to an emergency stop immediately before him.

Inside the aircraft, Dr. Charles Reilly felt a rising concern at the aircraft's sudden stop. He peered out the window but couldn't see what had caused the unannounced delay minutes earlier. Sensing someone standing over him, the scientist turned and was greeted by one of the senior airline attendants.

The woman's expression was an equal mix of worry and fear. "Excuse me, are you Dr. Charles Reilly?"

Thirty seconds later, the scientist found himself being escorted off the aircraft by airport security and marched toward a motorcyclist who was being restrained face down on the tarmac by airport guards. The motorcyclist had evidently ridden onto the runway in the path of Dr. Reilly's flight.

The man escorting the scientist motioned toward the pinned-down motorcyclist. "Do you know this person?"

"Of course he knows me, you idiots! You think I make a habit of breaking into airports to pull over planes?" Mark yelled, his voice muffled from his head being pressed against the ground.

Reilly's escort remained emotionless. "He said you were an adviser to the NSC, and it was a matter of national security. Homeland has verified your former status to us, but do you know him? He was carrying this in his back pocket."

Reilly was handed the business card with his name

handwritten over his cell number. He turned the card over to find the word *Shift* written on the back.

"Yes, I know him. He's harmless," Reilly confirmed.

Mark struggled to turn his head toward the scientist. "Jake is gone! They chased him into the desert. He went over a cliff. They found what was left of his Ducati down the bottom, but there was no body! He disappeared! The guys in black don't even know where he is!"

Reilly stared for a long moment as if to absorb the gravity of the profound news.

"Natasha found your card in her pocket," Mark said, still struggling against the guards. "He must have put it there before he took off! He wanted us to find you."

Reilly studied the single word handwritten on the back of his business card then slowly raised his eyes.

CHAPTER 72

"DO NOT BE AFRAID," it said.

The words ricocheted around the inside of Jake's mind. The voice was clear, precise, and came across in a gentle tone. Yet Jake didn't hear it with his ears. It was like listening to his own internal dialogue. Jake was receiving the words from an outside source, which wrapped his own English around them to convert the message into a comprehensible language.

"WE ARE THE ONES YOU SEEK," he heard.

Telepathy!? Jake's world was spinning.

He momentarily forgot about the events leading up to being chased off the cliff. Jake realized that he was standing in the center of a round room. At one end of the room stood the source of the voice. He blinked the figure into focus.

This can't be real!

It stood a little over four and a half feet tall. Its dolphin-like skin was light gray and hairless. Its head was relatively large in proportion to its body, framing two large, very dark, almond-shaped eyes. There were small holes on the side of its head where one would expect ears to be, and small slits for nostrils instead of a prominent nose. This being, or thing, Jake thought, would definitely not pass as human if it were to walk down a crowded street.

He felt like an atheist standing in the presence of God.

Am I really on board their craft?

Jake saw how these beings could look fearful. He had once heard them described as ghosts with evil, black eyes. But he felt as if he was in the presence of a supreme being; there was an unseen flow of energy emanating from its direction which, at some deep level of perception, he could feel flow past him like a comet facing an invisible solar wind. And yet, there was something eerily familiar about the little gray figure.

Hollywood wasn't too far off the mark!

"WE DO NOT COMMUNICATE THROUGH SOUND AS YOU DO."

The creature seemed to be wearing a tightly fitted, single-piece outfit that was only a few shades darker than its skin color. Jake saw no visible seams, buttons, or zippers. As it stepped closer, Jake could make out deep back pupils framed by a black iris within its huge dark eyes. Its irises were vertically elongated, diamond-shaped slits, more like a cat iris than a human's.

Jake was surprised he was so calm. As a boy, he'd sometimes had bad dreams about UFOs and little gray men. The dreams would follow talking with his father about his grandfather's time with the 509th Bombardment Group at the Roswell Army Air Field. Waking up in a panic, he'd look around his room to make sure nobody was there, and then he would duck his head under the blankets for added protection. But as he stood staring at the creature, he didn't feel scared or threatened in any way.

Jake had never given a thought to how he would feel if he were ever face-to-face with a non-terrestrial being. He perhaps expected to be petrified. Instead, being in the entity's presence made him feel at peace, as if it was actually possible to be wrapped in layers of reassurance and tranquility. He was in awe of the entity before him.

"A-Am I ..." Jake stammered.

"YOU ARE WITH US AS WE ASCEND." Again, words resonated in his mind.

"You mean ..." Jake felt as if the entity was looking into him, not at him, as if reading his thoughts.

"YES, WE HAVE MOVED AWAY FROM YOUR WORLD."

Shit, this IS real!

He felt a wave of excitement and exhilaration. The answer to the question of whether we were alone in the universe was standing right in front of him. A torrent of questions ran through his mind; there were so many things he wanted to know.

The creature read Jake's eagerness to look around. Gesturing with its right palm, it opened its four-fingered hand, indicating that Jake could take a closer look at his surroundings.

Jake wanted to absorb every tiny detail of the room. He detected no light source, yet it was emanating from everywhere. The large room was circular, approximately 40 feet in diameter, with a ceiling height of about 20 feet. Apart from the bench behind him, there was nothing conventional: no screens, no workstations, no control panels or equipment of any kind. The room was barren with no adornments at all; every surface was one color—light silver with a pearl and violet hue.

Jake felt slightly light-headed, blissful, almost euphoric.

Perceiving Jake's state of mind, the creature said without words, "THE SENSATION YOU ARE FEELING IS DUE TO THE OXYGEN CONTENT IN THE AIR, WHICH IS HIGHER THAN YOUR BODY IS USED TO. IT WILL SOON PASS."

With the creature's permission, Jake stepped away from the bench and approached one of the walls to take a closer look. He could distinguish a fine hexagonal imprint that extended in all directions within the texture of the wall. It occurred to him that there were no joints, seams, corners, or door frames. It was as if the room had been machined out of a single piece of light gray metal.

How did we both get in here? There are no doors.

Jake's heart was pounding. He turned back toward the entity. "Where are you from?"

"THERE IS NO NEED TO TELL YOU DIRECTLY WHERE WE ARE FROM. INSTEAD, YOU ARE TO EXPERIENCE THE ANSWERS FOR YOURSELF."

Jake was confused. "I'm not sure I understand."

A mind blast of information streamed in—thousands of images and thoughts at once. In that moment, Jake understood.

There were 30,000 potentially hospitable worlds within 1000 light years of the Earth. Theirs was the fourth planet that orbited the Zeta Reticuli binary star system, which were sun-like stars similar to the Earth's. Human scientists had already considered it to be an ideal system and capable of supporting life. At a distance of 39 light years, in astronomical terns, it was a pebble's throw away from Earth. Their star system was a billion years older than Earth's sun, giving their civilization a billion-year technical head start on *Homo sapiens*. Humans were using horse-drawn carriages and oil lamps a hundred years ago; they have since developed space flight, atomic weapons, robots, and lasers. Jake couldn't fathom the capabilities of a civilization a million years ahead of Earth's, let alone a billion years ahead. This being before him was orders of magnitude more advanced compared to *Homo sapiens* than Jake was to the apes.

Jake felt almost paralyzed by the sudden stream of information directed into his mind. "I get it. You're really not from around here."

He suddenly felt the need to sit. The world as he had known it evaporated as he staggered back toward the bench. Jake watched in amazement as the metal of the silver bench molded itself into a seat around Jake's legs and rear end as he sat, meeting Jake's immediate needs.

Looking up, he asked his next burning question: "Why are you here?"

The words once again sprung from ideas directed into his mind: "YOU HAVE NEVER BEEN ALONE."

Another onslaught of ideas and visions streamed into his thoughts.

In the distant past, the ancestors of other off-world races were called gods by early human civilizations. They influenced primitive humans, leading them to believe that these beings from the stars were their creators. These races manipulated the human genome, which would have been beyond early human civilization's understanding at the time. Their early teachings, moral and spiritual, were bent into what is now known as the world's religions.

These beings from the fourth planet of the Zeta Reticuli binary star system had been interested in the development, social behavior, and demise of Earth's indigenous inhabitants and civilizations as they evolved, as well as the effect the humans have had on the planet's biosphere and ecosystems over time.

Jake sat silently, processing the information.

They are studying us.

Jake remembered that there had been other slightly smaller beings in the room before. "What happened to the other ones?"

"BIOLOGICAL CYBERNETIC ENTITIES. THEIR TASK IS COMPLETE."

Jake understood the creature's meaning. The other beings were biological robots used by their civilization to carry out hands-on work. They were no longer needed now that Jake was on board and awake.

"Why me?" Even as Jake spoke the words, he couldn't believe the conversation he was having. "You should be communicating with our governments."

"MULTITUDINOUS REASONS."

Ideas seemed to flow around the words resonating in his mind, filling Jake's thoughts with accompanying concepts and images. If the off-world beings presented themselves now to the human population, which was 35 times what it had been during humans' first contacts with off-world beings in their early development, the calculated risk of degradation and the safety of the population, in addition to the horrific social problems that would arise, would not be in anyone's best interest. It would disrupt the fabric of human civilization and likely set humans back further rather than promote human development as a species. Instead, they have been content to observe from a distance.

The visitors found that the problem of communication with *Homo sapiens* had always been with the limitations of the human mind because human brains operate at different brainwave frequencies. To tune into an extraterrestrial mind, an individual needed to be in a deep meditative state, which is difficult for most humans, and near impossible to achieve while remaining fully conscious. Historically, when the ETs had taken humans into a craft, they were usually petrified, making communication impossible.

This is why the visitors won't present themselves before the general public; this problem with communication would prevent any messages getting through to the humans. Instead, the ETs chose to work with individuals on a one-on-one basis—with those that have been able to achieve alpha states of mind and move past their initial fears. Jake's practiced meditative states had amplified his extrasensory perception—a sense few humans have learned to utilize.

The mind machine, Jake recalled.

In his deep meditative state, Jake became super-receptive to the collective consciousness that permeates and binds all beings. It was in this alpha state that Jake perceived the visitors' awareness and answers to his inquiries.

The thrust of images into his mind was reminiscent of seeing his escape from the building. Jake tried to wrap his mind around the realization. "But in the building, those images … the visions … that was you?"

"WHEN YOUR BRAIN IS IN AN ALTERED STATE, YOU BECOME RECEPTIVE TO THE SUPER-CONSCIOUSNESS."

The concepts came faster now. Jake was in a situation in which he had no chance of surviving; the off-world beings assisted in showing him the only way of preserving his life. He did the rest. They have been here from the beginning. Every few generations there have been individuals who have shown promise in shaping the development of the human civilization. ETs have sometimes assisted those individuals to realize their goals. Jake needed help to escape from the building, and the ETs simply showed him a way out.

They have been here all along? Jake thought. *Significant individuals? But that could explain …*

"Albert Eisenstein, Isaac Newton, Nikola Tesla," Jake heard himself blurt out. "Socrates, Pythagoras … the Dalai Lama. Were you guiding them?"

"NOT ALL OF THEM."

The thought stream kept flowing through Jake. The journey he had chosen had the potential to commence a chain of events that could change the way human civilization understands nature's laws, energy, and ultimately their place in the galactic community. It was in the visitors' interests that Jake be successful in his endeavor because they sought to preserve Jake's planet, which nurtured ecosystems and life forms considered a rare gift in the universe. But ultimately the choice was his.

Jake understood that the being was not referring to his choice personally; instead the choice was up to all humans.

Jake felt a growing heaviness in the pit of his stomach. "Why even bother? I mean, nearly every generation of humans that has ever lived knows the meaning of war. We fight over land, we pollute our skies, we pollute our oceans. Our different races can't even get along with each other. How are we supposed to get along with civilizations from other worlds?"

"MANY THINGS ARE IN NEED OF CHANGE."

Mankind was travelling a dangerous course. Jake's mind was being filled with concepts of humans coming into an age of knowledge and industrialized development based on a culture of materialism and power. The pinnacle of human technological achievements, such as harnessing the energy within the atom, has in one form or another been weaponized. Thirst for power and cultural supremacy of differing nations has always led to bloodshed and wars.

"YOU ARE KILLING YOUR WORLD!"

The words grated along the inside of Jake's skull, wrapped in images of dangerous changes taking place in the oceans and the atmosphere. The increasing decay of the ozone by continued production of chemical substances that rise into the stratosphere, pristine rivers and lakes being polluted by over-industrialization, the release of destructive chemicals from combustion motors, and toxic by-products from atom-splitting to create energy. The images morphed into one another with the disorientated nausea of a slow-motion freefall.

A profound dread settled over Jake. Man's assault on the planet has been ongoing since the beginning of the industrial age. It has only increased in scale with the accelerated rate of population and technological advancements of the motor car, jet aircraft, and multi-stage space launch vehicles. This has been accepted as common knowledge by the human race, and yet the changes in their ways have been slow.

Mankind continues to walk these steps of unreason by breaching the laws of nature on a daily basis.

Earth's magnetism has been affected by the atomic explosions that have occurred since the 1940s. The explosions, whether done for testing or in anger, produced a weak repulsion against the Earth.

The planet has been forced out of its normal orbit by a degree not yet detectable by human scientists. The atomic explosions forced changes that will have a far-reaching effect that can, over a timespan that may surpass human civilization, produce catastrophic results.

Scientists have already observed the magnetic north pole slowly creeping over the northern ice islands of Canada toward Russia. Meanwhile the magnetic south pole has been moving toward South America.

Jake drew a breath; he was engulfed in myriad images associated with what he was being told. It felt like an intense dream while being awake.

Human civilization has advanced its evolution, but only in its technical sciences. Its spiritual evolution has been hindered by materialism. Human technology has reached a point where it could destroy the surface of its world with atomic warfare, which has dangerous downstream consequences for its solar system.

In a time that preceded current civilizations, a similar catastrophe occurred in Earth's solar system when a planet was populated by a biped, carbon-based humanoid species similar to humans. Their technology also advanced to an understanding of the workings of the atom. However, through the pursuit of power and warring among themselves, their planet was destroyed. A resulting explosion, its devastating power beyond a magnitude yet known by man, ripped the planet into billions of fragments. Its pieces still circled the sun between the orbits of Mars and Jupiter and are known to the human race as the asteroid belt.

Fragments of this ancient world still threaten the Earth by way of meteor strikes, which once annihilated a great proportion of Earth's life in the distant past. Scientists have tracked the skies in an effort to map any rogue asteroids that may one day threaten Earth's future.

For centuries, modern man has not possessed the values or ethics of a developed civilization. Because of this, the human race's chance of eternal survival has been slim. It has blocked its own way to cosmic integration.

The current civilization is the most important that has ever lived. Humans are on the verge of understanding new branches of science and physics which will bring with it more abundant and cleaner energies. Humans have taken their first steps toward a global government with the United Nations and European Union, and they already possess a global communications infrastructure with the internet. The visitors see great potential in the humans.

It is an obligation to all more highly developed species to assist less-developed civilizations, but not to influence their evolution. This duty is an obligation of all life in the universe, and is known to the visitors as the Creational Law.

Pouring through the avalanche of images and concepts that flowed through his thoughts, Jake's mind felt like it was weightlifting. He was still reeling from what the visitor had laid out before him. Jake felt a physical yearning to change the subject. The severity of what had been shared had been taken to heart; he had felt and breathed the information engulfing him.

I think I prefer talking, Jake told himself.

A moment passed. Slowly, Jake looked at the creature, fighting to build his confidence. "Can I see your ship?"

CHAPTER 73

"Jake is a very clever boy."

Dr. Charles Reilly was seated in Mark's living room examining the business card with his name handwritten on the front and the single word *Shift* on the back. Across the room, Natasha and Mark looked on with confused expressions.

The scientist sensed the next question coming. "This is a code."

"Code?" Natasha's voice cracked, and she looked increasingly puzzled.

"If you had been detained and searched by the government," Reilly went on, "not even our cryptographic algorithms would have broken this code because they're programmed to search out patterns, not colors."

Natasha and Mark exchanged a glance, still unsure of what the scientist was talking about.

"*Shift* is a code?" Mark asked.

"No, not *Shift* on its own." Reilly held up the card. "*Shift* written in red."

There was a long silence, and the scientist sensed that Mark and Natasha were lost.

"When light is emitted from a star in motion, its wavelength is stretched out. The faster the motion, the longer the wavelength. And as its wavelength changes, so does its color."

Mark nodded blankly.

"As its wavelength increases, it's said to become redder, or shifted to the red end of the visible spectrum."

"Redshift?" Natasha offered.

"It was the redshift in the light observed by Edwin Hubble that led to his discovery that all galaxies appeared to be moving away from each other. If all galaxies were moving away from each other, then once upon a time, all galaxies must have originated from a single point in space."

"The Big Bang?" Mark asked.

"Precisely," Reilly said. "It was redshift that proved there was indeed a moment of creation."

"But it doesn't necessarily prove there was a creator," Mark countered.

"No, it doesn't." Charles gave a patient smile. "But isn't it interesting that the three of us are together speaking of God."

Natasha's eyes rose to look at Mark then Dr. Reilly. "We stopped at a church when we were on the run. He didn't tell me why."

Dr. Reilly's smile grew wider. "Now what would be the odds of the three of us having a conversation that would lead to the creation event soon after you recently visited a church?"

"He left something there!" Mark blurted out. "He

knew that the two of you would work it out and wanted you both to find it because he knew something was going to happen to him!"

The words wrenched at Natasha's stomach. She glanced away, unable to face the two men.

The scientist's expression grew to one of concern. "Indeed. But I don't think what he left there will remain safe."

Without a word, Natasha left the room.

Mark turned toward Charles with a look of despair, realizing he hadn't chosen his words wisely.

Reilly's words grew somber. "I think we both know what is waiting at the church. But she needs to find somewhere safe to lie low until we decide what to do with it. Perhaps out of town with a friend."

❧

Mark found Natasha sitting on a bench in the backyard. Her tear-soaked eyes shone with loss and anguish.

He felt a fresh wave of remorse. "I'm sorry."

She looked at him as if he had slapped her in the face.

Mark cleared his throat, feeling suddenly uncomfortable. "Look, he's not like the rest of us. He has the mind of a mathematician, the curiosity of a scientist, and the soul of an artist."

Natasha's tears were now streaming; she looked away and covered her mouth, as if to muffle a silent cry.

Hesitantly, he sat beside her. "I've known Jake a long time. When we were in high school, we had this gym teacher who used to make us kids line up on either side of the basketball court. We played this game where the teacher placed a big, heavy medicine ball in the center of the basketball court then called out the name of one kid from each side. The first kid to drag the heavy medicine ball to their side of the court won. The ball weighed a ton—it was a test of strength."

Natasha remained silent, looking away.

"Then one day," Mark said, "the teacher decided to be a smartass. She called out every person from each team. It was chaos; there were 40 teenage boys wrestling each other, trying to drag this huge heavy ball to their side of the court. I was on Jake's team, and we were about to lose. The other team had the strongest kid in our grade. He managed to pick up the heavy ball and carry it to his side; he was inches away from winning. Jake rammed him head on and picked the guy up over his shoulders, while he held the ball, and used him to plough through all the other kids to our side of the court. I couldn't believe my eyes. We won."

Natasha was drying her eyes. He gently laid a comforting hand on her shoulder.

Mark's voice was determined. "My point is, ever since that day in gym class, I've witnessed him do things that defy human ability … again and again. Wherever he is, he'll find some way to make it back. Of that I'm certain."

CHAPTER 74

Jake Marcel swallowed his remaining fear as he followed the extraterrestrial entity through the curved corridor. He noticed that the creature was barely five feet tall, and yet the corridor was tall enough to provide generous headroom for the tallest of human basketball players. He still saw no discernible source of light despite the glow that bathed the silver walls and ceiling of the corridor.

He tried hard not to stare at the entity that walked beside him. The creature's movements were efficient and elegant; it moved with an incorporeal weightlessness.

Jake could barely contain the burning question he had come to ask: "The crashed spacecraft my grandfather found?"

"A CONVEYANCE TRANSPORTING SYNTHETIC BIOLOGICAL ENTITIES NOT OF OUR RACE" was the response.

Images flooded Jake's mind. In the years 1946 through 1953, there were five cases where extraterrestrial ships crashed on the surface of the Earth. In the crash colloquially dubbed the Roswell Incident, not one but two alien ships were involved, which collided and crashed in different parts of the land in the western North America.

The Earth's magnetic field is not stable; it's subject to cyclical variations with unpredictable eddy currents and vortexes even under favorable conditions. Whenever a conveyance powered by magnetic drives was engulfed in a strong field fluctuation, it disrupted the repelling field generated from the ship's drive causing the craft to glide uncontrollably off its path.

In the 1947 case, one of the ships was caught in an electrical atmospheric fluctuation, which caused it to collide with the other ship. The electrical fluctuation was caused by a strong electrical discharge during a weather event.

"If you've been studying us … can you help us?" Jake ventured to ask, his true meaning wrapped in the emotion that accompanied the words.

"WE HAVE CONVEYED WARNINGS ABOUT UNKIND INTELLIGENCES."

Jake's mind intently swirled with images of the 2002 Hampshire crop circle, which was accompanied by an image of an alien being not unlike the creature that led him along the curved corridor.

So it was a warning, Jake realized.

The ET species depicted in the crop circle, the species that entered into a treaty with the US Government, is in peril. An ancient species at a cellular level, they suffer from a genetic condition whereby the information stored in the nucleolus of their cells can no longer be readily accessed; they have lost their natural ability to replicate and regenerate.

To combat this condition, they developed medical technology to grow artificial tissue to replace their defective organs with synthesized substitutes.

Over eons, they had become artificial shadows of their former selves. Genetic breaks in their DNA were common among their species—genes from various compatible species in addition to artificial genes were used to fill the gaps in their DNA strings. So much of their original selves had been replaced that they were no longer naturally born organisms. Instead, they had become organic machines grown from synthesized materials. Knowledge and intellect was transferred to their synthetically grown brains; however, they had lost the ability to feel emotions.

As a result, they were fully functional, organic cybernetic organisms, but were incapable of feelings and emotions as humans experience them. They no longer felt alive as humans do.

The reason they were interested in human genetics is that *Homo sapiens* had DNA compatible with their own. They were harvesting intact DNA strings from humans and compatible Earth animals to splice with their own to repair their broken strings. They attempted to undo the species-wide genetic degradation caused by many millennia of cloning.

The abductions, Jake thought with a gasp.

The ET species interested in the genome of *Homo sapiens* were the same beings that met with Eisenhower in 1954 and signed a treaty with the US Government that would give them access to non-terrestrial technology. The agreement was for the visitors to move in the skies unhindered and to have access to a small portion of the human herd for their genetic study and needs, with returned humans having no living memory of the event.

In return, the US Government would have access to off-world technology for study and adaption to terrestrial applications. The Eisenhower administration didn't know it at the time, but the visitors ignored the terms of the agreement, hence the warning about unkind intelligences depicted in the crop circle.

The extraterrestrial species knew *Homo sapiens* to be simple-minded creatures; they gave false information about the workings of their advanced technology and thus received more out of the exchange than the humans did. They were well aware that humans would lack the scientific understanding of the technology they were given.

Jake shuddered, recalling Dr. Reilly's account of the 1954 Eisenhower meeting.

They never told us the complete truth.

Jake kept pace with the being by his side as he was led around the curved corridor. Similar to the room Jake had woken up in, the walls were silver and featureless without any corners, giving the impression of being molded from a single piece of metal.

Jake had a thousand questions he wanted to ask. "But what about our wars, can you help …?"

Before Jake could finish, his mind was again rocked by entering thoughts. "WE ARE NOT GOING TO STEP IN TO BREAK UP YOUR QUARRELS LIKE A PARENT WITH THEIR CHILDREN."

The subtext was profound. Humans need to learn from their own mistakes and care for their planet. Only when they demonstrate that they can care for their environment and each other will they be invited to join the cosmic community.

From the visitors' point of view, it was the misleading explanations that some religions espoused about the meaning of mankind's life that had been a disruptive influence, leading to bloodshed and wars on Earth for thousands of years. There had been no greater loss of life on Earth than that caused by persecution in the name of religion. The element of fear had been used all too often to control the population, preventing humans from developing and realizing their place in the cosmic community.

The visitor didn't need to explain. Humans tend to shrink the reality of the world they live in down to their daily routines and material possessions. Human cultural evolution restricts them from gaining an understanding of the universe in which they exist.

Jake knew that proof of intelligent life elsewhere in the universe would be a paradigm shift, forcing humans to look up from their petty skirmishes over land and religions. Humans would no longer see themselves as a collective of nations, skin colors, and religions, but for the first time look past their differences and regard themselves as members of a single species in a universe teeming with life.

It would no longer be a question of whether extraterrestrials exist, but whether humans were ready to believe.

Jake took a tremulous breath. "Can you give me something to take back, so I can prove there is more to our universe than just ourselves and our petty differences?"

For the first time, the creature that led Jake turned to meet him with his large eyes. The effect was hypnotic; its impossibly dark, cat-like pupils seemed draw Jake in. They were the peaceful eyes of a deep, philosophical thinker studying Jake with quizzical indifference.

The answer was in his mind in an instant.

The cosmic law of interplanetary contact was that the free will of any species never be infringed on. This natural law was intended to prevent one race from interfering with the evolution of another.

If a species were to achieve advanced knowledge too early in its development, it would not utilize such knowledge wisely, which would lead to otherwise avoidable catastrophes. This was the situation humans faced, having discovered the secrets of atomic science without the maturity to control it. Such knowledge had already been applied for destructive purposes in the form of atomic weaponry.

Mankind's technical advancements had always far outweighed its social development. To supply technical information to a developing species beyond its grasp of knowledge was a breach of this natural law. It increased the gap between humans' intellectual development and their almost nonexistent social development because mankind would rather play with their rovers on Mars than assist a third of the planet's population that lives in poverty.

Jake Marcel could only stare as his mind swirled with the barrage of incoming images and thoughts.

If Jake were to take something from the visitors' craft back with him, it would not be long before its underlying technology was reverse-engineered into a terrestrial application that would profit the possessing nation, or worse still, be developed into a weapon that could result in self-destruction.

Homo sapiens were at a stage of development when

every increase in knowledge was dangerous because of humanity's insane thirst for dominance and power. Thus, aiding the destructive tendency of humanity's scientific pursuits was not permitted.

A complete change in mankind's thinking was necessary before humanity would be allowed access to more advanced technology. Outside help beyond Earth's skies would only be possible when humans, a warring race, gave up their hunger for dominance, power, and materialism.

Humans had the potential to take the next step in their evolution, but their growth as a civilization was stunted by the greed of the very powerful few who influenced their governments and kept humanity dependent on their current energy sources.

Jake understood instantly: Oil.

It was unfortunate that the few elite within the human race were able to hinder the development of abundant, clean energy.

Humanity's next big step was to overcome this dependency on petrochemical energy, as mankind's grasp of physics was starting to understand the nature of the universe and how to create new energy sources.

They approached a closed door on the right side of the curved corridor. The being who led Jake slowed, stopped short, and then faced the closed entrance. The change in pace pulled Jake from his cyclone of thoughts.

Studying the closed passageway, Jake glanced back at his interstellar host. "So, where exactly are we?"

CHAPTER 75

"He's gone!" Natasha sobbed into her phone.

She was riding in the back of a taxi leaving a voicemail message.

"Jake has disappeared. Jack, when you get this message, call me. I'm coming to your parents' house."

The last half-hour had been a blur. Natasha had taken Dr. Reilly's advice to find somewhere safe to lie low for a while. On route to her best friend's parents' house, the iconic Las Vegas skyline had long since disappeared over the horizon behind her. Ahead was open desert knotted with ridges and bridges crossing ravines.

She questioned whether seeking refuge with her friend's parents was in fact the right thing to do. *Would I be dragging them into this as well?*

Natasha tried to gather her thoughts. The government had been able to find her somehow when she and Jackie were in the downtown café. What could they possibly want with her when they also witnessed Jake's disappearance?

She endured a sharp pang of loss as the image of Jake

going over the cliff played in her mind again. Natasha still felt disturbed by the agent in black asking if she knew where Jake had gotten to.

Where could he be?

The sensation of the taxi suddenly slowing snapped her back to the present. Leaning forward between the two front seats, she peered beyond the halted cars ahead to see what the commotion was.

The taxi driver sensed her apprehension. "It's not an accident. Looks like a roadblock of some sort. Police are checking all cars for some reason. A bridge is a stupid place to do it."

Natasha didn't hear the driver launch into a diatribe about the police causing more delays than necessary by blocking the bridge. A crushing fear gripped her as she looked down at her cell phone.

The revelation crashed like a wave: *My phone signal!*

The taxi hadn't yet come to a complete stop when Natasha leaped from the slow-moving vehicle. Finding her feet, she broke into a frantic sprint back toward the bridge entrance.

The driver's face registered confusion as he watched the girl run back in the direction they came from in his mirror.

Seven seconds later, Natasha felt herself skidding to a stop. Her heart seized when she saw it.

Rising from under the bridge like a leviathan was the angular silhouette of an Apache gunship, its menacing bulk bearing down on the petrified girl. Natasha stood in frozen terror in front of the huge, ferocious-looking attack helicopter.

CHAPTER 76

Jake's interstellar host gestured toward a closed archway on the corridor wall. Jake watched in dumbstruck awe as joints materialize before him within the polished silver surface. The joints formed the shape of a large spiral, each claw of the spiral silently retracting within the wall to form an opening like an iris.

As Jake stepped into the round room, he looked up to follow the domed ceiling. The room was 16 feet in diameter, its silver walls were identical to the ones in the room where he had woken up and bore the same fine, hexagonal indentations. Facing away from the door was a single high-backed chair positioned in the middle of the otherwise empty room.

Jake's gaze fell to the chair as he approached; it was composed of the same dull silver metal of the walls, angular with molded rounded edges and a single leg that attached to the floor.

If he was standing in a control room, it did not look

like any conventional aircraft, spacecraft, or military craft he had ever seen.

As Jake drew closer to the chair, the lighting in the room dimmed.

He paused then took another step. Pinpoints of light became visible through the walls and ceiling.

Instinct directed Jake to take a step back; the light levels in the room returned.

Jake's skin prickled with foreboding. He took three full steps to stand right beside the chair. The room again grew dim, the points of light became brighter, and a cosmos of stars blazed into existence around him to fill the room with an almost infinite spread of constellations. The walls darkened into the background of deep, black space.

The scene before him was surreal; he felt as if he were standing in the emptiness of space. Jake stared in open mouth wonder. He felt his knees go weak. "You've got to be eff'ing kidding me!"

Before him was the breathtaking vision of the Jovian system.

CHAPTER 77

Father Jordan had finished his late afternoon mass. With the church empty, he quietly packed away the trays and communion bowls for the next day's service. The deep echo of a knock at the church's front doors drew his attention. Surprised at the interruption, the priest closed the storage cupboards and emerged from behind the altar, making his way down the long aisle to unlock the front doors.

When the heavy door opened, Mark and Dr. Reilly set eyes on the same priest who had opened the door for Jake very early that same morning.

Dr. Charles Reilly spoke first. "Sorry to disturb you, Father, but a dear friend sent us. You may be keeping something safe for him, something he may have wanted passed on to us."

The scientist noticed a surprised flicker of recognition behind the priest's eyes.

Ten minutes later, Mark and Dr. Reilly found themselves sitting in the front pew before the altar. The scientist had quickly explained to the priest that Jake had disappeared and that a cryptic message left for them had led the doctor and Jake's friend to Father Jordan's church. After the priest confirmed that Jake had indeed visited earlier, and that Jake had asked him to keep an important package safe, he disappeared into the church's back rooms to retrieve the object.

"Jake said that the two of you would come looking for this. But you say he is now nowhere to be found?" the priest said, appearing from behind the altar carrying a wooden box.

Both Mark and the scientist were drawn to the object cradled by the approaching priest.

"Only bits of his motorcycle were left at the bottom of the canyon. There was no body," Mark said, his eyes never leaving the wooden box.

The priest considered the comment for a moment, and then placed the box on the pew next to Mark.

"When they came up out of the water," the priest proclaimed, "the Spirit of the Lord suddenly took Philip away, and the eunuch did not see him again, but went on his way rejoicing. Philip, however, appeared at Azotus and traveled about, preaching the Gospel in all the towns until he reached Caesarea."

Mark and the scientist exchanged a puzzled look.

"Acts chapter 8:39–40," Father Jordan explained. "My sons, people have disappeared before, so how is this any different? Have faith, your friend will appear again."

Mark turned to Charles and whispered, "Who is the eunuch?"

The scientist frowned but didn't answer.

With a curious expression, Mark turned toward the wooden box. It didn't look like something Jake would have owned. The box was handcrafted with ornate symbols of Catholicism delicately decorating its sides and lid.

He placed it on his lap then slowly opened the lid with both hands. The inside was lined with deep purple velvet and looked as if it had recesses to hold several long cups or chalices. Laid across the recesses was a metal object; its surface glistened with a familiar violet-silver glow.

Even though he had already seen the unearthly object, Dr. Reilly's eyes widened at the sight of the little I-beam. An object of enormous consequence, its very existence held the answer to mankind's oldest question. Never before had a single object had the power to rewrite everything humans knew about the history of the solar system and the development of mankind.

It was then that the ground rumbled beneath the church. Mark heard the deep thrum of a helicopter's turbine. The machine flew low over the church and descended beyond the building's front doors.

Instinctively, Mark closed the box and leaped to his feet. The scientist also found himself suddenly standing, his gaze following the sound of the helicopter as it landed. The priest stood, startled. Charles felt an uneasy premonition as he turned to Mark.

"We gotta run! Or they'll get the …" Mark swallowed, apparently unable to say the words.

Charles placed a soft hand on the young man's shoulder. "Believe me; if we can hear them, then they've already got us."

᭓

With fierce military precision, black-clad soldiers poured through the front doors of the church. Fanning out along the walls, they advanced on the three sole occupants of the building. Simultaneously, additional teams of black-clad figures appeared from behind the altar and unseen entrances from the sides of the building.

Mark spun wildly as he watched the armed figures converge from all directions to surround the party of three. His face froze in an expression of fear as one of the bulkier figures stepped toward him. It was the only soldier without a weapon raised.

The bulky soldier paused, looking directly into Mark's eyes.

Mark's expression turned to one of recognition. *You're the one from the bar!*

"Stand aside, soldier. We *are* walking out of here." Dr. Reilly's tone was defiant.

Bravo raised an eyebrow at the scientist. "Really ... how so? I count three unarmed civilians and four dozen fully armed, highly trained Navy SEALs and Delta Forces. Perhaps I miscalculated."

Turning to Mark, a dangerous smile crossed Bravo's lips. "Is that box from Jake?"

"Jake who?" Mark barked, more forcefully than he intended.

Mark again felt a patient hand on his shoulder; Reilly was shepherding Mark to stand behind the scientist. Mark slipped in behind Dr. Reilly, his eyes never leaving Bravo's.

"Let go of me! I can walk by myself," an angry female voice echoed from somewhere beside them.

The gun barrels trained on Mark and the scientist parted to make way for three more figures. Dr. Charles Reilly felt a fresh wave of remorse engulfing him when he saw Natasha being marched in by Alpha. Following closely behind was a man dressed in a black suit.

Natasha's eyes softened at the sight of Dr. Reilly and Mark.

The dark-suited man smiled at Dr. Reilly. "You know how this works, Charles. You wrote the field manual on collateral contamination and containment."

"Hello, Stephen." Reilly's voice was tinged with disappointment and defiance.

Natasha's eyes flashed confusion as she turned to Sabre then back to Dr. Reilly. "You know each other?"

It was as if her words had physically shot pain across Reilly's chest. "It was a different time."

Mr. Stephen Sabre drew a deep breath, apparently ignoring the question. "Well, it appears we have a situation here that could turn out most unfortunate for you and your new friends."

A tense silence settled within the lofty arches of the church.

Sabre shot a glance at Bravo, as if to say "grab the box."

Complying with the unspoken order, Bravo stepped toward Mark and pried the wooden box from his grasp. Mark's attention shifted to the assault rifle strapped to the soldier's arm.

"Wow, is that the MK16 SCAR-L with a custom grip and muzzle brake attachment?"

Bravo cocked his head in surprise, startled to hear that

Mark even knew the weapon's componentry terms. "Which military branch did you work in?"

Mark was confused by the question. "*Call of Duty.* I'm up to Prestige 3, level 48."

Looking appalled, the soldier waved off the answer and handed the wooden box to Mr. Sabre. A satisfied smile slowly crossed Sabre's face as he peeked inside the box. Immediately recognizing the object, he quickly closed the lid and handed it back to Bravo.

Natasha, Mark, and Dr. Reilly exchanged uneasy looks. Father Jordan stood in perplexed silence.

Sabre turned on his heel and headed for the church's front doors. "Bring them. Leave the priest."

Both Mark and Dr. Reilly felt gun barrels on their backs, pushing them to follow Mr. Sabre. Leaving the confused priest behind, Natasha, Mark, and Dr. Reilly were escorted out the front doors of the building by the horde of black figures.

Pausing at the top of the steps that led to the church's front doors, Dr. Reilly heard Mark whistle at the sight that met them. Amassed before the church was an army of black SUVs, an exotic looking helicopter, and an Apache gunship, both of which had evidently landed in the middle of street.

Dr. Charles Reilly had no illusions about what was about to happen.

CHAPTER 78

Colorful and hypnotic, the image of the Jovian system was unforgettable.

Jake Marcel did not have the vocabulary or command of the English language to express the scene of staggering beauty before him. His words were barely a whisper. "It's beautiful … I had no idea."

Jake was fixated on the imposing presence of Jupiter. Vivid and compelling, it was a majestic and mesmerizing vista, as if the room itself opened to the limitlessness of space dominated by the colossal curvature of Jupiter's form. The depths of its Great Red Spot, its Earth-sized hurricane, dominating his spectacular view.

"Oh, Natasha," Jake gasped. "My God! You're not going to believe what I'm looking at right now!"

Pausing for a moment, another of Jake's questions dawned on him.

"God!" Jake turned back to his short, gray companion. "Do you believe in God?"

The small visitor stood motionless; seconds later the

answer poured directly into Jake's mind in the form of concepts and ideas.

In essence, one common trait was shared by all life in the universe. These visitors from the fourth planet that orbited the Zeta Reticuli binary star system were searching for the same answers as humanity was. Some races in the universe were more advanced in their understanding of the one, the universal conscious, but others less so. Races that seeded life in the universe were one step closer to understanding the universal conscious, the way that Jake would one day understand how to be a parent when he bore offspring of his own.

Jake was not sure he understood, but didn't dare ask the small extraterrestrial being to clarify. Nevertheless, he tried to absorb the answer as he turned back to the celestial scene that seemed to surround them both.

Jake's gaze sailed from moon to moon that orbited the colossal giant, observing clarity and surface features he'd never seen in textbook pictures. Stepping forward for a closer look, he moved as if through a dream. His eyes traced the scar lines of ridges and fractures that laced Europa, taking in the brightness of its reflective, icy surface. He marveled at the massive volcanic eruptions that sculpted Io's surface.

Barely able to believe what he was seeing, he scanned the faint dusty rings that circled the immense planet. Unlike the prominent icy rings of Saturn, Jupiter's rings resembled a faint, flat halo. Even so, Jake gaped at something he never knew existed.

Rings around Jupiter?

In a state of wonder, Jake's attention was drawn to

an object that orbited the imposing giant. It was tubular, cigar-shaped, and dull dark gray. With no sense of scale, there was no way for Jake to discern its size.

His eyes bulged at the possibility. "That's not ours!"

With a sudden upwelling of astonishment, his gaze fell upon a second orbiting object, then a third. Three objects orbited the mammoth planet, all inclined at the same angle.

Are we on one of those things?

"How can we not have seen your satellites? We've got probes of our own out here!"

The small visitor remained silent.

Turning to his host, Jake repeated his former request. "You brought me all this way … You know that my race needs help. I'm not asking for your technology. All I'm asking for is proof that we're not alone, that we're part of a bigger galactic community."

Even as the words left his mouth, Jake felt it ironic that he was having this conversation with a member of a race not his own.

Jake's resolve hardened. "I want to show our scientists proof that other civilizations have overcome the problems we're now facing."

"WE CAN'T INFLUENCE YOUR GROWTH."

The words were deafening inside Jake's skull. The cosmic laws prevented intervention.

Every cosmic race had the right to develop and grow on their own, despite some races having met self-destruction upon discovery of nuclear energy in the distant past. Even the most insignificant sample of material that had been manufactured by the Zeta Reticulians would be at risk of being absorbed and adapted into terrestrial technology.

Homo sapiens would have the potential to do harm to themselves. Humanity was not ready for the responsibility that accompanies technology beyond their means.

Jake found the confidence to counter, "But didn't you—"

Before Jake could finish, he was silenced by the response entering his mind. "YES. WE HAVE ASSISTED."

The Zeta Reticulian had stepped in when Jake flew off the ridge. But Jake should not forget that it had been he who made the choice to speed toward the cliff. Given the circumstances over Jake's lifetime that led him to the cliff, preserving Jake's life had been the better option. The course of Jake's life had been influenced by events outside his control, and beyond the Earth's skies. Saving Jake was, as the human idiom proclaimed, the better of two evils.

The burning question now, however, was how would Jake prove his experience with interstellar beings without producing some tangible piece of extraterrestrial evidence. As Jake remembered how he'd been helped by the off-world visitor, he felt something far more fundamental resonate within him.

His sensei's words called out to him across the vast expanse of space: If you can't fight fire with fire, then use the fire against itself.

Jake felt the hair on the back of his neck stand on end. "I have an idea!"

CHAPTER 79

Mark stood with his face pressed up against a large one-way window that dominated the brightly lit room where was confined. He strained to peer into the dark space he suspected was on the other side. The single door burst open, startling him. Mr. Sabre appeared, taking an ominous step toward the room's lone occupant. In his wake followed a muscular guard.

Grabbing Mark by the neck, Sabre shoved his detainee into a chair that faced a stainless-steel table positioned in the center of the small cell. Without a word, Mr. Sabre sat down on the remaining chair to face Mark. The muscular guard stood at attention, blocking the closed door.

Shaking off the forceful shove, Mark was almost excited. "Is this one of those secret men-in-black interrogation rooms?"

Sabre ignored the question. There was a long silence as he studied the captive. Mark's notion of excitement evaporated into a slowly sinking sensation. He seemed to shrink as Sabre's stare bored into him.

Mr. Sabre's words dripped with disdain. "Tell me about Jake's communications with the IBEs."

Mark gave an odd expression.

"Interstellar ... biological ... entities," Sabre clarified, the pauses between his words punctuating his diminishing patience for the captive.

Mark's eyes shot up. "So you guys acknowledge that they do exist!"

Sabre leveled his gaze at him. "There are things out there that do transcend human understanding. But what I may or may not acknowledge is irrespective of your having the ability to spread the word."

The unspoken threat made Mark swallow hard.

Sabre fixed him with a penetrating stare. "Where do you think your friend has gone?"

Mark was enjoying the rare chance to teach an NSA agent something about classified information. "Well, we've seen a copy of the military's top secret ET Technology, Recovery, and Disposal Manual. Perhaps he went to have a meeting with them to discuss that!"

"It won't matter if you try to go after him," Mark continued, surprised by the confidence in his own voice. "You'll learn that he doesn't back down easily."

A satisfying smile crept across Mark's face. "But you know that already. He was able to dodge your F22 ... You got something else to go after him with?"

Sabre was unmoved by the comments. A subtle, refined warning came across in his tone. "Keep in mind, we are specialists in gathering intelligence, including extracting intel from unwilling participants. You think about that for a while. If you need a demonstration of our methods, you just let me know when I return."

With that, Sabre left the small interrogation room followed by his guard. Mark stared after him, his expression turning grim as the closed door was locked from the outside.

⁓

Natasha sat at the table alone in the interrogation room. She ignored the one-way window to her side, her focus trained on the small cell's single door.

As the door opened, Mr. Sabre stepped in. He studied Natasha with a practiced calm, but she saw danger in his eyes. It was as if his stare was encroaching on her personal space, inducing mental claustrophobia. He took the single unoccupied seat across from her.

After a short pause, Sabre spoke. "Why did Jake run to the canyons?"

"He felt like an early morning ride," she said, her blue eyes testing him. "Why am I here?"

He smiled, clearly appreciating the question. "You are here because one of our citizens seems to have disappeared off the face of the Earth. And we need to know where he's gone."

She felt a fury rise from deep within. *Almost to the bottom of a cliff because of you!*

Mr. Sabre continued. "Who was he there to meet?"

She stared at him, offering no response. There was a tense silence.

"Where is Jake?"

"You should tell me!" she declared, her piercingly blue

eyes boring into him with rage and resilience. "I'm just a messenger."

"Is that so?" he said, amused.

She glanced away.

"And what would be the message?"

Natasha slowly swung her gaze his way, like an artillery cannon traversing. "That we are not alone."

CHAPTER 80

"How's your health?"

Mr. Sabre stood in front of the closed door of the interrogation room that held Dr. Charles Reilly. The scientist sat calmly at the small table in the center of the cell.

"Why, Stephen? How long do I have?"

Sabre said nothing. Reilly sensed from his eyes that the NSA agent knew more than he was willing to reveal.

Dr. Reilly took a patient breath, his expression a mix of disapproval and disappointment for his former colleague. "What are you doing, Stephen?"

"No, Charles!" Sabre retorted, his tone intensifying. "I need to ask you, what do *you* think *you* are doing? Why were you helping Jake?"

The scientist gave a compassionate smile. He could see the dangerous combination of emotion in the agent's eyes: anger, confusion, betrayal.

The agent's tone was suddenly harsh. "We used to be on the same team!"

"And whose team is that?" Reilly asked. "Ours or theirs?"

The agent was fuming now. "*They* have kept the population shielded from the harsh truth for over half a century. You were the one who explained that public disclosure would show ancient connections between an extraterrestrial civilization, Earth, and the emergence of the human race that would collapse the fundamentalist orthodox belief systems of every religion on Earth."

More to the point, the scientist knew, was that the theological and philosophical implications would be immediate. The world's religious leaders would need to come to terms with a universe where humans were no longer the sole intelligent life. Current beliefs in creation and God would need to evolve to accept the existence of intelligent life elsewhere in the universe.

Dr. Reilly had led the group charged with managing contact with interstellar biological entities, or IBEs, as well as the study and integration of their technologies on behalf of the National Security Council. Agent Stephen Sabre had been assigned by the NSA to control and contain the secrecy that accompanied the scientist's activities and deep black programs.

"*Damn it!*" Sabre said, his patience wearing thin. "You wrote the manual on ET crash site retrieval and sanitization. And you know better than anyone with a seat on the NSC's SSG-36 what ET tech will do to the world energy infrastructure."

The agent didn't need to finish. Reilly understood he was speaking of the world's biggest industry—petroleum. Once the world learns that Reilly's team had reverse-engineered from the ET technology a viable, readily available, economically producible energy source, oil would be devalued overnight and bring an end to the petroleum industry.

Governments and groups who had invested trillions of euros and dollars into existing petroleum infrastructure would find their assets and resources instantly worthless.

Middle Eastern states that were reliant on oil export will no longer have a demand for their product. Dictatorships like Saudi, the UAE, Bahrain, and their neighbors would also lose their power over their citizens. Geopolitical unrest would be inevitable and spread across religions where tension between governments, citizens, and neighboring countries were already critically high.

This scenario had been repeatedly examined by the keepers of the secret, and they kept arriving at one inescapable conclusion: mass geopolitical unrest could erupt in the Middle East as a result of the devaluing of their resources and currency. Existing security treaties and alliances would force the hands of the superpowers to get involved on both sides. Although not public knowledge, there are several nuclear weapons in the region controlled by nervous Middle Eastern interests. After previous decades of tension and fighting, the resulting war had the potential to be nuclear. If it were to start, it would affect everybody on the planet. And if left to escalate, it could set back human civilization hundreds of years.

Dr. Reilly had always thought this catastrophic scenario was predicted by Einstein when in 1947 he remarked, "I know not with what weapons World War III will be fought, but World War IV will be fought with sticks and stones."

Sabre's growling voice pulled the scientist back. "The cost

of maintaining this cover-up is far less than the cost of letting it out in the open."

The scientist's voice remained cool and calm. "And what of the costs of Dr. Steven Greer, Dr. Vladik Primakov, and numerous other brilliant minds you've sanitized over the years? Were their lives justified in the cover-up?"

"Collateral fallout!" Sabre spat back. "*Acceptable* numbers when weighed against the potential thousands that could be impacted. *We* were working for the same cause."

"Perhaps once," Reilly said, his tone composed. "But we are not the same. I was exploring new possibilities in science and physics to produce new energy systems. You are a killer."

The agent was in a boiling rage. "The nation on Earth that first acquires this technology will be the dominant force on this planet militarily, economically, and politically. *We* took necessary actions that others didn't have the stomach, the balls, or even the conviction to prevent the possibility of—"

"Yes, the possibility of one single state or nation monopolizing this new technology," Reilly said before he could finish, his voice gentle. "But that's just it; we became the very thing we set out to prevent by keeping what we learned hidden."

Stephen Sabre stared at the scientist in disbelief.

"We're not in a cold war any more, Stephen. And the Earth is still in the 1800s as far as energy generation and transportation are concerned. Gas, oil, and coal are still our primary sources of energy, and the combustion engine runs our way life. They are also equally the primary causes of our air and water pollution."

Mr. Sabre reached the end of his rope. He exploded, "So you turned your back on your accomplishments?"

"From the particle beam weapon for the Strategic Defense Initiative program," the agent said, "to chemically driven, molecular-sized micro-processors that run billions of times faster than conventional computer chips. How do you justify walking away from your sworn oath of secrecy? Instead you've been helping to bring this all out into the open!"

"I also left our work on genetically engineered biotoxins and neurotoxic weapons for biotoxic warfare," the scientist said. "Let's not forget kinetic energy weapons or the multiple impact re-entry vehicles with six nuclear warheads to each ICBM. We created weapons that could take out six cities in the one shot."

Charles's voice was heavy with emotion. "I'm tired, Stephen; I've existed in the gray area between right and wrong for far too long."

Sabre looked at him as if he was insane.

"Let the kids go, Stephen. You have the specimen, you have the report, and the key people who could have disseminated the information are dead. And I don't have long to go."

The agent averted his eyes, saying nothing.

A moment passed, and the scientist smiled. "I'll take your silence as your intent to not release them. Well, then," Dr. Reilly said, "you know how chaos theory can be described by a butterfly flapping its wings in Africa causing a hurricane over the Atlantic?"

"The butterfly effect. What's your point?" Sabre hissed, forcing a smile.

"Well, Stephen, I suspect that the particular butterfly you seek is about to flap its wings."

CHAPTER 81

The depths of Jake's amazement at witnessing the splendor of Jupiter and its moons with his own eyes seemed limitless.

With a renewed vigor, he tried to gather his thoughts about his idea.

Casting his mind back to his physics classes in college, he remembered it took light eight minutes to reach the Earth from the sun. Similarly, it took light 43 minutes to reach Jupiter from the sun.

He raised a hand to feel the stubble on his chin. It was almost the same length that had shrouded his jaw when he and Natasha busted down the front door of his house that morning to make their getaway toward the desert canyons. That meant it hadn't taken the extraterrestrial spacecraft days or weeks to arrive at Jupiter's doorstep, despite it taking NASA's probes decades to traverse the same distance.

These guys must be able to travel at the speed of light.

Jake did the calculation in his head. "Okay, so at

light speed, it would have taken us about 35 minutes to get here."

As Jake stepped toward his interstellar companion to pitch his question and move away from the central control chair, the room began to materialize around him. With the walls now faintly visible, it was as if they stood in a glass room orbiting the Jovian system.

Jake didn't let the change in the room's appearance distract him. "How long would it take you to find one of our Voyager spacecrafts?"

"INSTANTANEOUS."

Jake thought hard, trying to comprehend this information. The Voyager space probes had been launched in 1977. The two probes had set out to explore the outer planets of Jupiter, Saturn, Uranus, and Neptune. By now, *Voyager 1* had left the solar system and was in interstellar space; *Voyager 2* would soon join it. It would take sunlight over five hours to reach Pluto, and both probes were twice that distance from the sun.

Instantaneous would mean that they had the capability of travelling many times the speed of light to reach the closest probe.

Jake opened his mouth to ask his question, but the Zeta Reticulian had already stepped past Jake toward the control chair. It waved its slender hand over the chair's arm, lighting up a series of previously unseen buttons on its surface.

Jake didn't need to vocalize his question. The small visitor had read his thoughts.

The floor in front of the chair reacted to the visitor's gesture. It was as if its metal, which was still opaque, had liquefied. It reached out of the floor to form a large ring the size of the opaque wall immediately behind it. When it had finished growing, it glistened a violet-silver as it solidified into what looked like a solid metal ring.

Jake watched in mute amazement as small balls floated from either side of the violet-silver ring to collide and explode. The blast's intense bright flash startled Jake and immersed the room in a wash of blinding white. The explosion, however, was contained within an unseen force field, the only hint of which formed a large sphere inside the metal ring, protecting the occupants in the room from the energy of the intense detonation captured inside.

At first, Jake didn't understand what he was witnessing. Contained within the force field, the explosion immediately caved in on itself to form a barely visible black dot that hovered at the center of the ring. The edges of the black dot appeared to glow as it grew larger to fill the area within the metal ring. The massive planet hanging outside was visible inside the glowing ring as it grew in diameter.

Trying to make sense of what he was seeing, Jake took a hesitant step forward. The glowing ring captured within the metal ring became energized and seemed to be spinning at such a high speed it gave the impression of glowing.

The image of the planet framed within the glowing ring zoomed in, as if it were a window descending through Jupiter's clouds, through its darkened core, and then out the other side to be filled with the blackness of space pinpricked by stars.

Jake blinked at the familiar shape that suddenly grew to fill the area framed by the energized, spinning ring. Although the light reflected off its surface was dim, there was no question in Jake's mind what he was looking at.

Floating before him was a human creation.

"The Voyager!" Jake's eyes bulged with excitement.

"You must have used antimatter somehow to spark off a matter-antimatter reaction to create," Jake said, swallowing hard. "An Einstein-Rosen Bridge. You made a mini black hole and turned it into a wormhole!"

So Einstein was right, he thought.

Jake was alive with wonder. "The only thing that can contain antimatter would be exotic matter, which is what the purple ring must be made of. But the energy needed to create a wormhole would be, well, some quadrillion times more than what we could ever hope to generate!"

Jake again studied the small visitor. *If these guys can harness the energy of a star, they must be at least 100,000 years ahead of us!*

"HUMAN UNDERSTANDING OF THE NATURAL SCIENCES IS COMING OF AGE."

The thoughts that poured into Jake's mind confirmed his observation. He had witnessed a ball-bearing-sized sphere of matter float across to touch a similarly sized ball of antimatter, interacting to release an unfathomable amount of energy that, for a fleeting moment, created a tiny star before his eyes. Being unstable, the star instantly collapsed into a single point of infinite density, and a mini black hole was born.

Although too small to see, the single point was actually a tiny ring formed by centrifugal forces as the black hole spun. The visitors' technology enabled them to use gravity waves to stretch the spinning ring to the desired size.

The wormhole, or Einstein-Rosen Bridge, was kept open and stable via the manipulation of gravity waves, allowing instantaneous travel between two connected points in space. It distorted the fabric of space between the probe and the visitors' spacecraft by shrinking the linear distance down to almost zero. The effect was like looking out a window. The Voyager probe appeared to hang in suspension on the other side of the portal.

Linear distances no longer held any meaning in the physics of wormholes, as the portals could be hundreds of light years apart. Travelling between these two portals was as simple as stepping through a doorway or, in this case, moving through the wormhole's energized portal on board the visitors' spacecraft.

In that moment, Jake knew he was in the presence of a very advanced, and very ancient, galactic civilization. He was reminded of science fiction author Arthur C. Clarke's third rule: "Any sufficiently advanced technology is indistinguishable from magic."

Humanity still has a steep learning curve ahead of it on the subject of physics because mankind is nearly as far away from the understanding of the nature of the universe as they were 500 years ago. Even so, mankind is well on its way to ascending what its scientists term a Type 1 Civilization.

The whirling thoughts from the Zeta conjured up a dormant memory from college lectures on the types of civilizations and how they could be classified according to the quantum of energy they create. Humanity is classified a Type Zero Civilization because it relies on extracting energy from dead plants in the form of oil, coal, and its petrochemical derivatives.

The ranking goes on to describe a Type 1 Civilization, which had the capability of harnessing the energy output of an entire planet; whereas a Type 2 Civilization was able to exploit the total energy output of a star, which is 10 billion times the energy of a Type 1 Civilization.

The very prospect of being able to create a wormhole was beyond what Jake could imagine. *These guys must be a Type 2!*

The scene was surreal. The purplish-silver ring encircling the portal gave the impression of a window looking out to the Voyager space probe. In the background, the breathtaking beauty of the Jovian system loomed.

The probe's 12-foot-wide, parabolic, high-gain antenna dish came to dominate the view through the portal. Jake couldn't tell if he was peering at *Voyager 1* or *Voyager 2*. It wouldn't matter, however, because Jake's plan would work with either probe.

The Zeta Reticulian already knew what the next question was going to be.

Jake swallowed. "Can we get closer? Can we go through to the other side?"

"THE OTHER SIDE OF THE JOURNEY WOULD BE A PROBLEM."

Visions accompanied the words entering Jake's mind. A carbon-based body, such as a human's, would have sufficient strength to withstand the gravitational shearing forces induced while entering the portal. However, the other side of the journey would be a problem for Jake because the exposure to deep space would be fatal.

"Wow, who would have guessed? A sense of humor!" Jake said, glancing at his host.

The small creature stared at Jake, its penetrating gaze able to peer into the depths of Jake's mind. Although there wasn't any change in its facial expression, Jake sensed that his host was mentally cocking its head quizzically at Jake's attempt at sarcasm.

The visitor gestured again with its hand over the arm of the central chair and turned to the portal. Jake followed its gaze.

The metal ring, along with the portal captured within, both grew. More astonishing was that the barely visible walls of the control room also grew. Jake watched in mute disbelief as the control room he was standing in grew to accommodate the expanding portal.

Wide enough to encircle the entire probe, the spacecraft with its three outstretched arms carrying an assortment of sensors and power supply was fully visible. The *Voyager* slowly moved through the portal into the control room, rotating as it gracefully hovered before Jake, its main antenna dish coming to rest facing the barely visible domed ceiling above.

Jake looked impressed and stepped toward the hovering probe. "Okay, not exactly what I was thinking. But this can work."

Attached to the side of the *Voyager* spacecraft was a 12-inch, gold-plated copper disk.

Jake had no illusions about what he needed to do.

CHAPTER 82

The United Nations complex in New York is in the Turtle Bay area of Manhattan. Perched between First Avenue and the East River, the complex serves as the UN's headquarters and consists of three primary buildings: the 39-story Secretariat Building, the General Assembly Building, and the Conference Building that looks out onto the East River between the General Assembly Building and the Secretariat.

A lone individual stood at the corner of East 45th Street and First Avenue across the street from the UN headquarters. His gaze climbed the gray facade of the Secretariat Building then swept across the curved lines and domed roof of the General Assembly Building to focus on a collective of media vans parked at the complex's entrance. Workers unpacked equipment from the vans and hauled the various items into the General Assembly Building.

The individual was oblivious to the heavy traffic that crammed the intersection, and went unnoticed by the pedestrians that streamed in all directions. His face sported a three-day beard growth. In his arms, he clutched his jacket, which was wrapped around a 12-inch, gold-plated copper disk.

✑

Dr. Charles Reilly labored to step up to the podium before the General Assembly of the United Nations. Hesitantly, he looked out over the myriad of curved desks that arched around and radiated out from the central podium. With the sea of seats filled by representatives of the member nations, the scientist felt the eyes of the world waiting for him to speak.

Being of no further use to Mr. Sabre, the scientist, Natasha, and Mark had been released from custody. Dr. Reilly set out to fulfil the task that Dr. Steven Greer was unable to complete. In the lead-up to obtaining the metallurgical report on the extraterrestrial sample provided by Reilly, Greer had arranged to address the General Assembly of the United Nations and present compelling evidence on the existence of an extraterrestrial presence in an effort to nudge the United States Government toward full disclosure.

Dr. Charles Reilly had contacted Dr. Steven Greer's office and offered to take Greer's place at the scheduled UN briefing. It seemed that the scientist had one last hand to play.

✑

Jake Marcel held his jacket firmly to his chest as he traversed the busy street and made for the gathering media vans. Crews carried camera equipment and mixer components past the security gates toward the General Assembly Building.

Trying to blend in, Jake placed his jacket on top of a freshly unloaded crate, lifted it, and then followed the procession of support crew through the security gates toward the General Assembly Building. The procession entered through the main entrance into the grand foyer then filed into an auxiliary corridor in the back-of-house area, bypassing a second security checkpoint.

Twenty seconds later, the procession approached the end of the corridor connected to the entrance of the main assembly arena. Another security guard stood at that entrance.

The guard focused on Jake as he approached, his expression of concern growing more intense as Jake drew near. Instinctively, Jake slowed his approach as the media crew filed through the entry.

Jake now noticed the guard had been looking over Jake's shoulder.

"S-S-Sir," the guard stammered, "you can't smoke in here."

Jake froze in place. He felt his heart drop as he turned to find Mr. Sabre flanked by a battalion of expressionless Special Forces guerrillas. A surge of apprehension ripped through Jake as he placed the crate on the ground and picked up his jacket.

Sabre closed in. A satisfied smile slowly crossed the agent's lips.

CHAPTER 83

D r. Charles Reilly wavered as he looked out into the cavernous expanse of the UN assembly arena. The loss of friends over the last few weeks weighed heavy in his heart. Searching the attendants for a familiar face, he found comfort in Natasha's soft features.

She gave him an encouraging yet pained smile.

The scientist drew an agonized breath. "An extraordinary man had been scheduled to give this address to you all today. However, in his pursuit of compelling evidence related to what I'm here to brief you on, Dr. Steven Greer had his life taken."

An air of uneasiness rumbled through the crowd.

Reilly glanced at Natasha, who sat at the side of the arena. Despite the aching sadness in her eyes, she gave a nod of encouragement as if to say "keep going."

Finding his breath, the scientist continued. "The recent discovery of an abundance of water on Mars has raised hopes for finding life elsewhere in the universe. Scientists do expect to find simple bacteria dwelling deep within the

Martian soil. Even so, the discovery of a single bacterium elsewhere beyond Earth's skies will force humanity to revise our understanding of where we fit in the cosmos. The revelation, when it comes, will be as controversial as when Copernicus, in the early 1500s, proclaimed that Earth was not the center of the known universe."

⚘

Jake Marcel stepped back toward the entrance with caution, grasping the object hidden by his jacket tight under one arm.

Sabre's penetrating gaze bore into him. "Welcome back, Jake. I trust you found the answers you were looking for."

The question startled Jake. "How did you …"

A harsh laugh escaped Sabre's lips as he extinguished his cigarette beneath his shoe. "These are trillion-dollar secrets that you are now a party to. The keepers of such secrets have access to unlimited resources to track you and your friends' movements. There is no limit to how far they will go to maintain the status quo … That is, this consumer-based, oil-addicted, celebrity-obsessed reality that you call life."

"People need to know," Jake replied with more hostility than he had intended.

The agent's tone was fierce. "People don't want the truth. It's too daunting. Too scary. The human race wasn't ready for it in the 1940s, and they're sure as hell not ready for it now. They're too obsessed with their own lives to realize there is more to our petty existence than watching TV and buying the latest fashions."

Creeping closer to the entry, Jake focused on the assault

weaponry held by Sabre's escort then the hip bulge in the agent's jacket. The guard by the entry stood terrified trying to process what was happening.

"There are two versions of reality that can unfold from here. One is where you go home, back to your life, and stay happy in ignorance. The other is where you walk into the General Assembly and help bring on the destabilization of all orthodox religious systems of the world. You will then threaten our way of government and send the political systems of every country back to the Bronze Age," the agent said, making no effort to hide his annoyance.

Jake's unease sharpened. "I've come this far. You'll have to kill me to stop me."

Sabre's eyes shone with a determination Jake sensed he would be unwise to test. "It may be morally indefensible, but absolutely necessary if it means protecting the population from realities they're not ready for."

Jake was defiant, as if tapping a hidden reserve of power. "Who are you to decide what the population is ready for?"

Sabre never raised his voice, but its intensity tripled. "You could not begin to fathom the gravity of what is to come. Do you really want to uncover revelations that will challenge our understanding of the fabric of reality? To twist the origins of the human condition? When we learned we were not alone, we also realized we were technologically inferior, hopelessly outgunned and tricked into signing a treaty with the wrong side. The most profound discovery in human history simultaneously became the most dangerous."

Jake took another hesitant step toward the entry to the General Assembly arena.

"You keep a very, very dangerous secret, Jake." The agent's tone left no room for debate. "You're making a mistake."

Jake's eyes burned with a hardened determination. "No, I'm correcting one."

Jake turned his back to Sabre and made for the entry. The sound of the agent's holster unclipping and his side-arm's safety being released caused Jake Marcel to instantly freeze in place. Jake heard the agent chamber a round.

Behind him, Sabre's lethal-looking sidearm was trained at Jake's head.

Jake stopped breathing as he waited for the inevitable.

CHAPTER 84

Inside the control room overlooking the General Assembly of the United Nations, Mark was rummaging through his bag. Standing over him was an impatient operations director, whose gaze darted between Dr. Reilly's address to the assembly on the floor below and Mark's hunched figure.

"Are you sure you have it?" the operations director said, visibly irritated. "We're about to miss our cue."

"It's got to be here somewhere," Mark said into the backpack. "Here it is."

Mark fished out an unlabeled USB drive and placed it into the waiting hands of the operations director.

❧

Dr. Charles Reilly sounded sick as he paused his speech and coughed. The ill scientist looked increasing frail. But Charles pressed on. "The evidence regarding this subject has been clear and overwhelming. There are, however, some very powerful interests that don't want the truth to come out. Regardless, we need to follow the truth no matter where it leads us."

❧

Grasping the object hidden in his jacket, Jake Marcel took another nervous step toward the entrance to the General Assembly arena.

Behind him the agent had his sidearm trained on Jake's skull.

Jake took another step.

There was no gunshot.

Jake began to walk, picking up speed through the entry.

Behind him, the agent slowly lowered his weapon and watched as Jake Marcel disappeared inside.

❧

Dr. Charles Reilly tried to steady himself as he took a long pause. Hushed murmurs spread through the crowd as the scientist composed himself.

"Sorry," Reilly managed, forcing a pained smile. "These lights are a tad bright."

Charles took another moment to gather his energy. "Physical, irrefutable proof of life elsewhere in the universe has always been elusive. Footage of alleged UFO sightings has been explained away as hoaxes or natural phenomena. And when there is footage captured of exceptionally high quality, it's dismissed as being doctored."

Dr. Charles Reilly paused again, blinking as his vision blurred. On the wall behind the speaker's podium hung two enormous projector screens that blinked to life. The large screens flanked a circular United Nations emblem on the wall behind the podium that dominated the assembly arena.

Guilt ripped through him has he struggled on. "The footage being played was procured from my former employers; it was filmed three days ago in the Nevada desert. It is genuine, authentic, and captured by cameras mounted on NSA and military assets. I will leave it to you to form your own opinion."

Dr. Reilly steadied himself as the video played overhead. Not being able to bring himself to watch the footage, he observed the mixed expressions on the seated faces before him. Murmurs of confusion now spread through the crowd as a video of a number of black SUVs chasing a motorcycle was projected onto the two large screens. It was quickly evident that the footage was shot by a chasing helicopter.

The confusion of the crowd seemed to deepen.

The scene now cut to a different angle that was zoomed in on Jake Marcel, his face shaky but clearly discernible. Now cutting to a third angle, the speeding motorcycle was tearing toward a deep cliff face. The armada of pursuing SUVs, however, had commenced braking and skidded to a stop.

The entire assembly sat in a silent mix of astonishment and horror as they watched the motorcycle, along with its rider, catapult over the edge into the canyon below. The crowd gasped with disbelief when the crisp image of a silver disk flying in the canyon appeared.

Natasha watched the footage with difficulty, feeling the shockwave that flowed through the crowd.

The video now cut to a tighter angle; the silver disk

looked approximately 100 feet in diameter—much larger than the motorcycle and rider catapulting into the canyon—and appeared to have changed its course to intercept the rider.

Gasps of disbelief quickly intensified in the crowd.

As the footage played from another angle, the rider was now falling; the motorcycle exploded on impact with the silver disk at the moment of interception. The silver object, however, appeared unaffected by the collision.

A millisecond later the disk became illuminated from within, its bright flash completely saturating the footage in brilliant white. In a blur, both the silver disk and rider instantly disappeared from the frame, leaving burning motorcycle fragments to plummet to the bottom of the canyon.

More gasps of astonishment came from the assembly. Natasha watched through watery eyes.

The sequence was replayed slower from another angle, again showing the bike and rider going over the edge of the cliff, the silver disk moving to intercept, the blinding flash, then the disk accelerating away at an impossible speed.

❦

Jake Marcel approached the speaker's podium of the General Assembly from a side aisle. With the object hidden within his jacket clasped under his arm, he was transfixed by the horrific yet spectacular scenes being played for the crowd.

From varying angles, the sequence replayed on a loop, each version showing a new detail or a closer view. Whispers of recognition rippled through the crowd as Jake reached the podium. Jake's resemblance to the doomed rider in the footage was uncanny.

The scientist coughed and faltered at the podium. The images being played were overpowering, their implications frightening. The scientist knew he had to deliver his next words very carefully.

His breathing was labored as he continued his address. "The question is no longer, are we alone in the universe? The question now is, how do we, as a United Nations collective, disseminate this new reality to the citizens of our globe in a calm, scientific, and evidence-driven manner? And not by militaristic, alarmist, xenophobic, or frightening means."

The scientist caught the outline of an approaching figure. Murmurs and whispers radiated through the crowd as the individual drew closer.

Dr. Reilly could barely focus. "There is no reason to believe that the extraterrestrial presence poses a threat to national or world security. If hostility or aggression accompanied their purpose here, it is likely that ..."

The scientist again faltered, losing his train of thought. He felt himself drifting toward unconsciousness as the outline of the approaching figure materialized into a familiar face.

Am I hallucinating?

The scientist tried to shake off the apparition. "It is likely that events congruent with hostility would have transpired long before now. It is our assessment that the extraterrestrials are not hostile, but are ..."

When Dr. Reilly looked again at the approaching visitor, he stopped in his tracks. His face instantly brightened.

It is him!

"I apologize, please excuse me." Dr. Reilly pushed away from the podium.

Natasha followed the scientist's gaze to find Jake Marcel approaching the podium. Instantly, she was out of her seat and on the move toward him.

Dr. Charles Reilly was filled with an unexpected rush of relief as his spirits lifted. Feeling frail, he stepped toward Jake. Natasha came to him with tearful eyes, losing herself in his embrace. She was crying and then smiling, lost in a torrent of emotion.

Closing her eyes, she was weightless in the moment. "It's really you!"

When she stepped aside, Jake's eyes shone with a determination that the scientist had never before seen. Jake uncovered the object that had been wrapped in his jacket.

The broad smile on the scientist's face turned to one of gaping marvel. Instantly, Dr. Charles Reilly knew what he was gazing at. He only needed a second to process its implication.

Jake was holding the inscribed, 12-inch, gold-plated copper disk that had been attached to a Voyager spacecraft, one of only four ever made. It was actually a gold record containing sounds and images selected to portray the diversity of life on Earth. The images etched in its surface identified the time and place of its origin should it one day, in the distant future, cross the path of extraterrestrial life. The other three, the scientist knew, were out past the orbit of Pluto. It seemed to imply one inescapable conclusion.

Jake met the visitors!

Dr. Charles Reilly told himself it was impossible, but

the fact that Jake held the inscribed disk in his hands was verifiable, undeniable, irrefutable proof that a human had visited one of the Voyager probes and returned. And since mankind did not yet possess the technology to complete such a feat, it only left one other possible explanation: Jake had received help from a more advanced extraterrestrial civilization.

The beaming scientist tried to keep his senses, but darkness was closing in. He lost his footing and felt his knees give way, but he was caught by Jake, who gently lowered him to the ground. The anxious crowd gave a communal gasp, and a voice came over the speakers calling for calm.

Charles felt a rush of hands lift him, carrying him away from the focus of the General Assembly. His eyes flickered; he returned for a moment as they set him down.

Charles's gaze located Jake. "My boy would have been around your age now."

A tightness rose in Jake's throat. "Dr. Reilly?"

"Jake," the scientist said, his voice fading, "you are in possession of a truth capable of altering history forever. An answer to a question that humanity has been asking since the birth of civilization."

"Stay with me!" Jake's heart was pounding.

"Listen to me, Jake." Charles's voice was frail. "It's a truth that will be welcomed by many, but equally feared by many more."

Jake and Natasha's eyes locked, an expression of pained dread on their faces, as the scientist continued. "Be sure the right people share it with the world in the right way."

A cold sweat gripped Jake as he held Dr. Reilly and tried to sound reassuring. "The paramedics are almost here."

Reilly was too exhausted to open his eyes. "One day you'll have a child of your own, and you'll feel what it's like to be as proud as I am of you."

Jake felt his heart sink.

Dr. Charles Reilly smiled. "You did what I couldn't. I can now finally join my wife and son."

His eyes welling with tears, Jake held the scientist's hand until it went limp.

Natasha covered her mouth, feeling Jake's loss.

CHAPTER 85

Jake Marcel and Natasha DeMorea sat in quiet reflection on a couch positioned in the corridor outside the Oval Office. Standing at attention to either side of them were two special agents who kept watch on the door that led to the president of the United States. Inside, the president and his aides were making final alterations to his speech before shooting a live, worldwide announcement from his desk.

Jake thought of Dr. Reilly: *The most brilliant scientist the world would never know.* It seemed a lifetime ago when the scientist first introduced himself outside Jake's office building.

A week had passed since the late Dr. Charles Reilly gave his address to the General Assembly of the United Nations before succumbing to his illness. The days since had been a flurry of media sensationalism and speculation about an imminent announcement the world would hear based on the recent UN gathering. Delegates of member nations were ordered to be tight lipped until it had been decided how to share the information presented. CNN had been running news stories around the clock on the nature of the announcement, going so far as to speculate that the stock market might temporarily close when the announcement came.

Natasha placed a soft hand on Jake's leg, noticing he seemed anxious. "What's the matter? Why do you look so nervous?"

"It's just that," he hesitated, searching for the right words, "in 10 minutes the president is going to address the entire world about ETs. And if you think about it, for the last 2000 years, we were the only life in the universe. For the first time in human history, everyone will learn that we have never been alone. Once people realize that there are other technologies, other sources of energy, oil is going to be worthless. The stock market might go into a freefall until we work out how to deal with it. It's going to be chaos."

She offered a soft smile, sensing the concern in his words.

"This is a turning point," Jake said, his voice conclusive, "and history will always remember this president as the one who had to deliver the news. I guess I'm nervous because from now on, everything changes."

CHAPTER 86

Televisions across the world tuned into a special live broadcast from the Oval Office.

With a reassuring smile, the president of the United States drew a deep breath. "My fellow Americans, people of the world, today we take our first steps on a journey into a new era. One age, the adolescence of mankind, has ended, and another age has now begun."

"This journey I speak of," the president said, his expression one of sincerity, "will be full of uncertainty and challenges unlike any our ancestors have known. But I firmly believe that our history, all the struggles we have overcome in the past, have prepared our current generation for what is to come."

"I now address you as citizens of this planet we call Earth because we are not alone. In recent decades, we have come to understand that the universe is populated with other beings, intelligent life such as ourselves of varying races."

The president paused, letting his words sink in.

"In the 1940s, our military forces recovered the remains of an aircraft of unknown origin from the New Mexico desert. Our scientists spent the following decades studying the craft and determined that it was a vehicle from the vast reaches of outer space."

"Since that time, our government has made contact with the benevolent entities of that spacecraft."

He paused again.

"Though this news may sound both fantastic and terrifying, I ask that you greet this with calm and optimism. I assure you, as president, that these entities are not hostile, and most races we have discovered are benevolent. Rather, what we can learn from them has the potential to allow our nations overcome the common enemies of all humanity: poverty, disease, and war."

"I cannot tell you that there will be no stumbling blocks or missteps as we navigate this new era ahead, but together with our interstellar neighbors, we can work at creating a better world. I believe that we have found the true destiny of the people of this great planet of ours; for all mankind to come together in peace as we join our cosmic community."

"In the coming days and weeks, you will learn more about these cosmic visitors, why they are here, and why our leaders have kept their presence a secret from humanity for so long."

"I ask you to look to the future not with apprehension, but with hope and courage. Because it is within our reach, to achieve in our generation, the ancient vision of peace and prosperity on Earth for all humanity."

"What has united us as human beings has always been

far greater than what has divided us, and for the first time, people from every part of this planet can live together, not as a multicultural civilization, but as a single species. And if we come together not as separate nations, but as human beings of planet Earth to face what is to come, if we pass through this time of great trial in a calm and scientific manner, if we confront without fear the challenges that will test our beliefs and resolve, then someday years from now, our children can tell their children that this was the time when humanity entered into the cosmic community."

"Let us not forget who we are: People of one planet, under God, indivisible, with liberty and justice for all."

"Thank you."

"God bless you."

"And may God bless every nation on Earth."

EPILOGUE 1

8ᵗʰ July, 1947
2:56 am

At the Marcel residence, Major Jesse Marcel had been showing his wife and young 11-year-old son, Jesse Marcel Jr., pieces of the extraterrestrial craft that had met its demise on a ranch outside Roswell, New Mexico.

The family were crouched on the kitchen floor examining crash fragments of different sizes and shapes spread out before them.

Marcel's eyes twinkled at his son. "Jess, one day, you'll understand the importance of all this. And one day, many years from now, when you grow up and have a family of your own, you will remember this night and tell your children about it."

The boy was struck with a deep sense of wonder as his eyes moved from piece to piece. There were splintered struts in the shape of I-beams, various fragments of shiny thin metal plates that would not bend, crumpled sheets of what looked to the boy like aluminum foil and strands of cord that appeared to be made of glass but were as flexible as rubber.

"Okay, Jess," Marcel said, "we've had a look. Help me pack all this up, I have to transport it back to base."

Young Jess raised his eyes to look at his father. Marcel could tell from the boy's face that he was not yet ready to part with the spacecraft fragments.

Marcel gave his son a soft smile. "Come on now, help me pack up."

With that, the family started to carefully repack the box that Marcel had brought to the house.

In a moment when Jesse's parents were gathering the fragments, the boy noticed they were not looking his way. He silently slid one of the fractured I-beams into the gap between the fridge and the kitchen counter while his father wasn't looking.

When his parents had filled the box, his father stood and looked around the kitchen. "That's all of it then."

A handful of nervous heartbeats passed as Jesse nodded in agreement with his father.

∾

The following morning, when hearing his mother talking on the phone, young Jesse silently approached the fridge. Reaching his small arm into the gap between the kitchen counter and fridge, he retrieved the object he had hidden there the night before.

Jesse stood staring at the gleaming I-beam in awe. In the daylight, its silver surface glistened a violet-purple. He ran his fingers over the raised markings that looked as if they had been stamped along its length.

In his other hand, the boy held a small cardboard tube that he had found in the garage. The size of the tube matched the width and length of the violet-colored silver component.

Holding his breath, Jesse slid the forbidden object into the cardboard tube and sealed its lid.

EPILOGUE 2

The Day of Major Jesse Marcel's Funeral

After the ceremony had concluded and the guests had left, Jesse Marcel Jr. returned to his father's tombstone accompanied by the priest who had presided over the funeral, Father Jordan.

They looked at the inscribed plaque that lay at the foot of the tombstone:

AND YE SHALL KNOW THE TRUTH, AND THE TRUTH SHALL MAKE YOU FREE.

Jesse crouched to the inscribed plaque and produced a small screwdriver from his pocket. Under the watchful eye of Father Jordan, he unscrewed the plaque to reveal a hidden compartment. From another pocket, Jesse retrieved a sealed cardboard tube, placed it in the compartment, and affixed the plaque back onto the tombstone to conceal the forbidden object.

He stood with a sad smile on his face as he looked to the tombstone. "I thought it was about time I returned this to you, Dad."

EPILOGUE 3

Jake Marcel Visits His Grandfather

"**C**an I be of assistance, my son?" said Father Jordon.

Startled, Jake Marcel instantly slipped the cylinder-shaped container that he had retrieved from his grandfather's tombstone into his jacket. He spun around to find the priest standing behind him, Bible in hand. Their eyes met for a few seconds before Jake responded.

At first, Jake opened his mouth to speak, but his words failed him. Instead, Jake managed to summon a semi-polite smile and sprinted for the cemetery gates.

Father Jordon watched from beside the grave of Major Jesse Marcel then turned his attention back to the tomb.

Still holding his Bible firmly against his chest, he immediately gazed down to the grave's metal plaque. A wave of shock rolled over him as he realized that the commemorative plaque had been disturbed. Now dislodged, the plaque was now being held in place by a single screw and hung askew.

Beneath the plaque had been a compartment hidden from view. The compartment, the priest realized, was now empty.

The priest hurried back to the rectory building that stood adjacent to the nearby church. Inside the priest's living quarters, he rushed to his study and found a leather-bound diary hidden within a drawer. Inside, he looked up a telephone number that contained a Vatican prefix. He dialed the number and waited for the line to be answered.

"Pronto," an Italian voice spoke.

"Good morning, is this Monsignor Carlo Botticelli?"

"Si," the accented voice confirmed.

"I apologize for calling at this odd hour, but the object I have been asked to watch over has been taken."

Vatican theologian Monsignor Botticelli sounded confused. "I'm sorry?"

"The object that belonged to the star visitors. I was to watch over it and call this number if anything happened to it. Well," Father Jordan hesitated, "it's no longer in its hiding spot."

For the Vatican theologian, the implications came almost too fast to process.

EPILOGUE 4

Vatican City

The world's religious leaders secretly gathered to discuss the implications of disclosure. Seated at a round table hidden deep within the chambers of the Vatican's Apostolic Palace, the Pope's private residence, sat his holy father the Roman Pontiff, the head of the Catholic Church, accompanied by Monsignor Carlo Botticelli.

Sitting around the table at the Pope's meeting were the imam, the religious authority of the globe's Islamic community; Chief Rabbi of Jerusalem, regarded as the authority of the world's Jewish religion; the Dalai Lama; and a highly revered swami, the Hindu spiritual leader.

Everyone sat in silence waiting for the pontiff to speak.

The Pope's eyes rose slowly to meet all in attendance. "Thank you all for coming to this summit on short notice."

The pontiff's heart turned grave then resolute. "We are here to discuss a phenomenon that has increasingly been appearing over the last 200 years. They are as fascinating as they are controversial, and in every instance, continue to divide public opinion. For many centuries, extraterrestrial spiritual beings have been a part of the faith of the world's religions. They have appeared in our history in the form of angels, servants of God who visited the Earth with messages of guidance and salvation. But now we must speak of extraterrestrial beings of a different kind."

The room's silence was laced with a tense anticipation.

"We have all known," the pontiff continued, "that there have been countless testimonies regarding unidentified flying objects, extraterrestrials, and spaceships of unknown origin. And we have been following the countries with organizations that collect the evidence from these unknown spacecraft when they have fallen from the sky."

"From our collaborations with these organizations that have studied the star visitors' technology, we have made the assertion that these beings are not the angels or spiritual beings from our collective scriptures. They are, instead, humanoid beings not unlike like us, comprising both spiritual and physical body."

The Pope sounded hopeful. "We can reconcile their existence with the redemption of Christ. As St Paul said, 'Christ is the center of the creation of the universe.' Therefore, there are no worlds without a reference to his teachings. From the Bible, it is thus possible to assure that Christ, considered as an incarnated verb, has influence upon all inhabited planets of God's universe."

The leaders in the room felt the true reason for their gathering come crashing down on them.

It was the imam who spoke first. "If we think God's

omnipotence and wisdom has no limits, then why should life be restricted to one of countless planets?"

The Chief Rabbi agreed. "Yes, it is absurd to claim that the countless worlds surrounding us are uninhabited deserts, void of life, and that the meaning of the universe lies only in our small, inhabited planet."

His Holiness the Dalai Lama could see what the men sitting around the table were thinking. "It is not only possible, but credible that in places inaccessible to mankind and his scientific instruments, there exist other beings able to know God as their Creator. And that their worlds represent the Creator's plan."

The highly revered swami considered the revelation. "And if they are indeed superior to us, can they not help and support us in our spiritual development? Perhaps they have already guided us in the past."

"Do we have any right to continue to claim," Monsignor Botticelli asked, "that just because of our limited senses and misguided intelligence, humans are the only intelligent beings in God's immense universe?"

A wave of assenting murmurs crossed the room.

The pontiff brought the room to order with a raised hand. "Indeed, St Padre Pio of Pietrelcina once stated that the Lord certainly did not limit his glory to this small Earth. He said that, on other planets, other beings exist who did not sin and fall as we did. And in 1999, His Holiness Pope John Paul II was asked by a child during his visit to a northern Roman parish if there were any aliens. His Holiness replied, 'Always remember, they are children of God as we are.'"

A pensive silence fell over the group. Each felt as if they

were discussing an ancient truth that had been imprinted on their souls.

"Which leads me to the essence of why we are here." The Holy Father's voice was soft yet powerful. "Since 1986, we have had within the safekeeping of one of our priests an artifact of compelling scientific and potentially theological significance. Being manufactured by elements and processes not of this Earth, it alone can prove the existence of intelligent life elsewhere."

The occupants of the room were stunned by the news that there existed an object to prove the existence of extraterrestrial life.

The Pope could see a mixture of amazement and shock on the faces of those gathered, and he certainly understood. The revelation was something that the Catholic Church had not planned to share with the world. But as fate would have it, the artifact was in the hands of the general public, and it would be only a matter of time before it surfaced for the entire world to behold.

"And you kept this hidden?" The Chief Rabbi asked, his expression scornful.

"At the time, we felt that the world was not ready," the monsignor explained. "We thought that the firm believers who put their blind faith in God could lose their grasp on reality. That they would not be able to relate their entrenched beliefs to an extraterrestrial presence."

"And you said it *was* within your safekeeping" The imam asked.

The Pope looked as if the words were physically difficult to say. "We have since learned overnight that the artifact has been taken. We are in communication with the agency that is trying to retrieve the artifact."

The Pope continued, his tone turning serious. "But we must consider the scenario where it is brought out in the open. Whether it be now, or 50 years from now, we will have to face our believers with the reality of intelligent extraterrestrial life."

The members of the Pope's gathering realized the implications instantly. It was conceivable that it was only a matter of time before the revelation would circle the globe and would no doubt be covered by CNN for all to witness. The public reaction would reverberate across decades.

The Chief Rabbi was looking more and more concerned with each passing moment. "Some of our faithful will be incapable of altering their beliefs to embrace a cosmic neighborhood. They will suddenly become unbelievers in reality."

The monsignor looked equally troubled. "True, some may see the ETs as manifestations of the devil who have appeared only to shake their faith. Some followers will be confused and self-righteous, unable to accept the evidence presented to them."

The Dalai Lama was more hopeful. "But imagine what we may be able to learn from them. Can they heal cancer? Did they also have environmental problems to overcome?"

The swami had questions of his own. "Yes, did they overcome problems of overpopulation? What political system do they follow? What is their faith based on?"

"But if they were to show themselves," the imam cautioned, "the Muslims will pray to Allah, hoping that it is the Mahdi who has returned to assess the unfaithful."

The rabbi was nodding to the imam. "I agree, Jerusalem will have an influx of people, since tradition holds that the Messiah would descend there."

"We had the same thought." The Pope now raised both arms. "The faithful won't be singing in St Peter's Square. We would expect our churches to fill with people asking the question, 'Has Judgment Day arrived?'"

The monsignor's voice was resonant. "But it will most likely be the scientists and politicians that will be the first to accept this fact and bring this news to the people."

Mutters of agreement and impending concern again circled the room.

"Disclosure of extraterrestrial life does not have to be theologically devastating. Christianity is robust and flexible enough to accommodate the discovery of extraterrestrial intelligence. The *Book of Moses*, chapter 1:33 talks of worlds without number that the Lord has created." The pontiff's words hung in the air for a long moment.

The imam considered the Pope's words then slowly raised his eyes to the gathering and said, "The Koran refers to Allah as the God of worlds, not just one world. Muslims are prepared for ET intelligence. The Koran states that among his signs is the creation of the heavens and the Earth and the living creatures that he has scattered through them."

The rabbi stared into the eyes of the imam for a long moment, then finally said, "Most Jews' interpretation of Genesis leaves open the possibility of life on other planets. If the news of the ET presence is shared, it will be more evidence of the power of God."

The swami could feel the strength of their will pushing

him in the Pope's direction. "The ancient Indian Vedas and other texts refer to aeronautics, spaceships, flying machines, and ancient astronauts. It speaks of unlimited multiverses and each multiverse having its own stars, planets, and life."

The Dalai Lama's voice was soft. "Buddhist cosmology includes thousands of inhabited worlds. But, the world's faiths were founded in the prescientific era, when Earth was widely believed to be at the center of the universe. Scientific and human understanding of the universe has progressed over the last 500 years. Organized religions don't need to be outgrown. This can be a great opportunity for the religious faiths to progress with humanity and lead our believers in these changing times."

There were nods of agreement around the table.

"To which God do you all pray?" the Pope asked.

The imam exchanged glances with the others before answering. "Whether we call him Allah, God the father, Buddha, or Jehovah, isn't the great spirit of eternal Creation one in the same?"

The Pope offered a warm smile. "Then let us all pray as a brotherhood that we choose the correct path to lead our communities."

The people seated around the table bowed their heads in silent prayer.

After an interval of quiet reflection, the swami spoke. "How do you think our followers would react if they saw all of us in the same room, praying together, discussing important matters in friendship?"

The rabbi knew there was logic in the Dalai Lama's argument for unity across the faiths. "We must find common ground if we are to lead our faithful in these changing times. If not, then the religious communities we represent will fragment and possibly collapse."

The pontiff was pleased with the direction their discussion was taking. "It sounds to me that we have found common ground. We all pray to the same Creator, and we agree whether one is born on Earth, or on another world that sustains life, we are all children of God."

Another round of agreements circled the table.

The Pope's eyes stared back at them all with fierce clarity. "Then I propose that when the news of ET life spreads across the Earth, we all guide our believers in accepting our interstellar brothers as part of the divine Creator's great plan."

EPILOGUE 5

The General Assembly Building of
the United Nations

Grasping the object hidden in his jacket, Marcel took another nervous step toward the entrance to the General Assembly arena.

Behind him the agent had his sidearm trained on Jake's skull.

Jake took another step.

There was no gunshot.

Jake was now walking, picking up speed, toward the entry.

Behind him, the agent slowly lowered his weapon and watched on as Jake Marcel disappeared through the entry.

For a long moment, the agent stared at the empty entry. The guard beside the door still looked white.

Mr. Sabre holstered his Glock, retrieved a cell phone from an inside jacket pocket, and tapped a speed dial number.

It was Thirty-Three's voice that answered. "Yes."

"Sir, as requested," Sabre said, "the target has been let through and has been given sufficient motivation to continue."

"Excellent work, Mr. Sabre."

The agent's tone was hesitant. "Are you sure about this, sir? This is in conflict with—"

"Yes, Mr. Sabre,"—his words were cut short by Thirty-Three—"please execute your orders."

Sabre was confused. "Understood, sir, standing down."

With that, the agent ended the call and shot a perplexed look back at the entry to the General Assembly arena.

EPILOGUE 6

Section 4 Boardroom

Thirty-Three watched the last few words of the President's speech on a wall-sized screen at the end of a boardroom nestled within Section 4's underground complex.

The president was speaking from behind his Oval Office desk. "And if we come together not as separate nations, but as human beings of planet Earth to face what is to come, if we pass through this time of great trial in a calm and scientific manner, if we confront without fear the challenges that will test our beliefs and resolve, then someday years from now, our children can tell their children that this was the time when humanity entered into the cosmic community."

"Let us not forget who we are: People of one planet, under God, indivisible, with liberty and justice for all."

"Thank you."

"God bless you."

"And may God bless every nation on Earth."

Thirty-Three used a small remote to switch off the large screen and swiveled back toward the boardroom's long mahogany table. His eyes gleamed with satisfaction.

"Gentlemen," Thirty-Thirty proclaimed, "today is a historic day for the human civilization, as today we begin our planet-wide disclosure. Mankind will take its next step in our evolutionary journey."

Seated at the long table were three nonhuman entities that had light gray skin and wore tightly fitted, silver jumpsuits that accentuated their slender bodies. Their heads were relatively large in proportion to their bodies and framed two large and dark almond-shaped eyes.

The three gray beings simultaneously nodded in acknowledgement.

www.ingramcontent.com/pod-product-compliance
Lightning Source LLC
Chambersburg PA
CBHW070731120726
47910CB00001B/59